HEAD
TO HEAD

D1542277

HEAD TO HEAD

LINDA LADD

PINNACLE BOOKS
Kensington Publishing Corp.
http://www.kensingtonbooks.com

PINNACLE BOOKS are published by

Kensington Publishing Corp.
850 Third Avenue
New York, NY 10022

All Kensington Titles, Imprints, and Distributed Lines are
available at special quantity discounts for bulk purchases for
sales promotions, premiums, fund-raising, and educational
or institutional use. Special book excerpts or customized
printings can also be created to fit specific needs. For details, write or phone the office of the Kensington special sales
manager: Kensington Publishing Corp., 850 Third Avenue,
New York, NY 10022, attn: Special Sales Department, Phone:
1-800-221-2647.

Pinnacle and the P logo Reg. U.S. Pat. & TM Off.

First Pinnacle Books Printing: March 2006

10 9 8 7 6 5 4 3 2 1

Printed in the United States of America

For my husband, Bill—the love of my life.

For my mother, Louise King, with love—thanks for always being there for me.

For my son, Bill and his beautiful wife, Paula Ladd—thanks for your love and support through thick and thin.

For my daughter, Laurie and her handsome husband, Scott Dale—thanks for your love and generosity, with a special thank you for being my first readers and for all your thoughtful comments, great ideas, and endless encouragement.

Prologue

LIFE WITH FATHER

Nobody knew what really went on in the embalmer's house. It appeared normal enough where it sat on a dirt road on the outskirts of town. Surrounded by dense woods of white oak, maple, and hickory trees, the house was constructed in 1902, but now the white clapboards had been repainted countless times through decades of families. A converted coach house stood at the back of the property, where a wide creek rippled over smooth, tan rocks. Both structures had been neglected and had weathered to gray, and the white curlicues along the ceiling of the porches and the once ornate banisters were peeling paint, giving a forlorn, abandoned look to the place. The dining room in the main house had a curved turret window seat that overlooked the wraparound porch, and above the dining room, on the second story of the turret, was a large master bedroom.

The property had belonged to the same family ever since the houses's construction; in each generation the oldest son was always the owner of the house and an apprentice in the lucrative embalming trade. Inside, the rooms remained timeless, spacious, and dark with faded floral wallpaper and massive mahogany furniture, which intimidated children in the dark of night. The attic was unfinished and dusty, with old trunks and books and the smell of mothballed clothing.

No one ever visited the house unless they wished to have a corpse prepared for a funeral and burial at one of the town mortuaries. The embalmer worked in the chilly basement of the house. A special door had been constructed under the side porch, where a ramp led into the laboratory workroom. The bodies would arrive in ambulances or black hearses, and the workers lowered their voices as they rolled them down the brick sidewalk to the cellar door.

The embalmer was a big man, rawboned and strong, able to lift by himself corpses of any weight onto the cold steel tables in the cellar. He had black hair cropped close to his scalp and a full beard, which he sometimes forgot to trim. He lived in the house with his wife and their child. He was a strict man who demanded that rules of family conduct be followed to the letter. If they were not, if the woman or the child disobeyed his decrees, he would walk slowly to where he kept the old razor strop on a hook inside the door at the top of the cellar steps. This means of punishment had been in the family for as long as he could remember. His father had used it to make a man out of him, and his grandfather had wielded it before that. It was black leather, worn thin now, with bits of brown showing through, and the metal buckle on the end was tarnished and half-broken, so that it left strange, irregular scars on flesh that looked like half-moons. The embalmer had many half-moons on his back. So did the wife and child.

By the time the child was old enough for the mother to teach him to read and do sums, they both had learned to behave in a way consistent with the embalmer's house rules. The mother kept the child close to her every minute of the day, and sometimes they sneaked out of the house and took a walk in the woods so the child could run and play. When they were far enough away from the house, they quit whispering, which was one of the rules—everyone in the house always spoke in a reverent whisper. They never stayed away long and made sure they returned home with plenty of time to prepare the evening meal, because the only time the embalmer left the dead bodies in the cellar was at night. A formal evening meal had always been the custom in the embalmer's household. Although they had never once attended church services, all three of them dressed in their Sunday best for the dinner hour, spent in the big dining room with its brown wallpaper depicting Chinese peasants pulling carts of rice, with cloud-ringed mountains in the background.

The meal routine was set in stone. The mother would give the child a bath, and then she would wash herself because the embalmer demanded cleanliness. Once they were dressed formally, she would lead the child by the hand to the kitchen, and the child would sit quietly at the kitchen table and watch her cook. If they spoke at all, it would be in whispers, because one time the embalmer had come upstairs early and caught them breaking the rule. But that had only happened once. After they healed from the punishment meted out by the embalmer, neither mother nor child ever again spoke above a whisper, not even outside in the woods as they'd done before.

At exactly five minutes after six each evening, the mother would place the food on the dining room table, on warming trivets lit by tiny, white tea candles. Then she would pull the heavy brown velvet curtains tightly together, turn off the electric light suspended over the table, and touch a flame one by one to the tapers in the five-light candelabras positioned in the exact center of

the sideboard and at the exact center of the table because the embalmer liked to dine by candlelight. Then
mother and child would take their places across from
each other, fold their hands in their laps in exactly the
correct manner, right hand on top of the left, with right
thumb resting inside the curled fingers of the left hand.
Silently, they would sit and listen for the embalmer's
slow footfalls as he mounted the cellar steps.

When he reached the wide entrance hall, with its twin
brown horsehair sofas and seven-foot antique Bavarian
grandfather clock, he would shut the cellar door, turn a
key in the ancient lock, and put the key on top of the
door header for safekeeping. His family would not say a
word as he climbed to the second floor to take off his
blood-spattered, black leather apron, wash up, and don
his black Sunday-best suit and white shirt and black tie.
Then they would listen to the main staircase creak as he
descended to the dining room and would grow tense
when he slid open the double doors from the foyer. He
would loom in the threshold, a huge, dark menace, and
neither of them would dare look up from their plate.

And so it was at six-thirty on the dot on this wintry
night in early November. It had turned cold suddenly,
after a month of Indian summer, gusting autumn winds
skittering oak leaves down the cracked sidewalk and
making frosty snowflake patterns on the windowpanes
in the early morning. It was too cold in the house, but it
had always been that way. Low temperatures helped
keep fresh the dead bodies in the cellar.

The embalmer turned and closed the doors behind
him, walked to the table, and as was his habit, checked
to make sure the mother had set it according to his
rules. The child sat very still as the father put his big
hand down and measured the child's dinner plate.
There was to be exactly the length of the embalmer's
thumb between the table edge and the bottom of the

Blue Willow plate, which had been in the family for one hundred years. The child let out a breath of relief when the embalmer found it exactly correct. He measured the child's glass then, making sure it was filled with milk to only a thumb's depth from the top rim, and then he checked that the dinner knife was a thumb's length from the spoon, with the fork in between but not touching. The woman used a Popsicle stick that the embalmer had cut to the proper length with which to measure, and she used it religiously in all her household tasks. The father checked the child's napkin and found it starched and ironed and folded into perfect thirds. He moved around the table and measured the woman's place setting, then his own.

"Very good," he whispered, patting his wife's bowed head.

The embalmer sat down, and his family watched him so they'd know exactly when to fold their hands in prayer. He prayed about duty and obedience until the hall clock began its hollow chimes announcing the seven o'clock hour. On the third bong, he whispered amen, and the three of them picked up their napkins and unfolded them together. He picked up the platter of fried ham and forked out a piece for the child and the mother, and then put the rest on his plate. He served the steamed rice and black-eyed peas precisely the same way; then they waited for him to lift his fork, and they all took the first bite together. Tonight they ate the rice first.

No one spoke—it was against the rules to speak while dining, even in a whisper—and if they finished the food served to them before the clock struck eight o'clock, they would sit without speaking and wait for the soft bongs to commence. On this night, an unimaginable catastrophe happened at eighteen minutes before eight o'clock. The child dropped a salad fork, and it clinked against the hardwood floor and scattered grains of rice on the faded red-and-brown oriental carpet.

Everybody froze. The mother and the child looked at the embalmer, saw the ruddy flush rise up his neck and darken his face. He put down his own fork exactly a thumb's length from his plate. He looked at the child, and the child made a low moaning sound deep inside his throat, eyes wide with terror.

The mother whispered, "Please, please don't."

The embalmer's eyes switched to her, and then he moved so quickly, she never saw the fist he drove into her nose. The blow hit her with a sickening crunch of cartilage, and blood spouted all over the white linen tablecloth and pooled in the child's plate of rice. The force knocked her chair over and onto its back, and she rolled onto her side, unconscious and bleeding.

The embalmer grabbed up the child and shook his thin shoulders until the child gasped for air. The big man dragged the child over to the mother and pushed the child's face down close to the woman's head. The embalmer mopped his hand over the mother's nose and mouth until it was slick with warm red blood, and then he brought it up to the child and rubbed blood, all over the child's face.

The father whispered harshly, "See what you did? You've got your mother's blood on you now, and you can keep it there until you learn your lesson. Your mother never disobeyed me before you were born. This is all your fault. We were happy before you were born. You are an ugly, stupid brat, and don't you dare cry. If I see one tear fall, I will put your mother back in that chair, and I will hit her in the face again. I will hit her over and over until you are obedient. Do you understand me?"

The embalmer slammed the child back into the

chair, and the child ate the blood-soaked rice while the mother's blood dried into a tight brown crust on this face. The child did not look at his mother again.

The child was five years old.

1

I got the call at 5:35 A.M. on my cell phone. As a Canton County Sheriff's Department detective, I get plenty of early morning calls but none like this one. The temporary dispatcher said, "Like, it's a real homicide, Claire! Awesome, like, can you believe it?" Guess that tells you a lot about what passes as excitement here at Lake of the Ozarks. I might live on the Lake Tahoe of mid-Missouri, but a haven for gangsters and murderers it ain't, believe me. My partner, Bud Davis, and I are more likely to investigate who stole somebody's yard gnome or who left an X-rated message on the answering machine down at Maudie's beauty shop. That last one comes to mind because I handled it yesterday, all by myself, too. But that's okay. For years, I worked Los Angeles Robbery/Homicide, or shall we say, Murder Unlimited, California Style, so the quiet life of purloined gnomes was one reason I immigrated to the Midwest.

My heart rate picked up because, hey, a murder is a murder. I sat up on the edge of my couch. I sleep on the couch a lot because I can't sleep anywhere a lot, and I forced my bleary eyes to focus on the dock in front of my teensy-weensy A-frame cabin. The lake cove was quiet and calm, dark green waters lapping dark green, forested shores. See why I came out here to live? The sky was trying to do the dawn thing it did every morning around this time, but the lake had pulled up its blanket of mist and was saying, not yet, not yet, please let me sleep, just ten more minutes.

"Guess what else, Claire, like, just guess?" Somehow I wasn't in the mood to guess much, but the question was rhetorical, anyway. Fact is, the dispatcher was an emergency temp named Jacqueline, Jacqee for short, which tells you a lot. On the other hand, she's the sheriff's youngest and flightiest of four daughters. My partner and I call her Dude-ette. She was home from college for the summer, and I guess nineteen-year-olds majoring in fashion design like to play guessing games with detectives at the crack of dawn. Thus, Dude-ette went on, oh, so excited: "And it's a Hollywood celebrity, can you believe it? Like, a real live celebrity down here at the lake that got herself killed!"

Now that one did make me wonder what Jacqee had been smoking down at the station house. "Okay, Jacqee, I'm awake now. Calm down, and tell me when and where."

"Cedar Bend Lodge."

"Oh, damn." Now I believed the celebrity part. Cedar Bend Lodge was the primo address on all fifteen hundred miles of the lake's mountainous, rugged shoreline. Worse news was that Nicholas Black, world-renowned psychobabbler, owned it. I'd never met the handsome and suave Doctor Black, of course, but word was he was more self-absorbed than his Tinseltown patients. Shorthand for: I am not eager to deal with him.

"Call Bud Davis. Is there a uniform on it?"

"Uh-huh. O'Hara. She's the one on duty."

"Does Charlie know?" I felt I needed to guide Jacqee

through the drill, she being a student of hem lengths and peasant blouses, and all.

"Daddy had to go to Jeff City last night, and like, talk to some dudes up there, you know, the governor and those guys."

Oh, them.

"Okay, I'm on my way," I said, then remembered who was on the other end of the line. "Listen, Jacqee, don't talk to anybody about this, got it? Nobody. Especially the press. Understand?" Redundant, yes, but it paid to be with Jacqee of the two *e*'s.

"Well, duh uh, you think I'm a dork, or what?" Yes, Jacqee, you are a dork, and more. The line went dead, the fashion expert affronted to her core, which probably wasn't all that deep, anyway. Oh, well.

I took my usual ten-second shower, combed my short blond hair straight back off my forehead and left it wet, threw on a black T-shirt and jeans and black-and-orange Nike high-tops, slipped on my shoulder holster with my 9mm Glock snugly buckled in place, and clipped my badge to my belt. The lead detective was on the way in two minutes flat.

The lake at Lake of the Ozarks was formed in 1931, with the construction of Bagnell Dam, and was still impressive now, more than seventy years later. I drove over that mighty edifice, windows down and caffeine deprived. Nicholas Black's resort was on a coveted point south of Horseshoe Bend, and I picked up speed on the deserted blacktop highways curving along the lakeshore. Later in the week the big Cedar Bend Regatta was supposed to begin, and crowds of tourists would venture out in the ninety-degree-plus July heat to watch. Just what we needed. A murder to get the race started.

I reached the stone gate of Cedar Bend Lodge in fifteen minutes and swung my black Explorer into the entrance road and accidentally ran over the end of a mammoth bed of pink and white impatiens and purple petunias. Uh-oh, a gardener 911 was probably going off somewhere. I guiltily regained the blacktop and drove through Doctor Black's meticulously manicured 18-hole golf course, pure emerald splendor for tourists with fat wallets and low handicaps. The main lodge loomed a minute later, built with waist-size logs and glinting with a zillion miles of dark plate glass. The famous five-star restaurant Two Cedars was the star of the black-and-gold reception lobby, but the four ballrooms, with cathedral ceilings and crystal chandeliers dripping glittery spangles, offering breathtaking lake views weren't too shabby, either.

Yes siree, Bob, Cedar Bend Lodge was impressive. The nine-by-twelve-foot front door with beveled stained glass in hues of ruby and emerald and topaz definitely welcomed people who had not come to Lake of the Ozarks to rough it.

I whipped under a portico the size of a basketball court and held aloft by flat, stacked fieldstone columns and slowed at the sight of a resort security guard. I stopped and wound down my window and flashed my badge.

I recognized Suze Eggers right off. She was the best friend of my next door neighbor, Dottie Harper. Suze strutted up to my car, all proud of the sharp black-and-tan uniform, which accentuated her lean, athletic body. I knew she worked security for Black, but to me, she had a gargantuan attitude problem. I sometimes wondered about her sexual orientation, although Dottie assured me she was as straight as the proverbial arrow.

"Well, well, Detective Claire Morgan, up with the birds and lookin' fine."

See what I mean? Maybe Dot was kidding herself about the gay thing.

"Hi, Suze, what's going on? Dispatch said there's been a murder."

"Oh yes, ma'am, you got yourself a murder, all right. All cooked up for breakfast."

Huh?

Suze grinned, made a deal out of pulling off her fancy tan hat with the Cedar Bend logo. She propped her palm on the roof of my car and leaned into the window. She smelled strongly of a unisex Calvin Klein cologne; I forget which one. I had to resist the urge to roll up the window and talk to her through the glass. She said, "Lady got whacked out at one of them fancy gated bungalows. You know the ones I mean? Out on the point goin' for a coupla grand a week." Suze seemed pleased about the murder. Not a healthy sign.

She stopped talking and ogled me a minute. It must've taken her a good long time to get her white-blond hair up into those stylish spikes that fell over just a little on the ends. She had thick, straight eyebrows over dark, nervous eyes. Maybe she was just excited. *Uh-oh, not good.*

"Fact is," Suze lowered her voice, and I guess she thought we were real cop cohorts now, "weird ain't near bad enough to describe this perp. He whacked her good, then came back for seconds."

Gangster speak was flowing now. A regular female Tony Soprano. I pictured her in front of a mirror, plastic water gun in hand, muttering things like "Fuhgeddabout it, or You talkin' to me? You talkin' to ME?"

"Did you find the body, Suze?"

Her eyes darted around some more. "Old lady found the body, one of the guests."

I said, "What about the victim?"

"She's a big-time VIP, just like the chick that found her. All them out there are loaded. They had condos next door to each other. The old lady says she gets up early and takes a swim out to that big floatin' dock Black's got out off the point, said she does the same thing every day. Anyways, minute she saw the dead girl, she went all hysterical and nearly drowned herself before she made it back to her place. She punched the panic button and held it down till I got there. Took me four minutes to get out there, and she was still screamin' her friggin' head off. I called in you guys right off. I did it by the book, Detective. I know procedures. I've been studying to be a cop."

Great. "Did you touch anything at the scene?"

Suze frowned and ran her fingers through her gelled hairdo. We both looked to see how much goop she'd raked out. She wiped the stuff on her pants. "I told you, I know procedure. I ain't touched nothin'. I went over and checked out the body to make sure the old broad wasn't seein' things."

"And you secured the perimeter after you called dispatch?"

"You bet. Guarded the road myself right here till the first uniform showed up. Name's O'Hara, I think. She got here in less than ten. She's that hot new chick that Charlie hired on."

I rest my case. I pulled the gearshift back. "Okay, Suze, where do I go?"

"Take the main road down 'bout a mile, I reckon. It dead-ends at Doctor Black's private gate, and that's something you can't miss, trust me. It's gotta big brass B on it. Hang a left there, and follow that road down to the water. It's got its own security gate, but your partner said to leave it open until you showed up."

So Bud beat me to the scene. That would cost me a dozen Krispy Kremes. "Listen, Suze, nobody goes down this road except for officers and the crime-scene team, got it?"

"Yeah, sure. Guests out here don't drag outta bed till

noon, anyways. Wild parties go on all night; then every-body sleeps in till their appointment with the doc."

I told Suze not to talk about the crime scene and then accelerated down the shady blacktop road. Hundreds of red roses festooned the split-rail fences along the way, and I could smell them, sweet and summery and vaguely reminiscent of prom corsages. I only went to a prom once, but I did get a rose corsage. It was a fake one, but it's the thought that counts, right?

It was still cool, but by nine o'clock, the sun would broil everyone alive. July was hot as hell in Missouri, un-like California's paradise weather. I drove past closed private gates guarding luxury condos hidden in woodsy tracts.

Now I was invading the most exclusive area, where bungalows nestled in jeweled glades and thick woods touched the water. Black must've hired a hundred or so ex-Disney World gardeners to landscape the place. Flowering orange trumpet vines decorated security cam-eras, and there were plenty watching from tall poles. Strangers loitering here would stick out like Michael Jordan on a junior high basketball team. Black's security, however, obviously had not done the trick. I'd have to interview every staff member to see if anyone had seen any unwelcome lurkers on the grounds.

Black's gate loomed up, all ostentatious and gaudy. Somewhere on the other side of that mighty portal wor-thy of Buckingham Palace, Nicholas Black had magi-cally transplanted a Hollywood-style estate smack dab to the Ozark hills. What I wanted to know was *why*? I'd ac-tually seen it from the water once when I was fishing with Dottie. The sun reflected off three stories of plate glass windows in a migraine-inspiring glare. The origi-nal Cedar Bend was built in 1962, and about five years ago Black had bought it dirt cheap out of bankruptcy and then spent several million remodeling the place.

Story was that he saw the view, liked it, and couldn't rest
until he owned it. A real Donald Trump, MD style. A
major celebrity, he was always in the news for something
and usually sporting a busty blonde on his arm. Another
penchant shared with The Donald. Not that he wasn't
devilishly good-looking himself, I had to admit.

I braked and studied the gate of the victim's condo.
Thrown wide open, no guard in sight. Great police work,
that. I turned in and, after thirty yards of steep descent,
saw the private bungalow. All logs, fieldstone, and glass,
beautifully framed by swaying blue-green cedars and
deep green lake water.

A dark brown sheriff's cruiser was parked next to
Bud's unmarked white Bronco. Connie O'Hara, pretty,
blond, twenty-five, and impossibly skinny in her brown
uniform, stood alone in the driveway. Charlie had hired
the young woman at my urging, and I was glad another
female had cracked the department. Young and un-
tried, O'Hara had potential, number three in the police academy and on the Kansas City force until her
highway-patrolmen husband was transferred south. We
practiced on the shooting range and sometimes worked
out in the weight room together. So far she was doing
just fine.

Then I saw the silver van and the two guys scram-
bling out of it. Oh, wonderful, Peter Hastings and Jake,
his obnoxious cameraman. I killed the engine and got
out. Within seconds Hastings had ambushed me with
Jake's camera rolling. I averted my face and kept walking. The brash producer was almost as disgusting as his
stupid TV show. Touted as honoring real cops, *On The
Beat* did more sensationalizing of crime scenes than
honoring anybody.

Why Hastings and his crew had trekked down to the
hinterland of the Missouri Ozarks to immortalize a
backwater sheriff's department was a more interesting

question, and nobody seemed to have a good answer. But watch out now, Hastings had hit the jackpot—a murder to exploit—and he was up for the job.

I nodded to O'Hara and tried to outstride the reporter, but Pete would not be deterred. Both men scuttled like cockroaches and cut off my path, and the camera was zeroed in close up when I ducked under the yellow crime scene tape and headed for the front door of the bungalow.

"Give us a statement, Detective Morgan? Reliable sources tell us this is a homicide. Can you confirm that for our viewers?"

Fairly certain he was fishing, I paused, and because Charlie had ordered us all to be polite to the TV crew, I addressed his questions. "I just arrived on scene, Mr. Hastings; any comment at this time would be inappropriate."

Hastings stuck a live mike over the yellow tape. "Is it true the victim's a famous actress here to kick a cocaine habit? Can you confirm that much, Detective? Can you tell us who she is?"

I hoped to hell it wasn't true, and I wanted to know who'd tipped off Hastings. Jacqee or Suze? "No comment. Tell you what, sir, it might be better to take that camera and wait at the entrance gate until we're finished here. Deputy O'Hara, please escort Mr. Hastings and his cameraman to the gate at the top of the hill and keep everybody out until we're finished with the crime scene."

"Yes, ma'am." Trying not to smirk, O'Hara ushered the newsmen away from the bungalow. Hastings muttered under his breath, and what he said was not pretty. I gladly left O'Hara to deal with the media morons and walked over the quaint, humpbacked little bridge that led onto a wraparound porch. Terra-cotta urns overflowed with brilliant scarlet geraniums along the planked walkway and deck. The house was spacious, built of rustic brown wood, and it jutted out over the water in an impressive feat of engineering. There were a few windows facing the road, but I bet there were plenty more facing the lake.

The surrounding woods were quiet. Waves gently lapped weathered pilings, and one ecstatic robin warbled his heart out somewhere high atop a tree. I could understand now why celebrities landed out here in the boondocks to screw their heads on straight. Quiet, peaceful, private, no traffic, no sirens, the place could ease the stress, all right. Except that now a murderer had come calling to our little utopia in the woods.

2

Bud Davis was standing inside the front door, grinning his big, cheesy grin. He spoke with a Georgia drawl that made the gals go all weak-kneed and faint, except for me, of course; I am immune. But most ladies were not, and he used the Southern charm like a fisherman uses a spinnerbait lure.

"Maybe you oughta keep a box of Krispy Kremes in your car since I always beat you to the scene." Thirty-two years old and handsome in a boyish way, Bud had thick auburn hair and a salon haircut that Tom Brokaw would die for. Although he'd had the misfortune to be named after his daddy's favorite beer, wardrobe wise, Ralph Lauren had nothing on him. How he had ever lowered himself to work vice in Atlanta I couldn't imagine, though I was glad he'd grown tired of the big city and moved up here, where he could enjoy hiking and hunting. Once I'd made him show me proof that he'd ever in his life had one hair out of place, and he'd come up with a Polaroid of himself undercover in a dirty flannel shirt, with greasy long hair and a nose ring. He must've gone through hell actually being grimy, as pathologically fastidious as he was. Point of proof: The guy keeps a couple of freshly starched dress shirts in the car in case of the dreaded sweat stain.

Bud's eyes were the color of ashes and lingered in distaste on my wrinkled T-shirt. Okay, so I'd worn it the night before. Hey, this is a homicide; I was in a hurry. So sue me. Bud didn't care for the way I dressed or for the way I cropped my hair. Last Christmas he'd disappointed me greatly with a year's gift certificate to Mr. Race's classy unisex salon called Winning Locks. I'd showed up once for an excruciating hour-long styling session with some guy who kept calling me girlfriend and admiring my high cheekbones and big blue eyes and telling me I ought to be a model 'cause I was so tall and willowy. I left looking like a complete jerk and gratefully forked over the gift certificate to an ecstatic Dottie, who had enough long, silky blond hair to send Mr. Race and his ilk into spasms.

I said, "Give me a break, Bud. It's frickin' 6 A.M. What the hell do you do? Jump up at dawn and primp your heart out in case a call comes in? You're not human anymore. You're a closet *GQ* model."

Bud laughed. "Mama always said ladies go for the well-groomed man. All it takes to look this good is a little preparation."

"Yeah, right, six to ten hours of it." I turned and watched the TV van accelerate up the road and out of sight. "How'd you keep Hastings out of the house?"

"O'Hara might've drawn her weapon. I told her to shoot 'em if she wanted."

"Hastings just informed me that the victim is a famous actress. Say it ain't so, Bud, please."

Bud grinned. "Well, it ain't Julia Roberts, but you ever heard the name Sylvie Border?"

"Soap opera?" The name clicked, but a face didn't. I wasn't even sure which soap she was on. I hadn't watched daytime TV since I went to college at LSU. That oughta tell you something about how interested I was in academics in college. The front door stood wide open, and I studied the entry foyer with its ornate brass chandelier suspended over a whiskey-colored marble floor, which reflected its glow. More down-home perks for Nicholas Black's two-grand-a-week guests.

"Black's assistant said Sylvie Border was here for some private counselin' with the Man, mixed in with a dose of downtime R & R on the lake."

"His assistant? Where's Black?"

"He's not here at the moment. Her name's Michelle Tudor, but she wants us to call her Miki. Ain't that cute? Miki with one *k* and two *I*'s. I hit her with the murder before she was completely awake this morning, but she got her act together real quick and informed me that His Highness flew to New York on his private Lear jet last night for, get this, Claire, an interview on this morning's *Today Show*."

"So Black's got an alibi? Well, we'll check that out before we cross him off our list. What about Miki with one *k*? Where was she?" What was it with these silly names? Whatever happened to Mary and Jane and Cathy? Didn't people know how to spell anymore?

"Said she spent the entire weekend at her kid's soccer tournament in Lenexa, Kansas; that's just outside Kansas City. Said her husband was there and fifty other people who could verify her whereabouts. Offered to come in for an interview the minute she gets back."

"When's that?"

"They're charterin' a flight. Should be about an hour from now."

"Suze Eggers said a neighbor found the body."

"Yeah, lady next bungalow over was swimming along the shoreline and came upon the vic before she realized what it was."

I looked at him. "*What* it was?"

Bud handed me a pair of protective gloves and paper booties. "You are not gonna believe the trouble this guy went to."

I snapped on the white latex gloves, then leaned against the deck railing and pulled the paper booties over my high-tops. Bud stood back and let me precede him into the foyer. Ever the gentleman. I stopped just inside the door and eyeballed the room. The chandelier was turned on, blazing down on a large, round oak table with a white marble top. Long-stemmed pink roses were just beginning to wilt in a fan-shaped crystal vase that looked like Lalique. A sickly scent that reminded me of mortuaries filled the air. A white card lay on the table. I bent and read it without picking it up. *Welcome to Cedar Bend, sweetheart. Relax, enjoy yourself, and I'll see you soon* was written neatly in small, back-slanted handwriting. It was signed *Nick.*

I walked through a curved archway into a long living room, which faced the lake. The day had finally dawned outside, and three large skylights threw oblong patches of sunlight over oak hardwood floors. Everything was spotless, pristine-looking, the carpet snow-white and plush under the couch. Half a dozen French doors brought in a spectacular view of the glistening lake.

On the back deck, lots of white wrought-iron furniture padded with thick blue-and-white-striped cushions were arranged in conversation nooks. Chaise lounges were lined up facing the water, among giant terra-cotta pots full of geraniums and marigolds. Now that she was out of prison, Martha Stewart would nod her approval and say, "It's a good thing, this place on the lake."

"Okay, enough with the suspense, Bud. Where is she?"

"Out here." I followed him across the glossy floor to a French door standing ajar. "No telling when somebody would've discovered the body if the neighbor lady hadn't gone in for a dip."

The back deck stretched about twenty feet out over the lake. There were steps leading down to a lower-level boat dock. I braced myself mentally. I'd had enough experience with spattered blood and brain matter in L.A., as well as various other gore, not to get sick at crime scenes, and I was well used to the incomparable stench of decaying corpses and the way it infiltrated my hair and skin until I could barely scrub it out. Unlike some officers and medical examiners, I couldn't look at dead bodies as hunks of red meat or evidence depositories; I saw them as wives, mothers, daughters, family members.

Homicide victims suffered terrible pain and unimaginable fear in their last moments on earth. Nobody deserved that, and now Bud and I, and other hard-eyed investigators like us, would prod and probe and invade Sylvie Border's body, dissect her life to find out who and what and why.

A water rescue boat sliced through the still waters, with a roaring engine, and headed straight at us. Twenty yards from the deck, the driver killed the motor, and silence dropped like a rock. There was only the gurgle and splash of water breaking on the pilings under the deck. One of the men was a state patrol diver who'd gone in after a bridge suicide last month. I didn't recognize the others. "I take it they're here for retrieval?"

Bud slid off expensive mirrored shades, folded them, and stowed them in his breast pocket as the rescue team donned scuba gear. "Take a peek over that rail and tell me what kind of psycho did her."

I leaned over the waist-high railing and peered into the water beside the lower-level boat dock. The lake looked about ten feet deep there, a little turbulent from the rescue boat's wake, but not enough to obstruct my view.

Sylvie Border sat upright in a chair sunk into bottom mud. She was completely nude, and her skin gleamed pale white, almost silvery, under the water. I couldn't see her face, but her long hair billowed up and down in underwater currents. The killer had not only submerged the victim in a chair, he'd also sunk a deck table, dishes, and silverware, entire place settings for three people, as if Sylvie were awaiting dinner guests on the bottom of the lake.

When a smallmouth bass slipped through long strands of waving hair and nibbled the victim's right cheek, I straightened and dragged my palms down my face. I said, "He's a freak, all right. What'd you think he was trying to say, leaving her at a table like that?"

Bud took out a stick of Juicy Fruit, bent it in half, and stuck it in his mouth. "He's a friggin' nutcase, that's what he's tryin' to say. Think about it, Claire. He had to've been down there in the water with her for a long time to get all that done. He's got goddamn salad forks and bread plates floatin' around down there."

I searched the bottom again. Whoever had done this knew proper dining etiquette, all right. The killer had to have spent lots of time down in the silent, murky currents with the dead woman, placing silverware and goblets just so. "He's got her taped to the chair." I squinted and tried to see where he'd bound her.

"Yes, ma'am." Bud pointed into the water. "Wrists, calves, neck, and ankles. Silver duct tape, and a lot of it."

I sucked air a moment and peered across to the Cedar Bend marina, trying to shake off macabre thoughts of the killer diving over and over to pose the corpse. "What do you have on the lady who discovered the body?"

"Some neurosurgeon's wife from the Big Apple, Jewish, plenty rich enough to come down to the sticks and stretch out on Black's thousand-dollar-an-hour couch."

"He charges a thousand dollars an hour?"

"That's what I heard." Bud popped a second piece of Juicy Fruit into his mouth, his one addiction other than silk Armani suits. "I'm telling you what, Black's got some kinda racket out here. O'Hara says the lady's name is Madeline Jane Cohen."

"Where is she now?"

"Next bungalow over. Waitin' for us to come interview her."

"Okay, we'll talk to her as soon as we finish up here." I examined the victim again, more objectively this time. I'd seen violent crimes before, even a couple of times when the vic was posed by the killer, but never anything quite this bizarre.

"Ms. Cohen's pretty shook up. Swam right over the victim. Then when she realized it was her nice little neighbor down there taped in that chair, she panicked, swallowed a bunch of water, and barely made it back to shore."

"The perp went to a helluva lot of trouble posing her like this. I guess you know what that means?"

"Couldn't've been too worried about bein' discovered," Bud said, offering me a stick of gum.

"Exactly. You oughta be a detective." I took the proffered gum and absently tore off the wrapper. "Think she was dead when she went in?"

Bud made a shrug, redonned his shades, and adjusted the aviator lenses. "Who knows what gets a maniac off? The ME can tell us cause of death soon enough." He pulled back a starched cuff and checked his watch. "They oughta be here any minute. I called Buckeye right off the bat."

"How many times you think he went down to get all that done?"

"Dunno. Plenty. Hey, maybe he's a window dresser at Pottery Barn or Crate & Barrel."

That Bud. He's a laugh riot.

"Have you checked out the bungalow?" I scanned the lake for pleasure boats. Nobody was getting anywhere near this crime scene, not on my watch.

"Nope. Got here right before you did. O'Hara pointed out the body. Accordin' to her, nothin's been touched, inside or out."

"The front door was open?"

"Yeah, Suze Eggers said the front door and the French door to the deck were both open when she got here."

"Okay. Let's see what we can find inside before forensics show. She'll have to stay put until the ME can supervise. I want retrieval videotaped."

"Buckeye's bringin' in his whole team. Said Charlie called from Jeff City and ordered them all out here since it's one of Black's privileged few."

I was more worried about rubbernecking tourists with Nikons. "What about next of kin? Does Sylvie Border have a husband?"

"Single, as far as I know."

"So she was registered out here alone?"

"Yeah, accordin' to Miki Tudor and the gal at the reservations desk. Been relaxin' out here for almost two weeks, with daily therapy sessions with the resident guru. Been spendin' a lot of time with him, from what I hear."

"Very interesting. Okay, let's get this over with."

3

Inside, the bungalow was spotless, perfection as usual from Black's top-notch maid service. The neatness didn't fit. Not that I frequented pricey hotels, or anything. My gut told me that wealthy socialites and cinema stars didn't spend time straightening up after themselves. Sylvie was probably the typical spoiled, pampered diva, and spoiled, pampered divas didn't hang up their clothes. I'd have to check on when the maids had done the bungalow last and what they thought of Sylvie. Where were the scattered newspapers and magazines and wet towels and flip-flops and half-empty cups of coffee? Like at my house.

"She didn't put up much of a struggle in here." Bud wadded up a gum wrapper and stuffed it in his pants pocket.

I said, "Could be the perp never came into the house. Maybe he sneaked up on her outside on the deck. Maybe she was sunning or napping on the chaise or soaking in the hot tub." I looked out the window. "The woods come right down to the bungalow, with bushes thick enough to hide somebody who doesn't want to be seen. It would've been easy to hide out there. She wouldn't have seen him."

"Yeah, sure," Bud said, "if he avoided about ninety security cameras and twice that many employees scurryin' around this place."

"Have a uniform walk the property after we finish in here. And crime scene needs to sweep the woods. Tell them to grid the woods behind the bungalow."

"Rained some over the weekend. Maybe the ground's soft enough to get a footprint." Bud held his blue silk tie with one hand while he carefully straightened the knot. He did that, maybe, say, one hundred times a day, a nervous habit that had grown since he'd stopped smoking. Bud said, "Might get lucky and get a shoe size. If he's a stalker watchin' her, he might've left a cigarette butt or gum wrapper behind."

"This guy's not that careless. He gets off on the act itself, treats it like a photo shoot, down to every detail. My guess is he thought this out in advance, fantasized it over and over. Control, effect, power, that's what he's into. Look how much time he took setting this up. He wants us to wonder why he offed her this way. That's his message to us, and all we've got to do is figure out the why. One thing for sure, this isn't any crime of passion. This guy has ice water in his veins."

I looked outside and saw the dive team readying underwater cameras. "It'd be easy enough to bring a boat in here. Cut the motor out a ways and glide in to the dock or bank. Or a canoe could've come in anywhere along here. If he'd waited until after dark, nobody would've been out on the water."

"Uh-uh. Security's too tight out here. You did notice the surveillance cameras at the top of the driveway?"

I nodded. "Tag the film for review, but I doubt if he'd be that stupid."

"Already done. Told the manager we'd be up to the main lodge sometime this mornin' to screen the tapes."

I shook my head. "This place is too damn neat. It looks like something out of *House Beautiful*. Or your house."

"So I'm neat. Is that a crime? Come look at the master bedroom. Looks like the maids bypassed it for some reason."

"They wouldn't do that unless they were ordered to."

"The guest room's spotless and so are the bathrooms. Both bedrooms have private decks with hot tubs, but the big hot tub's out on the back deck. Beds're made. Kitchen's clean, all the dishes put away. Except for her bedroom, Miss Border was a tidy lady."

"Or the killer wiped the place clean after he was done with her." A growing foreboding twisted up some knots in my belly. "My bet is he's not going to make any mistakes, make it as hard for us as he can. He's playing games, first with his victims, now with us."

"Victims? You think he's serial?"

"Yeah. He's got her staged like he's spent lots of time fantasizing, and my gut tells me he's had enough practice to do it right."

Bud said, "Like a little girl posin' Barbie dolls. That's what she looks like, a damn Malibu Barbie."

"Okay, let's see what we can turn up before Buckeye gets here. Maybe the guy got careless, but I doubt it."

"I'll take the desk." Bud headed across the oak floor to a slender-legged secretary pushed up against the far wall.

"Make sure you don't disturb anything. I want the crime scene photos to be exact. If he is playing with us, he might leave clues on purpose." I was lead in the case because of my experience in homicide, but Bud had four years vice under his belt with the Atlanta PD.

Undercover had given him good instincts. Too bad he
made Colin Powell look unkempt.

I searched the living room for anything even remotely out of place. An oversized sofa dominated the
room. Pale yellow sectional. Pricey leather. High quality
like everything else at Black's resort. Exact same shade
as the walls, it curved in a nine-foot arc around a brown
fieldstone fireplace. Five navy blue chenille pillows were
propped in perfect alignment against the plush back. A
glass-topped cocktail table was positioned inside the C
of the sofa, held aloft by a fantastic chunk of driftwood.
A shallow, black stone bowl was the only object atop the
glass. I knelt and looked under the glass. There were no
visible fingerprints on the glass surface. Probably wiped
clean by the killer. Buckeye would find them if they
were there.

Inside the bowl was a complicated television remote
control and a set of keys. I got out my ballpoint pen and
snagged the key ring. Three keys—all gold—one em-
blazoned with the cedar tree emblem of the resort, obviously the bungalow's key. A Mercedes car key. The third
looked like a tiny luggage key. A round gold medallion
dangled from the key ring, stamped with the NBC peacock logo. I wondered how the NBC head honchos in
New York would take the demise of their star. I carefully
replaced the keys. Maybe publicity drove the perpetrator. Maybe he was sitting in some dark hole, glued to a
television set, salivating for his fifteen minutes of fame.

A huge entertainment center held a 50-inch, flat-
screen TV and state-of-the-art stereo equipment I could
almost kill for. I had few pleasures outside work anymore, but music was something I enjoyed. Soft music at
night when I lay awake and remembered the bad things.
The entertainment center, constructed from gleaming
grained oak, was built between two giant, undraped side
windows. It was wiped down, too, with not a speck of

dust anywhere. Even the artificial silk ivy flowing from a brass pot was clean and glossy. I slid open the top drawer and sorted through an extensive selection of CDs and DVDs. Variety of films, including a dozen or more porno flicks. The second drawer was deeper and held nothing. I pressed the button on the DVD player. The drawer slid out, empty.

The adjoining kitchen revealed more polished oak and shiny beige marble. Fully stocked wet bar with cushioned stools near a window seat overlooking the deep woods. I stared through the leafy branches and heavy underbrush, wondering if the killer had stood out there in the darkness, fascinated by the famous TV star, making his plans, fantasizing about the sick things he'd do. Or had Sylvie known the person who sent her to the bottom of the lake? A friend, a jealous lover, an unknown enemy?

An answering machine was on the counter under a beige wall phone. Unplugged. Side-by-side refrigerator with ice and water and orange juice on the door. Inside, I counted six liter bottles of Perrier and five packaged bags of salad greens. Diet Italian dressing and half a bottle of California white zinfandel were stowed on the door shelf.

Sylvie either needed to do some grocery shopping or she was the typical Hollywood anorexic who could barely summon up strength for the obligatory, energetic love scenes that sent couples slamming themselves up against walls and rolling off the bed onto the floor. Methodically, I opened and shut cabinets, then searched under the sink for a wastebasket. Found it empty with a clean white plastic liner.

"George Clooney could've performed ER surgery in this kitchen," I said to Bud. "Either she hasn't been here much or she's not human. Or your mother does her cleaning."

Across the room Bud made a mock hurt look. "Hey, my mother made me what I am today. Cleanliness is next to godliness. Of course, you wouldn't know about either of those."

"Didn't you tell me your mom used to iron your underwear?"

"So? You got a problem with that?"

I had to grin as Bud meticulously went through every article on the desk. "She's been here, all right. Lookee here what I found, Claire: two weeks of mail, all stacked up, nice and neat. The last two days are still unopened. And"—he held up a single sheet of expensive beige vellum between two gloved fingers—"here's a cozy little note from the good Doctor Black, giving her grief for skippin' out on their appointment. Dated two days ago."

"Lovers' spat, you think?" Interested in that particular relationship, I joined him at the desk and picked up a couple of letters written on pale blue stationery. Both were addressed in the same nearly illegible handwriting, and I did a double take at the return address.

"Well, now, guess who these are from? Gil Serna."

"The bad boy actor Gil Serna?"

"They must've had a thing going on." Frowning, I considered the implications. "That's all we need, a big celebrity like him giving tearful, grieving interviews to Diane Sawyer."

The second blue envelope was unsealed, and I extracted a single sheet, careful to hold it by the edges. I skimmed the handwritten message. "Looks like our bad boy's got a little of the green-eyed monster. Take a guess whose ass he's threatening to come down here and kick?"

"Doctor Black, I presume?"

"You got it. And Gil baby's accusing her right here in black and white of having an affair with her shrink, not to mention cheating on Gil and ignoring his phone

calls. Which might explain why her answering machine's unplugged. Gil Serna seems a bit out of control.
Wonder where he spent the last few days?"

"How 'bout I find out?" Bud whipped out his cell
phone as if it were a magic wand. Sometimes I believed
it was. He could obtain just about any kind of information by punching a few numbers. Which made him very
handy to have around.

"Make sure Black's assistant is telling the truth. I
want verification as to exactly when Black left the
premises, how he left, and where he ended up. And I
want a crack at him before he has time to compare
notes with his assistant, or anyone else who can brief
him on what we know. If they were lovers, it'll be interesting to see how he reacts to the details of how Sylvie
died."

"I'm on it, man. Sounds like Buckeye's here." Bud
stood up when the front door opened and bantering
voices filtered into the living room.

Buckeye Boyd was the county medical examiner, and
I nodded at the motley crew of criminalists that filed
into the room. Excellent technicians they were indeed,
but they looked more like they'd crawled en masse out
of an Ozzy Osbourne concert. Lucky for us in the
Canton County Sheriff's Department, the real estate
around the lake was worth millions in taxes, which
funded us as well as any big city police department. We
were going to need all the forensics help we could get
on this case.

"So, Bud, you headed for a wedding, or what?" Buckeye said right off. He wasted no time entering his quip
war with Bud. "Man, I gotta remember from now on to
wear my tuxedo when I work homicides. Keep forgetting; don't know what the hell's wrong with me."

"You're just naturally uncouth, Bucko, my soiled little friend. You can't help it." Bud was good-natured

about Buckeye's abuse over his meticulous attire. He'd heard it enough. "Hell, you ain't changed that shirt in six years. Why don't you do us all a favor and let the little woman throw that thing away before it walks off on its own legs?"

Buckeye affected hurt. "Hey, this here's my lucky fishing shirt. My bass boat's gassed up and ready to roar soon as I get this one bagged and tagged and downtown. This is my day off, if you remember. I'm just here 'cause Charlie called down from Jeff City and requested my personal touch before you guys screw things up."

Bud retorted, "Screw up, us? Get real, man. We're so good, the victims request us."

I said, "She's outside in the water, Buckeye. Let's get this show on the road."

"Got a floater, huh?" Buckeye looked at me. He had snow-white hair, bushy enough to give him a benign, Captain Kangaroo look, but his facial hair was black— eyebrows, mustache, and short, jaw-hugging beard. He'd lived on the lake all his life, and his claim to glory was his Bass Tournament trophies. He boasted to any who'd listen that his autopsy skills came from years of filleting fish.

"Not exactly. One more thing. It's Sylvie Border, the soap opera queen."

"No shit? She's that gal that plays Amelia, right? The sexy one with hair like Jean Harlow's?"

"You know who Sylvie Border is?" I was surprised Buckeye was up on daytime television.

"Sure. She's my wife's favorite. Brigitte's been watching *A Place in Time* for goin' on twenty years. *Entertainment Tonight* did a segment not long ago about Sylvie gettin' Tinkerbell tattooed on her breast. Television crew went with her to the tattoo parlor and everything. She's got a little bitty yellow daisy on her butt, too, but she wouldn't let 'em show that one."

Curiouser and curiouser, I thought. "Is that the name of Sylvie's show? *A Place in Time?*"

"Yeah, it's the hot one right now. Comes on every day at one o'clock, just after the noon news. Brigitte says they'll win the Emmy for best soap this year."

"Get Vicky to do a comprehensive video sweep of the place and as many stills as she can get. Then dust it top to bottom. This guy set the whole thing up for us, but he's good, so get us anything you can. I'm hoping for footprints, so go through the woods with a fine-tooth comb."

Buckeye turned to his crew. "Hey, Vicky, the body's outside in the water. Get a move on; there's a ten pounder waiting for me this side of Hurricane Deck."

Bud was stabbing numbers into his cell phone. "Yeah, Buckeye, we've been hearing about that big bass for years. Maybe that ugly shirt scares him off."

"Let's get busy before ski boats start showing up and taking pictures of their favorite soap star," I said, not in the mood for jokes. "Nobody's to get wind of her name or crime scene details until I've questioned everyone involved. Understood?"

Bud had already gotten through to Gil Serna's publicist. He gave me a thumbs-up as I moved into the bedroom and waited for Vicky to set up her equipment out on the deck. Bud was talking animatedly into the telephone. He'd get whatever information we needed. Bud could sweet-talk a nun out of her rosary beads.

The bedroom was a mess. Odd, considering the immaculate condition of the rest of the place. The cream-and-rose decor was splendid and expensive. The rumpled, unmade duvet was sewn from silk damask. Thousand-dollar-an-hour Nicholas Black did spend a few pennies on his bungalows.

I had to smile when Johnny Becker ambled into the room. We called him Shag because the guy looked like

Shaggy in *Scooby-Doo*. Ancient gray T-shirt that might have been white once. Baggy, faded denim skater shorts that dropped past his scrawny knees. Orange-and-black Nikes like mine. Johnny was in his late twenties, undeniably a dude, a fact proven by about twenty earrings on his ears, not to mention his red dreadlocks sticking out in every direction. Charlie overlooked Shag's eccentricities because he knew his way around corpses and was undisputedly the best criminalist south of Kansas City. He drove Charlie totally and absolutely berserk and got a real kick out of it. Born and bred in the Ozarks, he was perfectly happy doing autopsies by day and Play Station games by night.

"Hey, Claire, you seen that awesome new Bruce Willis flick?"

"Still on your Willis kick, Shag-man?"

"Yep, he's my man." Shag set down the aluminum case he carried and looked around. "Man, did you get a load of the babe on the bottom out there? Somebody's really got his wires jerked loose to do something like that to a hottie like her." He shook his head, dreadlocks wriggling like anxious, hairy worms. "Oh yeah, Buckeye says for you to come on out. Vicky's done with the stills, and the divers are bringin' the lady up."

"Okay. No mistakes, okay, Shag? The media's going to eat this one up. Peter Hastings's already been out here snooping around."

"Yeah, they filmed us all the way in. No sweat. I'm the best, you know? Not to worry."

4

The water was clear now, and we all moved down to the lower dock to watch retrieval. It was like looking through a glass-bottomed boat at a scene from a horror movie. Three divers hung suspended under the surface around Sylvie Border, taking underwater pictures from every angle, while Vicky and Shag photographed from the deck. I couldn't take looking at the woman's waist-length hair floating eerily in the currents, so I watched for approaching boats instead.

"They're ready," Bud said.

I gave the signal to bring her up.

Nobody said much now, which was unusual at a crime scene. We all knew each other well, and sometimes it helped to make small talk, if only to alleviate the tension. The chair was sunk into the mud halfway up the victim's calves, and the divers pulled it loose with some effort, one man holding the back and one on each side.

The body broke the surface a minute later, and water streamed down the nude torso, straggling hair like bleached seaweed over her face and breasts. Bud and

Buckeye grabbed the arms of the chair with gloved hands and pulled it up onto the decking. Discarded like a sack of garbage, Sylvie's remains now would be examined, prodded, cut open, invaded by me and my friends. Though necessary, it seemed obscene.

I squatted down beside the chair. Both the victim's arms were taped to the chair, at the wrists and the elbows, the skin wrinkled and bluish from hours underwater. The fingernails were painted scarlet. A perfect manicure. Three nails on her right hand were split or broken. The left thumbnail was nearly torn off. "She didn't go down easy," I said.

Bud leaned down and studied the hanging thumbnail. "Maybe she got a coupla gouges in him before he finished her off."

"Jeez, this guy's the psychopath of the century." Shag's video camera whirred softly as he spoke. He edged around the body slowly, methodically recording everything we said and did. O.J. residual. Do everything by the book.

Buckeye went down on his haunches in front of the chair. "No visible cause of death. Probably means either drowning or strangulation. Get a close-up on those bruises," he said over his shoulder to Vicky. "Especially the big ones on the upper arms. And there's the tattoo of Tinkerbell I was tellin' you about. God, she just got that put on. I watched 'em do it."

I stared at the two-inch lime green and yellow fairy tattoo on her left breast and frowned. "Her thighs are marked up pretty bad, too. Look at those wounds on her torso that look like little half-circles. What'd you think made those, Buckeye?"

"Looks like he either hit her with something or gouged her, and some of them ain't from no perp." Buckeye pointed out a line of purple marks on the waxy flesh of one arm. "She was fish food all night long.

Turtles probably fed on her some, too, but not as bad as they would've if she'd been in the water longer."

"This is god-awful," Buckeye said.

I said, "Vicky, get your still shots of her whole body; then we'll pull back her hair and let you shoot her face." Vicky stepped forward, a quiet, thick-figured woman of forty with three teenagers at home and a husband who owned a boat dock. Quick and efficient and quiet, Vicky did the job solemnly, finished, and backed away. I got out my ballpoint pen and lifted a strand of wet hair. The face had been brutally beaten; so swollen and grotesque, it was beyond recognition. A five-inch swath of silver duct tape was wrapped around her neck and the decorative iron bars on the back of the chair, holding her head tightly in place.

"The skin on the face looks a little strange, Buckeye. What's with that?"

"Hell, nothin's gonna look right after a night underwater."

"Some of it's already sloughing off."

Buckeye said, "I suspect the fish went for the head first, so the face is more damaged than the rest of the body."

"God, they must've had a real feeding frenzy. We gotta get this psycho," Bud said, leaning back against the deck railing. He sounded as disgusted as I felt. He turned to Buckeye, all kidding aside. "What'd ya think, Buckeye? Why would he set her up at a table like this?"

"God only knows," Buckeye said, watching Shag film while I snagged back the rest of the hair behind her ears. "She's still got on diamond ear studs. Wasn't no robbery."

"It couldn't've been easy to choreograph that little scene at the bottom." I rose and frowned down at the victim. "He couldn't have done it in one dive. That means lots of coming up for air. Or full scuba gear."

"God, and she was so beautiful," Buckeye said.

"Think you can get anything off her?" I asked him.

"Most trace evidence's gonna be degraded." Buckeye grimaced and kept shaking his head. "Guess this'll put my fishing trip on hold for a good long time. I'll get what I can, but don't expect much. When Shag's done, let's take her in like this, and I'll remove the tape at the autopsy. Looks like he wrapped the goddamn tape around her neck at least a dozen times. We could get lucky with a partial print, but I doubt it."

"Guard that film with your life," I said to Shag and Vicky. "Develop it yourself. I don't want any ghoulish pictures showing up in the newspapers." I snapped off the gloves, eager to get the body out of sight. "Let's go, Bud. What'd you say the lady's name was who found her?"

"Cohen, Madeline Jane Cohen. I got a uniform over there with her. She's pretty shook up. She's been waiting on us since dawn."

Madeline Jane Cohen was sitting on her sofa in a circa-1932 black tank bathing suit, with a .22-caliber pistol atop her bare, varicose thighs. She wasn't pointing the gun at us yet, but she looked scared enough to shoot a hole through anybody that made a wrong move.

"Ma'am, you ain't gonna need that gun." Bud glanced at me and then approached the old woman with a certain degree of caution. Nothing like a frightened old lady with a loaded pistol to get your attention. A trail of wet spots led across the white carpet, where the woman had probably dripped water when she'd run to the phone. "Give the gun to me, Mrs. Cohen. You don't have to be afraid; we're gonna leave an officer here with you till your husband shows up. Remember, I told you that. Everything's gonna be fine and dandy."

"He's on his way," Mrs. Cohen said. Her voice was quick, nervous, hoarse—so were her movements when she obediently picked up the gun and handed it to Bud. "He'll be here by noon. He got the first flight out of LaGuardia. He couldn't believe it, either. Why, we've lived in New York over forty years, and never once has anything like this happened. Mort and I've been married forty-seven years in December, and never have I gone off by myself on vacation. And look what happened when I did. I swear I'll never step foot out of the city again. It's a lot safer up there with all those people around. Oh, God, that poor little girl. She was such a nice little thing. I asked for her autograph, and she gave it to me, and another one for my granddaughter, Katerina, too."

I said, "So you and Sylvie Border were pretty good friends?"

"Oh, no, no, I only met her a couple of days ago. I guess it was three days ago. Yes, it had to be on Tuesday because it was when I was coming out of the spa in the main lodge. I recognized her right away, because she's been on TV so much lately. I saw her getting a tattoo on *ET* right before I left home. She and Lorenzo—that's her boyfriend on the show—have been accused of killing her stepfather for his money. They didn't, of course, but it just looks so bad with them finding that Ginsu knife that killed him in their apartment and everything. Come to find out it was her own brother who did it, and she turned him in. He was an evil thing." Her words faltered, as if remembering this was real life and Sylvie was dead. Her eyes got real round.

"Sounds like you're a big fan," I said, trying to snap some reality back into her.

"It's the best soap on TV, but it'll never be the same again. Not ever, not without Sylvie. She was so good in

that role of Amelia. Everybody loved her." Madeline
teared up and covered her face with her palms. She
gave a little sob.

"My name is Claire Morgan, and I'm a detective with
the sheriff's department here in Canton County. You've
already met Bud. We're investigating Ms. Border's death."
I glanced at the flame-stitched wing chair beside me.
"May I sit down, Mrs. Cohen?"

"Of course, dear, please do. I'm just so nervous, I
can't think straight."

"That's understandable." I took a small notepad out
of my big leather handbag, sat down, and flipped it
open. "Why don't you tell us exactly what happened on
Tuesday when you first met Ms. Border? Did you notice
anything in particular about her that day, anything unusual?"

Mrs. Cohen shook her head. "She was just very nice,
very sweet. She said she'd wait when I wanted to run
back in the salon and grab something for her to autograph. She was gracious, very much so, just like she was
a regular person. So was Doctor Black. I can't tell you
how many times I've seen him on morning shows, especially *The Today Show;* he's on that one the most, might
even be a regular. He treats me more like an old friend
than a patient."

Bud leaned in toward Mrs. Cohen. "Doctor Black was
with Sylvie when you saw them?"

"That's right. They'd had lunch together. What a
handsome couple they made. She's so small and blond,
and he's so tall and dark."

"Had you seen them together before? Were they a
couple?" I wasn't hiding my eagerness much, but I was
interested in Mrs. Cohen's impression of that relationship.

"You mean, were they romantically involved?" Madeline made a birdlike shrug and shivered all over. Bud handed her a chenille throw off the end of the couch. It was the color of seashells.

"Thank you, dear," she said, becoming more relaxed. Southern charm works like a charm, just like I said. "I really can't say if they were or not. It appeared they were having a good time together, you know, laughing and enjoying each other's company. She held on to his arm when they left, but I suppose that doesn't really mean anything, does it?"

I nodded. "Is that the only time you spoke to the victim, Mrs. Cohen?"

"Yes, the only time I spoke to her at length. Except, sometimes when I was out swimming, I'd see her. I was a champion swimmer way back when. I won ten medals for the breaststroke back in the fifties. I still have a strong crawl." Bud and I donned suitably impressed looks and waited. "Usually that was in the morning, when she was drinking coffee out on the deck," Mrs. Cohen said, her voice growing hollow. "She'd always wave at me. That poor little thing, barely more than a child, and now she's dead. And why was she sitting at that table like that? She was sitting at a table under the water, wasn't she? I did see that, didn't I?"

I nodded and said, "That's what we're trying to find out, ma'am, who killed her and why. Did you hear anything unusual last night? Any screams or loud noises? Or did you see anyone hanging around?"

"No, no, I can't say that I did. But I take a couple of Tylenol PM every night around eight o'clock so I can get up early enough to swim before the boats get out on the lake. It's my arthritis that acts up. It's really quiet here, with all Doctor Black's security. How could this have happened? Right next door. I'll never be able to swim in that lake again. Oh, to think of her down in that water like that. Mort's coming to take me home. I can go home, can't I? You're not going to hold me, are you?"

"No, ma'am." Bud patted her shoulder. "But we'd like to take down all your personal information so we can get hold of you if we need to ask you more questions."

"Pretty interesting how Black and Sylvie were such a cozy little twosome," Bud said as we left Mrs. Cohen's condo. "What's say me and you go see if his girl Friday can really alibi her boss?"

LIFE WITH FATHER

The child sat on the bed beside the mother because she was getting over another beating. She'd failed to get the blood out of the father's white shirtsleeve. He'd punished her with the strop until she could not walk.

She whispered to the child, "He'll stay in the cellar until dinner. He won't come up here." When she reached out to him, she groaned in terrible pain. "Don't ever leave me, and I won't ever leave you. We'll always be together." She began to weep, softly so the embalmer wouldn't hear. The child glanced at the door in alarm, afraid for her but not crying; that was against the rules. She went to sleep after a while, and the child walked to the window and looked outside. It was a beautiful spring day. The red rosebush that the mother tended on the trellis by the side gate was heavy with blooms. She loved roses more than anything. She picked them and put them in a vase beside the child's bed, and they perfumed the room. The mother was lying still now, one forearm flung across her eyes.

Tiptoeing, the child moved out into the upstairs hall. It wasn't scary in the house in the daytime like it was at night, when they used the candles and shadows flickered up the walls like grasping fingers and the furniture crouched in wait like dark, devouring monsters. Downstairs, the sound of the embalmer's saw drifted up from the cellar in a distant whine, as if someone were crying. The father was busy. It was safe to sneak outside.

Once in the warm sunshine, the child breathed in fresh air, not used to being alone. The mother kept the child at her elbow at all times. It was against the rules to leave the house. Fear rose and made it hard to breathe, then receded when the sweet fragrance of roses wafted on the breeze. The mother loved roses. She would be happy if she had some beside her bed.

The child ran fast, reaching the lush rosebush and jerking off three roses before a car approached on the road. A black hearse pulled in the driveway, and the child hid behind the thick trunk of the nearest oak tree as the cellar door swung open under the porch. The father walked up the steps, and the child's breath caught with fear as the embalmer looked around the yard. Then the man driving the hearse called hello from the front yard, and the father walked down the brick walk to meet him.

Minutes later the embalmer and hearse driver pushed a gurney down the sidewalk and descended into the cellar with a dead body. The child squatted behind the tree and waited until the man had driven the hearse away, then sprinted toward the back porch.

Racing across the porch into the kitchen, the child made it to the entrance hall before the embalmer stepped out. "You think I don't know what you're up to, sneaking around, breaking my rules. You think your mother can hide you behind her skirts now?"

The embalmer grabbed the child around the waist and descended into the cellar. "You broke my rules on purpose, didn't you? You were spying on me in the cellar, weren't you? Well, I'm going to show you what I do all day in the cellar. It's about time you earned your keep, you lazy, ugly brat."

The words were mouthed in the embalmer's awful, vicious whisper, and the child was terrified. The cellar was big and dark except for bright circles of fluorescent light that shone down on two long metal tables. Naked bodies lay on both embalming tables, and one had strange black hoses snaking from the corpses into big brown bottles. It smelled terrible, like the iodine the mother put on the child's half-moon cuts after the beatings. Another smell came from the dead bodies, a strange, unpleasant odor, and the air was so cold that the child shivered uncontrollably.

The father forced the child to sit on the table beside the body from the black hearse. "I'll teach you to go outside alone. I'll teach you to be disobedient. You're just like your mother. Evil, pure evil." He reached over and dipped his hand in the blood pooled at the end of the slanted table. He smeared it on the child's face. "You've got the blood of this dead man on you, you ungrateful brat. Don't you move. You're not going to cry, are you? You know what happens when you cry. Go ahead, cry like a little baby."

The child didn't move as the embalmer began his work on the corpse; didn't cry when the scalpel slit open the veins and the blood began to drain.

The child was seven years old.

5

"I can assure you that I have nothing whatsoever to hide. Neither does Doctor Black," Miki Tudor said. Defensive as hell. She was so classic Grace Kelly, chin-length, ash-blond hair pulled back in a chignon with a tasteful tortoiseshell clasp. Tiny pearl earrings on delicate ears. A strand of large pearls draped around her neck, real ones, expensive, if I was any judge. Actually, I wouldn't know a real pearl from a peppermint Chiclet. Miki fingered the glossy necklace, revealing more nerves than she admitted.

"Nice pearls," I said.

"Thank you," she said.

Bud was ogling the young woman and making no bones about it. Not a new development. Bachelors admired attractive women. It was their nature. Ms. Tudor was ignoring his drool, highly insulted that law officers dared think that she or her renowned employer could be involved in a crime.

"Nobody's accusing either of you of anything." My voice stayed level. I'd learned to be patient. Why spook the lady before we got what we wanted out of her? Miki

Tudor wasn't the first person I'd questioned whose defenses were revved to full throttle. "We'd like to view the hotel's security tapes."

"I think you need a warrant for that sort of thing," Miki said, eyes unblinking and on me. Guarding her master like a well-heeled dog. A poodle in pearls.

"That's true in some cases. Most of the time we don't. Innocent people are usually eager to work with us. I doubt, Ms. Tudor, that you want to get off on a bad foot in a police investigation, especially when there's no real reason to."

Confident Miki looked a tad unsure of herself, so I pressed her.

"We realize this is a difficult time for the hotel staff, but if you cooperate with us, we'll get through it faster and easier."

Bud decided to ooze some Southern charm. He oozed well and knew it. He was oozing it better with pretty Miki Tudor than he had oozed it with elderly Madeline Jane Cohen. "Believe me, Ms. Tudor, we're not suggestin' you had anything to do with this. We just want to find the killer as soon as possible." His smile was white and winning, his eyes beseeching, his Rhett Butler accent heavily pronounced. Miki visibly relaxed, even dropped her hand and quit fidgeting. Maybe she didn't like female police officers. Most women didn't trust their own gender. I sure as hell didn't. Give me a male friend any day. But then I'd always been a tomboy, so there you go.

Miki folded smooth, tanned hands atop her white French provincial desk. Fingernails were immaculate, a French manicure, perfectly done. Miki Tudor defined cool elegance and obviously liked French stuff. Framed by a spectacular view of blue water, behind her white sails dotted the lake as entrants practiced for Cedar Bend's famous Independence Day Regatta, slated for a few days from now. She was a good-looking woman, and

I would bet a week's pay that Miki wore her large, tortoise-rimmed spectacles to de-emphasize her beauty. Under the big lenses, her china-blue eyes looked wary and fatigued. Miki was edgy and trying to hide it.

Miki could be concealing guilt, but my intuition told me it was more likely frayed nerves and a red-eye from Kansas City.

"We realize you haven't had much sleep, Ms. Tudor. Naturally, this is quite a shock to you. Would it be better if we postponed this interview until tomorrow? After you've had some rest?"

The offer surprised Black's personal assistant big time, not to mention Bud. I ignored his quizzical look and studied Miki's face. The young woman was incredibly readable. I liked to watch people's expressions and body language. My instincts were usually right on, and I had enough common sense to listen to my inner voice, as they say. Miki was tired. And now Miki was grateful; her big blue eyes welled up, and she became a weepy poodle. I noted, however, that no tears actually fell. A delicate lace hankie miraculously appeared in Miki's hand, and she daintily dabbed nonexistent tears away.

"Forgive me, detectives, I'm just overly emotional. I can't help it. I am exhausted and thoroughly stunned by all this. Nothing like this happens here at Cedar Bend. I thought it was impossible. And I know Sylvie. We'd become pretty good friends since she'd been coming here. We're both runners. Last week we ran three miles together every day."

She inhaled deeply, breath shaky. She shook her head. Her coiffure didn't move. She had no wrinkles, not even a frown line. Botox Betty. "I just can't seem to absorb this," she said and met my eyes in a show of vulnerability. Okay, I am a skeptical cop, I admit it. I watched her remember her duty to Cedar Bend and Doctor Black. She retreated into narrow-eyed, guard-poodle mode.

"We do everything humanly possible, and I mean everything, to protect our guests. Nick insists upon the tightest security, especially with his patients."

Nick, was it? Well, well. First-name basis between Doctor Black and girl Friday. Interesting to be sure, but that could mean anything.

"Man, that's terrible. Her bein' your friend and all." Bud leaned forward, Mr. Earnest. I thought for a moment he was going to reach out and hold her hand, but he didn't. He said, "But we really need your help today to catch this guy, if you feel up to it at all. Did the victim have any enemies that you know about? Did she mention any problems that cropped up since she's been here at the lake?"

"Well, actually, we weren't that close yet. At least not enough for her to bare her heart about her personal problems. Nick knows her much better than I do, really. He's just devastated. He could barely talk when I told him what happened."

I said, "Did he know anything about Sylvie's frame of mind the night she was killed?"

"No. He asked the questions," Miki said. "And I didn't know all the details. He wants to talk to you as soon as possible so you can tell him exactly what happened."

"When's he coming back?"

"Tomorrow morning, early. He has business meetings in New York today, and Larry King tonight. Black always honors commitments."

Right. I said, "I'd like to speak with him as soon as he returns. What time do you expect him?"

"He's coming in on the Lear, but he'll probably spend the night in New York. He's got a loft in TriBeca. His ex-wife lives in Manhattan, and he usually visits her."

"And his ex-wife's name?" I poised my pen over my notepad.

"Jude."

"Jude what?" I asked.

"Not *the* Jude?" Bud perked up considerably. "You don't mean the supermodel from Denmark?"

"Yes, she's quite well known."

"Yeah, I'll say. She was on the cover of *Sports Illustrated* a few years back. I remember it well."

Bud was downright giddy. After all, it was the swimsuit edition. He probably had it framed in his bathroom. "How long has Doctor Black been divorced?"

"Five or six years, I think." Miki leaned back in her swivel chair, obviously uncomfortable with the turn of conversation. "To be perfectly honest, I'd prefer that you ask him any questions about his private life. It's really none of my business and certainly not my place."

"Of course." I nodded, the understanding, fellow female detective. "If you'll tell me approximately when he'll be here, I can be waiting for him and get the interview over with."

Miki liked the sound of that. "Doctor Black's schedule is often disrupted, you understand. He's a very important man, but the flight plan calls for him to leave JFK at 5 A.M. New York time. That should put him down here around six o'clock our time."

"Early bird gets the worm, and all that," Bud said. He grinned. The Affable Male Detective.

Miki let down her guard enough to smile. "Doctor Black doesn't seem to require as much sleep as other people do. I can't imagine how he gets by on so little."

Curious as to why Black had so much trouble sleeping, I probed a bit. "He's certainly well known for analyzing movie stars. Does he have other interests that take up his time?"

Miki immediately warmed to the subject of her employer's shining accomplishments. "He just finished his latest book. His publishers predict another best-seller." She beamed, proud as a little poodly peacock.

"Another best-seller?"

"Nick's written four self-help books that have hit #1 on the *New York Times* best-seller list."

I did remember reading something about him writing books, and Bud sat up straight and grinned. "Maybe he'll put me and Claire in his next book."

Bud was so charming now that he ought to invest in a king cobra and a flute. But his remark wormed another smile out of somber Miki. "He just might. He likes to observe the people around him. He is a psychiatrist, after all."

"I'd like to meet him at the airport. Could you arrange that, Ms. Tudor?"

"He'll land at the hotel's private airstrip outside Camdenton and then come out here on the helicopter. Nick built a helipad out at the point."

"Just like the prez heading home from Camp David, huh?" said Bud.

A third smile was not in the cards. Put the cobra back in the basket. Stomp on the flute. In fact, Miki ignored him and concentrated on me. "Our VIP guests hate paparazzi. That's the main reason they choose Cedar Bend for their R & R. We provide private flights and complete confidentiality about their stay here."

I replied, "That privacy isn't going to last long when the press gets hold of this murder. It's only a matter of time until they find out what happened to Ms. Border."

"We're quite aware of that, Detective Morgan." All huffy and stiff-necked. "I'm getting ready to put together some kind of statement, but I want Nick to approve it before I talk to the press."

"You can't release information until we notify Ms. Border's family. Do you have information on the next of kin?"

"Oh, Nick's already taken care of that. He felt he owed it to Sylvie's family since it happened here."

That took me by surprise. "He's already spoken to the family?"

"Yes, I guess he has by now. He said he was going to call them."

"Then he's a personal friend of her family?"

"I don't know the answer to that question."

"We'll have to get their names and personal information. We'll need to interview them."

"I don't have access to information about Doctor Black's patients. You'll need to discuss that with Doctor Black himself."

I changed my tack. "As far as you know, Ms. Tudor, was Sylvie involved in any kind of trouble, here or elsewhere?"

"If she was, she didn't confide anything to me. But she wouldn't. As I said, we weren't that close. I very much enjoyed her company, however. I suppose I was a little in awe of her. She was very big at NBC."

"Was she dating anyone special?"

"She mentioned Gil Serna a couple of times," Miki admitted. Reluctant. Feeling like a traitor. "She did intimate once that they hadn't been getting along lately. But she really liked him. I could tell by the way she acted when she talked about him."

"How do you mean?"

"He called once when I was at her bungalow. We'd just gotten back from a run. She seemed really glad to hear from him. She was smiling, you know, real happy like, genuine pleasure, at least it seemed that way to me."

"Has he ever flown out here to see her?"

"Oh, no. And we definitely would've known if he had. She's only been here for a couple of weeks this time."

"This time?"

Miki stiffened as if she'd let a secret slip but recovered quickly. "She visits us two or three times a year, usually. She absolutely thinks the world of Nick."

"As far as you know, Ms. Tudor, are they more than just friends?"

Miki glanced away from me. Not good. Lying? "Not that I know of, but I certainly don't presume to keep tabs on Nick's private life."

"What about you?"

Miki was bewildered. "What about me?"

"Have you ever been romantically involved with Doctor Black?" Blunt inquiries sometimes shake people's confidence.

"Absolutely not. Never." Unequivocal. Firm. Offended. I believed her.

"That's right," Bud said. "You're married, aren't you?"

"If you must know, I'm in the middle of a divorce. But I'm not involved with Nick, and he's not the reason for my marital problems. I work for him. I respect and admire him more than anyone I've ever known, but that's as far as it goes. Ask anyone on the staff here, if you don't believe me. They can tell you our relationship is strictly professional and always has been."

"We have no reason to believe otherwise, Ms. Tudor. We're just asking the questions we have to ask. We're not trying to insult you or make you uncomfortable in any way."

"Of course," said Miki, her words as frosty as Christmas in Stockholm. "Now if you want to review our surveillance tapes, I can arrange that. But I've really spared you all the time I can."

6

"Whaddaya know. Look who visited our lady right before she ended up in the drink." Bud punched a button, and the sleek black Porsche froze in the act of turning into Sylvie Border's private drive. I stood with him in front of a wall of television screens in the security office of Cedar Bend Lodge. The tape clearly revealed Nicholas Black behind the wheel of the Porsche. Bud had paused the tape at the point when Black checked out the camera. The digital timer read 9:37 P.M.

"Muggin' for the camera. How considerate of the Doc. This places him at the scene the night of the murder," said Bud, nodding. "Okay, he showed up there around 9:30, and I'll bet a Double Whopper with cheese, Buckeye'll tell us Black was with her within the window of opportunity. Question number two—how long before Black pulls out in his fancy car?"

I said nothing as the motion-activated tape kicked on again. Black's Porsche appeared driving up from the bungalow, but the driver didn't face the camera this time. In fact, the face was averted when the car hit the main road and accelerated toward the lodge. Other cameras along the way picked up the car until it sped through the stone entrance gate and out of sight.

"He left at 12:30 A.M. That's a pretty long time to visit a patient at night, don't you think, Claire? Especially when they're not romantically involved."

I leaned against the desk, staring at the cameras and frowning. I thought about it. "Rewind it, Bud. Let's see if anybody else's in the car with him."

Bud walked around the console and worked a couple of buttons. The tape reversed, and the car rolled into view again, but it was too dark to see anyone in the passenger's seat. "He's got a cap on now." Bud pointed to the screen. "He wasn't wearin' one when he drove in."

"If it's him coming out. Could be somebody else."

"Could be a her. Or it could be Sylvie herself."

"Maybe. But unlikely."

"Yeah."

"Guess we better take a look at all the tapes, Bud. It wouldn't hurt to go back to the day Sylvie Border arrived at Cedar Bend and see if we can find anybody else paying a call on her. Might even pay to check out her previous visits, if Black keeps his tapes that long."

"Okay, I'll confiscate as many as I can. We can go halves on watchin' them. I like to share the fun with you, podna."

Oh, these Southerners.

"Miki gave us the okay, so have somebody get them together for us to review while we take statements from the staff."

The individual questioning took the rest of the day. I talked to countless maids, kitchen and room service people, and Bud rounded up everyone else who worked at the lodge. After a forty-minute session with an eighteen-year-old maid so scared she stuttered everything she said, I called it a day and checked out Sylvie's bungalow.

I wanted it secure and guarded from press vultures. Bud had gone back downtown to fill in Charlie, who was supposed to be back from Jeff City by five o'clock.

At eight minutes after six o'clock, I climbed into the Explorer and finally left the grounds of Cedar Bend. Tired, fighting one of the killer headaches I'd had for the last couple of years, I admitted things didn't look so good for Nicholas Black. So far, he was the only person seen going in or out of the victim's bungalow that day or the day before. And he'd visited her on five separate occasions during her two-week stay, not counting their therapy sessions up in the private quarters of his luxury digs. No one else had been seen anywhere close to the dead woman's bungalow. Sylvie hadn't shown up on the tapes, either, but I had a whole stack of videocassettes for homework.

Traffic was heavy as I drove across Bagnell Dam. Boats dotted the glittering lake, many trailing water-skiers in creamy wakes. Jet Skis zipped everywhere like pesky little gnats. July was the busiest month at the lake, and Cedar Bend's Regatta and Black's special Fourth of July fireworks display shot from barges out on the water brought visitors in droves. That wasn't counting the conventions at the big resorts. Cedar Bend's concierge told me four conventions were going on there this week, with fifty more slated before the huge New Year's Eve gala that Black threw for his friends and clients, with more fireworks, lots of champagne, and invited media.

Today I'd bumped shoulders with about a zillion guests all decked out in shorts and conventioneer badges and black straw Panama hats, but they'd have to have 007 infiltration skills to crash the exclusive bungalows on the point. Still, the convention rosters would have to be checked out.

My head pounded now. The traffic was horrendous, and I had to fight not to run my siren and slap the flashing light on my roof and take the shoulder home. One crawling minivan driver was so annoying that many unkind but highly descriptive remarks left my mouth in a low, muttering growl, but, hey, I didn't yell or scream profanities or make unpleasant gestures. I am classy that way.

Finally, finally, I pulled off Highway 54 and turned right on the private gravel road I shared with Harve Lester and Dottie Harper. Suddenly, it occurred to me that my fridge looked a lot like Sylvie Border's had, minus the salad and wine. I ticked off my mental grocery list. Let's see, no milk, no bread, no eggs, no bacon, no nothing. Food sounded good, but not enough to fight minivan drivers anymore. I thought I remembered a can of chili in the cabinet, but that might've been dog food left over for the stray black mongrel that sometimes came to call.

My mailbox appeared, looking old and rusted and forlorn beside Harve and Dottie's brand-new, silver, industrial-sized one, one big enough for a toddler to live in. Theirs had silver numbers that glowed in the dark; mine had numbers in faded black Magic Marker. They actually got mail. I drove on without stopping. Dottie picked up my mail and kept it in a cute little wicker basket on her front porch in case I ever showed interest in it.

Harve Lester and I had been friends for years, and although Dottie was pretty much a disenfranchised flower child with nothing in common with either of us, she took very good care of Harve. Hiring her as his nurse and live-in housekeeper had been the smartest thing Harve had ever done.

Harve and I were partners when I worked in L.A., and he'd fixed it for Charlie to hire me. He'd been shot in the line of duty and had no feeling below his waist. He was pretty much self-sufficient, but when Dottie had come along two years ago, it had made a huge difference in his life. She never left him alone for long, except for the weekends, when she ran around with Suze Eggers and lifted weights and kayaked and pretty much kept her athletic body in perfect condition. She was great, and a good friend to me, too.

When I couldn't take California anymore, Harve offered me the small A-frame fishing cabin he owned a quarter of a mile down the shore from his own house. Rent free. He'd inherited twenty acres of plum lakefront footage from his grandmother that was now worth a small fortune, and he loved it almost as much as he loved Dottie Harper. He never spoke his feelings aloud, probably because Dottie didn't share his feelings, and kept their relationship strictly platonic, but I knew him well enough to see it in his eyes.

Nearing Harve's place, I saw Dottie step out of the screened porch and wave. I braked and rolled down the window.

"Hey, Claire! Dinner's about ready! Come on in and tell us about that murder over at Cedar Bend."

Great. They already knew about the murder. That didn't bode well. Oh, yeah. Our mutual friend, Suze. "I don't know, Dot. I've got a lot of work to do, and I've got a headache."

"I'm making my special lasagna with extra mozzarella. And I'll fix you a toddy for your headache."

I hesitated and listened to my stomach react at the mention of Dottie's lasagne. Dottie did Italian right. A vision of cheesy lasagna bubbling in a pan did me in.

"Give me ten minutes to shower and change, and I'll be over."

Dottie gave a thumbs-up and disappeared back into the house. The screen door banged behind her, and I drove on to my little corner of the world. I got out of my car and stood looking out at my dock, where I tied up my little jon boat, but I saw fish pecking at Sylvie Border's ravaged face. I shut down the thought as I'd learned to do. Yep, the day was a downer, but whaddaya gonna do?

Twenty minutes later I was clean and dressed in a different T-shirt and cutoff denim shorts and sandals and was lounging in Harve's dining room chair, drinking an iced version of Dottie's famous, magnificent toddy. She'd concocted it for Harve when his muscles tightened up, and it took away my headaches and relaxed me more than anything else I'd ever tried. My mood picked up the minute Harve rolled into the room in his motorized wheelchair and gave me a big smile.

At fifty-one, he was as strong as a bull in the upper torso from fanatically lifting weights and hoisting himself in and out of his wheelchair. Although he'd had no use of his body from the waist down for years now, I'd never heard him utter one complaint. He was handsome, rugged looking. His eyes and hair were the same color, iron gray. Always positive, he actually kept my spirits up. He was my best friend in the world. "Havin' one of those fun days, are you?" Harve rolled into place at the head of the table.

"You got that right." I set the silverware around the table, and that made me think of Sylvie, too, so I picked up the salad tongs and tossed Dottie's secret recipe, her homemade Parmesan dressing, into fresh salad greens. She made the best salad dressing this side of New York City, and I popped a cucumber slice in my mouth. My stomach fussed at me for not eating all day. Sometimes my stomach hated my guts.

Harve said, "I heard you pull out a little before dawn. That's never a good sign."

Harve got up early, sometimes by four o'clock. He liked the quiet morning hours to work on his Internet business. He constructed Web sites and was damn good at it. In fact, he was a computer genius.

"How'd you find out about the murder?"

"Dottie heard it from Suze, and it was on the police band this morning." That Jacqee. She's, like, a big mouth, you know?

"It's real ugly, and Nicholas Black's shaping up as the primary suspect."

Harve whistled softly, but his eyes lit up with the old fire. Nobody loved a murder investigation more than Harve, and he was pretty good at solving them, too. He'd been my mentor at the LAPD.

I confided in him without worry. He was the one friend I kept no secrets from.

"Who got killed?"

"Ever heard of Sylvie Border, the soap opera star?"

"Oh, my God," Dottie cried from the kitchen. She held a piping hot nine-by-twelve pan of lasagna. She wore yellow oven mitts with red smiley faces on them. Her T-shirt matched the mitts. That pretty much summed up Dot. "That's Amelia on *A Place in Time*! How could anyone kill her? She's one of the good ones."

Harve made a sheepish shrug. "Dottie and I watch that show. It comes on when we're havin' lunch out on the porch."

"You and everyone else, it seems. This perp's a psychopath, Harve. We've gotta catch him quick." I told them the bare facts, and Dottie sank into a chair, still holding the lasagna. Her blue eyes were wide and shocked.

"Oh, my God." She breathed heavily, looking a little sick.

I said, "Sorry. I should've waited until after we ate."

Harve said, "No, that's okay. Do you really believe Black's that much of a sicko? He doesn't seem the type."

I shrugged. "We'll see. Supposedly, he was in flight to New York when the murder went down. I get a stab at him first thing tomorrow morning. How about doing a quick rundown on Black for me?"

In addition to Web site building, Harve used his computer savvy to track down people on the lam for individuals and law enforcement agencies. He prepared dossiers on anyone who was anyone and made twice as much money at it than he had as an LAPD detective lieutenant.

"I've already got a good-size file I put together on Black when he stirred up that big stink buying up the land around Cedar Bend Point. I'll pull it up after dinner. Tell you one thing, though, he's got a hell of a lot of interests other than psychiatry. He's big in real estate. He likes hotels, buys up resorts, and makes them exclusive by putting in a clinic for his high-class clients."

"I want to know his favorite color socks before I meet him tomorrow."

"You got it, sweetheart."

I picked up a knife and sawed thick slices off a loaf of hot, crusty Italian bread. I was salivating by the time Dottie picked up the serving spatula and cut the lasagna into squares.

I took a sip of my iced tea as Harve handed me my plate. "Black's on *Larry King Live* tonight. How about you two watching with me and giving me your impressions of him?"

"I can tell you one thing, Claire. He's a real cutie," said Dottie, shoveling a huge portion of the lasagna onto Harve's plate. She wanted him to gain weight. "I met him once. Did I ever mention it?"

"You met him in person?" I took a slice of bread and handed the plate to Harve.

"Sure did. I went to his book signing last year up in Kansas City. Barnes & Noble at the Plaza. He's got real pale blue eyes. Almost like ice, sort of, but then it feels like they burn into you, real intense-like. He said, 'Who's this book for?' and you know what, I couldn't even remember my name for a second or two. I felt really silly, like some little teenybopper with a crush." She shook her head.

"You still got that book?" I asked.

Dottie nodded. "Uh-huh. It's in my room. I've got his others, too."

"May I borrow them?"

"Sure. Remind me to get them before you leave."

I looked at Harve. "You ever meet him?"

"No, but with the big, fat file I've got on him, I feel like I'm his long-lost brother. You aren't going to believe all the irons this guy has in the fire."

"Can't wait to invade his privacy." I shut my eyes in ecstasy at the first bite of lasagna. My stomach wasn't kidding. I was damn hungry.

After dinner Harve and I sat down in his cluttered office, a converted sunporch overlooking the quiet cove. The first thing Harve pulled up on the computer screen was a head shot of Nicholas Black. Dottie was right. He was handsome, all right. I'd seen him before, of course, but just glimpses on television now and then. Up close and personal, he definitely had impact. Black hair, short, but a stylish corporate kind of cut, probably about $200 a la Bill Clinton's scandalous do by Jose out of Beverly Hills. Lean face, dark tan, high cheekbones. Gazing straight into the camera out of eyes that looked more sky blue than icy. Native American–looking. A bare-chested Sioux warrior on a rearing wild black stallion came to mind. Sex appeal. Aplenty. For sure. Even I wasn't immune, and I haven't slept with a man in years. The celibate detective.

I said, "He looks like he owns the world and everything in it."

"Yeah? Well, he's getting close."

Harve clicked the mouse a couple of times, and up popped Black's background data—page after page after page. I scanned it with real interest. Born in Kansas City,

Missouri. Maybe that was why he ended up down here in the woods. Parents deceased. No siblings. Undergraduate degree from Tulane University, master's degree from Columbia, three years in the army, and a medical degree in psychiatry from Harvard. I sat back and swiveled my chair. "Gee, and with his looks, he could have made something of himself. What's he worth?"

"He's loaded. He's bought up real estate all over the world, mostly hotels like I said, and either he's got damn good business instincts, genius financial advisers, or he's one helluva crook. Piles of cash in the stock market, even more moolah rolls in from his practice. He's got offices all over the world. At the moment, bucks are piling up from those best-selling books Dot reads."

"Have you read his books?"

"Hell, no. But Dottie's his biggest fan since she saw those icy eyes."

"I heard that," Dottie yelled from where she was loading the dishwasher in the adjoining kitchen.

I wasn't much of a reader, but I reminded myself to borrow one before I left. "His practice is worldwide?"

"Yep. He maintains small, exclusive psychiatry practices in New York, L.A., London, Paris, Rome, Tokyo, and there's talk of setting up one in Moscow. He's got trusted colleagues running them for him, but he visits each office regularly to see special patients. Busy guy. Must take days just to count his money."

"And here he is, holed up in good old Missouri, out in the middle of nowhere. Doesn't ring quite true to me. His assistant intimates he's been spending lots of time here at the lake."

Harve said, "It says here he's got a Lear jet to travel in. And a Bell 430 helicopter with a helipad, I might add. He's also got a motor yacht he had custom-built to use on the lake. He likes his toys and finds time to play with them."

"Money'll do that for folks."

"Wouldn't know."

"Me, either."

The television suddenly blared in the living room, followed by Dottie's excited cry. "Hey, guys, Larry King's coming on any minute."

Harve tapped in the print command for Black's dossier, and I followed him into the living room at the front of the house. It was a bright daffodil yellow. Dottie liked for everything to be yellow, different shades, maybe, canary, butter, sunshine, but all yellow. I chalked that up to her sunny disposition. Harve's penchant for technology showed up in the 71-inch TV screen surrounded not only by sound but every digital instrument known to man. Black wasn't the only man who liked toys.

I owned a 13-inch model, which wasn't hooked up to cable, but hey, it was color. I felt a hint of culture shock watching a screen the size of my plate-glass front window. When Black came on camera, I had a physical response that I didn't like. He was way, way too good-looking. I studied him with professional objectivity, as a suspect instead of a man, trying to figure out exactly what brought out that reaction in women. He looked dangerous, sensual. And those eyes were too intense given his otherwise relaxed, confident demeanor.

Larry King asked him right off about the book he was promoting. Black was at ease with the camera—articulate, urbane, with a well-masked accent I detected but couldn't quite place. It sure as hell wasn't Kansas City.

"Does he know about the murder yet?" Harve muted a toilet tissue commercial with little puppies sliding into four-roll packs.

"Miki Tudor, his assistant down here, said she told him. But I notice he's handling his grief rather well."

Dottie came in with a tray of coffee and cherry cheesecake. My stomach said, Oh yeah. She said, "You'd think he'd act more upset, or even cancel the show, since she's his patient."

I took a sip of the coffee. Decaffeinated. Yuck. "Yeah, if Black's upset, he's hiding it pretty good. Wonder what else he's hiding?"

"You'll have him in your gun sights soon enough. I almost pity the guy." Harve smiled at Dottie when she poured his coffee. "Why don't you record your interview with him and let me listen to you grill him?"

"I bet he uses a bunch of psychobabble stuff to throw you off," said Dottie, finally sitting down with her own coffee and cheesecake. "If you can remember your name when he puts those killer eyes on you."

Harve laughed. "Interesting use of words, Dot."

"I'll be forearmed by then, thanks to Harve's dossier. Maybe I'll ask him his take on the killer, since he's a psychiatrist."

"Good point," Harve said. "I forgot to mention he assisted the FBI on one case. He testifies in court sometimes, too. You'll read all that tonight."

"I've had some truly sad news today," Black said on-screen, instantly drawing all our attention back to the tube. "Shocking, terrible news."

I felt my muscles tense, and Larry King leaned forward, pleased as punch about the shocking, terrible announcement going out live on his show. Ratings, ratings, my kingdom for ratings.

"I hope to hell he's not thinking of telling—" I stopped midsentence when Black spoke again.

"The wonderful young actress Sylvie Border, a very close friend of both of us, Larry, died last night at my resort in Missouri."

King looked as stunned as I was. "What the hell does he think he's doing?" I jumped up, rattling my coffee cup. "This is going to whip up a frenzy around here."

"Oh, my God. Sylvie was on this show not a month

ago." King glanced off camera, presumably at his producer. "I can't believe it. She's so young . . . how . . ."

Black looked the picture of sorrow now. "It's a terrible tragedy. I can hardly believe it's true, either. I spoke
to her parents early this morning, and understandably,
they're taking this extremely hard. I want to encourage
the press to leave them alone, give them some time to
grieve in peace. That's why I'm bringing this up now.
I'm making a plea for privacy for the family."

Larry King shook his head and said, "What happened to her, Nick? Are you at liberty to tell us anything
more?"

"She was found murdered," Black said. King's sharp
intake of breath was caught on air. "I don't know all the
details. I was on my way up here already. I'm leaving that
to the police. I understand the Canton County sheriff is
handling the investigation. I know Sheriff Charles Ramsay
personally, and I have every confidence he'll find Sylvie's
killer."

"Thanks for nothing, Black." I was so angry, my voice
shook. "You've just sent every frickin' camera crew in
the country down here."

Dottie said, "Why'd he announce it on the air? He
ought to know better than that."

"He probably did it to get publicity for this new
book, and if he did, he's gonna regret it. I'm gonna
make sure he doesn't talk about it on any more television shows or at book signings, unless he wants me riding his back night and day until this case is over."

LIFE WITH FATHER

The mother was in excruciating pain, but she pulled the child by the hand across the upstairs landing. The embalmer had beaten her again with the strop because she'd objected to the child going down into the cellar, where the corpses were. She had been terrified, but the child had come upstairs from the cellar for dinner, all covered in blood and stinking of embalming fluid. The father kept the child in the cellar all day now, away from her. He called the child Brat now, all the time, and the child refused to talk and had eyes that were empty and haunted. She had to escape, had to get the child away. She packed one suitcase for their things, and as soon as the child was sent upstairs to be readied for dinner, she got the suitcase and pulled Brat along the upstairs hall. The embalmer had kept Brat down there until five-thirty, and she didn't have much time to flee. They had to get out now. She held her side where he must have cracked her ribs when he kicked her two nights ago. It hurt to walk, even to talk.

She whispered to the child, "Hurry, hurry, before he comes . . ."

But he was standing at the bottom of the staircase, waiting. She screamed in utter horror, and the child awakened from a stupor because screaming was against the rules. She ran for the back stairs, dragging the child with her, but the father took the steps three at a time and caught her by her long blond hair before she could slam the door. He jerked the child from her hand and flung the child against the wall. Breath knocked out, the child slid limply to the floor and watched the parents fight. The mother went wild then and attacked the man with all her remaining strength. She clawed at his face and eyes and screamed until she couldn't scream anymore, and he hit her hard with his fist and knocked her to the floor. He grabbed her up like a rag doll and forced her back against the wall. He held her off the floor, his fingers clutching her throat harder and harder. The child struggled up and screamed for the first time ever and ran and jumped on the father's back. The father shook the child off and rammed a fist into the child's stomach.

Gasping and coughing, the mother fled for the front stairs, but he reached her and held her with one hand while he hit her with his other fist; then he flung her down the staircase with all the force of his rage. She screamed, but it died when she hit the stairs and tumbled over and over until her head hit the floor below with a loud thud.

"This is your fault," the embalmer raged, jerking the child off the floor. At the bottom, the woman was moaning, and the child said, "Momma, momma," and the father said, "Go ahead and die, you whore."

Then he picked up the struggling child in one arm and dragged the mother by her left foot down the cellar stairs, her head hitting each step along the way. Thump . . . thump . . . thump . . . He went to the cold room, where he kept his corpses. He tossed the screaming child down the steps into the darkness, then picked up the mother and threw her down beside the child.

"Nobody leaves this house," he said, so angry his voice was breathless in a way the child had never heard before. "If I have to keep you down here forever, you'll learn not to break my rules."

The embalmer slammed the steel door shut, and the child cradled the mother's head and held it still and listened to the wheezing sounds coming from her chest. The cold, black darkness surrounded them like a dank and malignant blanket, and the child sat shivering in the dark until the mother's breathing stopped, and the child was alone with the dead.

The next morning the father opened the steel door, and light slanted into the cold room. The child was too chilled to move. The father draped a blanket around the child and, once they were upstairs in the house, sat the child down beside the roaring fire. The father was no longer angry. He sat in a rocker and watched the child shiver uncontrollably. Then he said, "You shouldn't have made me knock your mother down the steps. Now she's dead, and it's all your fault."

The child looked at the flames.

"But I'm not angry with you. It's probably for the best. I can fix her where she looks like herself again, so she's smiling and beautiful. You'd like that, wouldn't you, Brat? For her to look peaceful and happy?"

The child nodded, remembering how the mother's head was twisted and her mouth was frozen open in a silent scream. "That's good, Brat. That's the way you should behave. Come along. You can help me prepare your mother."

The embalmer picked up the child and returned to the cellar. He sat the shivering child on the tall swivel stool and walked into the cold room. When he came back out, he had the mother in his arms. He laid her gently on the steel table, straightened her broken neck with a gentleness he had not shown her in life. "See how beautiful she is, with all that long blond hair. Why don't we braid it so it'll look all neat and pretty? Will you help me do that?"

The child nodded, and together they took the rest of the hairpins out of the mother's big, soft bun. The father washed the blood out of it with the water hose suspended above the table and taught the child how to braid.

"There, see, that makes her look very nice. It'll only take a jiffy to stitch up those cuts on her face, and I can put make-up on the bruises. Watch. See how I can make her smile." He closed the dead mother's mouth and prodded the cold, stiff lips until they curved in a caricature of a smile. "See, look how happy she is now."

The child thought she did look happier now.

"You must never tell anyone that you killed your mother," the father told the child then, leaning close and speaking in a stern voice. "They would come and take you away and bury you alive in a deep, dark hole in the ground. You'd never see your mother or me again."

The child stared at his mother's strange grimace, afraid.

"Now you can help me prepare her, like we've done with the others, but this time it's special because it's your own mother. This is an honor for both of us."

The embalmer gathered the sharp tools and rubber hoses and chemicals he'd need and rolled the towel-covered instrument tray beside the child. "You can hand me the tools I need. You can make up for killing your mother by being my helper." He pointed at an instrument on the tray. "Now hand me that big scalpel."

The child picked up the scalpel. It felt heavy and

cold. The father took it and began to work. The child took the mother's cold hand and squeezed it tightly but didn't cry as the father cut into her soft white flesh.

The child was eight years old.

7

The Cedar Bend helipad was located at the tip of the point, where Black kept his private quarters and office. I was seething inside when I arrived there early the next morning, but I was the picture of calm tranquility, pure Zen, as Miki the Poodle ushered me through palatial marble halls to Black's lavish tan-and-black office. Ten leather-framed Rorschach inkblot designs lined one wall, and I studied each one in turn. In my present mood, they all looked like the devil to me. I stood in front of a windowed wall and watched the sun come up.

Not long after, the dull, insistent buzz of rotors infiltrated my glass sanctuary, and the Bell 430 helicopter Harve had described the night before came barreling into sight. Surprise, surprise, guess what color it was? Nicholas Black probably raised black-and-tan coonhounds, too.

I watched the copter bank right as graceful as a gull, then straighten and head home. Black was precisely on time. Well, good. The sooner I got my hooks in him, the better. Thanks to Doctor Ain't I Somethin', media vans were rolling to the lake in swarms, like killer bees but with deadlier stingers.

I stood in Black's penthouse office. It had its own third-floor wing, did I mention that? Gee, I'm impressed. The craft set down expertly on the round concrete pad, and I watched the wind from the rotors blast the calm water out in concentric circles. A security guard in uniform rushed to open the door for Black, but it wasn't Suze Eggers. Maybe Eggers annoyed Black, too.

Decked out in a dark blue suit, white shirt, and red tie—nothing casual here—Nicholas Black stepped out, still talking into a cell phone. He thrust off a briefcase to the security guard, who trotted after him like a trusty beagle, as he bent low and made his way swiftly up a wide dock of bleached wood lined with about a dozen berths, each with its own Cobalt 360. All black and tan, of course.

My God, I'd been transported to Palm Beach. Where were the polo ponies and Prince Charles? Did I mention my penchant for sarcasm? Yeah, well, ostentatious wealth is a big trigger, let me tell you.

I watched him until he disappeared somewhere below. My mouth watered in anticipation. My fingers twitched. My eyes lit up. Armed with a fifty-page dossier about him memorized in my head, I was ready to put my foot on his chest and force him to confess.

I wondered if Miki Tudor was the one on the phone with Black. I turned and observed through an open door that Miki was at her pretty little white desk across the hall, her usual sleek self dressed in white with pearls all shiny around her neck. It looked like she was doing her nails, but she could have been admiring her big diamond ring. But I'd know if they'd talked again after she apprised him of the murder; I'd already requested both Black's and Miki's phone records.

I rolled back my shoulders like the kick-boxer I am, ready, willing, and eager. I was good at interviews, even with psychiatrists. I waited. Impatient. Resisting the

urge to pace, I stood still. The complex was connected
to Black's private quarters, essentially a French chateau
with a massive glass atrium walkway. Maybe he went
next door to Buckingham Palace to admire all his stuff.
That might take some time. Maybe he was on the phone
to the president, advising him on the war against terror.
Maybe he was wiping his fingerprints off everything he
touched, just in case he killed somebody else and threw
them a tea party under the lake.

"Sorry to keep you waiting, Detective."

A deep, masculine voice out of nowhere. I spun
around and found Nicholas Black right behind me.
The mirrored doors of the elevator slid soundlessly together, creating a seamless wall of mirrors. Clever, clever.
I bet it was a one-way mirror, too, so Black didn't walk
into any surprises. He came straight to me, the briefcase
in his left hand, right hand extended to shake. I took it.
His clasp was firm and dry. So was mine.

"Nick Black. Fill me in on what you've got so far."

"Claire Morgan, Canton County Sheriff detective."

"I know who you are. Miki told me you wanted to
meet me here as soon as I got in. Sorry, I'm an early
riser." He smiled and gestured at a chair. "Please, sit
down. Would you like some breakfast? Or a cup of coffee? I'm having one. Miki makes terrific coffee."

"Gee, how nice for you."

Black raised an eyebrow, and I decided to tone it
down. He was a tone detector. Time to shift to the polite, "let's be civilized and have coffee together" mode.

Like an apparition in the mist, Miki floated in wearing her all-white business suit, including hose and strappy
high heels, and carrying a silver tray that held a coffee
urn, a silver creamer, and two white cups and saucers.
Fine white china with a narrow band of black and gold
around the rims. No monogram or design. Simple but
elegant. The same kind of china used under the water

with Sylvie and everywhere else at the resort. I settled into the tufted, tan leather armchair across from Black's massive ebony desk. It was polished to such a gleaming patina that I could see the clouds in the sky behind him reflected in the top.

I thanked Miki and balanced the cup and saucer on my lap, atop a crisp white linen napkin. I watched her leave, then said, "Ms. Tudor is a very efficient assistant."

The way I said it was designed to make him think I suspected more was between them than an employer/assistant relationship. Black obviously picked up on it, because he studied me a moment, then chose to ignore the remark. His reaction was more effective than acknowledging my insinuation. He knew that. I knew that. He said, "Miki's a treasure, all right. I don't know what I'd do without her. She keeps everything running around here."

He does like his lackeys, I thought, *Sycophants Unlimited,* and then stopped myself. I was exhibiting the kind of chip-on-the-shoulder attitude that could jeopardize my case. I didn't usually react so strongly to people, but the man brought it out in me. He might be phony, but he wasn't stupid, so I changed my approach. "I appreciate your seeing me first thing, Doctor Black."

"Please, call me Nick. And I'm glad to talk to you. Sylvie was a special person. Very special to me. I want her killer caught and punished. I promised her parents I'd see to it."

"Are you in the habit of making promises you have no way of keeping?"

Black's eyes delved into mine, searching, analyzing. I felt like his patient but stared back without blinking until he said, "I intend to cooperate in every way possible. Her parents are distraught, understandably so. They asked me to intercede with the authorities and the media on their behalf, and I felt obligated to do so."

"Then you are well acquainted with Sylvie Border's parents, I take it?"

Black picked up the silver creamer and dribbled about a teaspoon of cream into his cup. Every movement was easy and graceful, while nonchalantly masculine. He held the creamer toward me. I shook my head. "I take mine black."

His eyes lingered on my face a moment too long; then he replaced the creamer on the tray. He didn't add sugar. He was one handsome fella, yes, sir, and mercy me. Charisma radiated from him like heat off the burning desert sands. I wasn't so out of the romance game that I couldn't feel it. Sexual chemistry was alive and well, and almost a tangible presence, as if it stood personified between us and laughed when I tried to step around it. I wondered if he felt it. Because I sure as hell did. But it wasn't ever going to happen.

I raised my cup, took a ladylike sip. Not that I'm much of a lady, but I do know how to sip—I just put my foot down at crooking my little finger. The coffee was good and strong, brewed to perfection, no decaffeinated crap for Nicholas Black. Perfect Miki strikes again.

Black resumed the conversation. He said, "I don't know them extremely well. We've met on several occasions, and I found them to be nice people. I knew them well enough to want to break such horrible news in person before they heard it on TV."

"Did you also feel obligated to break the horrible news to the whole world on CNN, or was that simply a publicity stunt to promote your new book?"

Black's facial expression didn't waver, but I watched something move in those blue eyes, something that hinted at danger. "I sense a certain hostility in you, Detective. Do you think I killed Sylvie? Is that what this is all about? Or do you just exhibit this chip on your shoulder as a matter of course?"

"Oh, it's a matter of course, I guess. Especially when I've just brought up a beautiful young woman who spent the night under the lake being nibbled by carp. And you were her only known visitor the night of her murder."

He didn't look away, but he waited until he'd taken a drink and replaced the cup on the saucer, then said, "I suppose I'm the primary suspect until you verify my alibi?"

"Everybody's a suspect until we verify their alibi. Tell me about the last time you saw Ms. Border alive." I pulled my notepad and pencil out of my purse and moved to the edge of my chair like Lois Lane at the *Daily Planet*. He made me wait. Choosing words carefully?

"It was the night before last, just before I left for New York."

"And where was that?"

"I went down to her bungalow."

"What time was that?"

"I guess it was around nine o'clock, but it could've been nine-thirty, or even ten."

"When did you leave?"

"I stayed about thirty minutes or an hour, I guess. She was getting ready for bed. She said she'd gone running earlier in the evening with Miki and was tired. We sat outside on the deck and watched the water."

I jotted without looking up. "Are you sure about these times, Doctor Black?"

"Fairly certain. I'm guessing, so they could be off some."

Lie number one and still counting. I said, "What was the purpose of your visit to Ms. Border's private bungalow?"

I watched him now for hesitation or signs of guilt. He stared back as if he knew what I was doing and how to get around it. I had an uncomfortable feeling he could hold his own in any police interrogation. Then again, I am not half-bad when I'm really motivated.

"She called up here and asked if she could borrow my car over the weekend, so I drove it down to her bungalow."

"Did she say why she wanted to use the car?"

"She said she needed to go to the grocery store and then pick up some things at the mall."

"Did she ever use your car before that night?"

"Last weekend, on Sunday afternoon. Shopping. Sylvie loved to shop."

I heard the sorrow thicken his voice now, and it seemed real enough. On the other hand, the surveillance camera showed his car leaving around midnight. Maybe I could make him dig that hole a couple of feet deeper. "How did you get home that night?"

"I walked along the lake. It's quicker than following the road back. It was a beautiful night with a full moon and lots of stars. I like walking at night. It helps me think."

He had adroitly covered himself with a viable story. "What did you have to think about, Doctor Black?"

"I was a little worried about Sylvie. I have other cases that dwell on my mind, as well."

"Why were you worried about Sylvie?"

"She wasn't happy, and she wouldn't say why."

"And what time did you say you left her bungalow?"

"About ten or ten-thirty. I had to get back and pack. We took off at midnight."

"We?"

"My flight crew and myself."

"Did you have sex with Sylvie that night?"

For the first time, anger sparked in his eyes, then turned into the blue ice Dottie had described.

"Certainly not. I told you already that she was a

friend, Detective. A good friend and a patient. We never had sex, nor would I ever have sex with any patient. I'm sure you know that would violate the doctor/patient relationship."

I'd riled him, and that was a good thing. Riled people made mistakes and said stupid things. "I meant no offense, Doctor. I'm just doing my job."

He relaxed and smiled, teeth white and even, a veritable Crest commercial. I wondered if they were capped, or at the least, bleached. "I have nothing to hide. Eliminate me as soon as possible so you can move on and find out who did this."

"Thanks for the tip on police procedure. I think I'll take you up on that and see if I can't find the killer." I can get a little sarcastic sometimes.

"You're a very angry lady, aren't you? It'd be interesting to find out why."

"Sorry. I don't believe in paying a thousand dollars to lie around on a couch and tell somebody my secrets. Seems like a stupid thing to do." I smiled ingratiatingly. "And besides, what I am doesn't matter in this investigation, Doctor Black. It's you we're investigating." For effect, I looked down at my notes. "Did Ms. Border act oddly or say anything out of the norm when you saw her that night?"

"Actually, she did. Like I said, she was unhappy, and she'd been upset all week. I'd noticed how stressed out she was in our first session, but we'd been making progress. She was relaxed and happy for a day or two; then all of a sudden, she reverted back to the way she was when she got here."

"What was she upset about?"

"I'm afraid that is privileged information, Detective."

We stared at each other, assessing, probing, panting. *He's enjoying this*, I realized, *but the trouble is, I am, too. Not good. Not smart.* I found myself wanting to best him, put him down. How unprofessional was that? I shrugged out of that coat and said, "Did she mention anyone, having a fight with a boyfriend, somebody harassing her, anything like that?"

"Since it has already been reported in the press, I can say that she's having a love affair with an actor. She said he'd called earlier that evening, and she'd hung up on him."

"Did she seem angry?"

"Not particularly, but Sylvie is a good actress. I always keep that in mind when I treat actors."

"Was it usual for her to put on an act with as good a friend as you claim to be?"

"We were good friends," he said calmly. Casually, he crossed his legs, put his elbows on the chair's armrests, and steepled his fingers. I had a feeling that was one of his favorite contemplative psychiatrist positions. He could probably daydream about buying more big toys doing that, and patients wouldn't be the wiser. I also had a feeling I'd gotten the last spark of anger out of him that I was going to get. He went on, "When she didn't want to talk about her problems, she'd hide behind facades. We all do that. Even you, I suspect."

I gave no reaction. So what if it was true?

"You look familiar," he said suddenly, and I tried not to react but with more difficulty.

"I've seen you somewhere before; I'm sure of it. I thought so the first minute I saw you."

"Maybe I gave you a speeding ticket."

"I'd definitely remember being stopped by you, Detective." His eyes were ravaging my person as he tried to remember. Our mutual friend, Mr. Sexual Awareness, flexed his muscles this way and that, back in our faces big time. "We crossed paths somewhere, trust me. I've got a knack for remembering faces."

I'd had enough of that subject. "You're mistaken.

We've never met. Can anybody vouch for the time you arrived home from Ms. Border's bungalow on the night of the murder?"

Black shook his head. "I never keep my personal staff past five o'clock unless something special is going on. Most of them have families to get home to, and I try to remember that. Do you have a husband and children to get home to, Detective Morgan?"

"Did anyone see you walking home from Sylvie's bungalow? Another guest, perhaps, or a room service waiter?"

"Not that I am aware of."

"Do you know the whereabouts of your black Porsche at this moment?"

For the first time, his surprise registered clearly. It seemed genuine. "I assumed it was still at Sylvie's place."

I took advantage of his disconcertment. "How long have you known Ms. Border?"

He hesitated and spoke so carefully that I knew he was hiding something. "I've been treating her for a couple of years, but I've known her for a long time. Since she was very young."

I sensed I was on to something at last, so I attached myself to the subject like an octopus sucker. "In what capacity, Doctor Black?"

"She modeled some in New York, before she got her big break on the soaps. My ex-wife introduced us."

"Your ex-wife is the supermodel known as Jude. Is that correct, Doctor Black?"

"You do your homework. Yes, she is, but we've been divorced for years."

I jotted that down. I'm good at jotting. I came at him from a different angle. "Was Ms. Border in love with you?"

His arresting blue eyes reacted, but not enough for me to get a bead on the reason why. I really, truly hate interviewing psychiatrists. Actually, I hate psychiatrists period. They were trained to take any question or comment without reacting. They were dynamite on the witness stand, and Nicholas Black was better at it than most.

"As I said before, I never become involved with patients. Never. I can't state it more unequivocally than that."

"Not even emotionally?"

"Like you, Detective, I've trained myself to remain unemotional." He was studying me again, and I tried not to fidget. "Have you ever lived in New York, Detective?"

Yeah, right, like I was going to start answering his questions. "What kind of person was Ms. Border?"

"Basically, she was a good kid. She had some problems, including a drug habit that got her in trouble, but I was helping her get clean."

"Any other kinds of problems?"

"Come now, Detective, you know as well as I do that I'm not going to tell you anything discussed in my confidential therapy sessions with Sylvie."

"Not even if it would help us find her killer?"

"Perhaps, if I thought it could catch the animal who did this to her, and if I had permission from the family. But neither of those things is likely to happen."

"How did Sylvie seem to you that last night?"

"I told you. She was sad and upset. I think she was depressed about her boyfriend."

"You mean Gil Serna."

"You're very good, Detective. I'm impressed."

"I try. Was it Gil Serna who called that night and upset her?"

"Yes."

"Why?"

"He thought she was down here to have a fling with me."

"But that was groundless, of course."

"Of course."

"What time did you say you arrived at her bungalow?"

Black smiled, as if well aware I was probing his story for inconsistencies. "Sometime between nine and ten."

"How long did you stay?"

"Thirty minutes to an hour."

"Was Sylvie serious about Gil?"

"Enough so that Sylvie was going to buy him a Porsche for his birthday. That's another reason she wanted to borrow mine. To test-drive it."

"You didn't mention that reason a minute ago."

"No, I didn't."

"That's an expensive car. From what you've said, the two of them didn't sound happy enough together for her to spend that kind of money on him."

"Everyone is different in the way they choose to show their love for another."

"What is Gil Serna like?"

"He's insanely jealous. She kept trying to make him feel secure in her love but without much luck."

"Insanely? Is that your professional opinion? Do you think Gil Serna is capable of murder?"

"You know what they say. Everybody's capable of murder under the right circumstances. I'm sure you've encountered that kind of person yourself, Detective."

The remark hit too close to home, and I fought back rising memories and the pain they brought with them.

Black noticed that, too. He frowned slightly and narrowed his eyes. "If Serna is the one, Detective Morgan, I hope you can prove it."

"Rest assured, Doctor," I said.

"You're very confident, aren't you? And now that I've met you, somehow I think you will solve this case. You've got steel in your eyes. Were you born around here?"

"If you don't mind, sir, I prefer to ask the questions."

"Fine."

"Did you say Ms. Border was making progress under your care?"

"Yes. She was feeling much better. We'd made some important breakthroughs. She was rethinking how she felt about things."

"She had a tendency to blame herself for her problems?"

"Sometimes, especially in romantic situations. She was insecure."

"Yet she seemed to have it all—looks, money, fame."

"Sometimes people hide their misery behind those kinds of facades. It's called self-preservation."

Something about the way he looked at me made me wonder if I should slap on some more bricks and mortar to my own facade.

"Has the cause of death been determined?" he asked suddenly. This time I could see his pain quite clearly. He had cared about Sylvie Border, and a hunch told me there was more to their relationship than what he intimated.

"Not officially. Why do you ask?"

"Miki described how she was found. It cuts me to think she suffered long."

My cell phone began to play the "Mexican Hat Dance" song, and I pulled it off my belt.

Bud said, "It's me, and we got a hit on the surveillance tapes. A busboy showed up at Sylvie's place around ten-thirty, went in the gate, and didn't come out. Guess who has a rape record and didn't show up for work today? Our old friend Troy Inman. Meet me at the station, and we'll go get him."

"I'll be there in ten."

Nicholas Black watched me stand up and replace my

phone. "Something important has come up, I presume?"

"Doctor Black, I'd like to continue this later, if you'll grant me the time."

He stood and retrieved a white linen business card from a gold desk holder. He took a pen and scribbled something on the back of it. "This is my private cell phone number. You can reach me on it at any time. I'll do anything I can to help you find out who did this."

I nodded, glad to hear it, and took his card, because I wasn't done with him yet, not by a long shot.

8

"Where the hell is this place?" Bud asked me twenty minutes after I'd left Nicholas Black's resort palace. We avoided maybe a million potholes as we jounced down a gravel road about ten miles outside the town of Camdenton.

"Inman lives about half a mile down this road in a trailer court. I ran him in on a domestic last January right after the Super Bowl. He beat up his wife when the Rams lost in the last three minutes of the game."

Soon the King Camelot Court loomed up in all its glory. The regal name was lost on the place. Most of the trailers were the small travel kind, shabby, rusted, and dirty. I had a feeling that rent was paid with first-of-the-month welfare checks.

Resident children had a playground in a weed-choked field in the middle of the trailers. The teeter-totters teetered and tottered on their last legs. The slide looked lethal. The whole place looked dangerous. Three little girls about seven sat in the dirt under a rusty swing set sans swings. One was wearing a red two-piece bathing suit, one had on blue baby-doll pajamas, and one had on dirty white shorts and no shirt. It was a pathetic place to raise kids. Unfortunately, I'd seen other places just like it or even worse in my line of work.

"Jeez, what a dump," Bud said.

"Over there, under the oak tree. The silver one."

A man wearing jean shorts and a red T-shirt that said SCREW YOU, LADY, PLEASE? saw me looking and ducked back inside his house. "What'd you bet crank rocks and quarter bags are hitting the toilets all over this place?"

Bud said, "Yeah, we oughta cruise through here once a week. Drug control without leavin' the car."

We pulled up near the nasty little trailer. "Tell me, Morgan, how's our boy finance a snazzy trailer like this on busboy's pay?"

"It's better than the rest of them. His wife's a cocktail waitress at the Blue Pelican Country Club. She makes good tips."

"Yeah? She oughta take them and get the hell outta here."

By the looks of the front yard, it appeared that Inman tossed all his garbage and beer bottles out the window instead of paying for trash service. I searched dingy windows for signs of life.

"Park down behind those bushes, and let's walk up. It'd be better if he didn't see us coming, especially if he's been hitting the booze."

I climbed out, unsnapped my shoulder holster, just in case. Inman was a big, mean guy with a temper—a real charmer. He messed with me last time, and I'd busted my hand breaking his nose. I listened. Everything was quiet except for the voices of the little girls under the torn-up swings. They were playing red rover. A little hard to do with just the three. Maybe they had imaginary friends.

Bud came up beside me and spoke in a low voice. "You ready?"

"You take the back, in case he runs. I'll take the front."

"Listen, Claire, don't go in alone if there's trouble. Wait for me." Bud looked at me as if he expected me to agree to that. Bud thought I took chances.

I said, "No sign of his truck. Maybe he's not here."

Bud slipped around behind some thick forsythia bushes. I took a deep breath and sidestepped garbage and other junk all the way to the front door. The soles of my sneakers crunched on hundreds of rotten acorn shells. I hoped all the beer bottles scattered around didn't bode ill for this takedown. Everything seemed unnaturally quiet, as if nature were holding its breath to see if we could surprise Inman. Even the birds had shut their beaks, probably irked by Bud's less than stealthy trek around back. The sixth sense that served me well quivered, and I drew my Glock and held it down alongside my right thigh. I edged up on the little porch, keeping my body to one side of the door.

"Open up, sheriff's department."

I hit the aluminum screen door with a doubled fist. It rattled like crazy but brought nothing alive inside. I tightened my grip on my weapon. "If you're in there, Inman, open up. Don't make this hard on yourself."

No answer. Cautiously, I opened the screen door and found the scarred door ajar. I pushed it open with my toe. The smell of cigarette smoke and stale body odor hit me in the face. Inch by ugly inch, Inman's home materialized. A ragged, overturned brown recliner. Broken dishes scattered around on the filthy green shag carpet. A woman lying on her back, arms outflung, blood all over her face. A broken Budweiser bottle lay beside her head.

I checked out behind the door, eased in with my back flat against the wall. Gun ready, nerves on edge, I surveyed the place. Kitchen empty and in a shambles.

The blood spatter visible on greasy white cabinets looked like three scarlet carnations overlapping each other. He must've hit her in the kitchen, then dragged her into the living room.

I tried to see if the woman was breathing as I moved toward her. Then Inman came at me out of the hallway so fast that I couldn't evade him. I ducked right, but he got a hard jab on my right cheekbone, which sent me sprawling. I hit the wall hard and slid down but managed to keep my grip on the gun. A six-foot-six giant of a man, Inman jumped me again, grabbed my gun hand, and slammed me back against the wall.

"You ain't puttin' me in jail again, bitch." His breath smelled fetid from booze and cigarettes and something else I didn't want to identify. He wrenched my wrist and squeezed until the Glock dropped from numb fingers.

I clawed at his hands as he jerked my feet off the floor, but I thrust my knee up between his legs as hard as I could. He wheezed and grunted in agony and let go. I stomped his instep and rammed my fist into his Adam's apple. I felt it give under my blow, and he went down hard, gurgling and holding his throat. Bud barreled in the back door and jumped him, flipping him over, and kept a knee on his back while he pulled his arms behind him and clamped on the cuffs.

"Goddamn it, Claire, I told you not to go in without me. Are you all right?"

He was looking at my face, and I touched my right eye and found it puffy and painful. There was blood on my fingers, but not much.

"The bastard blindsided me," I said, going down on one knee beside the woman. It was Inman's wife, and her breathing was shallow, the cut on top of her head deep and oozing blood. She had a pulse, but it wasn't much of one. I grabbed a dish towel off the counter and pressed it down on the wound.

Bud knelt beside me. "You sure you're okay, Claire?"

"Yeah, but she's not doing so hot."

"She still alive?" Bud stood up, jerked out his phone, and dialed for an ambulance.

"Yeah, but she's lost a lot of blood. Let's get that piece of shit out of here so the EMTs can work on her."

9

Bud and I were summoned to Sheriff Charles Ramsay's office at eight o'clock the next morning. Charlie was not in a good mood.

"What the fuck happened to you?" he asked me in his gentle way.

"I was injured on a domestic call last night. It's nothing. They put a Band-Aid on it."

"It looks like you were hit by a dadgum freight train." Charlie was prone to cursing. He was versed in every profanity known to mankind but drew the line at uttering the Lord's name in vain. After all, he was a Southern Baptist. So he said weird things instead, like *dadgum* and *goldurn*. He eyed my blackening eye and butterfly bandage as if personally offended.

"He got the jump on me for a minute, but I was able to take control of the situation."

"Where the hell were you, Davis? Out taking a piss somewhere?"

"No, sir. I helped apprehend the perp when I heard him attacking Morgan."

"Well, that's fucking good of you."

"I happened upon the perpetrator before Bud was in place," I said.

"You just happened on him, did you? Seems to me I warned you on several occasions about going in alone, Detective. Don't make me call you on it again, or your ass is off the force. Is that clear?"

"Yes, sir."

Charlie grimaced and jerked open his top drawer. He took out a bottle of Pepto-Bismol and chugged it like a root beer. I shifted in my chair, grossed out, until he wiped the pink stuff off his upper lip with the back of his hand. "Okay, now tell me what the hell's going on out at Cedar Bend."

Charlie looked at us, expecting answers or else. He was an honest man, a man who did his job efficiently and by the letter of the law, and he insisted we do the same. He hated criminals but treated them fairly, and when some innocent victim got killed on his turf, he took it as a personal affront. Gruff and profane, he'd won every election he'd been in in the last twenty years and would continue to as long as he wanted the aggravation. He'd given me a job when nobody else would, and I never forgot it.

Bud pulled out his notebook and flipped over the first page. "911 got a homicide call at 5:32 A.M., July second, and the first unit arrived at approximately 5:37. Deputy O'Hara secured the scene."

"Hell, Jacqee told me that much over the dinner table. Has Buckeye finished the autopsy?" He looked pointedly at me, and I felt his gaze on my swollen eye. It hurt pretty bad, but I was gobbling up Excedrins like candy.

"No, sir. We're scheduled to observe as soon as we're done here. Buckeye wants all three of us there, and he wants it videotaped. This is a difficult one, sir."

Charlie grimaced and made a growling sound deep in his throat. Then he belched behind his fist and seemed to feel better. Ulcers were hell. He glared at me, and I tried to look as pleasant as I could with a black eye and swollen jaw. Charlie ran his hands through hair that was graying at the temples and thinning in back. He hid the impending baldness with a severe military cut he'd worn since he served in Vietnam years ago. Some of us called him W. C.—behind his back, as we wanted to remain in the land of the living—because of his Winston Churchill bulldog jowls and the way he had of lowering his head when he glared at subordinates. Sort of like right now. His eyes were blue, slightly blood-shot, and at the moment, alive with tension. "Why the hell don't you run off those media assholes hanging around outside, detectives? They chased my car into the fucking parking garage like rabid jackals."

"Yes, sir. I'll take care of it." I am prudent. I didn't remind him that he okayed Hastings's request to ride patrol and film everything he saw. "As you know, sir, the victim is a celebrity. Peter Hastings knew it before I got to the crime scene."

"Shit, this is a circus. And Black announcin' it on CNN made it worse." I knew for a fact that Black was one of Charlie's major campaign contributors, so he wouldn't get down on the doctor until he was sure he was guilty. He mumbled something that Bud and I couldn't hear, which was probably a good thing.

"Okay, what else?" Charlie scowled, his face flushed redder than usual. He snatched off his black glasses and started rubbing the thick lenses violently on the end of his black tie, another sure sign he was about to blow.

"The victim was Sylvie Border, sir. She's a soap opera star."

"Hell, I know that," Charlie snapped. "I've seen Vicky's

pictures of her taped to that damn chair. And I better not see any of them in the damned *Enquirer*, or heads are going to roll."

"Yes, sir." I filled him in on what we'd done so far. He did not seem overly impressed with our investigative prowess.

"So you're telling me that your only suspects so far are my good friend Nick Black and some junkie wife beater who doesn't have the imagination to set up a victim like this."

"Yes, sir." Bud was not exactly sheepish, but he was close.

"Well, get the hell out there and find out who did it. If Buckeye's going to videotape the autopsy, then I'll watch it later. I've got a meeting with the lake's Chamber of Commerce, who's been calling me all night about what the national press is doing to tourism around here. Shit."

Thus ended our interview, and we slunk out. He'd be in a better mood later. Maybe. No, probably not.

I met Bud at the coroner's office fifteen minutes later. Autopsies were not my favorite pastime, especially right after breakfast. Luckily, I forgot to eat breakfast and sure wouldn't want to afterward.

"Mornin'," Buckeye said as I entered the lab, the cheerful coroner ready to dissect. The smell always hit me first, antiseptic, chemicals, and cold death. Sylvie was still sitting upright in her chair, still taped up, still beaten and ravaged by marine life. Bud was leaning against the next steel table, arms crossed, eating a jelly donut. He didn't seem to mind autopsies as much as I did. I put on my surgical mask and gown. I'd already donned latex gloves and paper booties in the corridor. Bud was similarly attired and holding his donut with a paper towel now. You'd think he could put it down.

"Okay, let's get started." Buckeye looked around,

then let out a yell that made me jump. "Shag, get your butt in here! We're ready to go!"

Shag rushed in with the video camera. He was eating a donut, too. What was the matter with these guys?

"Okay, okay, I'm here. No need to bust my ass." Shag stuffed the rest of the donut in his mouth, pulled on gloves, then grinned at me as he positioned the camera on the corpse, still in a sitting position. Which in itself was a rarity, I'd say.

Buckeye ignored all that. As I said, Shag was so good at his job that he got away with murder. Not exactly the best term at the moment. Sorry.

Buckeye began to speak into the microphone he wore on a headset attached to a tape recorder clamped to the breast pocket of his shirt. "This is a female Caucasian, age twenty-five. Name is Sylvie Anne Border. I'll get her weight and height after I remove her from the chair to which she's been secured with silver duct tape."

We all gathered around for the show. The bright light hanging over the table poured down on the body as in a theatrical production. Buckeye knelt and started at the feet. "Skin and muscle are showing deterioration from being submerged in water, with more degradation appearing from the neck up. She is taped with wide silver duct tape at the ankles, calves, wrists, and throat. The body has not been touched since removal from the lake. Observing this procedure are Canton County Detectives Claire Morgan and Bud Davis, and my assistant, John Becker. I'll start by removing the tape binding the victim's ankles."

Buckeye picked up a tool off the table beside him that looked like a grocery store box cutter. Maybe it was. He knelt and carefully split the tape down the back. We all watched silently as he removed it with industrial-strength tweezers. It came loose slowly, and I tried not to notice that some skin came away with it. I was praying for fingerprints, but I had a feeling the perp knew and loved gloves for acts of murder.

The tape around the calves was removed next and placed on a clean sheet of white evidence paper. Buckeye picked up a pen and wrote where the tape had come from. Shag would run the tests on it after the autopsy was completed. Everything took a long time because Buckeye was experienced and did not make mistakes that would compromise the investigation. He was as good as any forensic pathologist I'd worked with in L.A., and I'd worked with some of the best.

Buckeye was slowly making his way to the head.

"I am now ready to remove the duct tape from the victim's throat. It appears to encircle the neck and back of the chair at least a dozen times, running from clavicle to earlobe." Buckeye moved around to the back of the chair and pulled a gooseneck lamp to angle directly at the neck. He pulled the long blond hair away from the nape, looking for the best place to slit through the tape without disturbing possible trace evidence. I waited patiently. Well, not exactly patiently. I wanted to be anywhere but here, but what can you do? I shifted my stance but kept my eyes on Buckeye. Bud leaned close as Buckeye began to peel away the final length of tape.

"The tape is thicker at the middle of the neck," Buckeye was reciting into the recorder, eyes intent on the back of Sylvie Border's neck. When he suddenly stopped and frowned, instrument still in hand, we all leaned forward to get a better look, even me. "There appears to be a lateral wound under the tape at about the fifth vertebra. Uh-oh, it appears the head is coming off."

I jumped back about the time the head tipped forward and ripped free from the remaining tape. Buckeye caught it by the hair, and my stomach did a forward somersault. We stared at Buckeye in disbelief as he stood and held the head in one hand by a shank of long blond hair. He looked like some Viking marauder of old, presenting a trophy of war.

"Oh, my God," I said.

"It appears the victim was decapitated before being taped to the chair," Buckeye announced uncertainly. I was glad I had not eaten a jelly donut. Shag filmed on unfazed, but Bud looked sickly green, and Buckeye continued, uninterrupted by the unexpected surprise. "The head appears to have been placed on what seems to be a paint stirrer, then taped tightly to the body and the back of the chair to hold it in place."

"Holy shit," said Bud.

My feelings in a nutshell.

I watched Buckeye place the head carefully on the steel table, and I thought of Nicholas Black and the pain I'd seen in his eyes when he talked about Sylvie suffering. This was going to hit him hard. Oh, God, and the family would be devastated.

"This does not leave this room. Is that understood?" I sounded breathless. I was breathless. I was sick. "This cannot get out to the media."

Everyone looked at me and nodded. Reluctantly, I dragged my gaze back to the table. I prided myself on my ability to face the worst crimes without flinching, but I sure as hell had never seen a decapitated head fall off in an autopsy. I tried for professionalism. I tried to think like a hardened detective would think under these circumstances. There was no blood around the head. She'd obviously bled out in the water.

I watched silently as Bud helped Buckeye move the headless body to the table, placing it just below the severed head. I stared at the Tinkerbell tattoo and wondered about the daisy one. A sense of unreality flooded me. Again, I thought of Black. Why did I keep thinking about him? And not as the murderer but as someone who had loved this person. His affection for the girl had seemed real to me. But that didn't preclude him from offing her. Look at O.J. and Nicole. I wondered if Sylvie was alive when the killer did it; then I wished I hadn't wondered.

"I need some air," I said. "I'll be back in a minute."

"Okay," said Buckeye. "Stop the camera, Shag."

I walked across the room to a lab sink, took off my mask, and splashed cold water on my face. I had never interrupted an autopsy before, and I wasn't really sick. Horrified was more like it. Sylvie had been so young. I don't know how innocent she'd been, but she sure as hell didn't deserve having this done to her.

"You okay?" Bud asked a moment later.

"Yeah, let's get this over with."

The rest of the procedure was not so dramatic. Sad but routine. Buckeye noted every bruise and abrasion, weighed internal organs, and took tissue and blood samples for the laboratory. All necessary, all important in finding the killer, but none of that made me feel any better. As long as I lived, I'd never watch another soap opera without seeing Sylvie Border's head fall off her body. Unfortunately, I'd have to be the one to tell Nicholas Black about it. Like it or not, I had to see his reaction.

LIFE WITH FATHER

For the first few months, the child was afraid of the dead people in the cold room. The father said they wouldn't hurt anybody, and it was nice for children to visit their mother. The father had fixed a nice cot in the cold room for the mother instead of storing her on one of the steel shelves along the walls, where the other corpses were wrapped in plastic. Sometimes Brat lay beside her and covered them both up with blankets. Brat brought her red roses and other flowers, too, sometimes, and put them in a vase made out of a Coke bottle beside the cot, but it was too cold in the room, and the blossoms always shriveled and turned black.

As time passed, the child's fear of the dead people receded. Lonely in the big house without the mother, Brat began to spend more and more time in the cold room with the mother and her friends. The embalmer left the door to the cellar unlocked now and seemed pleased that the child enjoyed watching him work. He took over the school lessons that the child's mother had always taught, and he carried Brat's red winter parka and green sock hat downstairs and hung them on hooks outside the cold room and told Brat not to forget to wear mittens when visiting mother.

But Brat was happiest with the mother. She looked so peaceful now, not sad at all, and the father treated her gently and with respect when he came to see her. Brat grew to consider the dead people as friends. When the heavy steel door to the cold room was shut, and the father couldn't hear, the child would talk to them. Brat would read the tiny paper tag tied to their big toes and then call them by name and make up stories about where they lived and who was in their family. In time, they would get used to the child's chatter, and they would open up and tell Brat all sorts of interesting stories. The child would make up songs to sing to them and sometimes hold their hands and try to make them dance.

When a new corpse came, it was like making a new friend, and it was always so sad when one had to go off and be buried. But the mother never left, and the child stayed near her most of the time. The father was very pleased and said the child was a good child now and knew how to obey the rules.

Then one night the father came into the cold room when the child was having an imaginary tea party with his mother and her friends. The father smiled, and the child thought he looked strange and unlike himself. His breath smelled like the bottle of whiskey he kept on his nightstand.

"Come sleep with me, Brat. I'm lonely without your mother."

The child backed away and hid under the mother's cot. The father knelt down on one knee and jerked Brat out and said sternly, "If you don't obey me, I will take your mother and bury her out in the woods where you can't find her. You'll never see her again."

Terrified at the thought of losing the mother, Brat

took the embalmer's hand and was led upstairs to the turret bedroom. The father undressed them both and snuggled up with the child under the covers. When the child was warm, he began to touch Brat's body and do things that hurt. Brat hated it, and when the father rolled away and lay still, Brat slipped out from under the blankets. The father stirred and said sleepily, "If you're going down to visit Mother, don't forget to put on your coat and hat."

The child crept back down to the cellar, holding the places that hurt from what the father had done. Brat took the parka and hat and mittens off their hooks and put them on, then told the mother and the others what had happened in the bed. They all agreed the father was a bad man and should be punished. The mother said the father deserved to die for what he'd done to Brat. The child nodded and snuggled up against her, shivering with cold, and now hatred.

The child was nine years old.

10

"Dadgummit, can anything worse happen?"

I didn't answer Charlie's question. I wasn't sure if it was rhetorical, but I treated it as such. Things seemed to be proceeding down a really rocky road, and who was I to say there weren't more potholes for us to plunge headfirst into? Bud must've felt the same, because he just chewed on his Juicy Fruit and volunteered nothing.

"The head just fell off, just like that, right in the middle of the autopsy?" Charlie said as if he were incredulous. Of course, he was incredulous. I was incredulous.

"Luckily, Buckeye caught it."

"Yeah, Bud. Lucky Buck." Charlie was not above sarcasm, either. "Okay, Claire, where do we go from here?"

I wasn't expecting the question, but I was prepared. "I think I oughta interview Black again, maybe show him the autopsy pictures and see his reaction. They're awful enough that he shouldn't be able to fake it if he's guilty. He said he'd be available any time. If he's innocent, I'd like to rule him out."

Charlie looked at Bud. "What about you?"

"I think I oughta fly up to New York and interview Black's ex-wife."

"The model?"

"Yeah. It's a dirty job, but somebody has to do it."

"You're really funny, aren't you, Davis?" said Charlie. "What do you say about that, Claire?"

Charlie looked at me, and behind him, Bud put his hands together in prayer mode and mouthed "please." The truth was that it was necessary to see if the woman could tell them when and if she'd seen Black on the night of the murder and how he'd acted. "Yes, I think her statement could be helpful in clearing Black. And somebody needs to interview the cast of Sylvie's soap. They might know something about a stalker or obsessed fan. And I think I should go to New Orleans for Sylvie Border's funeral. I want permission to put in a request for the NOPD to videotape the service and see if we can catch the killer admiring his handiwork. Seems to me he's the type. I also want to interview her family and friends, especially Gil Serna, if he shows up."

Charlie shook his head. "There goes a year's budget worth of travel expenses." He considered their game plans, filling his black pipe with some kind of tobacco that didn't smell too horrible. The smokeless premises did not apply to the sheriff. Nobody even mentioned it; they just took their cigarettes outside and did the sidewalk thing. "Okay, but don't be puttin' yourself up at the Ritz. And fly coach, dammit."

The minute they gained the hall outside Charlie's office, Bud said, 'I'm a travelin' man, goin' to NYC. Gonna see a pretty woman and pick myself up a couple of tailored suits."

"You better pick up enough clues to clear Black, or Charlie's going to lose his biggest campaign contributor."

"Maybe I can catch a show on Broadway while I'm there."

"From what I hear, there's a lot you can catch on Broadway."

Bud laughed as we braced ourselves for the reporters camped outside the front door. He said, "Same goes for some of those dives down in the French Quarter. I wouldn't drink the water."

Sylvie Border's family had to wait until the body was released before the funeral could be scheduled, and that wouldn't come until after Buckeye had all the blood and tissue samples he needed for testing purposes. I wanted to get a hair and saliva sample from Black, too, just in case, before he lawyered up and refused to cooperate. It was nearly seven, but I didn't want to wait to confront Black.

My Explorer was parked in front of the sheriff's office, and the reporters yelled at me en masse as I got in. I waved to Bud as he took off to pack his clothes for the trip to New York. He gave me the victory sign, but I wasn't feeling nearly so good about what I had to do as I pulled my cell phone out of my bag. The white linen business card with Black's personal cell phone number was still sticking in my visor. I dialed the number and waited, curious if he really was available at that number at any time, day or night.

"Yes." His voice was deep enough and distinctive enough for me to recognize it right off.

"Doctor Black, this is Detective Morgan from the sheriff's office."

"Hello, Detective. What can I do for you?"

I hesitated. "I need to talk with you. It's urgent. Are you available this evening?"

"It can't wait until tomorrow?"

"No, I prefer to meet with you tonight. It won't take long."

"Okay. Go to my office, and I'll have Miki direct you to me."

I closed the phone, found myself dreading the coming interview. I put the autopsy file on the seat beside me. I needed to see him look at the gruesome pictures, but I wasn't monster enough to like it.

Twenty minutes later, Miki and I walked down the Cedar Bend dock that led out to the helipad. The yacht that had been custom made for the mighty Black was my destination, but it was anchored somewhere out on the lake, so there was a fancy-shmancy Cobalt 360 cruiser to ferry visitors, with a young, good-looking hunk in a tan-and-black uniform idling the motor.

"Nick's hosting a dinner party on the yacht tonight. They left around four, but Tyler'll take you out there in the launch." Miki was all business today. Not even a supercilious look to make me feel inferior. She turned and clicked away on her high heels, and I watched to see if she got one of her stilettos stuck in the cracks of the dock. She didn't, of course—that would be gauche—and I wondered how she avoided that.

Jumping down into the bobbing cruiser, I said as much to Tyler. He laughed. "I don't know how any of you ladies walk in those things."

Sticking out one of my black high-tops, I drew another laugh. The witty detective making friends with the hunk. As he expertly maneuvered the cruiser out of the slip and hit the open water, I moved up under the canopy with him. He smiled at me, all blowing black hair and big brown eyes. A very pleasant boy. I liked him.

"What's all this stuff?" I asked over the roar of the motor, pointing at the big green radar screens with lots of blips on them.

"That's our satellite tracking system. Every boat at Cedar Bend has a device embedded in the hull that sends out a signal. They're all equipped with these screens, too, so we'll know where each boat is at any given time. Some of our guests get lost out on the lake, and Doctor Black wants to make sure we can find them if they get in trouble. All the boats are numbered. See this blip here, number one?" Tyler said, pointing at a moving green dot. "That's us. We're headed out to the *Maltese Falcon*. That's the big guy."

"I take it Black's a Hammett fan."

"Yeah, he's a fan of everything back then. Have you seen his forties memorabilia yet?"

"No, can't say I have."

"He keeps it at his ranch out in L.A. You ought to ask him about it. It'll make his day. He digs that stuff big time."

Yeah, what I was going to show him was not going to make his day. I watched all the little dots moving around the radar screen and wondered if there were ever any flaws in Cedar Bend operations. Other than a famous actress being beheaded, the doctor seemed to run a very tight ship, so to speak.

The yacht loomed up after about twenty minutes, anchored out in the middle of the lake. Red, white, and blue lights were strung all over it like Christmas at the mall. It had a festive air, and as we tied up alongside and cut the engine, I remembered that the big Fourth of July fireworks display was tonight. No wonder Black was busy. There was music playing on board. "Bridge Over Troubled Water," which was damned appropriate under the circumstances. Tyler helped me off on a boarding ramp at the side of the yacht. I thanked him, and as he roared off toward the resort again, I made my way toward a white-uniformed sailor type waiting at the top of the steps. His black nameplate said Geoffrey.

"Detective Morgan, I've been asked to take you to Doctor Black's office."

"Okay," I said, feeling like James Bond being escorted into Goldfinger's lair, or was that Doctor No, the guy with the big boat, that dragged 007 and a built Bond girl over some sharp coral reefs? But, hey, better get my feet back on the ground. I'm a small-town detective with no knives in my shoe, no rockets in my car's exhaust pipes, just a real nasty autopsy file in my hand. I followed Geoffrey the sailor man along the deck, beside a gleaming rail. In fact, everything was gleaming. We passed some big, gleaming plate-glass windows, and I saw Black having dinner inside the salon with four or five guests. Gee, all candlelight and soft music and orchids. He was leaning toward a pretty woman with red hair and glittering diamonds at her throat and large breasts spilling out of her golden gown. But what else would Mr. Suave be doing? He looked more interested in Buxom Red than in the fact that his dear friend got murdered on his property. I guess fat cats take things in stride.

"Please wait here, and I'll tell the doctor you've arrived. May I get you something while you wait?"

"Nope. I'm fine."

Geoffrey bowed, all crisp white fabric, tanned skin, and shiny brass buttons. Good-looking appeared to be a prerequisite for employment at Cedar Bend. I moved around the stateroom. It was supposed to be the aft quarters, but it was also an office. Large windows wrapped around the end of the stateroom and revealed a night sky with about a million stars and a long line of sparkling lights stretched out over the horizon like Buxom Red's diamond necklace. I wasn't sure exactly where I was, but that would be night owl traffic crossing one of the bridges. An open door revealed a good-sized stateroom for a boat, bigger than my living room. Same windows and same view and a bed big enough for King Kong and Babe the Blue Ox to get it on in. I had a feeling the red-

head might hang her tiara on that bedpost overnight
and really heat up those black satin sheets with the good
doctor.

"How do you like the *Falcon*?" Out of nowhere.

"You make a habit out of sneaking up on people?" I
was slightly annoyed that he'd pulled it off again. He
was dressed in a tuxedo and looked damn good in it,
too. Bond didn't have much on him, no sirree. I had on
jeans with a rip in both knees and a big blue-denim
shirt over a black tank top to hide my shoulder holster.
For some reason, I just didn't fit this yachting lifestyle.

"Didn't mean to startle you. Please, sit down," he
said, rounding the teak desk. There was an expensive
Dell laptop to one side, the top closed. The spangled
night sky was his backdrop, but his face was shadowed,
the desk lamp with a black shade not fully illuminating
him. I had a feeling that mood was everything with him.
Then he got a load of my face. "Good God, what happened to you?"

"Ran into this criminal type who wasn't glad to see
me."

He frowned, not finding me amusing. "Have you
seen a doctor?"

"It's nothing."

"Why don't you let me take a look at it?"

"Thanks, but no thanks. Like I said, it's nothing."

He sat down; so did I. Time to be nice. I could be
professional, despite my clothes. "I appreciate your
time. I didn't realize you were entertaining guests."

"It's a business meeting, some colleagues from Moscow. I'm thinking of opening an office there. Would you
care to join us?" He kept looking at my black eye.

"Sorry, not in the mood for parties."

"Are you ever in the mood?"

"Not since we found Sylvie's body, and you won't be
either in about ten seconds."

His gaze dropped to the file on my lap; then his eyes met mine and glinted blue in the lamplight.

"Victim's autopsy report," I said as I slid it across the desk. "You told Sheriff Ramsay you wanted to see it. He gave his permission and asked me to bring it out here in person."

When he picked it up, I braced myself. I'd put the picture of the severed head on top, and I felt about two inches tall. But I knew his reaction would tell me a lot. He took a moment, maybe bracing himself, too, then opened the folder. He came out of the swivel chair hard enough to send it banging against the windows behind him. I came to my feet, too, and he looked at me with complete and utter horror. I pretty much knew in that moment that he didn't do it. I watched him stagger out of the room and a minute later heard water splashing. I could also hear the sounds he was making, muffled, choked up.

The heartless detective does her job. Feeling like a dirty dog, I sat down and waited for him to compose himself. It took about five minutes. His face was pale when he came back, and he shut the folder without looking at the picture again. When he put his eyes back on me, they were so cold and controlled that I felt like shivering.

"I guess you enjoyed that, Detective? I guess you'll say, 'It's just part of my job,' right?"

"I didn't enjoy it, but it went a long way to make me eliminate you from my suspect list. You can't manufacture a reaction like that."

"God, you're as cold as ice, aren't you? What kind of person are you?"

"You don't have to worry about that, Doctor. Do you want to hear what the autopsy showed, or do you need to go back to your party?" It was a well-aimed jab, and his jaw hardened, a flush running up under his skin.

"Let's hear it."

"What we know now is that she was beheaded before she was put in the water. It appears he used some sort of stick to attach the head to the body, a paint stirrer, in fact."

He looked revolted, got up, and turned his back to me and stared out at the night. "Go on."

"It appears to have been quick and clean with a long blade, like a sword or cleaver, or something like that. There were other wounds, bruises, and abrasions, especially on and around the face, and there was some damage done by marine deterioration."

He kept his back to me. "Was she raped?"

"Yes. With an object. Buckeye thinks it might've been the paint stirrer."

"Oh, God." He rubbed his face with both hands, then brought his fingers back through his hair.

Sometimes I hate myself. I hated myself right now. His voice was tortured, and I found myself wanting to round the desk and comfort him. I didn't move. That was a job for Buxom Red.

Black suddenly turned to me. "Something awful must have happened to you to make you this unfeeling."

Boy, he hit that nail on the head, but I took a moment to roll up the protective window I used at times like this. "I'm sorry you think I'm unfeeling, Doctor Black. But you're wrong. I feel very badly about Sylvie. I want to get the person who did this awful thing to her. If it's you, I'll get you. If it's someone else, I'll get them. I won't stop until I do, I can promise you that."

"Nicky, darling, is something wrong?"

Uh-oh, Buxom Red at the door, oh so concerned, smelling like two hundred dollars an ounce and wearing fifty times that much jewelry on her impressive self.

"No, everything's fine. I've just had some difficult news."

The woman sashayed into the room like a cat ready to rub the heck out of somebody's legs. She looked at me like I was a grub worm that had wriggled its way in from the deck. I stood, gentleman to the core, and Black made the introductions.

"Gillian, this is Detective Morgan. Detective, this is Gillian Coventry from my London office."

"How do you do?" I said. "I won't keep you from your guests any longer, Doctor Black."

"I'll take you back in the launch myself."

Well, that surprised the hell out of me. "No need. I can wait for Tyler to come pick me up."

Black looked at me for a long moment. Maybe he was offended. Maybe he wasn't used to anyone ever turning him down. "I need to head back, anyway," he said. Did that ever get a look out of Buxom Red!

"Oh, Nicky," she purred. The cat analogy was still working. "The fireworks haven't even started yet."

Interpretation: "I want to sleep with you, Nicky poo, in the worst way. I can make you scream with pleasure all night long." Suddenly, I wondered where Ms. Coventry had been the night of the murder. She was a little scary acting, but then I'm not used to society types. Was she jealous enough to get rid of Sylvie?

"Have you been visiting us here at the lake very long, Ms. Coventry?" I asked, watching her closely and wondering exactly what she did in London. I could think of a few things, but they weren't kind.

"She got in this morning," Black said sharply, obviously well aware of my suspicions. "She never even met Sylvie."

The dim lightbulb deep in Buxom Red's brain suddenly came on. "Do you suspect *me*, Detective?" All shrill and bent out of shape. Curls and breasts aquiver with outrage. It was a sight to behold. Dolly Parton hit by a stun gun.

"I suspect everyone, ma'am. It's my job." Deadpan Jack Webb.

"Gillian, I'll try to see you later tonight or early in the morning before your flight out."

Gillian balked, but he sweet-talked her across the stateroom, out into the hallway. Then he came back and took my arm in a tight grip and led me to the launch. No sweet-talking going on now, no talking going on at all. I stepped down into the stern of the launch and sat on a padded cushion as he manned the controls. I watched him jerk loose his black satin bow tie, then grab hold of the helm with both hands, probably pretending it was my throat. He pushed up the throttle with not a lot of finesse, and the bow rose sharply, as if the pricey craft was shocked at the mistreatment, then leveled off as we gained speed across the water.

I held on to the side, glad our little evening together was about over, and more relieved than I should have been that he didn't appear to be guilty. Ten minutes later I was still wondering why I cared if he was or not when he suddenly cut the motor. The launch stopped on a dime and rose as the wake washed forcefully against the hull and rocked us like two babes in a cradle.

Not good. Alone in the middle of a very deep and dark lake with a possible killer who was really, really mad at me. I reached inside my shirt and unhooked my holster. Black noticed the little snap it made.

"What are you going to do now, Detective? Shoot me?" He spat the words out. Sharp. Angry. Not his usual impeccable diction.

"Maybe. Depends on you."

"I didn't kill her." He was approaching me, and I

wondered if Sylvie had been killed in a boat. This boat.
I wondered if there was a sharp saber stowed away
somewhere in the upholstery for enraged moments like
this. Neither of us looked up as the fireworks started in
the distance. A huge starburst exploded in the sky
above us, bathing us both in pink light. Another followed quickly and painted us green.

I said, "I don't know if you did or not, but I will soon
enough."

"You're pretty damn sure of yourself, aren't you?"

"Yes. Now, why don't you start the motor again and
let me get back to work?" Another burst of color, and we
turned yellow before everything faded to black again.

"I want to read the autopsy file first. Out here on the
water, where I won't be disturbed. You got the shock
out of me you wanted, just the way you planned. Now
give me the goddamned file. Her father's going to
want to know how she died, and I want to tell him the
truth."

I handed over the file, without a word. He took it with
him to the cockpit, sat down at the helm, and switched
on a lamp above his head. I watched his jaw working as
he leafed through the photographs one after another.
He didn't react visibly this time, but he read each page
carefully, pulling certain pictures back out in order to
check them against the written accounts. It took at least
half an hour, and I sat in the rocking launch and said
nothing and watched the magnificent fireworks. He
never looked up at the show in the sky, not once. He'd
made me feel like the aforementioned grub worm, and
I deserved it. But hey, that's why they pay me the big
bucks.

When he finally finished, he handed the file back to
me without comment, started the motor, and headed
back to Cedar Bend. When we got there, he left the

launch and stalked down the dock, and it was Tyler who came running with a big smile, eager to help me off the launch and back to where my car was parked. At least somebody liked me.

11

"You sayin' you dint know Sylvie was a Montenegro?"

I was sitting in the upstairs window of a safe house overlooking the Sacred Heart Catholic Church, with two undercover guys. Both were beefy and florid, of Cajun stock, which reflected big time in their accents and mannerisms. I almost expected them to break out a fiddle and washboard at any minute and play me a foot-stomping version of "Jambalaya." But they were all business and scary as hell, and I prayed they weren't on the take, or I might end up as a human anchor somewhere in the Gulf of Mexico.

I'd flown to New Orleans early that morning for Sylvie Border's funeral, had reported in at the NOPD, and had been assigned to two gorillas posing as Homo sapiens. Don't get me wrong, but sometimes gorillas are just what you need when you're snooping around in a strange city. Especially when your partner got all snazz-ied up and flew off to New York to meet a supermodel. Thinking Sylvie's family would reside in the Garden District or in another upscale neighborhood, I was sur-prised when Thierry Baxter (Baxter sounds more like

Indiana than a French Cajun, right?) and Jean-Claude Longet drove across the Mississippi River Bridge to Algiers. Even I knew that place's reputation, which, by all counts, was where all the criminals in the state of Louisiana lived and prospered happily ever after. It was also where Sylvie Border grew up.

"Nope. Never heard of the Montenegro family until today."

"Some call 'em Cajun Mafia, but Sylvie's daddy built it up all by hisself. He be de head of de family, and he already got out feelers to see who went and whacked 'is baby girl." That was Thierry. He did most of the talking for the dynamic duo.

"Well, fellas, that puts a whole new slant on my case. Do you think she was hit by another crime family?"

"Dunno," said Thierry. "But Jacques Montenegro'll fin' out." Thierry and I had high-powered binoculars. There were a couple of surveillance guys from the FBI operating a video camera and a Nikon in the bedroom next door. Law enforcement cooperation at its finest. The feds were too busy to sit around chatting with me, but they said I could borrow their funeral tapes if I went through the proper channels.

For at least twenty minutes, Thierry had been identifying thugs, murderers, counterfeiters, and smugglers by name as they entered the church to pay their respects to the departed soap star. Jean-Claude soon excused himself and took a circuitous route out of the building and headed for the funeral, dressed in a black suit that made him look like a night-painted German tank. "I best get me o'er dere. It's pret' bad 'bout dat Sylvie. She was a sweet li'l thin', dint like paparazzi knowin' 'bout her daddy."

The consensus seemed to be that Sylvie didn't deserve to die, certainly not in the way she did. But Mafia connections often ended up badly—I'd watched the

Godfather movies a couple of times. I perked up when Nicholas Black arrived in the typical long black limousine. Ah, this high-on-the-hog living was really something. I focused my field glasses on him when he got out of the back. "What about Nicholas Black? Does he have any kind of affiliation with the Montenegro family?"

Thierry shook his head. "He don' come 'round much. You can check dos FBI films. They on all de time."

"The FBI's on the family around the clock?"

Thierry nodded; then he took off when the funeral seemed about to begin. Five minutes later I watched him through the binoculars as he climbed the church steps and disappeared inside. I wanted to be late so I could stand in the back and watch the mourners without being seen, so I hung around for another ten minutes. I was not looking forward to the next hour. I had a thing about funerals—didn't like them, didn't go to them, and I rarely wear dresses. Okay, I never wear dresses, but out of respect for Sylvie's family, I put on a circa-1980 sleeveless, ankle-length black dress with a broomstick skirt. I added a black short-sleeve linen blazer over it to hide my shoulder holster, because I'll be damned if I'll prance around Algiers without a weapon on me. Even at a funeral. Even if I melt into a puddle in this muggy, hellish Louisiana heat. Hell, everyone who'd entered the church had a gun bulge somewhere on their person. I'd even left my sneakers at home in lieu of these too tight black patent flats, but I drew the line at panty hose. No way. I'd lost a lot of weight since I'd last worn the dress, so it hung on me like I was a metal coat hanger or a scarecrow. Oh well, that's the way the ball bounces.

Thierry had reminded me to cover my head, so I'd picked up a black silk mantilla at a Dillard's on the way to the funeral. Draping it over my head until I looked almost female, I entered the church and nodded at the six big goons standing guard at the holy water font. They were all suitably somber, their guns respectfully tucked out of sight. Thierry was one of them. Jean-Claude was nowhere in sight.

The church was nearly full; the drone of the priest told me that the funeral mass was well under way. I crossed myself with holy water the way I'd seen on television and lurked in the back. The deceased's family sat together in the first few pews, and it didn't take me long to notice that Nicholas Black was seated in the row behind them. He seemed to be alone. I didn't recognize anyone else, until I heard loud weeping and picked out Gil Serna on an outside aisle. He was taking it hard. People were beginning to turn around to see who was bawling. He had some woman with perfectly cut and highlighted hair with him, probably his press agent, and a husky, bald guy, probably his personal bodyguard. Stars didn't go anywhere without their "people." I had hoped he'd come. It would give me an opportunity to interview him without Charlie having to pay for a flight out to La La Land.

The casket was closed, of course. I wondered if Black had filled the father in on the gory details. Sylvie had about the same number of flower sprays that Rudolph Valentino'd had at his funeral in the 1930s. Across the altar, down every aisle, everywhere you looked. It smelled like incense and roses, and there was quite a bit of crying and shuffling in the cavernous sanctuary. The service continued, and in deference to the black patent torture devices on my feet, I took a seat in the back row, behind a pillar. I saw Jean-Claude guarding a side entrance that led to the adjoining cemetery. What did they expect? An armed assault on the coffin?

After the Mass concluded, the casket was picked up by the eight pallbearers. To my surprise, Nicholas Black was one of them. More surprising, Gil Serna was, too.

He wept like a baby all the way to the grave site. Certainly appeared to be grief stricken, but then again, he was an actor. Actors did tears.

Outside, I stood back at the perimeter of the onlookers and waited for the opportunity to approach the family. Chairs for the family and pallbearers were placed around the giant Montenegro family crypt, and the mourners began to file by and offer condolences. About the time I reached Sylvie's parents, Nicholas Black caught sight of me and tried to head me off, probably afraid I'd offend the grieving family. After all, I was that cold-hearted bitch he didn't like much.

"Jacques, Gloria, this is Claire Morgan. She's the detective in charge of the investigation," he said very low and respectful instead of whisking me away. He added something in what sounded like flawless French, which, of course, I didn't understand and which, of course, ticked me off. Whatever he said, it piqued their interest. "Have you found out the animal who did this to my baby?" Jacques Montenegro said, eyes rimmed with red from weeping and lack of sleep. He was tall, elegant-looking, and slight. Delicate, sort of. Well, he looked like a Frenchman.

"Not yet, sir. But I will. Please accept my condolences."

"Thank you."

Sylvie's mother was pretty, a small woman with graying blond hair and dark eyes. She didn't look at me or say anything, just kept wiping her tears with a white handkerchief embroidered with red roses. I started to ask if I could come by later and ask them some questions, but Jacques beat me to it. He gestured for me to lean down close.

"I have questions for you, if you please," he said near to my ear. Couldn't say any mafioso had ever whispered in my ear before. "Please come to my house after this is

done, and we will talk." His Cajun accent was less pronounced than that of my undercover friends, and more
educated. He wasn't going to say *gar-rawn-tee*, I guaran-
tee it.

"Yes, sir, thank you," I said, deciding things were
moving along rather well.

Black took my arm then, which was becoming an annoying habit of his, and escorted me away from the family as if he owned me. His voice remained low and
guarded. "Why didn't you tell me you were coming
down here?"

"Excuse me? Since when do I have to check in with
you to do my job?" I tried to pull my elbow free. He didn't
let go, holding me gently, but firmly. Now I was really
getting pissed off. I started to let him have it, but then
that would cause a scene. I'd save that for later.

"I flew down on the Lear. You could have come with
me."

"How thoughtful of you, Doctor Black. Is that so you
could keep tabs on me?"

"You might need it around here."

"You don't know me very well, or you'd know I can
take care of myself."

Black examined my bruised eye for a long, significant moment; then he frowned down at my outfit.
"Where'd you find this nun getup? The Salvation Army?"

I said, "Ha-ha. You slay me." An unfortunate choice
of words.

Black said, "I wouldn't suggest pulling that gun you're
wearing under the blazer."

"Oh, darn, and I just love to shoot up funerals."

Black did not find me amusing. Imagine. "You can
ride back to the house with me if you like."

"I thought you weren't close with Sylvie's family."

"Who said I was? Jacques wants me to come out so he
can talk to me, just like he wants to talk to you. I'm not

staying long. You might as well ride along." I was about to say I had a ride, thank you very much, when he added, "Gil and his friends are coming with me."

"Why not?" I said, all graciousness and smiles.

Gil Serna blubbered all the way to the Montenegro estate, so I didn't get a chance to question him, even though Black introduced us all around as we left the church. I sat across from Gil's blond, good-looking female agent named Mathias Grobe—yeah, that was really her name—who absently patted him on the knee and murmured little things that I couldn't understand. The big, bald bodyguard guy was named Jimmy Smith. Go figure. Not Jimmy the Rat nor Jimmy the Hammer nor Jimmy the Terminator. Plain old Jimmy Smith, and I wasn't sure there was anything inside his head, judging by the blank stare coming out of his squinty little black eyes. Maybe he should have been called Jimmy the Lobotomy. I'm unkind; I know it. Sorry.

Nicholas Black sat beside me, and I tried not to think about how handsome he was. It was irksome that I noticed the size of his hands, the way his fingers were long and tapered and tanned where he rested one on his crossed knee. He was close enough for me to pick up a hint of a clean-smelling cologne. Nothing I recognized, but I'm not into expensive fragrances. Okay, okay, I admit it. I'm attracted to him. I've got hormones. He rings my bell just a little bit. So what? I just could never act on it, not as long as he was a suspect. Not even if he wasn't a suspect. Hands off. Off limits. Bad news. Possible killer. And although I was rusty with men, courtship, dating, and anything remotely connected to any of the above, I sensed he was attracted to me as well. I wasn't that rusty. Or maybe he was just figuring out the best way to off me. Never can tell.

"Mr. Serna," I said at length, realizing I had to broach the subject sometime, and it might as well be now, when his tears had lessened. "I'm going to have to ask you a few questions. I realize you're upset now, and that this isn't a good time, but I'm due back in Missouri tonight. May I have a few minutes of your time later, after we arrive at the house and you've had time to compose yourself?"

Mathias looked offended at my dastardly forwardness, and Jimmy the Baldy looked like nobody was at home in his head. Then he looked straight at me and left me no doubt. Gil was distraught, but he nodded and turned to stare out the window. He could've been acting; he did Academy Award–caliber stuff, but I didn't think so. It's hard to cry so long, even if you're not putting on a show. Trust me, I know. On the other hand, he could be crying because he cut off his girlfriend's head and now regretted it.

The Montenegro estate was the proverbial sight to behold. More like an armed camp and *Gone with the Wind* set backed up to the Mississippi River. It looked like it had once been a real antebellum plantation, but there was an eight-foot concrete wall surrounding the grounds, which had to be at least twenty acres of live oaks dripping gray Spanish moss. The guards at the front gate actually looked inside our vehicle, checked the trunk, then waved us through the iron gates. I bet they didn't even do that at Madonna's house. Michael Jackson's, yes.

The house had the obligatory white columns in front, actually around all four sides, supporting long, shaded verandas on both floors. I could smell the white waxy blossoms of a giant magnolia tree beside the front porch as soon as I got out of the car. The scent of roses was even stronger in the hot, motionless air. I was having a

mild and sweaty heatstroke in my black blazer but re-
sisted the urge to fan myself with my Glock automatic.

We were ushered inside a long, wide foyer that ran
the length of the house, and I greeted the air-conditioning
like a long-lost lover. Through an eight-foot back door,
which stood open, I could see a long green lawn that
stretched to the river. A barge was moving right along,
the top of it visible over the levee. Drugs and prostitu-
tion obviously paid well in New Orleans.

People, all dressed in black, all hushed voices and
reverent manner, were milling around the bottom floor,
which was comprised of a living room, dining room, den,
office, and huge kitchen in the back, probably needed
to serve all the armed henchman standing around. I
know because I checked it out as soon as we got there. I
like to know where the exits are when visiting godfathers.
Everything was beautifully decorated in pastels, not the
heavy dark wood associated with the Francis Ford Coppola
movies. Of course, they were Italians. Louisiana gangsters
obviously liked the Florida motif and hired interior dec-
orators from Palm Beach.

The family was receiving in the pale blue and yellow
parlor, and I noticed they greeted Black very warmly. As
he'd told me, he didn't intend to linger. He sought me
out where I was watching everything from a spot on the
staircase. Not very subtle, but an overview. "I've got to
get back. Would you like to fly back with me, Detective?
I've got plenty of room."

"This isn't a pleasure trip, Doctor. I've got work to do
here." Now that sounded rather boorish and prim. I
don't know why, but I had a lot of trouble being civil
when he was around. Usually I was a pretty civil person.
Maybe I was subconsciously nipping in the bud that attraction thing. It was doing the trick. His eyes were about
the same degree in temperature as an Alaskan glacier.

"Please let me know if I can be of further assistance to you in the investigation." He gave me a smile that said I'll remain studiously polite even if you're a bitch.

I went to the window after he left the room and made sure he really was leaving like he said. Not that I didn't trust him one bit, but I didn't trust him one bit. I was glad I went the extra mile when I observed the Montenegro's black chauffeur come up and give him a warm embrace. Very interesting to a trained investigative mind like moi's. They smiled and chatted a little too long for strangers, and I stepped out on the veranda and stood hidden within a group of people admiring the view, hoping to hear what they were saying. "Don't make it so long next time, Nicky. You missed big 'round heah."

Well, well, did that ever justify my bitchiness. Black obviously did have more of a relationship with Sylvie and her family than a psychiatrist should. I wondered if he was into something illegal down heah in Cajun country. Drugs, maybe. Drug distributor to the stars, perhaps? Maybe that's how he afforded multiple mansions and custom-built yachts and Lear jets. Maybe that's why Sylvie got murdered on his property. I filed this new information to think about later. Gil Serna had finally stopped crying.

We sat down together on a navy velvet settee in one corner of the foyer for our interview. I was very solicitous.

"Mr. Serna, I am so sorry for your loss. I understand you were involved romantically with Ms. Border."

Big tears welled up in his big chocolate eyes. Oh, Lord, waterworks again. His tear ducts were going to get on their knees and beg for mercy if he didn't stop soon. "I was in love with her. Oh, God, God, I can't believe this happened to her. How could it've happened to her? Oh, God, this sucks."

"That's what I'm going to find out. When was the last time you saw her, Mr. Serna?"

"Just before she left for Cedar Bend. I didn't want her to go. I wanted her to stay with me. I had a week in L.A. before I had to go to Italy to shoot my new movie. The working title's *Trojan*. It's a period piece, sort of like *Gladiator*. If she'd stayed, this wouldn't have happened. She'd be okay. I could've protected her. Jimmy Smith's with me night and day. I wish I'd sent him with her. I told her she should've had a bodyguard, but she said she didn't need one down there with Black." He looked at me like it was my fault.

I nodded, anyway. "I wish she had stayed with you, too. She was a lovely young woman."

"And she was good, too, really good, down deep inside, you know, down in her heart. I'm not good; you know my reputation's shit, but she was good for me. She helped me control my temper."

"You have a temper, Mr. Serna?"

"Yeah, everybody knows about it. You didn't know about it?"

"Did you ever lose it with Sylvie Border?"

"Sure, a couple of times." He looked at me; his eyes were dry now, beseeching me, trying to pluck my locked-up heartstrings. Actually, I think I saw him play this scene in his last movie. Right before he shot a police officer between the eyes. "But I never laid a finger on her. I couldn't. I loved her. I couldn't stand to be away from her very long. She made me better. I'm no good, but she made me better."

"What can you tell me about her relationship with Doctor Black?"

He frowned and rubbed his jaw. It was unshaven, but maybe that was his *Trojan* look. "I figured they were having an affair. Who wouldn't want to be with her, who wouldn't? But she flat denied it, said he was her doctor and her friend, and that she liked him a lot and he was helping her, but she always said that's all it was. Strictly professional, and now that I met up with him and we hung around some, I believe it. I didn't, though, when she went off to his resort for her sessions. I called constantly. She made me crazy sometimes, when I got to thinking about her with Black. He's known for being with beautiful women; that's a well-known fact."

Yeah, I noticed that. Buxom Red came to mind. "So you had no real evidence linking the two of them romantically?"

"No. She said he was just a friend."

"Do you know anyone who might have wanted to do her harm?"

"No, no, I've been racking my brain, trying to think. People liked her. She was kindhearted and good. You know what she used to do? Last winter when we were in New York, she used to buy up all these winter coats and scarves and hats and stuff and take them downtown where the street people hung out. She made me take her and Jimmy Smith to keep us safe. She liked it. She used to make ham sandwiches in my kitchen, a whole basketfull, and take them down there, too. She's just awesome, man." He realized the tense should have been past and got a little glazed in the eyes.

I asked him a few more questions and found out that he had been on the set with a whole movie crew the evening she'd been killed. I'd check that out to make sure, but that was one helluva good alibi. I made sure he would be available for further questioning if I needed him, and he said they were going to shoot interior shots for *Trojan* on a soundstage in Los Angeles for a couple of weeks and that's where he'd be. Our conversation seemed to have calmed him down a bit, and I left him in Mathias's hands, dry-eyed and somber.

As for Sylvie's parents, I waited for most of the

mourners to depart before I approached them. They seemed to be nice people, other than their bloodstained and murderous criminal activities, and both were totally crushed by their daughter's death. She was their only child.

"Sylvie was so sweet," Gloria said softly. "Always there when we needed her. She called often, came home a lot. We're very proud of her, making it in acting. That wasn't easy, you know, to land that role of Amelia. She was up against sixty-five other women, and she got it. That was the happiest day of her life."

Jacques teared up but fought down his emotion. I waited a moment, aware of the herd of gun-toting henchmen watching from the doorway. "Mr. Montenegro, do you have any idea who might have killed your daughter?"

"No, not yet. I am making inquiries."

"Will you let me know if you find out anything?" I said, not really expecting him to, especially if it was some of his Mafia cronies, but I still gave him my card. "I'm also curious about Sylvie's relationship with Nicholas Black. Is he a close friend of your family?" Now I'd see if he admitted Nicky had been around more than today.

"No," he said, gazing straight at me for the first time. "The only time we've talked is today and when he called about Sylvie the morning after she died."

Liar, liar, pants on fire. Even Black had admitted more association than that. "Did she ever talk about him to you? Indicate that they were involved in any way?"

He shook his head. "Is Doctor Black a suspect in Sylvie's murder?"

I evaded with my ultraskillful detective acumen. "He was one of the last people to see her alive. It's important for me to understand their relationship."

Montenegro didn't like my questions about Black,

not one bit. "I think you better look elsewhere for my daughter's murderer, Detective. Nicholas Black couldn't have done it."

I was brave. I said, "How could you possibly know that, Mr. Montenegro?"

Montenegro got a look on his face that would probably cause most of the burly, armed men standing around to wet their pants. Gloria Montenegro recognized it for what it was and quickly said, "They were not involved. Sylvie would have told me if they were. We were very close. She was in love with Gil Serna, but he was jealous, and she got tired of his possessiveness."

"Do you think Gil Serna is capable of killing her?"

Jacques Montenegro gave an impatient shrug. I was irking him. I did that irk thing to people sometimes. "He's tough in his movies, but just look at him over there, sniveling and weeping on that woman's shoulder. He's weak. He wouldn't have the guts to kill anybody. Acting isn't real life."

Deep thoughts from Mr. Mafioso, but I guess a man like Jacques Montenegro judged men differently than everybody else. Unsettling, with me asking him questions. I finished the interview shortly after that, realizing they weren't being exactly forthcoming with their answers. I expressed my condolences again and left, not knowing much more than I did before I got there. One thing I did know, Nicholas Black and the Montenegros were lying about their relationship, and it was up to me to find out why.

12

I took a cab to the airport, sweltering like a tamale warpped in black in my staid funeral attire. Everyone, however, treated me with a great deal of respect. They probably thought I was a nun, like Black said. The airport was crowded, bustling with lots of southern accents, tourists in tank tops, and Louisiana foodstuffs, like pralines, beignets, and crawfish cakes. I thought about renting a car and buzzing up to Baton Rouge for old time's sake; then I remembered Katie Olsen, my roommate at LSU, and what had happened to her, and nixed that idea.

My gate was situated about a million miles down the concourse, of course, probably because I wore torturous shoes. Why didn't I bring a change of clothes? Maybe I'd stop at one of the souvenir booths and buy a shirt that said FRENCH QUARTER or NEW ORLEANS SAINTS or VAMPIRES LOVE THE BIG EASY. That last one was more my style because it showed Anne Rice's handsome Lestat with blood dripping from his pointy fangs. Maybe we should get something similar to encourage tourism at Lake of the Ozarks, except we could use a werewolf, or something, maybe a maniac killer who seated their victims at underwater dinner tables. This sobered me, and I increased my step.

At my gate I sat down in an empty row of seats against a wall and massaged my pinched, screaming feet for a while. I leaned my head back and shut my eyes, but opened them when somebody sat down right beside me. Annoyed, I was about to complain that there were plenty of seats available that weren't on my lap, but then saw that it was Nicholas Black. Well, hell's bells.

He said, "Hello, Detective."

I hardly recognized him because he'd changed out of his silk Italian suit and crisp white shirt and psychiatrist demeanor, and into a plain white T-shirt, faded denim jeans, black running shoes, and a good old boy demeanor. Gee, he looked like a real person and everything. I said, "What's up, Doc? Slummin' it with us peons? Thought you flew off on your own special little jet plane with your own special little flight crew."

"Are you always this unpleasant?"

I pretended to consider. "Yes, sir, I usually am."

Black seemed tenser than necessary and exhibited a less than chipper mood. "I need to talk to you. It's important."

"Didn't I give you my cell phone number?"

"I said it's important."

"Okay, shoot." I watched him watch the people hurrying by with their rolling suitcases or duffel bags thrown over their shoulders. Maybe he just joined me to people watch, but I admit I was curious. His flight should have taken off a couple of hours ago—a lot of time for a very busy man who must keep to a schedule. Which meant he had gone to the trouble of finding my flight number and hanging around until I showed up.

"I have some information for you," he said, not looking at me. He kept scanning the crowd until I got nervous and started eyeballing our fellow travelers, too. I didn't see any lurking Montenegro types, but they could be in disguise.

"Okay." Sometimes I didn't mince words.

"You have to swear that you won't divulge this to anybody."

"Sorry, no can do. I'm an officer of the law, remember? I divulge facts to lots of people, including my partner, the sheriff, the district attorney, the judge, and the jury, to mention a few."

"Then I can't tell you. But it's a substantial lead that might take you straight to Sylvie's killer."

"Is that so? Maybe an obstruction of justice charge would loosen your tongue."

Black kept up the frowning, thought about it awhile, then obviously decided he didn't like the sound of an obstruction charge, even though it probably had a snowball's chance in hell of sticking with the DA. "I found out today that Sylvie had a stalker. One that's been bothering her ever since she was in high school. I've got the name, and the address is down in bayou country south of the city. It's not far, a couple of hours, tops."

Did that ever perk up my little ears. I got out my trusty detective tablet. "What's his name?"

"I thought you might want to visit and ask him a few questions while you're down here."

"You thought right. Give me the name and address, and you can be on your way."

Black shook his head, leaned back, and propped a foot on his knee. "No can do. I want to go along. You'll never find his place out in the bayous without me to guide you."

I studied his face for a long moment, hoping to make him squirm uncomfortably for pissing off a police officer. He stared back, Doctor Cool. I said, "How do you know this area so well?" Translation: "Are you involved in Jacques Montenegro's crime syndicate?"

"I went to Tulane, and I also did part of my residency at Charity Hospital in New Orleans. I have friends down around the Lafourche area."

That was true, at least the college part, but that didn't rule out crime connections. Maybe that was when he threw in with the bad guys? So I said, "Thanks, but no thanks. It could be dangerous, and I don't have time to baby-sit you."

Black barked a laugh, as if my remark was oh just so idiotic, and the arrogant look that followed clearly said that he didn't need anybody to take care of him, especially me. I read between the lines well, you see. What he said, however, was, "You don't know the bayous, or you'd welcome somebody who knew his way around them." He hesitated, as if he was still contemplating throwing in a baby-sitting reference about moi, but he quickly came to his senses and didn't. But I'm not stupid, and I did know enough about bayou country to know it was downright spooky down there and that he was probably right, so I said, "I think a better course of action is to call the NOPD and get a couple of armed officers to come with me."

Our eyes met for a long moment; then he said, "I wouldn't do that if I were you. I have no way of knowing this for sure, of course, but I wouldn't be surprised if Jacques Montenegro didn't have a couple of NOPD officers on the payroll. The last thing you want is for Jacques to find out about this guy and have him hit before you can question him. From what I hear, Jacques doesn't waste a lot of time asking questions before he passes sentence. That's why I waited and told you about the stalker, instead of going to the New Orleans police."

Black was pretty good with this Mafia stuff. "So you're the good guy in all this, right? Just doing your civic duty, and the detective ought to be grateful?"

"Something like that."

"How long is this going to take?" I asked him, and he smiled, smelling victory.

"We'll probably make it out before dark, but if not, I have an old friend who'll put us up for the night."

"Now you're telling me you have an old swamp buddy who's gonna let us spend the night with him?"

"Yeah. It's not a Four Seasons, but it'll do."

"I'm not spending the night anywhere with you."

"Then we better get going."

A long-term stalker was the lead Bud and I had been looking for. Of course, Black might have his own reasons to identify a new suspect for me to go after while he neatly wiggled himself off my hook. But he was right about Montenegro getting to his daughter's stalker first. The guy'd be dead before he opened his mouth.

"I'll have to call Charlie and obtain permission. And I'm going to tell him that you're my source and that you are insisting on going along."

"I'm not going to kill you and dump you in the bayou, if that's what you're afraid of."

"I'm not afraid of anything, but Charlie'll have your ass if you try anything funny." Just for his information.

"I'll be a good boy and not murder you, I promise." Man, scorn was alive and well in New Orleans, Louisiana.

Fishing my cell phone out of my bag, I crossed the busy concourse a good distance away from Black and punched in the sheriff's number. I watched Black walk to the nearest coffee shop and stand in line. Charlie picked up on the first ring. "What the hell do you want?" was his gracious answering etiquette. He obviously had caller I.D.

"Hello, Sheriff. It's me."

"I know who the hell it is. What's up? I'm on my way to a fuckin' press conference."

"I want permission to take a later flight or maybe stay another day down here. Nicholas Black just told me that he's got a lead on a stalker who's been hounding Sylvie Border for some time. The stalker's place is out in the bayou. He wants to go with me, says he knows the bayou country and can be useful."

"How does Black know about a stalker?"

"He won't name his source, but apparently, he's got a lot of college friends down here, and I suspect he heard it from one of them. I want you to know I'm going off into a swamp with him, in case I never come back."

After a beat, Charlie gave a small sniff. "I doubt if he's going to up and murder you, Claire."

"That's easy for you to say."

"Nick's not a killer. I've known him too long."

"Maybe you're more trusting than I am. I just want you and Bud to know where I am and who I'm with, and that I don't trust Nicholas Black as far as I can spit." Yes, I was a little ticked at Charlie's cavalier attitude. So what if the guy chipped in beaucoup bucks for Charlie's election campaigns? Give me a break here. "Do you want me to check this out while I'm here or come on home?"

"Check it out, I guess. Bud's still in New York, partying it up on my nickel, no doubt. Just call in and keep me posted. If I'm not available, tell Jacqee."

Oh, right, I'll entrust confidential information to Ms. Airhead UCLA. "Yes, sir. I'll be sure to do that."

I placed the phone in my bag and waited for Black to seek me out. He strolled over a few minutes later with two black coffees and a sack of beignets, whatever the hell that was. "Everything set with Charlie? Did you give him my best?"

I watched his dimples deepen when he smiled, but I

looked away and strode off down toward the main ter-
minal ahead of him. "Let me guess, we're riding down
to the bayous in a black stretch limousine so we won't
stick out among the natives."

He caught up and matched my stride. "What makes
you think Cajuns don't ride in limos?"

I smiled, sort of, but when we exited, he led me to an
old, beat-up gray Chevy pickup truck. I looked it over as
he opened the door with a flourish, a real gentleman. I
said, "Hertz must be going bankrupt offering these
kinds of rentals."

"I borrowed this from a friend. As you said, we don't
want to be conspicuous."

"You got a lot of friends all of a sudden, don't you?"

I got in, hoping I wasn't settling into my personal
beat-up gray Chevy hearse. Black slid into the driver's
seat, turned on the ignition, and edged us out into the
traffic. The windows were down because there was no
air-conditioning, and I wondered if Doctor Millionaire
could survive without his upper-upper-class perks. No
conversation passed between us until we were out on
the interstate and heading south toward the Gulf of
Mexico. After a while he glanced over at me and then
reached behind my seat and retrieved a plastic Wal-
Mart bag. "I picked you up a change of clothes. You
don't want my Cajun friends to genuflect and say a Hail
Mary."

"Enough with the nun jokes, okay?"

Inside the bag, I found a pair of denim short shorts
and a lime green halter top and white slip-on Keds.
"What is this, Daisy Mae Day? And where do you suggest
I clip my weapon, to my halter strap?"

"You can hide it in your purse like Charlie's Angels
do."

"Yeah, and if pigs could fly, I could solve all my cases
in one hour like Charlie's Angels do."

"It's hot in the swamp. All the women dress this way."

"In your dreams I'm gonna wear this."

"Yeah, that's true, too."

I had the urge to laugh at that, so I looked out the window and wondered if I was losing my objectivity.

About fifteen miles down the road, Black pulled into an Exxon truck stop and while he gassed up the Chevy clunker, I went into the bathroom and turned myself into Daisy Duke. Big mistake. When I came back out, a long line of truckers sat chugging coffee and eating cheeseburgers at the counter. They turned collectively and stared at me aghast, as if Mother Teresa had suddenly turned into Pamela Anderson. They watched me the whole time I thumbed through the T-shirt rack and finally chose one that had an alligator eating Jerry Springer on the front. I wondered if that would help me feel at home in Cajunville. I also chose a plain white one like Black's, so we could be twins, and a pair of low-rider jeans and some white tennis peds, a can of Deep Woods Off, and a good-sized citronella candle. I've seen bayou movies, thank you very much. The truckers had obviously been on the road too long, because they were still watching me browse around in my skimpy, Playmate getup, as if they'd never seen a woman before, and so was Black, now that he'd pumped and paid for the gas. Annoyed, I tore off the $6.99 price tag and slipped the Springer shirt over my head. Show's over, fellas. Tune in to *Baywatch* reruns to get your jollies.

I took my goodies to the checkout desk and added two Snickers bars and two bottles of water in case Black and I needed sustenance along the way. After all, he bought me coffee and those strange beignet thingies, which I found out were doughy fried rolls with powdered sugar all over them. I paid the kid at the counter, who also had on an alligator T-shirt, but his was eating Burt Reynolds. I returned to the ladies' room and clipped my holster and badge on the front of my new jeans and arranged the big T-shirt to hide them. Now this was just so much better. I shouldered my leather bag and was ready to go stalker hunting.

13

We took Interstate 10 and crossed the Mississippi River on the Huey P. Long Bridge. Traffic was heavy until we turned onto Highway 1 South and into the far outlying areas of New Orleans, where lots of shipyards, manufacturing plants, and shabby strip malls edged the road. Then we got into low marshes and drainage ditches and decrepit houses with lots of barefoot children playing with chickens. The highway narrowed and thinned out, and we flew along without much chitchat. Black pointed out a landmark here and there, but I was more interested in talking about this supposed stalker.

"So are you going to tell me the stalker's name, or do I have to guess it?"

"His name is Marc Savoy. He went through middle and high school with Sylvie. Apparently he adores her."

"And how did you say you found out about him?"

Black kept his eyes on the road but grinned at my less than subtle attempt to make him spill the beans. Like I said, I hate psychiatrists. "I guess I can tell you now. Father Carranda called me and told me that Savoy showed up after the funeral, got all hysterical, and tried to force open her crypt."

I turned in the seat and stared at him. "You're not serious."

"Yes, I am very serious. That's why I thought you might want to talk to this guy."

"How do you know Father Carranda? Oh, let me guess, you were friends in college."

"Yeah, that's right. I went to Mass at Sacred Heart sometimes. Father Carranda said the two of them went to the parish school, and that Marc adored her and followed her around like a puppy. They were good friends and dated some until Sylvie moved to New York and got the soap gig."

"Did this Savoy guy stalk her in New York?"

Black nodded. "Apparently, he went up and hung around, wanting to start things back up, but Sylvie'd moved on and pretty much gave him the shaft. Savoy didn't give up hounding her until Jacques Montenegro sent a couple of guys to pay him a visit. They hadn't heard much out of him since then, but this thing at the church was too sick to ignore."

"Yeah."

Black glanced at me. "You need to stop for anything?"

"No. I'm fine. How much farther?"

"Lafourche Parish is about twenty miles ahead. We can rent a bateau there."

"Bateau?"

"Sorry. Boat. It's what they call them in the bayous."

"You sure we aren't looking for the pirate Lafitte?"

"You know New Orleans history?"

"I went to LSU. Our favorite bar was Lafitte's. They had a picture of him painted on the ceiling."

"*You* barhopped? *You* actually had some fun once?"

I ignored that. "Some of us are serious about our work."

"And I'm not. Is that what you're saying?"

"I'm not saying anything."

I must've ticked him off, because he didn't say anything while we drove through little towns named Larose and Golden Meadow. We finally pulled into the huge metropolis of Leeville. It had regular streets and houses and churches and everything, but unfortunately, we didn't stop there. We kept going until we were out in the real boonies, with forests of trees draped in Spanish moss and cypress knots and egrets flapping off of sunken logs. We took yet another dirt road through live oak trees that nearly touched the truck door, and I felt like I had been transported to Jurassic Park. My imagination came to its senses when the truck's tires crunched onto a driveway made of small white shells and Black pulled up in front of an old, rickety gas station/boat rental that had a po' boy restaurant inside.

"We'll leave the truck here and rent a boat down there," Black said, putting on a St. Louis Cardinals cap and pointing to a boat ramp on a brackish-looking body of water. The famed bayou, I supposed. I couldn't get over how different he seemed out of his doctor garb. I suddenly wondered if I'd been duped by his identical evil twin, who was a regular guy.

While he went inside, I gathered up my shopping bag and purse and walked down the hill to where three or four picnic tables sat under a huge live oak tree with long streamers of gray moss hanging over olive green stagnant water. Wow, scenic. I guess I was used to Lake of the Ozarks and its relatively clear water, so I was not exactly impressed, and from the hordes of insects buzzing on top of the water, I was glad about the Deep Woods Off. Three boats were beached not far from the tables, or should I say bateaux. They looked like jon boats to me, and I was glad to see the outboard motor in the stern of each. I wasn't in the mood to wield a paddle.

A man and woman and little boy sat on the picnic table closest to the boat ramp eating po' boys and drinking Dixie Beer. The woman looked over at me, but when our gazes met, she looked quickly away as if scared to acknowledge me. She had that frightened look in her eyes, one I'd seen a lot in my line of work. I knew a battered woman when I saw one. I sighed and took a seat on the picnic table farthest away from them. I stared out at the water and thought about Marc Savoy and his relationship with Sylvie Border; then I decided I ought to contact Bud while Black was out of earshot. I pulled out my cell phone and hit his number on speed dial. It took him too long to pick up, but on the fifth ring, he answered.

I said, "Whatcha doin'?"

"Hey, podna, I was wonderin' where you went to. Have fun at the funeral?"

"Oh, yeah, a blast. Where are you?"

"Well, I'm gonna get grief for this, but I'm shoppin' right here on Fifth Avenue."

"Hope Charlie doesn't hear about this. Fact is, I've been doing some shopping myself. Got a Jerry Springer T-shirt I'm planning to give to you for your birthday when I'm finished with it."

"That's what I need up here." We both laughed, and he asked, "You still in the Big Easy?"

"Actually I'm getting ready to enter the Black Lagoon with the Creature."

"Come again?"

I told him what had gone down, and he whistled. "And Charlie actually okayed this little side trip?"

"Yeah, you know how buddy-buddy he is with Black. I just wanted to tell you to drag the swamp and pump the alligators' stomachs if you never see me again."

"You sure this is a good idea?"

"Nope, but I don't think Black's dumb enough to murder me here, with everybody knowing it was his idea to play Swamp Fox. I'm going to be vigilant, believe you me. Anything turn up at your end?"

"I got in to see his ex-wife, and she's got an ironclad alibi. I'll tell you about that later. I'm goin' up to the set to interview the cast of *A Place in Time* after they wrap for the day."

"When you do, toss around the name Marc Savoy and see how they react. That's the name of the guy we're looking for. See if he was ever up there bothering Sylvie."

"Got ya. When you headin' back?"

"Probably tonight."

"Ya'll be careful, you hear?"

"You'd fit right in down here, Davis."

We hung up, and I wondered what Black was doing for so long up at the boat rental; then I wondered if he owned this place. Hey, maybe he even owned the swamp and was planning to put up a five-star resort on stilts.

"What da fuck you think you doin'?" It was the man's voice. I looked over at them, and he had the little boy by the ear. He twisted it until the boy fell on his knees and cried out. "Get me a switch, you, right now, heah me, boy?"

I felt my muscles tense, but the mother looked down at her plate and said nothing. The little boy looked about six, and he ran to the nearest bush and broke off a little branch. He was crying when he ran back with it.

"Hell, you little shit, dat ain't big enough for what I gonna do to your butt." The man's voice was mean, bullying. I felt my teeth do a grinding job. "You go get a bigger one, boy, one dat'll leave you black and blue."

The little boy looked at his mother, then ran off again, and the mother stood up. Uh-oh, I thought, as she said in a quivering voice, "Bobby Ray, Ricky din't mean nothin'. He just don't like eatin' onions on his—"

"You backtalkin' me, Shelley? You darin' to backtalk me?" Bobby Ray said, then backhanded her so quick and hard, she fell to the ground. I stood up and walked over as he stood above her, ready to throw in a kick or two. The little boy stood frozen by the bushes, probably well aware what his momma was going to get next.

"Ah, sir, excuse me," I said in my polite police voice.

Bobby Ray turned around, and I could smell the booze on his breath from three feet away. He had these long, ugly sideburns that grew down and out on his cheeks like Elvis's, and wore a dirty sleeveless undershirt with three globs of mustard down the front and tight black Wrangler jeans on his scrawny little butt. His face was flushed with the excitement of beating his wife, his eyes slightly beer-bleary, and he glared at me for interrupting his fun.

He said, "What da hell do you want?" He was spoiling to beat somebody unconscious, and I decided that today it might as well be me. Or vice versa, if things went as planned.

I said, as conversationally as I could, "I just couldn't help but notice that you're a big, stupid asshole."

"Huh? What'd you say?" Bobby Ray was confused. Maybe no one had ever described him out loud before.

"I said you're a big, stupid asshole."

He stared at me in disbelief, so I went on. "You know what else I think, Bobby Ray whatever your name is? I think you beat up on women and little children because you're yellow to the core. Know what I mean? You're nothing but a coward, and I bet if you ever had to face a man you'd tuck your tail between your legs and run like a rabbit. I bet you don't even have the guts to mix it up with me. C'mon, I'd just love to clean your clock."

His mean little eyes widened, shocked; then they lit

up as if I'd offered him a winning lottery ticket that said
he could beat me to a bloody pulp. He put his head
down and charged me like a bull, but he wasn't exactly
Mike Tyson, so I sidestepped him, got my arm around
his neck; and helped his head into the aforementioned
live oak tree. His skull hit it hard, and he went down in
a heap and looked up at me, all dazed and confused.
This was the moment in cartoons when you'd see little
stars and tweety birds flying around his head. Ricky ran
to his mother, and she gathered him in her arms.

With some effort, Billy Ray seemed to realize that some
strange woman had actually fought back and rammed
his head into a tree. It must have made him angry, because, oh happy day, he jumped up and came at me
again. I pivoted left and sent my right foot into his chest
with my best kickboxing, Tae Bo, Billy Blanks technique.
He hit the tree again, his back this time, fell to his knees,
and went down on all fours, groaning. *Please, please, come
at me again,* I thought unkindly. I am not a violent person, but sometimes people need a comeuppance.

"There you go, Bobby Ray; you're not so tough after
all. Some women don't like being kicked around, just
won't stand for it. I'm kinda like that. See, it doesn't
feel so hot getting beat up, does it? I know, why don't
you go cut me a switch, and let's see what I can do with
that?"

Bobby Ray looked at his wife and son, then in one
last burst of bravado, charged me again. He was only
slightly drunk and a little woozy from the brand-new
gash in his head, so it was pretty easy for me to jab his
eyes with my bent knuckles and then punch him as
hard as I could in the stomach. When he bent over, I
shoved him into the end of the picnic table for good
measure. He went down, then sat up, but not for long
because Shelley grabbed a full bottle of Dixie Beer off

the table and smashed it over his head. This time he rolled onto his back and lay still. Ricky grabbed the switch and hit him in the chest a few times, then burst into tears and ran back to his mother.

I said to Shelley, "You shouldn't be with him. He's gonna kill you someday."

"Thank you, ma'am," she whispered, as if the jerk on the ground could hear her and would punish her later, but she looked pleased in a frightened way, too, because she'd finally got a chance to hit him back. "I've been fixin' to leave him. I tried to get away before, but he always finds me and beats the shit outta me. He's gettin' worse, and now he's startin' in on Ricky, too. You saw."

"Yeah, that's the way it usually happens. There's a national domestic violence hotline number, 1-800-799-SAFE. Have you ever tried calling them?"

"We don't got no phone. And he don't let me go out alone, not even to visit my momma. Momma's so scart of him, I don't go 'round there no more."

I looked up the hill and saw Black walk out of the boat rental office. When he saw me standing over an unconscious and bleeding man, he started to run down the hill. "Look, you need to get some help. There are places you can go where you'll be safe."

Black reached us about then, and I couldn't help but notice he had a shotgun gripped in one hand. He looked down at Bobby Ray, then turned to me and said, "I can't leave you alone for a minute, can I?"

"Look at her face. The jerk was beating up on her and the kid."

Black looked at Shelley's face and said, "Are you all right? I'm a doctor. Let me take a look at that eye." He examined the cut just below her right eye, and we both noticed the yellowing bruises healing on her throat and upper arms. Black said, "Look, my friend is right. You need to get out of here and away from him, or there'll be hell to pay when he wakes up. Can you drive?"

When Shelley nodded, he dug out the keys to the truck. "Take that truck up there, and drive to Charity Hospital in New Orleans. Ask for Julie Alvarez. She works in the emergency room. Give her this card, and tell her I sent you. She'll help you get to a safe place. Think you can do that?"

"Yes, sir. I don't know how to thank you." Shelley kept looking down at Bobby Ray as if he were only pretending I'd put his lights out. "But I can't just take your truck. It ain't right to do that."

"It's okay. Leave the keys at the hospital with Julie, and I'll have somebody pick it up."

I watched Black lead her and the boy up the hill and get them settled in the truck, and I had to admit I was distinctly impressed with the doctor's bedside manner. Maybe Black did have a good side to him. He watched the woman reverse the truck, turn it around, and take off in a spray of white shells. Then he joined me where I was standing guard over Bobby Ray.

"Tell me, Detective, do you accost everybody you come into contact with?"

"If they're beating up a woman or a little kid, I do."

"Well, next time wait for me, and I'll help you." Black knelt and fingered the gash on Bobby Ray's forehead. "He's not going to bleed to death, but he'll be out for a while."

He stood up, and we actually shared our first true smile. Then he said, "Come on. Let's get the hell out of here before somebody calls the cops."

14

I sat at the bow, facing Black as he guided the jon boat through gross-looking, dark green water. He was a real Chatty Cathy now, telling me over the low growl of the motor how great it was to be back in the bayous and that it'd been too long since he'd visited his old friend Aldus Hebert, who was quite a character. He said the bayou was as primordial and primitive and beautiful as ever.

Primordial and primitive, all right, but the beautiful part was iffy, to say the least. Truth be told, I was more interested in the shotgun lying across his knees. I didn't trust his motives in suddenly showing up with a loaded weapon, so I got down to brass tacks in my usual subtle manner.

"Why'd you bring that gun? Thought you weren't going to shoot me."

"I never go into the bayous without a weapon," he answered; then he grinned, all relaxed and at home, Mr. Swamp Man himself. "Sometimes alligators attack boats like this and turn them over, you know."

"Yeah? Maybe I'll blow their heads off if they do."

Black laughed. "You're losing your sense of humor, Detective."

I lightened up by demanding, "Who's Julie Alvarez?"

"Julie's a nurse at Charity. She was battered herself when she was young. Now she helps other women escape from men who hit them."

Actually, I'd gained some respect for Black, begrudging, yes, but real enough, so I said, "That was pretty cool what you did for Shelley and Ricky. Lending them the truck, I mean."

"You did the hard part. I wish somebody had come to my mother's defense that way."

The fact that he opened up about his private life surprised me a little, but he didn't look like he was going to elaborate, so I didn't ask any nosy questions. I didn't like people prying into my personal affairs, either, so I changed the subject. "How are we going to get back to the airport?"

"I'll call for a limo."

"I knew you'd be in a limo again before this trip was over."

He didn't rise to my sarcasm, so I spent the next ten minutes spraying about half a can of Deep Woods Off on every inch of my exposed flesh. Then I glanced around the creepy place and said, "Do you know where you're going? This place all looks the same to me, cypress trees and dragonflies and that weird gray moss hanging off the trees."

"I know where I'm going. We call dragonflies mosquito hawks down here."

"We? Sounds like you've spent more time down here than just college days."

"When I'm up north, I call them dragonflies. Satisfied?"

I frowned and ran my fingers through my hair. The stupid Jerry Springer T-shirt was hot, and I pulled out the material in the front and waved it around, trying to get cool.

Black watched me a few seconds, then said, "You'd be cooler without that T-shirt."

I returned his big, suggestive smile. "The T-shirt's just fine."

Black laughed and shook his head. "Know what, Detective? I've never met anyone quite like you. Unpredictable, unpleasant, uncooperative, un-everything, but hell, I like you, anyway."

"Gee, thanks. Now I can sleep nights."

It took almost forty minutes to reach Black's friend Aldus Hebert and his cabin in the swamp. I fidgeted the whole time, unsettled by the big water moccasins slithering around and the alligator eyes, like tiny twin periscopes, watching us chug past.

The minute the old homestead came into sight, Black perked up considerably. "There it is. The house has sat out here in that clearing going on seventy years. There's Aldus on the porch." He raised his arm and waved.

I half-turned and looked at the old man sitting in an even older rocker on the front porch of a small, weathered-gray house with a rusted corrugated tin roof.

Aldus stood up and returned Black's wave as the jon boat bumped up against his dock, and at least ten mongrel dogs came running and sniffing and barking.

"This place really jumps after dark. It's the swamp nightspot, with lots of foot stomping and dancing and drinking. You'd fit right in," Black said, warming up some of his own sarcasm.

"Uh-huh. These dogs bite?"

"Not unless you threaten Aldus."

Black climbed out of the boat, and I jumped ashore, ignoring his helping hand. So I'm the self-sufficient type, and I like to keep my gun hand free.

Aldus came down the steps and out to meet us, and

Black gave the old man a big bear hug. "Man, it's good to see you," he said, then lapsed into what I assumed was Cajun.

"*Garde voir le beau belle!*" Aldus cried, shaking his bushy gray hair and beard all around and reminding me a little of Charles Manson on a good day, without the swastika carved into his forehead. He obvious had a penchant for yelling out everything he said. Maybe he was used to calling out to passing boats. Oh, excuse me, I meant bateaux?

"What'd he say?" I asked Black.

"You don't want to know."

"Au contraire," I said, proud that I happened to know a few French words myself. "Tell me."

"Okay. He said, 'Look at the beautiful girlfriend.'"

"Well, tell him I'm not your girlfriend," I said.

The old man chattered some more in Cajun, his dark eyes gleaming as he looked me up and down and round and round like he was ready to put in a bid.

"He spends a lot of time out here alone," Black explained.

"Ga, ga, ga," Aldus said then, speed-talking Cajun and wriggling his eyebrows like a real, true-life lecher. Indeed, the guy was a regular Hugh Hefner of the Bayous, with denim overalls and no shirt instead of a black silk smoking jacket. Somehow he just didn't fit the profile of someone Black would bother to associate with.

"Who is he to you, anyway?" I asked.

"I told you. He's an old friend. His grandson and I interned together, and we used to come down here to fish."

"Why doesn't he speak English? We *are* still in the United States, right?"

Black ignored me and introduced us in English.

"Aldus, this is Detective Claire Morgan from Missouri. Detective, allow me to introduce my friend Aldus Hebert."

Aldus shouted something in Cajun, shocked me by grabbing me quick-like and smacking me a good one on the mouth. I almost pulled my weapon.

Instead I suffered the ordeal with a tight smile as we all moved up onto the porch. Aldus led me to the rocker; then he sat beside Black on a bench across from me.

"Ask him if he knows where Marc Savoy is. We don't have all day," I said.

"Will you be patient? You don't rush in on Cajuns and start demanding answers. They consider that rude. They're hospitable people. He'll be offering you something to drink in a minute. Take it and be gracious."

"I'm not thirsty."

"Yes, you are."

I turned my attention to the old man. "Mr. Hebert, I'm here on police business, and I'd like to ask you a few questions."

Aldus was looking at me now, grinning like an idiot, despite my serious tone. Obviously, he was quite proud to be a horny old goat.

I said, "Do you know where we can find Marc Savoy?"

Ignoring my question, Aldus asked me something in Cajun.

I sighed and looked at Black. "Well?"

"He asked you if you'll go to the dance with him tonight."

I frowned.

So Black said, "This is pretty serious, Aldus. We think Marc Savoy might've killed Sylvie Montenegro. Do you know where he is?"

The mention of murder seemd to sober Aldus. "Marc Savoy a strange bird," he said in English and asked us what we'd like to drink. Black told him sodas, so Aldus went inside and brought out three Pepsi-Colas in ice-cold bottles. We all drank.

Aldus turned to Black and said, "He live out in de swamp still, in dat old stilt house of 'is daddy. You know de one. We stop dere when you came fishin', and his momma go fix up a bucket boiled crawfish for supper."

"Yeah, I remember her. They lived about a mile or two due west of here, right?"

"Okay, then let's be on our way," I said, my patience winding down.

It took us about twenty minutes to reach the old shack stilted out of the water. There was an aluminum canoe tied to the dock just off the front porch. The place was really out in the middle of nowhere, I assumed even for Cajun homesteads. The three buzzards perched on the roof didn't bode well, either. About twenty yards from the dock, the wind shifted and the smell hit us, and it was like plunging into an open vat of putrefaction.

"Somebody's dead in that house," I said and pulled my weapon. I searched the surrounding cypress trees for rifles sighted on us.

Everything was real quiet, except for the slow flapping of wings as the buzzards lazily took wing. It was as eerie as hell, but I knew that smell very well. Death, grotesque and unmistakable.

"Wait here, and let me go in first," Black offered, but I ignored that and jumped out of the boat as soon as it bumped the rickety wood landing. I climbed the steps cautiously and flattened my back against the wall at one side of the door.

"Open up, police," I called out.

"No one with a nose could stand being inside that house for longer than a few minutes," Black said from right behind me, but he held the shotgun at the ready.

He was probably right, but I couldn't be sure of that, so I kicked in the door and led with my gun. Inside the one-room shack, the stench was revolting, and I covered my nose with my shirttail. Black followed suit.

The person who I assumed had been Marc Savoy sat in an overstuffed chair in the corner. A deer rifle was propped between his knees, and a huge black hole gaped where his mouth and nose had been. It was sweltering hot in the room, and bluebottle flies had found their way in through holes in the window screens and were swarming on the oozing wound, their buzzing loud in the silence.

On the wall behind the corpse was blood and brain tissue, spattered over about a thousand photographs of Sylvie Border taped to the old pink-and-yellow striped wallpaper. Actually, all four walls were covered with images of Sylvie. Some were pictures torn from high school yearbooks; more were from movie magazines and *Soap Opera Digest*. There was a framed prom picture of the two of them and an eight-by-ten of her in a blue-and-white cheerleader's uniform on a table beside an unmade cot. Marc Savoy had lived in a shrine dedicated to Sylvie Border.

I squatted down and examined the corpse. Obviously, Black had seen a few dead bodies himself, because he wasn't too squeamish to join me by the man's remains.

He said, "Looks like a suicide. Is there a note?"

"I looked. There's no note. Don't touch anything. Let's go outside, and I'll call the sheriff."

Black followed me out, both of us sucking in the fresh air, but the odor crept all over our flesh and clothing like some kind of living fungus.

I hoped I could pick up reception way out there as I fished out my cell phone. Black watched me and said, "Maybe he followed Sylvie to Cedar Bend, murdered her because he couldn't have her, and then couldn't live with the guilt."

I held the phone in one hand and looked at him. "Is that what you think happened?"

"Sounds reasonable."

I stared at him, and he stared back. "Or maybe it went down this way. Your Cajun Mafia friends took the law into their own hands rather than wait for the cops and courts to screw it up. Maybe you're covering for them?"

Black didn't move, but I could almost see the anger rising up inside him. "That is ridiculous, and they're not my friends."

Surprised he'd finally lost his cool, I smiled and said, "No need to get all defensive, Black, not unless you have something to hide."

Face dark and furious, Black watched me dial 911. I identified myself as a Missouri law enforcement officer, reported the crime to the Lafourche Parish Sheriff's Department, and told them exactly what we'd found and when and where.

LIFE WITH FATHER

Since the child had been sleeping in the father's bed, the father had forgotten to enforce some of the rules of conduct. He now let Brat go outside and play in the woods and along the little creek at the back of the property.

One day Brat was swinging on an old tire swing near the coach house at the end of the old driveway when a little girl about six years old came running across the lawn. At first, Brat wasn't sure she was real.

"Hi," she said. "What's your name?"

Brat dragged both feet to stop the swing and stared in shock at the little girl. She had long blond braids and was very pretty. Brat had never seen another child, except for the five-year-old little boy who had drowned in a public swimming pool and whom his father had embalmed.

"My father calls me Brat."

"That's a funny name."

"Are you real?" Brat asked, reaching out to touch her.

She said, "Why are you whispering?" Then she said, "I like your swing. Can I swing on it?"

Brat got off and let it dangle between them, but the little girl with braids was too small to climb on, so Brat lifted her up. "Now push me," the little girl demanded. "Real high. I like to go high as the birds. I have a pet squirrel named Mr. Twitchy Tail. He comes right down out of the tree and eats acorns out of my hand. You can feed him, too, if you want to."

Brat nodded and pushed the swing higher and higher, and the little girl laughed and laughed until Brat laughed, too. It felt strange to laugh. Brat couldn't remember laughing before, but the father was busy in the cellar and no longer watched so closely. Brat liked the little girl. Maybe she could be a friend.

They took turns on the tire swing until a woman's voice called from the distance.

"That's my momma. See, here she comes."

Brat looked and saw a woman walking quickly toward them. She had blond hair twisted into braids like the daughter, and she smiled, one that was big and white and happy. "Why, hello there," she said to Brat. "You must be the child who lives in the big house. I work for your father now. I'm your new cook."

Brat remembered the father needed a cook and nodded.

"We're living down in the old coach house. Come with us, and we'll have chocolate chip cookies and milk."

Brat nodded and went along with them. It seemed very peculiar to be outside with other people, but they were both very pretty with their long blond hair like Brat's mother's, and they didn't seem to care that they had to do all the talking. The little girl gave him some acorns, and Brat sat very still until a brown squirrel with a big, bushy tail scampered down on the porch rail and grabbed one out of Brat's hand. The little girl clapped with delight and said that Mr. Twitchy Tail liked Brat and that Brat could feed him any time he wanted.

That night Brat told his friends in the cold room about the woman and little girl and Mr. Twitchy Tail, and they were very pleased about Brat's new friends. When the cook had brought out the cookies, Brat had stolen five more off the pretty yellow plate to take home to the mother and her friends, but a new dead man had come in the black hearse today, a skinny old grandpa with wrinkled brown skin that clung to his bones like a skeleton. He looked like he needed a cookie more than Brat did, so Brat broke his in half and shared so the poor old man wouldn't be left out. The old man was grateful and said he had five grandchildren, all boys, and they liked to fish in his pond behind the barn and swim in the creek where tadpoles darted around and dragonflies landed on the surface of the water. Brat liked the old man and wished the grandsons would come to visit.

From then on Brat spent lots of time with the little girl and the cook, without his father finding out, and it was the best time of his life. Then one day when Brat and the little girl were taking a shower with the hose in the cook's backyard, the embalmer walked around the corner where they were playing. Brat's happy smile froze and faded to horror, and the father said, "You run along home, right now, you hear me, Brat!"

Brat dropped the hose and obeyed, but the cook said, "That's a terrible thing to call a child."

"Then just let me tell you what he did to his mother, and maybe you'll understand," the embalmer said in his angriest voice.

Brat felt sick inside but kept walking across the wet grass toward the main house. But then he looked back and saw the cook listen to the father, then place the little girl behind her and look after Brat as if she saw a monster.

Later that evening, the father found the child hiding in the cold room and dragged Brat upstairs to bed. He said he was disappointed that Brat'd gone off and talked to those people in the coach house. He said he'd been forced to tell them how Brat had pushed his own mother down the steps and killed her, and to advise the cook that it would be wise to keep her child away from Brat.

Brat felt a terrible burning inside him, like a boiling hot river of fire, but waited until the embalmer slept, then crept from the main house and ran to the coach house. Inside the glass front door, the cook and the little girl were packing boxes. They were leaving, and Brat beat on the door and cried, "Don't leave me here, don't leave me. Please, take me with you. I'm not bad, I'm not. I didn't hurt my mother."

The cook ran to the door and said through the glass, "You go home now and leave us alone, or I'll call the police." She jerked down the shade, and no matter how long Brat knocked and pleaded, she would not answer.

Later Brat trudged home and went down into the cold room and told the dead friends, and they said, "They aren't real friends like us. They don't care about you. They were liars and just pretended. They like to hurt you like your father does. They're evil like him."

Brat felt the fire blaze hotter inside his belly as thoughts came about going back to the coach house and hurting the cook and the little girl, beating them with the razor strop over and over. The flames inside him grew hotter and hotter until he knew he had to go back tomorrow and beat them. But the next day, when Brat went down the hill with the razor strop, the cook and the little girl were gone, and the front door stood ajar. So he lured Mr. Twitchy Tail up on the porch with the acorns the way the little girl always had. Then Brat grabbed the squirrel by the tail and twisted its neck, then slammed it over and over and over on the front steps until the fire inside him went out. He then walked back home, feeling much better.

When Brat told the mother about the pet squirrel, she said, "It deserved to die for being friends with that terrible woman and little girl who hurt you so much. Besides, it's not so bad being dead. I like it here in the cold room with all my friends around me. It's good to be dead. Maybe you can bring Mr. Twitchy Tail down here to play with us."

Later that night, after the child had returned to the cold room from the father's bedroom, the little squirrel did come to visit and curled up in the child's arms, like it used to do on the front porch of the cook's house.

The child was ten.

15

It turned out that the Lafourche Parish sheriff knew exactly where Marc Savoy had lived. His name was Roy Lebonne, and he showed up with a coroner named Joe Billy Preston. Both of them knew Black by name and spoke to him in Cajun, which made me a trifle nervous.

I stood back and watched them work the scene, but it was killing me not to go inside and make sure they weren't screwing up the evidence. I am controlling that way, I admit it. They were friendly enough, had Cajun accents, and assured me that it was well known that Marc Savoy was in love with Sylvie Border and had chased her around since high school like a love-struck *chien*, which translated as dog. They told me that rumor had it that he'd once been visited by her father's friends in the Montenegro crime family and been beaten nearly unrecognizable in his own house, and that after that he'd kept to himself out here, where he could worship Sylvie in peace and quiet. I wondered again if the Montenegros hadn't decided Savoy was guilty, then paid the poor guy a second, more deadly visit.

But I was out of my jurisdiction and my element, so I listened and nodded and didn't share my expert opinion. Black hung around for a while, and when I told him I preferred to catch a ride back to town with the sheriff and take a commercial flight home instead of sharing his jet, he got all bent out of shape and said, "Fine, do whatever you want to, but I'm going back over to Aldus Hebert's house and spending the night. If you change your mind and want to fly back with me, that's where I'll be." Then he took off without saying another word.

I felt bad because he was the one who put me on to Marc Savoy, and then I got mad at myself. I was getting personally involved with him, and so I vowed then and there that I'd just have to get myself un-personally involved with him. By the time we got the body tagged and bagged and deposited into Marc Savoy's old canoe to tow behind us, night had fallen. I did not like the swamp in the daytime, and I sure as hell didn't like it pitch-black. All the way back to the Lafourche Parish Sheriff's office, I waited for the Creature from the Black Lagoon to rise wrathfully and pull me down into his underwater lair. When we passed Aldus Hebert's house, I heard the lively strains of a hopping zydeco band playing "Jolie Blond" over the sound of the police boat's motor. I looked to see if I could see Nick Black among the figures dancing under strings of lights in the front yard but couldn't make him out. I thought about stopping, but spending the night there with Black was just asking for trouble, and I had enough trouble as it was.

I didn't get away from the Lafourche Parish Sheriff's office until well after midnight and caught a ride with one of their deputies to the airport, where I took the first morning flight home. I'd had enough of the New Orleans heat and humidity and bluebottle flies. I slept on that flight and the commuter one, too, then some more when I finally fell onto my own couch and crashed. By late the next afternoon I felt fairly refreshed and ready to get back to work.

I spent some time preparing my written reports on the trip and then dropped in to see Harve around seven-thirty that evening. I handed him Sylvie Border's autopsy file and left him at the kitchen table to sort through it while I opened the fridge and got out a can of V8 juice. "Dot gone fishing?"

"Yeah, she and Suze promised to bring back a whole mess of crappie for dinner. Stay, and we'll hash this thing out."

"I think I'll pass this time. I want to check out the crime scene at night. If the perp got her after dark, I want to retrace his steps and see things the way he saw them."

Harve glanced up from the file. "Good God. The head was taped to the chair?"

"The duct tape held it in place. You know, Harve, I thought something looked funny about the head at retrieval, but none of us suspected it was actually severed until Buckeye cut through the tape."

"So why the hell would somebody cut off the head, then reattach it? Doesn't make a lick of sense. I've heard of decapitations before and using the head as a trophy, but nothing like this."

"Maybe he did it in a rage, then regretted it? Tried to fix it." I popped the V8 tab and took a sip. Harve was nursing a Heineken.

"There's not much rage in this murder. The body's been beaten with some kind of object that leaves those half-moon shapes but not too badly, except for the face, and some of that damage might've been done by the fish."

Suddenly, fried crappie didn't sound so appetizing. I

would definitely skip Dottie's fish fry. "Have you seen any cases similar to this?"

Harve shook his head. "We've both run across cases where the victim's positioned in a specific way, especially in serials, but that's usually done for a reason. We can check out the FBI's database of recovered body parts. I've got a friend at Quantico who'll do a search for me. Might find something that ties in with this one." He frowned. "I just can't figure why the perp reattached the head."

"Reattached the head? Gross. Don't say any more; it's almost time to eat." We hadn't heard Dottie slip in from the back porch. She was dressed in khaki shorts and a light blue sleeveless tank top with a heart made out of red glitter on the front. Smiling, she held up a good stringer of bass and crappie. "Possum Cove's a treasure trove, and my dirty little secret. I found a fishing hole just below Suze's place that's teeming with fish just for me. Lots of brush and a rickety old dock. I'd give anything if I could get you over there, Harve. You'd be in the box seats of Nirvana."

The box seats of Nirvana? Dottie said stuff like that all the time. Not fish heaven, not angler's paradise. But box seats in Nirvana. Dottie was a unique person, and she beamed at me. "You're staying for dinner, aren't you? I gotta hear your impressions of the delicious Doctor Black."

"I'm gonna have to pass, Dot. I want to go back to Sylvie's bungalow and look the place over again. Yeah, and by the way, Black's pretty much everything you said he'd be."

Dottie slung her catch from Nirvana into the kitchen sink, with a clatter of the metal stringer. "I bet even you felt the chemistry, right? What'd I tell you? He's something, right?"

"*Even* me?" Mock hurt. But sometimes the truth hurts. I hadn't been out with a man since I'd known her. What else was she going to think? "He's involved in the case, so that means hands off even if I was interested, and I'm not." Sometimes I tell little white lies. "I don't think he did it, but some things about him just don't add up."

Harve looked at me with interest. "Like what?"

"Like he said he hardly knew Sylvie's family, but I saw him embracing some of their help, who acted like they wanted to kneel down and kiss his ring."

"You thinking he's working for the Montenegro family?"

I said, "He throws around an excessive amount of money, even for a doctor/real estate developer. Maybe he supplements his lifestyle with drugs and dirty money. Maybe he launders it for them."

"Who's this Montenegro family?" Dottie washed her hands and dried them on a dish towel as she approached the table. When she reached for the file folder, Harve put his palm on it before she could pick it up. "You don't want to see these, hon. It's got the autopsy photos in it."

"Oh, Lord, no, I don't. Thanks for warning me. But who are the Montenegros?"

"Sylvie's dad turned out to be a crime figure in New Orleans. Some people say they're a Cajun Mafia."

Harve said, "And that opens all kinds of cans of worms."

"Jacques Montenegro informed me he's *making inquiries*, to quote him. This may kick off a Mafia war. The feds'll be thrilled. They're already surveilling them."

Dottie looped an apron over her head and tied it behind her back. She flopped a bass on a wood cutting board and lopped off its head with a meat cleaver. "So you think Doctor Black is involved with a crime family?"

She shook her head as she cleaned the fish. "Who would've guessed that?"

"My hunch is that he might've been more seriously involved with Sylvie than he's letting on. Maybe he had an affair with her while he was married and doesn't want it to get out. She's a patient, and he's got a reputation as a psychiatrist to protect. Bud's in New York right now interviewing his ex-wife. It'll be interesting to hear what she has to say."

"Please stay and eat, Claire." Dottie turned around and gave me a beseeching look. "I want to hear everything. We never see you anymore. By the way, I put your mail on your front porch swing, about three days' worth."

"Thanks. I'll take a rain check on the fish, I promise. I'm not finished with the paperwork on my New Orleans trip, and Charlie wants this one done strictly by the book."

Twilight was settling in over the lake, a dark purple haze that looked like a gauzy curtain. When I arrived at Cedar Bend, I found Black had installed a new security post, which was manned by two guards at the entry gate. They were stopping people going in and out of the resort, and I rolled down my window and held up my badge. It wasn't Suze Eggers this time, and I wondered if Black had fired her since Sylvie had died on her watch. "I'm Claire Morgan, primary on the Border case. I'm headed out to the crime scene."

The new guard was big and tough and looked like he'd been around the block a few times. I had a hunch he was either retired military or big city cop. He had these watchful cop eyes, blue and unreadable. He looked like somebody I'd want backing me up in a sticky situation. Nicholas Black was getting serious about his security staff.

"Yes ma'am. If we can be of assistance, let us know."

"Thanks." I looked at his nameplate. It said John Booker. "You're new, right, Booker?"

"Yes, ma'am. Just came on this week. Nice to meet you."

"Ditto. Anybody else come through here requesting admittance to the crime scene?"

"No, ma'am. Lots of press trying to get through, but we've kept it cordoned off on Doctor Black's orders."

I attempted my best nonchalant tone. "What about Black? He been down there?"

Booker shook his head. "No, ma'am. Not to my knowledge."

I thanked him and took off down the road to the murder site. Tourists were everywhere on the lake, obviously not turned off by a grisly murder on the premises. The media was discussing nothing else, but we'd held them off pretty well so far. They hadn't found out the condition of the body, and they weren't conjecturing on possible killers yet.

Sylvie's gate was padlocked. I didn't have the key and didn't want to return to the main lodge, so I ducked under the yellow sheriff's tape and made my way down through the trees on foot. The grounds had already been swept by Buckeye's people, with very few results. A hair caught on the bark of a tree and a couple of old cigarette butts were now being examined and tested. I was more interested in how the perp approached and got into the bungalow.

I had my flashlight, and I stepped through the thick undergrowth and leaves. It was rough terrain, overgrown, but there were animal paths and rain washes cut into the hillside where I could place my feet on gravel and not leave footprints. So could the murderer.

It was completely dark now, and I stopped just above the bungalow and listened. Night sounds. The loud, discordant chorus of crickets. I could hear music, very faint, from the bungalow that Mrs. Cohen had stayed in. "You Light Up My Life." Mrs. Cohen was gone. Somebody who liked the oldies was staying there now. I wondered if they knew about the horrible murder next door. And what they'd think if they knew a detective was creeping around in the dark, listening to their radio.

Twenty yards below I could see the bungalow where Sylvie Border died. Solar lamps glowed dimly every four feet along the front porch, and I remembered the lights were also positioned across the back. Still, the deck was very dark. The chandelier in the foyer was on; I could see it through the fanlight. The rest of the bungalow lay as dark as a grave. This is what the killer saw if he came down through the woods. Where was Sylvie when he was standing here? In the house? On the deck? Asleep in bed?

If Black had left between 9:30 and 11:00 P.M. like he'd said, what would she have done after he left? He said she was tired from a run. Would she soak in the hot tub on the back deck? Or in the one in the bedroom? Maybe she took off her clothes herself before she got into the hot tub, was naked before he attacked her. Maybe he watched her, got aroused, and decided to rape her and then kill her.

I moved laterally down to the lake until I could see the back deck. The hot tub was clearly visible. If I were Sylvie, once Black was out of sight, I would have soaked in the hot tub and relaxed my muscles before I went to bed. Hell, that's what I needed to do right now. There wasn't much I wouldn't give to have my own private hot tub.

This time of night the bungalow was completely secluded, dark, and private enough to bathe nude without being seen. Unless somebody was standing where I was, shielded by bushes.

Across the cove I heard a boat motor start up, then

idle. Then I saw a boat move out into the lake. I could see the light attached to a pole in the stern for night fishing. I could see figures moving along the marina deck, where there were a couple of restaurants catering to casual diners. I could smell hot wings cooking on the grill and the faint fishy smell of the lake. The point farther out at Black's digs was quiet, no helicopters landing or taking off. Just the soft music from next door. "The Way You Look Tonight" suddenly went off as if offended that I was listening. Now all was quiet except the crickets and the lapping of the water against the pilings. I wondered if these were the last sounds Sylvie had heard, those and the sound of her killer's voice.

I climbed over a fallen log and wound my way to the edge of the water. It would be easy for me to splash through the shallows and climb up the side of the back deck. If Sylvie had been in the hot tub, gazing over the water toward the marina, she'd never see me. I did it easily, and without any sounds that would alert someone to my approach. It was dark around the bungalow, lots of shadows not illuminated by the solar lamps. I moved silently to the hot tub. It had been emptied, probably by Buckeye's people. I turned and looked out over the lake. He got her here, while she was in the hot tub; I felt sure of it. That's why she was nude. She may have even been drowsing, with her eyes shut. Just enjoying the peace and quiet.

I heard a board creak behind me but a second too late and only got a faint impression of a dark figure before something hit me in the back of the head. Everything went blurry, and I fell to my knees. Hands grabbed me around the waist and jerked me up, and I knew I was in trouble. I shook off my grogginess and kicked out at his groin as hard as I could. It was too dark to see my assailant, but I heard him grunt with pain. I twisted loose, got him again in the jaw, and clawed for the gun in my shoulder holster. Another guy grabbed me, but I landed a good punch to the face, which nearly broke my hand, before he got me a good one in the side of my head and my lights went all the way out.

I wasn't sure how long I'd been unconscious when I came to, but I knew I was on the lower-level boat dock close to the water and somebody was tying my wrist to a deck chair. I lunged up at him, yelling and fighting, and grabbed the guy's hair with my free hand. He cursed and fought my hold, then slung me backward so hard, I went off the deck into the lake, chair and all. I hit cold water, pulling desperately to free my bound left hand as the heavy wrought iron chair sank quickly, taking me with it. My feet were free, so I kicked and twisted, pulling at the rope holding my wrist. The knots weren't tight, and I knew I could work myself free, but panic threatened, anyway, stark and overwhelming, in that awful, dark silence where the fish had fed on Sylvie's body. As I jerked and pulled, I could see the solar lamps on the deck above me, and a stream of bubbles burst from my mouth when I finally wrenched my hand free.

I shot desperately upward and broke the surface, gasping and choking. I sucked in air and grabbed hold of the pilings, and then I heard a voice, Nick Black's voice, low and angry, answered by other voices before the sound of running feet thudded up the steps and receded into the distance. I got my elbows on the deck and tried to hoist myself out of the water, but then Black was there, right above me, hauling me out by the back of my shirt.

As soon as I hit the deck, I jerked away from him and scrabbled sideways. Breathing hard, hands trembling, head hammering, I pulled my weapon and held it trained on his chest.

"Get down, get down on your knees. Do it, do it!" My voice was hoarse, and I was shivering with cold, but I could see him better now. He held his arms straight out to the side, then went slowly down on his knees, as if he'd had some practice at it.

"Easy, easy, Detective. Don't shoot me. I didn't do this."

"Get your hands behind your back! Now! Now, I said!"

Once he was flat on his stomach, I cuffed him, frisked him for weapons, and found him clean, then staggered sideways, a little weak-kneed, and leaned against the railing, looking around for his accomplices.

A moment later I ducked and shifted my aim to the shoreline when somebody ran into sight. He yelled, "Security! Drop your weapon!"

"Police!" I yelled back. "I need help over here!"

The guy splashed across the water and climbed onto the deck in exactly three seconds flat. It was John Booker. "What happened?" he said, holstering his gun and looking down where Black was on his belly at my feet. "Is he all right?"

"I don't give a shit. He just attacked me."

"No way, Detective. He's with me. We came down here when we found your vehicle abandoned at the gate. Black wanted to make sure you were all right. I went in the front, and he took the back."

I stared at him in disbelief, quivering with wet and cold and anger, still holding my weapon trained on Black's back.

"Look at the surveillance tapes if you don't believe me. We just got here minutes ago."

I took Black in to jail, anyway. I had him finger-printed and thrown into a holding cell for assaulting a police officer. Nothing in my life had ever felt better than seeing him behind those bars. Booker's story checked out, but that didn't mean I bought it. Booker brought in the surveillance tape and ran it for Charlie;

then one of Black's slick lawyers, wearing tasseled loafers, showed up and had a private conference with Charlie. I wasn't invited. I waited in the interrogation room, calmer now, except that my head still pounded and my hands shook. I kept them around a mug of hot coffee so no one would see.

As soon as Charlie walked into the room and I saw his face, I knew Nicholas Black was going to walk. I stood up and dared Charlie to let him go.

"It wasn't him, Claire. He can prove it."

"Yeah, right. He just happened to be there at exactly the same time somebody assaulted me."

"That's right. He was at the main lodge with the fuckin' mayor of all people when security informed him your vehicle was sitting empty at the gate. Said he wanted to make sure you were okay, and he excused himself from the meeting as soon as he could, and the two of them opened the gate and drove down the hill. The guard named Booker went in the front door, but Black heard something and ran around the side deck, and that's when he saw you struggling with a couple of guys. They ran, but when you got dumped in the lake, all he thought about was getting you out of the water."

"Bullshit."

"Maybe. The tape shows him coming in with the guard clear as day."

"Maybe the guard's in on it with him. Ever thought of that, Charlie? He works for him, doesn't he? Or maybe he hired those two thugs, then arranged it so he could show up and save the day at the last minute so he'd look like a hero. I'm telling you Black's got something to do with this. I heard him talking to them, for Christ's sake."

"Go home, Claire. Get some rest. You got the wrong man this time."

"Go to hell, Charlie."

"I didn't hear that. You're tired. You're upset. Go home and think it through. Then we'll talk."

I wanted to shoot him, so bad I had to hold my arm down to keep from drawing my weapon, but I didn't. I left in time to see Black and Booker being picked up by a long black limousine. I was going to get Black for this. I was going to get him if it killed me.

16

It was midnight by the time I got home, damp and muddy and enraged. Dottie was waiting on my front porch with a pot of homemade chicken noodle soup. I loved Dottie like a sister, but I wasn't in the mood for company. Actually, I wasn't in the mood for anything, other than murdering somebody with my bare hands. I suppose Dottie was safe. I like her soup.

"Harve and I heard on the police band," she said, jumping up and exhibiting wringing-of-hands concern. "Oh, God, look at you. Are you all right?"

"Well, I've been better." Truth was, I wasn't sure. I was still shaky and nasty with lake slime. I walked into the kitchen, more agitated than anything. Dottie followed. "Did Black do this to you?"

"Yes, but nobody'll believe me."

"I believe you."

I could always count on Dottie, and I was grateful. Truly, I was. She was a good friend, but I wanted her to leave me alone. I needed to think, to relax muscles that were knotted hard. I needed that hot tub. "Thanks, Dot. I do appreciate your bringing the soup. But I'm not hungry. I'm real tired and, frankly, pissed off so bad I'm not going to be good company." She nodded. She understood. "Let me help you get out of those filthy clothes. You'll feel better if you do."

I let her, and then I got in the shower and let hot water pour down on my face for so long that Dottie came back in to make sure assailants hadn't gotten me again. I dried off, put on an oversized T-shirt and red tights, and slouched down in my trusty old vinyl recliner with my favorite pillow. Dottie was watching me like I was an unexploded cherry bomb. I sank my head into the pillow and closed my eyes. The old recliner was my security blanket. I'd had it so long, my body fit its contours, and it felt like somebody trustworthy was holding me in the palm of his hand.

Dottie moved into the kitchen and stirred the soup bubbling happily on my stove top. "I'm going to turn the burner down real low, but you'll have to keep an eye on it. And I brought over a hot toddy, which will relax you. You're going to need something to help you sleep after all this." I opened my eyes as she came around the counter dividing my living room and galley kitchen. She was dressed in cutoff jeans and a big turquoise shirt and had her hair twisted up in a red clip. She was barefoot. She was always barefoot. She handed me a big white coffee mug and said, "I know you don't want to talk about it right now, but I'm here if you need to. Ring the dinner bell, and I'll come running. Sometimes talking helps."

She meant the big black bell I had attached to a pole on the dock in front of my house. Harve had one just like it. We used it for emergencies, but more often if either of us wanted company. Fact was, at the moment, all I wanted was for Dottie to leave. I wanted to weep uncontrollably into my pillow. I wanted to rid myself of the abject panic I'd felt roped to that chair. Most of all, I wanted to shoot Nicholas Black between the eyes. "I can't talk about it yet. I'll come by tomorrow and see you guys. Tell Harve not to worry. I'm okay. I'm just angry, is all."

"Okay." Dottie got the message. But she was loving and nurturing, and it felt good when she put her hands on my shoulders. "Lean forward, and I'll loosen up some of that tension before I take off."

Dottie was a licensed masseuse, and I obeyed. The moment her fingers began to knead my shoulders, I relaxed and the whole sordid story poured out, almost against my will. She listened, made no comment, just made little comforting sounds. She was one hell of a listener. I guess that's why I open up to her when I won't to anyone else, not even Harve. Harve worries about me too much.

Finally, Dottie said, "Do you really think Nicholas Black would do something like that?"

"I heard his voice, and he was talking to the guys who jumped me. He was right there. Maybe he didn't do it himself; maybe he hired them to scare me off. He hires people for everything." I got up, my fury whipped up again, angrier than I'd been in years. I began to pace. I stopped in my tracks when we heard Harve's bell echoing out over the water.

"Harve's anxious about you," Dottie said, heading for the front door. "I need to get back and fill him in. You'll be all right. Eat some soup. Lie down and let the toddy work, and you'll feel better." She sounded more sure of it than I did.

"Yeah."

"Do some yoga. That always calms you down and clears your mind. If you need us, call or ring the bell."

"Thanks, Dot."

She hesitated and searched my face. I couldn't have looked too hot. "You want me to stay the night? Harve'll understand."

"No, no, I'm fine, really."

I walked out to the front porch and watched her run along the path toward Harve's house. Dottie ran everywhere, barefoot or not. She was the fittest person I knew from all that running and lifting weights. I vowed to start a new routine with free weights as soon as I calmed down. Even my kickboxing practice was going to get more rigid. I was tired of getting jumped and hit in the head. What was the matter with me? Where was my sixth sense? Where were any of my senses?

I walked into the kitchen and turned off the soup. Food just wasn't going to cut it. I kept thinking about why Black would order such a thing. To frighten me, make me back off from him? Well, I'd be damned if I'd back off. Now I wanted to get him, and I would if it took the rest of my life.

I'd learned yoga when I lived in California, and it had helped me get through the mess I'd been in out there. I was too on edge to do anything else, and I was tired of pacing. Assault and near drowning have a tendency to shake me up. I had to calm myself down in my head, where I was reliving everything over and over.

I always did yoga on the dock, which stretched about fifteen yards out into the lake. *Old Betsy*, my trusty jon boat, was rocking at the end, tied to a piling with a dusk-to-dawn light on the top. I walked outside under a canopy of black velvet and glittering stars and began to feel better. I was safe at home. I had my cell phone clipped to my waist, right beside my Glock automatic. Usually, I didn't do my stretches with my gun attached to my person. But hell, this was a special occasion.

About six feet wide, the dock expanded to twenty feet near my jon boat. I'd replaced the rotten boards and sanded them smooth so I could do my yoga poses outside, where I could hear the lapping of the water and cricket songs. I liked to exercise at night under the stars. I'd formed my own routine of poses in an attempt to strengthen and keep limber every muscle in my body. It took just thirty minutes, and it worked. I never missed a day. It helped me think. But I was adding weights to my repertoire tomorrow, without fail.

I warmed up with some easy standing poses, then slowly loosened up my legs with some downward-facing dog positions and warrior stances. My mind had a tendency to empty of thoughts during yoga sessions, and it was working admirably until I heard something behind me. I was out of my stance in two seconds flat, on my belly, Glock out of my holster and trained on the shadowy figure just behind me. Oh, God, not again.

"Don't shoot; it's me." Nicholas Black stepped from the shadows into the light. "I want to talk to you."

Stunned, I kept my weapon trained on him while I searched the dock and beach for his toadies. I didn't see anyone. Lucky for Black, he had enough sense to keep his hands in the air. "What is this? If at first you don't succeed? You here to finish me off, is that it?"

I could hear my own breathing, short, fast, belying my calm words. I cursed over finding myself in a vulnerable position. How the hell did he sneak up on me again? If this kept up, I was turning in my badge. "Get down on your belly, with your arms spread wide." I started to say *Now!* but he obviously knew the drill and obeyed without further urging.

I patted him down for weapons and found nothing under his black T-shirt and jeans but lots of hard-packed muscles. "I'm not armed," he said, and I again searched the lake and shoreline for accomplices. "How did you know where I live?"

He ignored my question. "Look, I need to talk to you, privately, confidentially."

"Where's your vehicle? How'd you get here without me hearing you?"

"I kayaked in."

"You kayaked here from your place across the lake?" That was rich. I didn't believe him.

"I do it for exercise."

"Then do it for exercise while you get the hell out of here and off my property. I have nothing to say to you."

"I have some information that you need to know. I want you to come with me."

I actually laughed at that one. "Oh, sure, that's gonna happen. Want me to help you attack me, too?"

"I didn't assault you, and I can prove it. Come with me, and I'll show you."

"Prove it here, Black. I'm not going anywhere with you, and if you don't clear outta here, I'm gonna run you in again. This time I can get you for trespassing."

"I didn't hurt you." His cheek was against the wood planks, facing me and muffling his voice. "But I know who did. And I know why."

I kept the gun trained on him, my eyes continually searching the darkness. "Is that a fact? Well, hey, go right ahead. Hit me with it."

"Not here. Come out to the yacht, and I'll explain everything."

"You cannot really believe I'm that stupid, can you?"

He sat up, and I retrained my aim to the midpoint of his forehead. It felt good. I'd been fantasizing about this scenario since I'd left the sheriff's office. He actually smiled. "Put the gun away. Believe me, I have enough sense not to make any sudden moves. I can prove I'm innocent, and what I'm going to tell you will help you solve Sylvie's murder."

"Cut the crap. If you have something to tell me, tell me right here, right now."

"We have to go now. Tomorrow will be too late. There are people waiting out there you need to interview. They'll be gone before daylight."

"Not if they had anything to do with using my head for a boxing bag, they won't. What people?"

"This has got to remain confidential, for reasons you'll find out when you talk to them. They can tell you things you have to know to solve this case. And I want it solved."

"What people?"

"I'm going out on a limb to come here tonight. People can be hurt if certain things come out. And don't ask me what people, dammit!" He shook his head, a little testy himself. "What happened to you tonight was inexcusable, and I want to prove to you that I had nothing to do with it."

"Sorry, Jack, you're just shit outta luck. I'm not stepping foot on your yacht tonight. We'll just go back to the station and have a little tête-à-tête in the interrogation room. Won't that be fun? Stand up. Keep your arms out to the side."

Obeying, he rose without effort, light on his feet. He was in good physical shape, too. Anybody who could kayak twenty miles across the water had some upperarm strength and stamina. "I was afraid you wouldn't listen. Charlie's due to call you any minute now. What time is it?"

"Time for me to arrest you again. Maybe this time it'll stick. You know, trespassing on private property, Peeping Tom, stalker, stuff like that."

"I've already talked to Charlie about this. I had a feeling you wouldn't go with me."

"Gee, you're a bright boy, now, aren't you?" Frowning, I watched him suspiciously until my cell phone rang. I pulled it out with my left hand and flipped it open.

Charlie's voice sounded in my ear. Impatient. Annoyed. "Get out to Black's yacht, Morgan. Right now. He's ready to give a statement, and he'll only give it to you. Alone. He's sending somebody to pick you up. Be expecting them."

"Yeah, he's already here, and I've got my gun pointed at his head. You're crazy if you think I'm going anywhere alone with him."

"Then call a backup and ride over with them. Bud isn't back from New York, which makes me wonder what the hell he's doing up there. Winin' and dinin' that model, probably. That trip's gonna cost the department a helluva bundle." Wow, Charlie, thanks for the concern. He was more worried about Bud spending a couple of thousand than about me getting worked over. "Just get to Black's fuckin' boat and find out what he wants to say. Nothing else is gonna happen to you. He gave me his word. Do it and report back to me as soon as it's done." He hung up.

I stared at Black. "Charlie might trust you, Black. You like to buy people off with your money. Maybe you're Charlie's biggest campaign contributor. Maybe he owes you and is willing to turn his head and let you slide now and then, but make no mistake, I can't be bought. If you think I'll let you off if I find you're involved in this at all, you're nuts."

"Maybe that's why I want to talk to you, Detective. Charlie's a good guy, but he plays politics. I can't risk that, not with this information. And I haven't bought off Charlie, either. We've been friends for a long time. He knows I'm not capable of killing Sylvie or hurting you. That's why he doesn't mind ordering you to talk to me. Like I said, people can get hurt."

"And like I said, what people?"

This time he hesitated a long moment. He looked out over the lake a second and considered. I waited, pretty sure he was getting ready to pull something. I kept my finger on the trigger. If I lived to be a hundred, he would never get the jump on me again. "Jacques Montenegro is on the *Falcon*. He wants to talk to you.

It's important. It'll clear up some details that'll help you find Sylvie's killer."

Well, knock me over with a feather. He got me again, because that was the last thing I expected. I guess there was some hanky-panky going on between Black and the Cajun boys, after all.

"Now can you see why I came here tonight? Why he wants a private meeting alone with you? It won't be good for any of us if his presence at the lake gets out."

"Right, and it especially won't look good for you. Being Montenegro's host and benefactor, and all. It might even indicate that you have some serious Mafia ties, right? No wonder you're slinking around in the middle of the night."

Black said nothing, which pretty much meant I was right. And was I ever tempted now. Man, was I tempted. Just the intrigue alone was enough to make me want to go see Montenegro. Even Al Pacino wouldn't have me offed at a meeting set up by the local sheriff. At Black's request, at that. I'd be safe enough, and if I didn't turn up tomorrow morning, heads would roll. Montenegro would know better than to pull anything cute, and it was certainly in Black's interest to get me home safe and sound.

"Okay, let's go. Get down in the boat."

"The kayak's a two-seater. We can take it."

"Gee, thanks, man, but I don't think so. I prefer to be in the driver's seat. So step down in the bow, and keep your hands where I can see them."

I must be out of my frickin' mind, I thought, as I stepped down into *Old Betsy's* rusted, twenty-year-old, camouflaged stern. Somehow I thought Black was on the up and up. Why, I couldn't say, but I could handle myself well enough with a gun in my hand. And it wasn't going to leave my hand, trust me.

I jerked the cord on the outboard, and of course, it wouldn't start right off the bat. It was obstinate. It liked to be coddled.

Black twisted around to look at me. "Is this thing gonna make it to my yacht? I can call for the launch to pick us up."

"Just shut up and keep your hands on top of your head where I can see them."

I finally got the motor running, and even though it smoked and knocked hard enough to make somebody answer a door, I knew it'd make it. And if it didn't, I was one hell of a mechanic. I operated the stick with my left hand and kept my right hand busy with my gun on Black's back. The next few hours were going to be interesting, if I got through them alive.

17

As it turned out, the *Maltese Falcon* was anchored in the deepest part of the lake, about five miles outside my own cove, due north, making Black's kayaking feat not quite so impressive. Even I could kayak five miles. Dottie could probably do twenty or thirty, if she had a mind to. The yacht stood in the darkness, with its strings of bright lights outlining the deck railings and cabin lines, looming like a last vision of the *Titanic* before it went to the bottom. *Not a good analogy under the circumstances,* I told myself as I nudged my ugly-little-stepchild craft up alongside the sleek and gleaming black-and-tan launch. Poor *Old Betsy,* probably felt like calling a plastic surgeon. But I was getting over being knocked into the lake tied to an iron chair. It's amazing how holding a gun to the head of a man like Nicholas Black can make you feel empowered. Go figure.

"It's okay," Black called up to the concerned-looking security guard standing at the top of the ladder, as if the Doc often arrived home in the dead of night with a cop prodding him at gunpoint. Maybe he did. Stranger things have happened. To me.

"You can put your gun away now," he said once we were on deck.

"Thanks for your permission, but I'm sort of attached to it tonight. Please, lead the way."

He led the way, and the guard grinned like he was glad somebody finally refused something to the big boss man. I found that sort of endearing, but I motioned him ahead of me, too, just in case he was smiling because he was planning to jump me. Black headed for his private quarters and I didn't see anybody else, not even the crew. The motor yacht was anchored for the night; everybody was tucked into their little black-and-tan beds.

"Rogers, return to the bridge. Everything's under control here."

"Yeah, Rogers, and if you hear gunshots, call 911."

"Yes, ma'am." I liked Rogers. He was all right.

Inside Black's quarters, in front of the wall of windows and a little balcony, sat Jacques Montenegro. He had on a gray Tommy Hilfiger sweatshirt and chinos, and no doubt expensive Docksiders without socks. He was sitting behind Black's desk as if he owned it, and he just might. Three of his big, burly lieutenants sat in easy chairs around the office. None of them were my friends Jean-Claude and Thierry. They all had on black sweatshirts and snug black sweatpants. Murderous, burly guys definitely should not wear snug black sweatpants. It just didn't do their figures justice.

"Don't get up, gentlemen. It's easier for me to shoot you sitting down."

Two of them laughed. The other didn't get my wit, I guess. He was sporting a black eye and swollen nose, and I suspected his crotch was throbbing a little, too. Montenegro smiled; oh, my, he was Mr. Debonair. "Good evening, Detective. I'm glad Nicky could persuade you to come here for a little chat."

"Your friend Nicky didn't do squat. I'm here on orders from Sheriff Ramsay, so say your piece and get it over with." I emphasized the name because, truth be told, I am sort of a smart-ass, and I was also a little embarrassed because someone in my present company had slapped me around and tied my wrist to a chair, and now I couldn't even shoot him. For some reason, that brings the sarcasm just boiling to the top.

Nobody laughed now. Black moved away and stood by a large porthole on the starboard side as if he were contemplating diving through it when the shooting started, but I could still cover them all with my gun. Unless they all drew on me at once. I decided that was unlikely, and besides, Rogers would call 911 if they did.

"Please, Detective, sit down. I understand you've been through something unpleasant this evening. I feel unhappy that it happened to you."

"Wow, thanks. I feel unhappy it happened, too. Even a little miffed, maybe."

Nobody laughed at that, either. Maybe I was a lousy comedienne, or maybe they had a lousy sense of humor.

"I've already had a talk with my men. It won't happen again."

"Are you saying you ordered me assaulted, Mr. Montenegro?"

"Not expressly. You see, with Nicky's permission, I sent my men to Sylvie's bungalow to gather her belongings so I could take them home to her mother. You surprised them there, and when you fought back so violently and caused them some injuries, they understandably got angry and a bit carried away." Jacques shifted in his chair and took a drink out of the short glass in his hand. I detected some underlying annoyance when he continued, "And, I must admit, we're not pleased that you insinuated to the Lafourche sheriff that we put out a hit on Marc Savoy, when it's quite obvious that he committed suicide. We have enough troubles at the moment without dealing with false accusations. When you surprised my men, they were afraid you'd find out who they worked for. They were protecting me, you see. The idea was to tie you up so they could get away without you pursuing them. When you came to and put up a fight, you got knocked in the water, but that was never intended to happen. It was unfortunate, especially since it upset Nicky so much. The truth is, however, that you were never in any real danger."

"No kidding? Wish I'd known that when I was holding my breath at the bottom of the lake." I looked at the Three Little Hoods. "Remind me to arrest their asses before I leave."

The guilty parties watched me impassively like they were really unconscious but had learned to sleep with their eyes open. All three probably had combined brains the size of one tiny chickpea. I'd had enough of the clever repartee.

"Okay, let's cut to the chase here. You went to a lot of trouble to get me on this boat. What do you want?"

"I had the feeling when you visited my home that you think Nicky killed Sylvie. I'm here to assure you he did not."

I gave a little laugh, incredulous, but nowhere close to amused. "I guess I'm just to take your word for that, right? Lay off him because he's your special buddy. Sorry, pal, I'll need a better reason than that to take him off my suspect list." He really was off my list, but they didn't need to know that.

"How about this for a reason? Nicky is Sylvie's uncle, and he'd never lay a finger on her or any other member of his own family."

Well, Montenegro threw me for a loop on that one. I was stunned, and I don't do stunned often. I bet they could tell. I glanced over at Black. He nodded and said, "Jacques is my older brother."

"Your brother. You and Jacques Montenegro are brothers." Sometimes I repeat myself when I'm unsettled. It gives me time to think up more clever remarks.

"That's right," Jacques said. "Unfortunately, however, Nicky isn't interested in the family business. He likes all this psychology mumbo jumbo. He keeps his association with us secret for obvious reasons. Sylvie was the same way. She didn't want the notoriety of the Montenegro name to overshadow her career." *Or ruin it*, I thought.

His handsome face fell slightly, sorrow written all over it; then his features went hard again, and his dark eyes glittered. "Whoever killed her is going to pay. But it wasn't my brother. Nicky and Sylvie were very close. You're wasting your time suspecting him and keeping your investigation off track. I came here to tell you the truth so you'd start looking in the right places instead of following this dead end. I have met with my colleagues in my own circles." Which meant crime families from New York to New Orleans to Sicily, I assumed. "I have been assured none of them were involved in Sylvie's death. My personal opinion is that a stranger killed Sylvie, and Nicky concurs with me. As Sylvie's father, I'm requesting that you work closely with Nicky, use his expertise at profiling, or whatever he likes to call it, and find the savage who did this. I want him caught, and then I want him dead. We can help you with that, if need be."

So much for fair trials and all that unnecessary bother. But I was taking it all in, trying to unboggle my boggled mind. I was shocked to learn of the relationship, even more shocked that Nicholas Black had managed to keep his real identity under wraps, considering his own fame and newsworthiness.

"I'm not ashamed of my family, Claire." Black used my first name, which seemed odd under the circumstances. "It was just easier when I was young to start out without that familial identification, especially when I enlisted in the army. I'd never have made it there if my true background was known. I used Black because it's a derivative of Montenegro. I didn't kill my niece or anyone else. I didn't try to hurt you tonight." He frowned at the three stooges. "Jacques is right. I was furious when I got there and saw what they'd done. It was stupid. Nothing like that will ever happen again."

"Not unless I happen to detect in the wrong direction."

"It won't happen again," Jacques said in a voice that pretty much meant death by agony to the offending party. Mr. Burly, without a sense of humor and with a torn-up face, squirmed in his chair, and I knew he was the one who had played Dunking for Donuts with me.

I began to ascertain that I just might be out of my league here. Hell, before the last week or so, I could count the number of underworld figures I'd met personally on one hand. I felt a bit uncomfortable, even with the Glock in my grip. Perversely, I was fairly certain I was safe. Black was now on a first name basis with me. Surely, he wouldn't call me Claire, then knock me off. It just wouldn't be polite.

Holstering my weapon, I put my hands on my hips. I could see my reflection in the dark windows behind the Godfather, and sans my weapon, I didn't look very intimidating in red yoga tights and T-shirt and no shoes. Everybody was staring at me as if it was my move, so I said, "Okay, tell me everything you know. From the beginning."

"Please sit down, Detective, and let me tell you about my daughter."

The sad story went on for almost an hour and

would've had me in tears if I hadn't been jerked around so much, but it told me little more than I already knew. Other than Black's relationship with the family, it pretty much bore out my findings. With Black eliminated as a suspect, though, it put everything in a different light, but I wasn't quite as ready as Jacques Montenegro to accept the assurances of his mob friends that Sylvie's death was not a contract hit. Maybe it was a little theatrical for a professional hit man, but there probably were dramatic killers for hire out there some place.

After the story was over and all my questions were asked and answered, truthfully, I hoped, Montenegro and his merry men took their leave. I glared them out of the stateroom, not liking the fact that they were getting a pass on hassling me, a licensed officer of the law. But I was more glad, I guess, that the attack hadn't been by some nut job still lurking out there and waiting to get me in a new, resourceful way.

"This'll just take a minute. Make yourself comfortable," Black told me as he followed the men out of the office.

I nodded, but it wasn't until I relaxed into one of the long white divans heaped with satin pillows that I realized how sleepy I was. I heard the launch come to life down on the deck, felt the slight sway of the yacht, and decided to shut my eyes just for a moment. I was gone in seconds. Dottie's hot toddy had finally kicked in.

Somewhere in the never-never land of my mind, I could hear a phone ringing. It was playing the "Mexican Hat Dance." Hey, that's the tune I set my phone on. Groggily, I reached for my belt, where I clipped my phone. I couldn't find it. I heard an unfamiliar voice.

"She's still asleep. This is Nick Black. May I take a message?"

Nick Black, I thought; then I thought, *Nick Black?* I sat up and looked around. He was sitting behind his desk, holding my canary yellow cell phone in his hand. "She's okay. She came out here to interview me last night and fell asleep on my couch. I'll have her call you back." He punched off and laid the phone on the desk. He was dressed in a starched white shirt and blue tie, clean-shaven and obviously dolled up for an important meeting. He smiled. "You're a popular lady. That's the third call I've answered for you."

"Why didn't you wake me up?"

"Actually, I tried. Whatever your friend put in your drink was potent enough to knock you out like a light."

"How did you know Dot fixed me a toddy?"

"I was waiting outside for her to leave so I could get you alone." He walked to a sideboard with a silver coffee urn. He filled a cup and brought it to me. "You like it black, if I remember correctly."

I took it and shoved my hair back off my face. I was at a disadvantage, but the strong black coffee helped. "What time is it?" I asked, noticing how the sun was glittering off the water outside the windows. "How long did I sleep?" Then, "Who called me, and who the hell said you could answer my phone?"

Black laughed and refilled his own cup. He leaned against the black granite counter and took a sip. He was always so calm, so collected, even when he'd been lying facedown on my dock, arms and legs spread. I wondered if all psychiatrists were like that. He shot out an arm and looked at his big, gold, expensive watch. "It's almost noon. That means you've been asleep almost ten hours, and I answered your phone because I knew whoever was calling would be worried."

"You should've given me the phone."

"I shook you, and you didn't stop snoring. I assumed you needed the sleep."

"I don't snore."

"It was a joke."

"You're not funny."

"Give me a chance. Sometimes I'm a real card." Dead-pan.

I frowned, but it hurt my bruises.

"See?" he said.

I remained sober. "Who called?"

"Sheriff Ramsay. I assured him that you were all right and I wasn't a danger to you. Then Dottie called, and I assured her that you were all right and I wasn't a danger to you. She said she made her potion extra strong so you would sleep through the night, and I asked for the recipe. Then some guy named Bud called, from a plane on his way home from grilling my ex-wife in New York, and I assured him that you were all right and I wasn't a danger to you."

So maybe he was a card. I wanted to smile but decided one time was one too many. I looked around. "Are we still out on the lake?"

"Yes, but we're going to have to weigh anchor and head back soon. I'm already late for a staff meeting." I raised an eyebrow. "I didn't want to wake you, and your boat wasn't ready."

"What do you mean my boat wasn't ready?"

"I ordered it gassed up and readied for the trip back. I have a mechanic on board who's been tinkering with it. It sounded a little, well, like it was dying on the way out here last night. I wouldn't exactly call it reliable."

"We don't all have yachts, *Nicky*." More sarcasm. See what I mean?

Black ignored it. I guess it was a little childish, but like I said, I was at a disadvantage. He was springing stuff on me left and right.

"You're welcome to use my shower. And I've laid out some clothes on the bed that you can wear home."

"That's not necessary. I need to get going right now."

"Come on, Claire, be sensible. Take a shower, have some breakfast, wake up a little. By then we'll have your skiff in the water again."

Skiff? I thought. *Nobody called jon boats skiffs, and whatever happened to bateau?* "Okay, but give me my phone."

He handed it over and motioned to the adjoining stateroom. "Help yourself. I'll order breakfast. Or would you prefer lunch?"

"Suit yourself. I doubt if I'll eat anything. I'm not hungry."

The stateroom was as big as the office and also had one of those cute little balconies that overhung the water. The balcony doors were shut, so I opened them, and I could hear a couple of men talking somewhere above decks. I wondered how big a crew Black had on this yacht, then moved into a black marble bathroom with gold fixtures straight out of a pasha's palace. The shower stall was all glass and mirrors, with fluffy black towels stacked around everywhere, and I decided Black was a little carried away with black. I locked the bathroom door, checked for hidden cameras just to make sure, then got in the shower. I made it as hot as I could stand it and washed my hair with a shampoo that smelled like gardenias. I knew Black didn't use it, so I assumed he was always prepared for ladies to stay over. I wondered idly how many other women had washed their hair in the huge shower, most of the time probably with him as their loofah brush. Maybe he should have had one of those counters on the shower door like in department stores and Web pages.

There were black terry cloth robes hanging on gold hooks, so I slipped one on, then found brand-new combs and toothbrushes in a drawer, all wrapped and hermetically sealed in cellophane. I chose one of each and used them quickly. Wide awake now, I was eager to get back to the station and talk to Bud. A black cotton T-shirt and matching black cotton slacks with a draw-string waist were on the bed, both in my size. Nicholas Black aimed to please.

I combed my hair straight back, didn't even consider looking for make-up to hide the bruises on my face and my puffy eye. The other guy looked worse and no doubt walked funny. That was the important thing. Then I re-membered that I was aboard Black's yacht and decided that it might be a good time to snoop around. I opened drawers and found lots of neatly stacked clean clothes, but in the bathroom I found his hairbrush and a small vanity glass, which might have his fingerprints on it. I tugged a few strands of hair out of the hairbrush bris-tles, put them in the glass, and tucked it down the front of my bra between my breasts, where Black would have to molest me to find it. Not to worry. We weren't that good friends yet. There you go, all done, slick as a whis-tle, just in case I needed a sample for DNA testing.

I walked out into the office area. No one was there, so I retraced my steps taken the night before and found Black on the top deck, seated at an outside table set for two.

"I'm ready to leave," I told him, looking over the side for my boat. It wasn't there.

"Have some orange juice first. Sit down. We need to talk."

I looked at him a moment, curious as to what he had to say. I sat down, and a woman came out in a black-and-tan uniform and poured me more coffee and fresh juice. The juice was in an icy black goblet. Jeez. I thanked her when she set large black plates in front of both of us. Fresh fruit, pancakes, scrambled eggs, sausage, and bacon, all prepared to perfection. My stomach noticed and threw a fit of growling. I frowned, pretending it was my bad mood raising the ruckus.

"Good, you're hungry," Black said. "So am I."

"When will my boat be ready?" I asked him, digging in with more relish than he did. It had been a long time since I'd eaten anything. I tried to remember if I'd turned off the chicken soup on my stove. I thought I did.

"Soon. It needed some serious attention." He watched me eat, smiling a little, and then I saw him looking at my bruises.

"The first ones are fading, but last night's look pretty horrible."

"I bruise easily, especially when a big fist smashes into my delicate skin."

He was not amused. In fact, he looked angry. "They're idiots, and apparently, you need to learn to duck and weave."

"Oh, are you the one who's gonna teach me?"

"I did some boxing in college. It looks like you need some lessons."

Highly offended was I. "He blindsided me, if you must know. And there were two of them."

"I can teach you awareness, too."

"And I can teach you humility," I said. "And how to live without a staff of hundreds to wait on you."

"I'm more self-sufficient than you think."

Okay, enough small talk. Time to ask the pertinent questions. "Tell me about your family, Black. Did Jacques inherit his Godfather status from your father as the oldest son? Are you waiting to take over when things go bad, like Michael Corleone? Or are you like poor Fredo, who got whacked out on a lake like this one?"

I was half-joking, sort of, but Black didn't take it that way. He looked out over the lake a moment, and I could tell he wasn't amused and wasn't eager to talk about his family. Too bad, I was. He made a decision and looked at me.

"Jacques made his own way. Both of us left home as soon as we could."

"Why?"

Hesitation, longer this time. Then he said, "My father was abusive to my mother until I got old enough to step in and stop him."

He'd mentioned his mother to me before, down in the bayou. "What happened?"

His eyes flashed with anger at my persistence. "If you must know, one night he was beating up on her, and I broke both his arms with a baseball bat. I left home after that, lied about my age, and joined the army. But he never hit her again."

"How old were you?"

"Sixteen."

"Are your parents still living?"

"No, they're both gone now."

"So Jacques went one way, and you went another."

He nodded.

"I'm surprised you told me all this."

"I want you to trust me. You'll see I'm all right, once you get to know me better."

Uh-oh, trouble, I thought. I laid down my fork. I thought it best to ignore that sappy crap. "I'm looking for Sylvie's killer, and that's all I'm looking for. Your brother's affirmation of your innocence last night was really sweet, but you're still a suspect in this case as far as I'm concerned. Until I prove to myself that you're not guilty."

"I can wait. If anyone can solve this, you can."

Flattered I was. Annoyed I was. Yoda I sounded like. Time to go. "I'll be in touch."

He rose when I stood up. "My pleasure, Detective."

My boat was in the water beside the launch now, but I hardly recognized it. It had been checked over all right. Newly painted, a couple of seats added for fishing, and it fired up with a smooth little purr when I pulled the cord. I looked up at the railing above me and found Black watching. I was pleased, and not above showing it, not where *Old Betsy* was concerned.

I gave him the okay sign with my thumb and forefinger. He gave a little salute and then disappeared from sight. I wasn't twenty yards away from the motor yacht when it began to move toward Cedar Bend and Nicholas Black's staff meeting.

LIFE WITH FATHER

The father was nice after the cook left. He and Brat often worked together on the corpses in the cellar, and he gave Brat presents. He bought Brat an IBM laptop computer and some games that went with it. Brat loved the laptop and sometimes took it to the cold room so the mother could play. The father took him on rides in their brand-new green Dodge station wagon, which they kept in the barn, and sometimes Brat even got to practice driving down deserted country roads at night, when there was no one to see them. Around this time, the father began to give Brat special injections, which he said would make him behave and obey the rules.

"You're turning into such a tomboy, Brat. You've got to be more ladylike, like your mother was. I'm going to help you do that, make you soft and sweet, just like you used to be."

Then one day the father drank too much whiskey, and he gave Brat another injection; then he stripped off Brat's clothes and taped Brat's wrists and ankles to the steel embalming table with a roll of silver duct tape. "I've talked to you about being more ladylike until I'm blue in the face, and now look what you've forced me to do. This is not something I want to do, Brat, believe me, but you've left me no choice."

Brat struggled against the tape binding him, but the father picked up the scalpel. "Someday you'll thank me," he said, and Brat screamed in agony when the scalpel sliced skin.

Two weeks later Brat could walk again, slowly and painfully. Groggy from painkillers the father injected, Brat went into the cold room, and the dead ones gathered around to see the horrible thing the father had done and stitched up, then hid under a white gauze bandage. "He must die," a young mother who'd died in childbirth said. "I'd never do something so horrible to my child," Brat's mother said. "Yes, he is evil. He must die." "Yes, Brat, he must die," they all agreed.

So Brat went into the kitchen in the middle of the night and got the big meat cleaver out of the cutlery drawer, carried it upstairs to where the father was snoring in a drunken stupor, and held it high over the embalmer's head, then brought it down in a hard chop on the father's neck. The head separated from the body, and a fountain of blood drenched Brat's arms and face and the bed and the wall, but Brat continued to hack the father's body into a bloody pulp of tissue and gore until the red river of fire inside him flowed slow and cool and blue again.

Then Brat took a shower, packed the cleaver and the razor strop and the laptop and computer games and other necessary things in a duffel bag, then went downstairs and got the big brown strongbox that the embalmer hid behind the corpses on the top shelf in the back of the cold room. The father did not believe in banks, and neither had his father before him, nor his grandfather before that. The strongbox was packed to the brim with money the family business had saved for years and years, thousands and thousands of dollars, and Brat took it and put it on the bottom cellar step, then returned to bid good-bye to his friends in the cold room. Brat told his mother good-bye and that she would never see him again, but his mother said, "You said you'd never leave me, and I said I'd never leave you." Then she wept, and Brat could not bear to hear her cry or leave her behind, so Brat took the cleaver out of the duffel bag and severed her head and put it in a brown paper sack from the Kroger store. He whispered, "Don't worry, Mother. We'll be together forever, I promise."

Brat took the mother's head and the duffel bag and strongbox and other necessary things outside and put them in the green Dodge station wagon, then went inside and poured gasoline on the father's butchered body and drenched the carpets in every room. Then he lit a match and watched the house burn for a little while, before he drove away into the night.

Brat was fourteen years old.

18

"Okay, Claire, let's hear it, beginning to end."

I sat directly across the desk from Charlie. Bud sat next to me. We were in Charlie's cluttered office, and outside the closed door, the other deputies tried to look busy while they eavesdropped. After all, we were discussing the biggest case to ever hit Lake of the Ozarks. All the secretaries huddled around the coffeepot, buzzing about glimpses they'd gotten of themselves arriving at work in the morning on video clips running nonstop on cable news networks.

Once when I was little, I went to a traveling circus held out in the middle of a high school football field. It had three rings, the whole works, with trapeze artists performing high above the ground and elephants tramping around the track. That's what this reminded me of, a Ringling Brothers show with Nicholas Black, Sylvie Border, and me as the featured acts. So far the spotlight had been on the other two, and I felt like I was swinging on a trapeze without a net, just waiting for the spotlight to find me. The audience would gasp, and I would fall to my death. Guess that tells you what kind of confident mood I'm in lately.

From the street below, a car's horn suddenly blared, and a bunch of angry shouting ensued. Charlie shot to his feet and jerked down the blinds. "I am so fuckin' sick of those vultures circling around. I'm damned tired of facing a media gauntlet every time I come to work." He glared at Bud and me as if we should do something about it. "And dadgummit, keep your voices down so Magdalena won't overhear."

Magdalena Broussart was his secretary for going on fifteen years, a wonderful little lady who reached Bud's chin, wearing four-inch heels, but who also kept the department running like a well-oiled engine. Unfortunately, she had a penchant for watching *Murder, She Wrote* and thought she was Jessica Fletcher. Double unfortunately, she had about fifty close bingo-playing lady friends in their seventies who lived vicariously through her knowledge of police business, and anything they heard from her spread through their ranks like wildfire. The bored old lady network, so to speak.

I wanted Charlie to stop glaring at me, so I began my sordid tale from the moment Black showed up at my house in the kayak. Charlie's bushy white brows came together at that point. I paused to give him time to spill out a string of vitriolic curses, but he didn't, so I went on to the point where I met with Jacques Montenegro on Black's customized yacht. Charlie had been saving his wrath up for the point when I told him who'd grabbed me and knocked me into the water, pacing around and threatening to have them arrested for assaulting one of his people. I found that a sweet offer but mentioned that it'd probably just cause more publicity and accomplish nothing. I'd calmed down considerably from the night before.

While he cursed some more and with a great deal of feeling and imagination, I considered whether to tell him that Black was Jacques Montenegro's brother. I decided not to tell him because I felt Black was right about Charlie. It would put him in an uncomfortable situation politically and lose him his biggest campaign contributor, all in one neat little package with a bow on top. I didn't want to do that until I proved Black had something to do with Sylvie's murder. And even I had to admit, that was a long shot.

"Black wants to help us with the investigation," I finished, glancing at Bud. "You know his background. He's studied lots of cold cases and has been moderately successful at profiling killers. He wants permission to look over the evidence, give us his opinion; then he promised to back off and leave the rest to us. He swears he's innocent and had nothing to do with Sylvie's murder. At the moment, I think he's probably telling the truth. I just can't prove it yet, one way or the other."

"Nick's no psychopath. I don't think he's got it in him to do something this sick," Charlie said. "I've known him for ten years, for Pete's sake." Of course, we all knew psychopaths were harder to identify than by the way they treated their friends who were sheriffs. I didn't point it out, but just look at Ted Bundy and O.J. Simpson and Jeffrey Dahmer. Not to mention that guy who killed all those young boys in Chicago and buried them in his crawl space. John Wayne Gacy had not only been named after a national hero, he'd been a clown to earn extra income, at children's parties, no less. I wondered what was in the crawl space under Black's many mansions or taped to chairs on the bottom of the lake under his yacht.

"Well, I'm waitin'," Charlie said, impatience showing. He kept a foam stress reliever on his desk, shaped like a little white Progressive Insurance car, and when he wasn't drinking Pepto, he was squeezing it. Right now, he was working it like crazy in his left hand. He'd be one hell of a cow milker, if the poor heifers could survive his zeal. "What do you think, Claire? You want his help? It's up to you; you're the lead."

That wasn't exactly true. It was up to him, and we both knew it. Guess he was being nice. "People say he's pretty good. We could release some of the facts to him, and if he can tell us anything helpful, that's great. And if I'm working closely with him and he's guilty of the murder and playing us for some reason, maybe he'll slip up, and I can nail him. Either way, it could be to our benefit. In any case, I can handle myself."

Charlie considered me and glanced at Bud, who considered me, too. I knew exactly what they both were considering. I felt my face grow hot and hoped I wasn't flushed as red as I felt. I clamped my jaw. Okay, I'd been jumped and compromised by great big thugs, like some green little recruit. It rankled, but it wasn't going to happen again. I had been on my home turf and had underestimated the situation. How the hell was I to know Black had underworld nursemaids?

"I can handle myself," I said again, frowning this time.

"What about the ex-wife?" Charlie turned to Bud. "She ruled out as the perp?"

"Rock-solid alibi. Had a soiree that night at her Manhattan loft, with lots of ritzy people there. That's what she called it, a soiree as in la-de-da. Lasted until three in the morning. Even had an off-duty NYPD officer hired for the evenin' as a security guard. He vouched for her."

"Nicholas Black, too?" I said. "Did he show up?"

"Nope. Not only did he not show up for the party, she said she hadn't seen or heard from him in over a month. That said, she oozed so much devotion to him that I was almost embarrassed that he left her. She clearly loves him, said she didn't want the divorce, but he did. Said they still love and respect each other. Said they couldn't make it work because at that time their careers meant more to both of them."

"Is she as beautiful as she looks in *Vanity Fair*?" I asked, thinking no one could really be that drop-dead gorgeous.

"I found myself staring at her and forgetting where I was. Body to die for. Voice like warm honey. Black's nuts to kick her out of his bed."

At that, Charlie got a trifle testy. "Shit, Davis, get your mind out of your pants for once, and get on with this. I don't give a flyin' fuck if you want to screw her." Sometimes Charlie zeroed right in on the point.

"Yes, sir. I did some digging around at the airport. Found out Black wasn't on his jet when it landed that night at LaGuardia. He flew in on a commercial flight later, nonstop from New Orleans."

Charlie slammed his right fist down on the table. I didn't jump; he usually did it at least once at each meeting, so I watched for it. "And you just now gettin' around to mentioning that? Claire, did you know about this?"

I did know it, of course. Bud's good about keeping me posted. "Maybe he went to New Orleans to notify the family. I'll check it out."

"Oh, will you? Gee, thanks, Detective, for doing us all a favor."

Maybe Charlie's where I get my sarcasm. Sometimes he was better at it than even I was. Especially when he was red-faced and furious and looking for somebody to vent on. "I'd say it's a bit suspicious for him to send his private plane on to New York and take a commercial from New Orleans. More sarcasm. Told you he was good at it.

"It'll be easy enough to check out," I put in quickly.

"FBI's been taping everybody going in and out of the Montenegro estate."

"Well, check it out and make it quick. I think Black's innocent, and I want you to declare it to the press as soon as you can, before the media hounds blow his involvement totally out of proportion and start throwin' around allegations about his contributions to my campaigns. Every magazine and rag on the rack has a picture of Sylvie with Black. This is turnin' into a fuckin' nightmare."

"Peter Hastings is stalking our officers," Bud said. "O'Hara found him filming outside her house this morning and demanding answers about the crime scene. She shut him down but said he's determined to get the goods any way he can."

"Well, he ain't gonna get the goods if I have anything to say about it. I mean, nobody says nothin' to the press. Is that clear? I don't want anything to break until I give the go-ahead. Understood?"

"Yes, sir," I said.

Charlie glared at Bud. "Yes, sir," Bud said.

"And I want a press conference tomorrow morning at 5 A.M. on the dot. Let the vultures get up at the crack of dawn. They make our lives miserable; we'll just return the favor. Bud, you're gonna do the talkin' for us. Make sure you say nothin' about nothin' when you answer the questions. Got it?"

"Yes, sir."

We left Charlie yelling into the phone at some unfortunate soul and made our way to the little cubbyhole we shared on the third floor, where I had about three weeks of paperwork piled up. I sat down in my squeaky wooden desk chair, and Bud sat across from me at his own desk. Our desks butted up against each other, detective togetherness. His was clean and neat like his designer fashions; mine looked all rumpled and day-old like my T-shirts and jeans. The window beside us looked down at the street in front of the building, and he spent a few minutes watching the satellite dishes lined up like giant metal umbrellas.

"I can't believe this," he said.

"Yeah," I answered, logging on to check my e-mail. I had 172 messages, most of which looked like X-rated spam. No wonder I put off checking my e-mail.

Bud lowered his voice. "Well, are you going to tell me why Black answered your cell phone?"

I looked up. "You think that's your business?"

Bud affected a hurt face. "Well, of course." He gave his famous grin, all charm, eyes glinting, and I had to smile, until he said, "Seems to me the two of you sure are getting awfully cozy out there on that boat of his."

"What the hell's that supposed to mean?" Defensiveness dripped like battery acid. I couldn't help it.

"That's supposed to mean, are you sleeping with him? and if you are, cut it out, because you're compromising the investigation."

"Get real. I'm not sleeping with anybody. You know me better than that."

"He seemed pleased as punch to let me in on the fact that you were still asleep and he didn't want to disturb you because you needed your rest. Said you didn't take good enough care of yourself."

"So? He can say whatever he likes, and you'll still know me better than he ever will. Not that it's any of your business, but I'm not involved with him, sexually or any other way. I fell asleep on his couch because I'd been up all night, and I made the mistake of drinking one of Dottie's hot toddies before he showed up at my house. It just happened. It was stupid, I admit it. I felt like a fool when I woke up there. I feel foolish now."

"Just watch yourself. That guy's smooth, and I don't trust him. He's too damn cool with the bad guys." Bud held up a piece of Juicy Fruit. Peace offering. Trying to make amends. I took it, glad that question had been asked and answered. I knew it would come sooner or later. "You still think he's capable of killing her? You've spent time with him now, seen him informally, slept on his couch."

Bud had to get in one last jab. It was in his nature. I hesitated in answering his question, realizing that I wasn't sure. Black was an enigma that it'd take time to figure out. "I'm not sure what to think yet. He's not cleared in my mind, not completely, but somehow I don't think he did it. It'll be interesting to see what he comes up with concerning the crime scene. It's worth a try. If he's trying to throw me off or create a red herring, I'll see through it."

"Why don't I sit in when he pontificates on the murder?"

"He made it clear he'd only deal with me. Said he doesn't trust anybody else."

"And you swallowed that bullshit?"

"I wouldn't trust people around here, either, if I were him. He won't open up in a crowd. I can work him better alone." Bud didn't look convinced, but he wasn't going to no matter what I told him. His distaste for Black was visceral. I changed the subject. "What about Inman? Any verification of his whereabouts at the time of the murder?"

"Caught him on a liquor store surveillance camera about the time of the murder. And his deadbeat neighbor had a beer with him out on a picnic table behind the trailer after he got home. Pretty well covered his slice of opportunity."

"He's not getting off on assault and battery. If his wife won't nail him on it, I will. My bruises ought to convince a jury."

Bud shook his head. "You've had one hell of a week,

Morgan. Maybe I oughta stick closer to you. Be your avenging angel."

"All I need right now is to get these reports done and in to Charlie; then I'm going to meet Black again. He wants to go over the photos and reports of the crime scene and give me his take on how it went down. That'll be interesting, to say the least."

"Yeah? Sure you don't want me to come along for protection?"

"You're not gonna let me live down gettin' jumped, are you?"

"I thought you were invincible. Now I worry about you."

"They got the jump on me, is all. There were two of them. It'll never happen again, trust me. Now, if I were you, I'd start practicing for the early bird press conference. Better you than me. Just don't mention my name or address."

"Yeah, right." Bud was grumbling, but he'd be great with the reporters. Nobody loved the cameras more than Bud, except, of course, Nicholas Black.

19

Black called me later on my cell phone and wanted to meet that night at his place. I said, "No, come to my house, or forget it." I didn't like to be ordered around, even if he'd done a complete rehaul on *Old Betsy* and made her look brand spanking new. He was sitting in the swing on my screened front porch when I got home at seven o'clock. People seemed awfully free to come over uninvited and use my swing. Maybe I ought to get a lock on the screen door or a pack of ill-tempered rottweilers as greeters. He was dressed casually, but not as casually as when he was a Swamp Cajun. He wore a black polo shirt and khakis. He looked good. He always looked good, unfortunately. He had a brown wicker picnic basket with him.

"I thought I'd bring dinner. I have a feeling you don't eat unless somebody reminds you."

True, but where did he get off pointing out my shortcomings? "Look, Black, if I want a nanny, I'll move to England. This is strictly business we're working on, and that's all it is. Don't try to turn it into something personal."

He smiled, as if he hadn't heard me. "Philippe made us fried chicken, Caesar salad, baked potatoes. Bottle of Dom Perignon."

Philippe, also known as the French whiz chef at the five-star restaurant in the lodge, had suddenly turned into Colonel Sanders with a large wine budget. Gee, now I was really impressed. My stomach growled as I unlocked the front door, belying my sarcastic thoughts, and I realized he was right. I hadn't eaten anything all day. Pissed that he was right, I checked my phone answering machine. Black didn't seem to take offense at being left on the front porch, holding the picnic basket.

I watched him take it to the big oak tree in my front yard, where I had an old picnic table and a swing attached by chains to a giant limb. He was unpacking the food and white china onto my scarred redwood picnic table when I pressed the play button on my answering machine. I began to get that old feeling of suffocation that I'd had when I'd been married. For the first time in years, I felt my space was being invaded. I didn't like it.

"Hi." Dottie's voice. "Come over soon and fill us in on what happened with Black last night. I've got this weekend off, and Suze and I are flying to Dallas, so don't forget to check in on Harve and make sure he's got everything he needs. Thanks a bunch. Be back on Monday or Tuesday, depending on the flights. Love ya. Oh yeah, glad the toddy helped you sleep."

Yeah, it helped all right. For about ten hours straight. Good thing Black and his friends didn't want me dead that night. But it was my own fault. I shouldn't have gone with Black alone. I wasn't using the best judgment where he was concerned, but that could be fixed.

I walked outside and relented somewhat on accepting his culinary bounty at the first whiff of crispy fried chicken.

"I'm afraid I forgot the goblets," he said. "Do you have something we can drink out of?"

"Sure," I said, and retrieved two jelly glasses with Mickey Mouse on them. Dottie had brought them home from a weekend jaunt to Disney World in Orlando with Suze, but they also had them at the Kroger store in Osage Beach. I sat down as he filled the jelly glasses up to the base of Mickey's ears. We ate in a relatively comfortable silence, but I didn't like the way he was examining me, like I was some kind of specimen wriggling on a pin. I didn't touch Mickey and the champagne. He took a drink of his, and I was glad to see he didn't sniff it and swirl it and taste it like a connoisseur. I always thought that looked like an affectation, but I was a country girl. He said, "I think I'm going to need a couple of glasses of champagne before I look at those pictures."

"You don't have to look if you don't want to. I understand now how close you were to Sylvie. If you'd like to change your mind about this, I'd understand completely, believe me."

"Have you had a similar experience?"

I had and he'd picked up on it, but he wasn't going to find out about it. "I've dealt with family members of murder victims before. It's never easy. Luckily, most of them aren't required to look at autopsy and crime scene pictures."

"I'll have to look at them again, really study them, but I wish to God I didn't. I've been preparing myself all day." He drained Mickey but didn't pour more. He set the glass aside. "Did you tell Charlie about my brother?"

The question came out of the blue, but I was expecting him to ask at some point. I shook my head. "I said I wouldn't unless it became necessary, and I'll keep my word. If I need it to come out at any point in the investigation, I'm not going to hesitate to make your relationship known. You do understand that, right?"

He nodded. "Thanks. It'd complicate my life and hurt a lot of people in ways I don't like to think about."

I didn't comment. What could I say? It was his deep, dark secret. I had a few of my own that I dreaded ever coming to light. I could cut him some slack as long as it didn't affect the job I had to do.

"Do you have the files? I might as well get started. It'll take a while."

I had the crime scene photographs and reports in a mailing envelope locked in a drawer inside the house. I got them and handed them over to him. He gazed out over the lake for a couple of minutes, took a deep breath, and pulled the pictures out. He looked through them one by one, studying each one, and it was almost painful to watch how each photograph hit him like a physical blow. He got through them, blew out a breath, then met my gaze. "Give me a moment, will you?" The vulnerability in the request was palpable.

Without a word, I got up and walked back into the house. He was looking at ghastly, hideous pictures of someone he loved, had nurtured, and protected as an uncle since she was a baby. What a horrible thing to have to do. I was not sure I could do it, not this soon. My cell phone rang, and I punched on, watching Black sit at the picnic table, thinking. The crime scene pictures were turned facedown now. He sat unmoving, staring out at the glass-topped green water of the cove.

"Claire? It's me."

"Hey, Buckeye. What's up?" I knew him well enough to know that he was not calling with good news. No coroner ever called homicide detectives at home with good news. I braced myself. Black was still looking out over the water.

"Bad news," he said.

"Tell me." All tensed up and prepared to be hit with something that would complicate the case. My sixth sense was working now.

"I got the tests back matching Sylvie Border with her father's DNA. That and the two tattoos give us a positive ID on her body."

I frowned. "Yeah, so?"

"Yeah, but I also got her dental records from New Orleans." Buckeye stopped and so did my heart. "The teeth don't match." He paused again. "The head didn't come off her body, Claire. It belongs to somebody else. The DNA didn't match up, either."

I was shocked enough to sink down on the sofa. I stared out the window at Black. Oh, God, now I was going to have to tell him this, too.

"Claire? You get that? Understand what I'm sayin'? I knew the cut marks didn't match up on the head and torso, but I thought he'd discarded tissue at the decapitation. And the head was so ravaged and torn up that she wasn't recognizable. I didn't expect this. It threw me, I can tell you that. We've never gotten into anything like this."

"Yeah." I cleared my throat, all thick now and swollen as if I'd stuffed a bale of cotton down it. I was having trouble believing my ears. "You're absolutely certain about this?"

"No doubt whatsoever."

"How? How'd he do it? I don't get it. Where's the other body? What'd he do with Sylvie's head?"

"It looks to me like the head he put on Sylvie's body might've been frozen at one time. I'm doing tissue tests right now."

My stomach rolled. "Any idea who the head belongs to?"

"No, that's your job. We can run the DNA through the database and see what comes up."

"Yeah, we'll do that."

"And there was no match on the hairs and drinking glass you brought in to the hair we found on the tree behind the bungalow."

"Okay. Thanks, Buckeye."

"Sorry, but I thought you'd want to know right off. I should've considered this possibility from the get-go, but, man, it never even occurred to me the remains were from different females."

"Yeah. Me, either."

"I'll give you a call as soon as the rest of the results come in."

He hung up, and I stared at the phone and tried to absorb the ramifications. The screen door slammed behind me, and I lurched up to my feet, almost guiltily.

"What's wrong?" Black said. He stood a few feet away, the envelope in his hand. "Claire? Are you all right?"

He was calling me Claire again, and I wished he would stop it. It gave us a closeness I didn't want, not right now. I kept visualizing the awful look on his face when I'd shocked him with the autopsy picture that night on his yacht. I didn't want to see it again. I didn't want to tell him this. This was a hundred times worse. I could keep it to myself. Make it confidential evidence that only the murderer would know.

"Claire, tell me. Is it about Sylvie?" He looked concerned. She was his niece, for God's sake. Her head was missing. I had to tell him.

"Who was that on the phone?" His eyes were intense and never left my face. I swallowed hard and forced myself to return his gaze.

I took a deep breath, but my voice sounded hoarse. "The coroner. I'm sorry, but it's very bad news."

Black said nothing at first. Then he said, "Tell me. She's already dead. I've seen all the pictures now. Nothing can be worse than that was."

Oh, yes, it could. "He got back the DNA and dental records." I kept trying to find the right words. There weren't any good ones; I just had to say it. "The DNA for the head didn't match the body. Neither did the dental records."

"What?" he said. He gave a little confused shake of his head. "I don't understand."

"It was Sylvie's body," I said. "I'm so sorry, but the DNA and dental records from the head didn't match up to hers."

I saw comprehension dawn in his eyes, saw it turn to horror, saw blood drain out of his face. He staggered backward until he hit the door, then stopped, pain and disbelief suffusing his face until I could barely look at him.

"I'm so sorry, so very sorry to have to tell you something like this." I felt helpless. I wasn't sure what to do, but I didn't have to do anything. He turned and went outside.

I followed, remaining on the porch as he stopped and braced both hands on the edge of the picnic table. For a few seconds there was no sound except the chattering of some squirrels in the woods behind my house and the low buzz of a faraway motorboat.

I jumped involuntarily when he suddenly exploded, swiping one arm across the top of the picnic table. Dishes and food flew everywhere in a shattering of glass and clanking of metal, and then he began to make the most horrible sound I could ever remember hearing, a keening so full of grief and fury that I felt a little sick as he overturned the table, sending it rolling down the small incline of my front yard to the rocky beach below. He turned away from me and walked jerkily across the grass about twenty yards before he sank to his hands and knees on the ground.

I turned away, unable to watch, unable to go to him.

I wanted to, needed to, but knew I could not. He was still in shock. He wasn't able to face me yet, but he would be eventually. I couldn't help him now, anyway, couldn't comfort him, no matter what I said or did. He wasn't ready for that yet. I knew. I'd been in that awful, black, lonely, terrible place once. I'd do now what I wanted others to do for me when I went through what Black was suffering now. Leave me alone until I had worked through it on my own, give me some space before pressing emotional buttons and wanting to be let in.

So I tried not to look outside; I didn't want to know what he was doing. I worked on my reports on my cantankerous old IBM computer, not knowing if he was still out there or if he had gone away somewhere by himself. When Black was ready to talk, he'd let me know. It was almost an hour later when I heard him come in the door. I looked up.

He looked terrible, pale, shaken. "I'm going to find the son of a bitch who did this to Sylvie, and I'm going to kill him." Uttered very calmly, very collected, very determined, very vigilante. He meant it.

"That's not the kind of thing you say to a police officer," I said in a low voice. "So, I guess I didn't hear it."

"No matter how long it takes, I'll get him."

"Yes, and I'll help you. Getting yourself thrown into prison isn't going to bring Sylvie back."

The way he looked at me spoke volumes, and I sensed then, despite all his polish and cultured sophistication, that just like his older brother, he might be capable of violence, of vengeance, whenever the need arose. Certainly not the kind of violence that Sylvie suffered, but I felt he could kill cold-bloodedly if he felt it necessary, if he needed to protect someone he loved. But I could, too. I had.

Somewhere in Nicholas Black's past, he'd been

pushed too hard, I suspected, and had pushed back. He was being pushed too hard now, and he was dangerous. Especially with his connections to the Montenegro family and organized crime. It was up to me to bring him down and back to his senses.

"You offered to work with me professionally. To help us solve Sylvie's murder. Are you telling me now that you're reneging on that offer and going out to play Rambo?"

Black didn't answer. In this instance, noncommittal was not a good signal. He finally spoke, softly. "I want to help you investigate this. I've thought of little else since it happened."

"Okay, good, because I want you to. Now listen up. I've got a good friend. Name's Harve Lester. I trust him implicitly. He's waiting for me at his house just down the road. He's like a mentor to me, and he's got one of the best detective minds that I've ever known. Come down there with me and meet him. If you're as good as they say, the three of us working together might just come up with something significant. We might solve this and bring this guy in."

His hesitation was a little too long to suit me, but he came up with the right answer. "Okay, let's go."

20

Black insisted that we take his Cobalt Cruiser down to Harve's. Fine with me. It'd be faster. I'd sent Harve an e-mail while Black was pulling himself together, telling him I'd be over later, most likely with Nicholas Black in tow. I also explained about Buckeye's discovery so we wouldn't have to go into it in front of Black. He'd suffered enough, and more problematic, he was angry enough. Surprisingly, I no longer looked forward to slamming a steel door shut on him.

Tied up at my shabby little dock, in all its glory, bobbed one of Cedar Bend's Cobalt 360s, the twin of the one sported about by the hunky Tyler. Designed for the whims of pampered guests, it was all long, clean lines, with the same global positioning system/radar unit, not to mention the main cabin outfitted with a table and berth, refrigerator/freezer, stove, and microwave, and the head compartment with a shower. Just in case you wanted to whip up a home-cooked meal or doll yourself up while catching a bass, I guess. Dottie would go ape over this rig.

Black was quiet and introspective, but man, who

wouldn't be? All the arrogance and self-confidence had been stripped from him. I hadn't seen him act vulnerable before, and I liked him better for it. More importantly, I was 99 percent sure he wasn't a murderer. I found myself wanting to eliminate him completely as a suspect. He wasn't all bad, and there was still that attraction problem, but I was throwing cold water on that spark, right here, right now. It was that strange chemistry between certain men and women that makes your heart pound when they walk into the room and your fingertips tingle when you touch them. Not that I planned to touch him, unless I had to frisk him again. No, ma'am, no tingling was going to happen, not while I was investigating this case.

"There's Harve's place. We'll tie up at the end of the dock."

Black maneuvered the boat in opposite Harve's ancient bass boat with the expertise of a man who'd had lots of practice on the water. I glanced up at the house and waved to Harve, who was watching us from his desk in the sunroom. I jumped out and secured Black's boat to the dock pilings. Black followed, glancing at Harve's old boat, which looked pretty darn pitiful beside the Cobalt. The Cinderella story, before and after. Yep, Harve's boat needed a fairy godmother to show up toting some kind of powerful wand.

Black said, "Your friend doesn't still take that thing out on the lake, does he?"

My protective gene began to spin and vibrate. "You're a little uppity when it comes to boats, you know that, Black? It floats. You can catch fish out of it. But to answer your question, Harve's handicapped. He can't go out anymore, so his nurse uses it. Dottie loves to fish more than anything."

"Dottie of the knock-you-out-like-a-light hot toddy?"

I nodded. "She's a lady of many talents. Nurse and

companion, and angel as far as I'm concerned. She's off on the weekends, or you'd get to meet her. Actually, you did meet her once, at a book signing."

"Is that right?" He looked at the wheelchair ramp leading up to the back door. "How did your friend become disabled?" Black stepped back down in the boat and retrieved his dark glasses and a black Windbreaker. He already had the file folder in one hand.

Well, there was a question I didn't want to answer. "He was a cop. Got hit in the line of duty."

"So he's a hero."

"Yes." *More than you know,* I thought, as we walked up the sidewalk, with me leading the way. I could tell him how it happened, I guess, but that would unnecessarily open doors into dreaded nightmares, and I wasn't willing to do that. Tonight had been one heavy scene. We didn't need another one.

"Hey, I'm back here!" Harve was still in the sunroom, and he rolled his chair into the doorway, with his usual welcoming grin. He was always glad to have company when Dottie took off on her minivacations. But it was good for her to get away. Even angels needed occasional R & R.

"How you doing, Harve?" I leaned down and hugged the guy. He smelled of Old Spice and Domino's pizza. He wasn't as obsessive as Bud about his appearance, but he kept himself well-groomed and neat whether Dottie was around or not.

"Ready for company. Doctor Black, I presume. I'm Harve Lester. Welcome to my humble abode. I've heard a lot about you. My nurse reads your books. She'll die when she finds out she missed you."

"Nice to meet you, Harve." Black took the hand Harve extended and glanced around the sunny room with its lemon yellow walls and white woodwork. So often people didn't know how to treat the handicapped, acted like they were deaf or dumb, or nonexistent, but Black was completely at ease. He smiled. "Nice place you have here. A good place to work, I'll bet."

"The land around this cove's been in my family for fifty years. Gave me a good place to retire to."

He swiveled his chair around and rolled across the hardwood floor to the desk in front of the windows. We followed, and Black asked, "You serve somewhere here in Missouri?"

"I was one of Los Angeles's finest, and proud of it. Didn't Claire tell you? We worked Robbery/Homicide at the same time."

Black gave me a searching, psychiatrist look. As if I were one of the inkblots he liked to hang everywhere. "Claire holds her cards pretty close to the vest, Harve, but I suspect you already know that. Maybe you can give me the scoop on her."

"I sure as hell know better than to do something like that." Harve laughed, but he knew where my secrets were buried like no one else. Although they were joking around, I felt uncomfortable enough to nip that conversation in the bud.

"Let's get started. I can't stay long. Black, take a seat." Sometimes I'm bossy.

There was a round table with a white tile top near the windows, and Black and I both took matching Windsor chairs as Harve eased his wheelchair on the other side. Harve had been studying the autopsy photos, because they were spread out in plain sight. Out of respect for Black's shaky emotions, I gathered them quickly together and turned them facedown. Black looked at me, blue eyes grateful, almost tender, and I felt embarrassed that he looked at me like that in front of Harve. Or at all. As if reading my mind, he smiled slightly and carved all those damned dimples of his. Something moved inside me that was downright saccharine. So I concentrated on Harve.

"You got my e-mail, right?"

Harve nodded, then looked at Black. "I understand you have quite a reputation in forensic psychiatry, Doctor Black. I'll be interested in your take on this perpetrator."

"I'm Nick, okay? I can't seem to persuade the detective here to go that informal, so maybe you'll do me the favor."

"You bet. Nick it is." Harve shook his head, but he was a straightforward, hardened, and experienced retired police officer, and he got right to the point. "I realize you've had some real bad news tonight, and I want you to know right off the bat that I'm sorry for your loss." He glanced at me. "Claire told me the victim was your niece, and she also said you didn't want anybody to know it. Whatever your reasons are for hiding the connection, they are none of my business. Rest assured that nothing we talk about here will ever leave this room."

Black looked surprised, but I wasn't sure if it was because I'd told Harve or because Harve was willing to keep the secret. "I appreciate that, Harve. It's a complicated situation, but I have very good reasons."

"So what do you think?" Harve said. "Have you gone over the evidence?"

"First off, I want both of you to know that I can't solve this case for you. All I can do is help you understand who the offender is and why he behaves the way he does. I don't track down killers or apprehend them. That's not my job; that's Claire's job. But I've had some success identifying why offenders choose to perpetrate crimes when and where they do." Black glanced at me, as if reassuring me that if we danced this case together, he wasn't going to step on my toes. "I study the victims' lives and figure out who they were and why somebody wanted them dead."

"Victimology," Harve said.

Black nodded and drew in breath. "Unfortunately, this time I already know a great deal about Sylvie. That doesn't mean she shared everything she did with me. Not even in our sessions did she open up completely. She was intimidated by her father and afraid I'd tell him her secrets. I wouldn't have, of course, but she still held things back, things she felt were private. I'm particular about my privacy, too, so I understood how she felt. I know she trusted me, but I was her uncle, and if she was into anything sleazy or illegal, she wouldn't have wanted me to know."

"Do you have reason to believe she was into something sleazy?" I said.

"No," he answered a little too quickly, but that could just be the protective uncle coming out. "Not really, but I've treated enough young starlets who led similar lives to know they're tempted by drugs and alcohol and sex from the moment they hit Hollywood until the day they're deemed too old to be in films."

"What's that, twenty-one?" I said.

"Yeah, Hollywood's driven now by youth and weight. And that's another thing these young women face: they're forced to be dangerously underweight to get good parts, and that leads a lot of them to bulimia and anorexia. Sylvie was bulimic for a while, and you wouldn't believe how many women I've treated for these kinds of problems. On top of that, the entertainment scene has a tendency to gobble these young women up, because they're quickly surrounded by sycophants, suck-ups, and hangers-on, who encourage them to do whatever they want, whatever feels good." I thought that might apply to Black as well, but I didn't say so.

"And they're young and naïve, with money to burn, and they experiment no matter how grounded they were before they hit it big. Sylvie was into coke for a while. That's when Jacques asked me to get her down to Cedar Bend for rehab and treatment."

"She did rehab here at the lake?"

Black nodded. "It's a good place for the big stars to go through detox. I have trained staff to help them kick the habit, while I work with them one-on-one. You'd be surprised the number of well-known people who've been here for treatment. Some really big names that you'd recognize."

Harve said, "I've been studying the police reports. What strikes me is the complete lack of physical evidence."

"Me, too. It's rare to find nothing helpful, no hair, no threads from clothing. That could be why he chose to leave her in the water."

Black's voice revealed nothing now; he'd internalized his emotions and was under steely, and I mean steely, control. He had put aside his personal feelings; he was ready to do whatever it took to find Sylvie's killer. I doubted if he'd react with passion again until we took down the offender. Then he might very well kill the guy.

Harve, on the other hand, seemed almost excited. He loved nothing more than solving a difficult case. And he was damn good at it. "The most significant clue in my book is the unusual posing of the body. He had a reason for putting her at a dinner table. I don't know if the fact that he left the victim underwater is pertinent. Maybe, maybe not. Like you say, that could have been merely to eliminate trace evidence. That's the key, I think, to understanding what's driving him."

"Exactly," Black said. "My sense is that he's done it before. He's probably a serial, but a sophisticated one who plans the crimes down to a T. As you probably know, most serial killers are white males in their twenties and thirties who come from lower-to middle-class backgrounds. Physically and sexually abused, sometimes emotionally. A common thread we've found is that nearly all of them set fires as children. They also have a tendency to torture animals, and most of them wet the bed."

"So chances are we're looking for a young man," I said. "Are they likely to know their victims personally?"

Black shook his head. "No, it's usually a random selection, just a stranger at the wrong place at the wrong time. They kill, then have a cooling-off period, when they get off by reliving the murder until the thrill fades and they need to live out their fantasies again. It's a psychological drive. The motive isn't greed or passion, but a sadistic need to dominate the victim. That's what I see the most in this guy and the things he does to his victims."

When Black's swallow went down hard, Harve turned to the computer on the desk behind him. "Claire asked me to do a database search for similar crimes, and so far five murders have come up where the victim was found decapitated. One was in North Carolina about this time last year. Some hikers discovered a decapitated female body in heavy vegetation along the Cape Fear River, but the head was never found. The Greenville detective in charge told me they assumed it had been swept out to sea by river currents."

I tried to be diplomatic. "Did any of the cases have the remains of two different victims at the crime scene?"

"No," Harve said. "But that doesn't prove anything. Most of these cases were covered by small town police departments without the means or experience to catch something like that. Buckeye's an experienced criminalist, and he discovered the discrepancy almost by accident." Harve was being considerate to Black, too.

I was surprised Black could discuss this so soon, but he was completely focused now. "Small town police departments wouldn't know the difference unless the victim was a local they recognized or they had dental records to prove identity. It could be why the offender confuses the identity, to hide his tracks."

"What about missing persons?" I said. "Did anybody go missing around Greenville in the same time period?"

"I haven't checked that out yet, but I'll get on it right away."

I said, "It's like a game he's playing. My gut tells me he's done this lots of times. Did you find victims as obviously posed as in this case?"

"Not yet. One was found on a riverbank, with fishing gear scattered around. In Illinois, a middle-aged woman was tied to a tree, with her head in her lap. Another body was found in an alley in a Pensacola suburb. The head was found two blocks away, tied to a stop sign by the hair. None of the scenarios had much in common."

"Was there a commonality in cause of death?" Black asked.

"One. All the victims were alive when the head was severed."

I tried not to watch Black's jaw working convulsively as he ground his teeth. Black needed a breather, so I got up and went into the bathroom to give him some time to compose himself. I can be thoughtful sometimes.

21

By the time I returned to the table, Black had his emotions under strict control. He looked at me and said, "It sounds like a ritual thing. And he's got a reason for beheading his victims. That's why he's taking the heads. We've got to figure out why he's doing it this way. I agree with Claire that it's a game, one he's become very good at. How does he keep them? How does he transport them? Where does he kill the other victim? He's got to have a home base that he works out of, some place where he feels safe and secure. Where he thinks discovery is impossible."

"Are you saying he might have a stash of victims somewhere?" I said, a little grossed out. "To use when he's ready to kill again?"

Black nodded. "I think it's highly possible. Many serials keep the bodies nearby, like Gacy did in Chicago."

"And Dahmer," Harve added.

I said, "But how could he move around the Cedar Bend complex with all your security people and cameras and still have so much time to set up the scene, almost like a stage set?"

"Sylvie's an actress," Black said. "He could have been putting her in some kind of scene. Some play or movie that he likes or that means something to his sick mind. Most of these offenders act out their fantasies; that's how they get their reward. And most of the time their fantasies continue to evolve and get more complicated and more violent."

"It'd help to know who the other victim was. If we can pinpoint where she went missing, at least we'll have a starting point." Harve looked at me. "Any missing persons reports at the lake?"

I shook my head. "I checked that again earlier tonight. But if she was a transient or homeless person, chances are no one would report her missing."

"Same applies to young runaways," Harve said. "One case I ran across they identified a runaway teenager, a fourteen-year-old girl, when they published a picture of a toe ring found on the body. She was clean except for that. The killer overlooked it."

"Was she from this area?" Black asked.

"No. She went missing from southern Indiana, a little town called Clarksville. Her head showed up in the mountains around Salt Lake City, Utah."

"Well, one thing we know without a doubt is that the killer is acting in an unusually cold-blooded manner." Black sat back in his chair and steepled his fingers. Thinking. I'd seen him do that before. "Except for some battering, little true passion was involved. No overkill. All clinical and precise. In my experience, that probably points to a stranger as the offender. I think the crime scene was too impersonal to be anybody involved with her, like Gil Serna or any other boyfriend. Or me, if you've still got me on your list."

I didn't say anything. He may still be on my list, but he was at the bottom of it. Instead, I said, "Do you think the perp chose her because she was famous?"

"I've been considering that, and it's possible," Black said. "That'd mean the killer's eager for publicity, wants to watch his handiwork on television, enjoy it all over and over again. It could be that he's worked his way up to this point in his fantasies and feels invincible."

Harve nodded. "If that's the case, he's pacing the floor, waiting for the gory details to surface. He's probably angry we've kept them under wraps."

"That could compel him to act again, sooner than he might've originally planned," Black said. "Force the police to acknowledge his handiwork by killing in a public place. Or notifying the media himself. Several cases I've been involved in, the serial killer chose a particular reporter and worked through them to ensure he got the publicity he craved."

"I think he chose Sylvie on purpose," I said, thinking about it from a different perspective. "He would never have selected a place like Cedar Bend, otherwise, not with all the security you provide your guests, if he didn't have a certain victim in mind, someone staying there. Why not choose a place that was easy to get into, a victim who was helpless, like a derelict off the streets? Why put himself in danger of discovery when he didn't have to?"

"Then why Sylvie?" Harve asked, and both men turned to look at me.

I said, "She's famous, for one thing, and that makes her newsworthy. Maybe it was something to do with the TV show she played on. Something her character did that offended him. Or turned him on. Some people are abnormally obsessed with soap operas and believe the people on them are real. Maybe he hated her character, wanted to kill her and stalked her until he got her down here when she was alone and vulnerable."

"Sylvie played the good girl on the show," Black said. "Moralistic, and always doing the right thing and expecting everyone else to do the same."

I raised an eyebrow. "That could annoy a psychopath."

"Have you found out anything from the other cast members on her show?" Harve asked me.

"Bud's been checking into obsessed fans and digging for any stalking incidents, but he hasn't come up with anything out of the ordinary. Marc Savoy's been ruled out because he was with some fishermen at a local bar when the murder went down. Bud picked up Sylvie's fan mail and interviewed the other actors on the soap when he was in New York. He's going through it now for any leads."

While I'd been talking, Harve had rolled his chair into the kitchen and had returned with three longnecks of ice-cold Heineken. He set them in the middle of the table with a clink of glass. "What about the use of the duct tape, Nick? Is that significant in your estimation?"

"If it's over the mouth, sometimes it's an attempt to silence the victim. Like when an abused son gets tired of hearing his mother nag and berate him, something like that. Same with over the eyes. Blind the victim so they won't see the offender perpetrating the crime. In this case, I think it was more a means of control first, then later to keep the head in place." I watched the realization hit Black again that it wasn't just a victim, but that it was Sylvie taped to that chair in the lake. Harve met my eyes as Black pushed back his chair and walked out onto the back porch. He'd done fine for a while, but even Nicholas Black was human.

I said, "He's still shaky. He's been through a lot tonight."

"Get him outta here. It's too soon, whether he thinks so or not. Let me go over all this again and sort it out in my head. Come over tomorrow, and we'll rehash it some more. Tell him I'll send over the reports on similar cases when I get them all printed out."

"Okay." I stood up and glanced outside. I couldn't see

Black on the porch. "Need anything, Harve? Groceries or anything?"

"No. Dot fixed me up with some casseroles and frozen pizza."

"When's she getting back?"

"Monday or Tuesday. I miss her, but she deserves time off. I'm not always so easy to live with."

"You're a teddy bear, and Dottie knows that better than anybody. Take care. Ring the bell if you need me."

As I was leaving, Harve said, "Don't be too hard on the guy. It's pretty obvious that he loved that poor girl."

"Yeah, I know. See you tomorrow."

Black was outside in the yard when I came down the steps, just standing there, hands on his narrow hips, staring out over the dark water. I'd always heard he loved the lake, and now I believed it. It had a calming influence on me, too, especially at night. I looked out over the quiet cove and watched a boat near the opposite shore. A lantern glowed faintly at the stern, and it made me want to be out on that smooth black water, too, just floating and stargazing, not thinking about gruesome murders and missing body parts.

I said, "We're calling it a night. Harve's tired and wants to get some sleep."

"Let's walk back to your place."

Already a few feet down the path toward the dock, I stopped in my tracks. "What about the boat?"

"Harve can have it."

"Harve can have it?" I repeated.

"Sure. It's handicapped equipped; all our Cobalts are. Then he can go fishing with his nurse if he wants."

"You're giving him your boat, just like that?"

"I've got a dozen of them docked at the marina. If I need more, I'll order them. Harve's helping me find Sylvie's murderer. Think of it as a token of my appreciation."

"He's a proud man; he might not take it."

"Then it'll be up to you to convince him. Tell him it's for Dottie to use."

I stared at him, but I thought about how often Harve longed to go out on the lake with Dottie, how many times he'd said he missed going fishing. It was just too dangerous in a wheelchair in the bass boat. But Black was right; he'd be comfortable in the big cruiser, and he'd be perfectly safe.

Black said, "It's a beautiful night. Let's walk. I think better when I walk."

The night was dark, still, and peaceful, and little was left to be said. He took long strides, a sign of inner agitation. But hey, I was five-nine; I could match him, almost. I didn't interrupt his thoughts. I knew what he was thinking about, and I wanted him to think about it. I was running into dead ends left and right. I welcomed his input.

When we reached my house, we walked down to the dock, and he took out his cell phone and politely requested that Tyler pick him up at my dock. While he gave directions, I righted the picnic table he'd overturned and sent tumbling down the hill earlier. I sat down on top of it with my feet braced on the attached bench. Black came over and stood in front of me.

"Thanks for giving the boat to Harve," I said, realizing I was more choked up at the gesture than I realized.

"I like him. He's a good guy. Was he your partner in L.A.? Is that how the two of you became friends?"

I did not fall for that. "He's been a good friend to me, he and Dottie both."

"What happened to you in L.A., Claire? Why can't you talk about it?"

The probing shocked me. Most people took the hint when I shut the door on a subject.

Frowning, I stood up and decided it was time to head

for the hills. That's right, flee when things become dangerously personal. Chicken, well, yes, exactly. Apparently, Black decided me exiting stage right wasn't going to happen. He grabbed my wrist and spun me back around.

I jerked against his hold on me, pissed off, but he pulled me close enough that our noses nearly touched. My heart began to pound. Black was breathing hard and his voice dropped to that husky, I-need-to-throw-you-down-right-here-right-now-and-ravish-you timber. "I want to kiss you."

Right to the point, no hedging here. I swallowed hard. Time for the womanly bravado I'd practiced for so long. "Sorry, pal, that ain't gonna happen."

"Like hell it isn't."

He brought his mouth up against mine, no soft little nibble but hard and edgy and determined, but his grip loosened almost immediately as if, uh-oh, he realized he'd made the wrong move, and I was going to be ticked off, but he was nowhere near to forcing me. This was a good time to knee him in the groin with good results. I could pull away any time I wanted, could stalk off, even slap his face or slap him in cuffs again if I wanted to. Unfortunately, I didn't want to; I wanted this kiss as much as he did. He didn't need more encouragement, and when I didn't resist, he put one arm around my waist and pulled me up tight against his chest, his other hand caught in my hair and holding my head steady. It had been so long since I'd kissed a man, even longer since a man had sent a sexual fire ripping down my spine to explode where it counted. It felt good, wonderful, like seeing the sun rise over the promised land you vowed never to visit again.

My lips opened to him, and he took full advantage, ravishing my mouth and cheeks, then moving to the base of my throat, where my pulse hammered in a staccato that was downright embarrassing. I felt my resolve go limp. I didn't know how long the embrace lasted, but I finally fought my way back to reality enough to realize I was engaged in something incredibly stupid and unprofessional. The truth hit me like a cold shower, and I pushed him back. He didn't resist my rejection, so we stood a couple of feet apart, both of us breathing hard and audibly, as if we'd run a full marathon. Sexual chemistry, there it was again, but now I *really* knew what it meant.

Then, I'm sorry to say, I was the one that went for him, grabbing the front of his shirt and jerking him back to me. Our mouths ravaged each other some more, and the embrace got crazy with lots of groping under clothes and tongues and groans and moans. Then I came to my senses again and jerked back away from him, how I do not know. Maybe it was the Cobalt roaring into sight at the far end of the cove.

"This can't happen," I got out somehow, but who was I kidding? It takes two to tango, and I'd been skipping around that dance floor pretty damn fast.

"It already happened." His voice wasn't quite normal, either, which made me feel better, but he was calmer than I was and not trying to touch me. "And it's not going to stop."

I was letting him lead me down the garden path that he'd chosen, and I stomped on my carnal brakes while I still could. "Look, Black. I like you. I didn't at first, I admit it, but you're not the kind of man I thought you were. I don't think you had anything to do with this crime, but I have to prove that. The kissing was great, I have to say; I enjoyed it, too. But that's all it can be. The end, over, done with."

Black gave a low laugh. Totally not amused. "I can wait until this case is over, if that's the problem. Just hurry up and solve it." He let me think about that for about two seconds; then he kissed me on the forehead and said, "Take care, Detective. I have to go to L.A. to-morrow, so don't get yourself killed while I'm gone. Remember, duck and weave. I'll call you when I get back from the coast."

Then he was striding down my dock to flag down his ride under my dusk-to-dawn lamp. I sat down on the picnic table, furious at myself for getting drawn into a personal relationship with a man like Nicholas Black. It was a stupid thing to do. If I couldn't keep my hormones from raging when I was around him, and it was pretty damn obvious I couldn't, then I'd have to keep my distance. Charlie would have my hide if he found out I'd been playing kissy face with a murder suspect. I cringed just to think how Charlie would ream me out if he ever heard about this.

LIFE AFTER FATHER

Brat didn't kill again for almost two years. The brown metal strongbox was so full of cash that it would last Brat and the mother a lifetime; Brat had stopped counting after two hundred thousand dollars, all in neat bundles of hundred-dollar bills held together with rubber bands. Three days after Brat had killed the embalmer and burned the old house, he saw an old silver travel trailer sitting in the front yard of a farmhouse on a rural highway. It had a white sign on the hitch that said FOR SALE in red letters. Brat knew it would be a perfect place for his mother to live in peace and quiet. It had a living room for a TV and computer, a kitchen where they could eat together, and a little bathroom with a shower stall, a tiny sink, and a toilet. The big bedroom at the back would be perfect for Brat, and the small one would give the mother privacy to entertain her friends when Brat brought them home. The elderly farmer said, "Yes, sir, it would be a nice surprise for your mother and a bargain for just four hundred dollars," and then helped Brat hitch it to the green Dodge station wagon free of charge.

After that, they drove and drove, mostly on county roads where nobody noticed them. Brat discovered KOA campgrounds and other camper parks, where nobody ever bothered them or came around, and they could hook up water and electricity and have a nice, peaceful life. They never stayed long, because Brat was searching, searching, constantly searching. Finally, after many months and many miles, Brat found the woman they'd been searching for. They followed her for over a week, to make sure she was the right one, until the mother said, "Yes, dear, she is the one. She's the perfect one." They smiled at each other, and Brat was very happy they were still together.

Brat thought about how to kill the woman for a long time. The cleaver and razor strop were in the mother's bedroom, where she could keep an eye on them, hidden under the money in the locked brown strongbox. The perfect woman to kill lived in a small house that had two apartments, one upstairs and one downstairs. She lived upstairs and had to climb long wooden steps built on the side of the house to get to her front door. Every day for ten days, Brat watched her leave for work at a soup kitchen on the corner, then come back home and climb the steps. Every time she came into sight, hatred filled Brat, and the hot river boiled up over its banks and made Brat's skin hot to the touch. When that happened, the mother refused to give good-night kisses. That's how Brat knew it was time for the woman to die. The mother was getting impatient and angry and was refusing to talk anymore.

One night when Brat and the mother were watching from the station wagon, hidden in the shadows along the woman's street, the woman came outside to smoke a cigarette on the long flight of steps. The mother said, "Go on, go on, Brat. Don't be afraid; she's the one," and so Brat sneaked silently up behind the woman, and when she stood up to go back upstairs, Brat hit her as hard as he could with the tire iron the embalmer had kept in the station wagon next to the spare tire. Heart thundering, the hot liquid boiling higher and higher, hotter and hotter, Brat watched the woman. She lay still at the bottom of the steps, and nobody came; nobody heard Brat dragging her by her long blond hair across the grass, then along the side of the road to the station wagon. The mother was pleased and said now they'd have a new friend to talk to.

Except that, uh-oh, the woman wasn't dead. She woke up and started groaning, and Brat had to tape her hands and legs and mouth shut with silver duct tape until they got home. Brat put her on the mother's bed, and soon the mother said what had to be done, that their new friend wouldn't like them, wouldn't talk and be friendly until she was dead, so Brat got on the bed with her and put both hands around her throat and pressed down until something went crunch in her neck and her eyes closed and she quit struggling. Brat jumped off her, and the hot liquid fell to a simmering heat in Brat's belly, until she moved again and her eyelids fluttered, and then the flames inside leapt out of control, and Brat dragged her to the tiny shower stall in the travel trailer and held her down on the floor. "The cleaver, use the cleaver," the mother said from her place on her bed, and Brat did it, and then finally, finally, the woman lay still.

Shaking all over, Brat got into the station wagon and drove all night, while the woman's blood ran down into the shower drain. When they came to a wide river, Brat turned down a road and severed the woman's head and put it on the pillow beside the mother's, then wrapped the woman's body in the shower curtain and dragged her up rocks to a ledge over the rushing water. Weighting her down with big rocks, Brat pushed her off the ledge and listened for the big splash, and when he returned to the trailer, the mother and the woman were having a good time, gossiping like old friends.

"You two sure are chatterboxes," Brat told them with a big smile. "How'm I gonna get any sleep tonight with all this yakkin' and laughin' goin' on, huh?" But now his mother had somebody to talk to during their long drives, and when the mother was happy, Brat was happy.

Brat was fifteen years old.

22

Sylvie's head turned up three days later. Attached to a new body. In Los Angeles. On the soundstage where Gil Serna was filming interiors for *Trojan*, no less. Even more interesting, Gil Serna had up and disappeared. I arrived at LAX late that same afternoon. I begged Bud to take the assignment, but he had his hands full handling the infestation of press people. Maybe this latest development would send them hightailing it back to L.A., where they belonged.

So I got hold of Jim Tate, a guy I went to the academy with, and he agreed to pick me up at the airport. I was glad to see him again, especially since I knew I could trust him. He hadn't changed much, still short and square with enough muscles to lift a small Brahma bull over his head. He had a receding hairline shaped like a W over his eyebrows, but he had taken emphasis off it with a blond buzz cut that made him look like retired military. He was honest and smart, and lived for the weekends with his three sons, who raced pickup trucks on dirt tracks out in the desert somewhere. Married and divorced twice, he had made his work the center of his life.

Tate already had permission from his superior officer to admit me to the soundstage, which was a few blocks off Sunset Boulevard, near Paramount Studios, the way paved by Charlie Ramsay's call to a friend of his, who also happened to be the L.A. Chief of Police. I requested Tate as my liaison and got him. The news of the grisly discovery had not hit the airwaves yet, but the clock was ticking.

"We need to get you in and out of here before the networks get hold of this and the media goes nuts."

"My feelings exactly." Jim knew better than most about what had happened to me and Harve. He had been on the scene that night. He glanced at me. "Except for those bruises, you're looking pretty good. You doing all right, kid?"

"It was nice and quiet down on the lake. Until this happened."

"Harve doin' okay, I guess?"

"I see him almost every day. Then this case popped up, and all hell broke loose."

He said, "Somebody in the media's bound to recognize you sooner or later."

"Yeah, I've been waiting for it."

"It's been three years. People forget. Maybe you'll get lucky."

"I've never been a lucky person."

He didn't try to convince me otherwise. Point made.

"What can you tell me about this one?" I said.

We took a ramp onto the 405 North fast enough to stand Tate's tan Ford truck on two wheels. Racing trucks around a track did that to a fella. I held on but didn't complain. Los Angeles was not the place for fainthearted drivers or scaredy-cat passengers. "Cast and crew all left the set on Friday around four o'clock. Security locked up the place for the weekend, but that doesn't mean jack. Anybody can scale the walls: they're low stucco with bougainvillea vines all over them for footholds. And a gap was found in a fence on the back lot."

When we reached Santa Monica Boulevard, Tate swerved onto it like a bat out of hell and flew west. The car in the merge lane was forced into the middle and almost hit a new bright blue Chevy Malibu, but Tate didn't miss a beat with his story. "When everybody showed up Monday around noon, they found the vic on a bed on one of the sets. They recognized Sylvie Border right off, freaked out, one and all, real mass hysteria, and put in a garbled call to 911. It sounds pretty much like the same MO your perp used."

"Silver duct tape around the neck?"

"Yeah. Hands and ankles, too. Pretty grisly stuff, even for out here. Blood everywhere, like that goddamn *Interview with the Vampire* movie."

"The victim nude?"

"Yes, and blood's congealed all over her; it looks like she's wearing a shiny red wet suit. Looks like he made an effort to smear it all over her face."

"Pleasant. Anybody spotted on the set over the weekend?"

"One guard said that that psychiatrist, you know that guy, Nicholas Black, came by late Saturday night, asked him if Gil Serna was around."

My stomach sank at the mention of Black's name. "Nicholas Black was at the soundstage where they found her? You sure it was him?"

"Sounds familiar, right? The guard said he stopped Black at the gate and wouldn't let him inside. Black told the night guy that he couldn't find Serna anywhere and was worried about him."

Great move, Black. Show up at the second murder scene asking questions. "Has Serna resurfaced yet?"

"Nope. He seems to have disappeared into thin air after he left work on Friday, which doesn't look particularly good for him. His coworkers are saying he hasn't been the same person since he found out Sylvie was dead. Said he went kind of crazy with grief and couldn't concentrate on his lines, couldn't function much at all."

"Who saw him last?"

"The night watchman said he left on Friday afternoon about four-thirty but then came back later, around seven in the evening. Said he forgot something. Guard said he didn't see him leave, or anyone else come or go, but he went on rounds in the back lot several times, during which Serna could've left without him noticing."

It took us about forty-five minutes to get to the Paramount soundstage where the second murder had taken place. The entire block was cordoned off, but media people were lined up like crows on a telephone line. Tate reached in the backseat and tossed an L.A. Lakers cap into my lap.

"Put on your shades and wear this, and they aren't gonna recognize you."

Gratefully, I shoved the cap down low over my face and climbed out of the truck. Years had passed, true enough, but Hollywood reporters remember scandals like Hollywood actors remember Oscars. Tate flashed his badge to the uniforms keeping the milling throng of reporters at bay, and we wound our way through a series of movie sets, stepping over cables and dodging lights and boom microphones and cameras, until we reached a scene lit up by three floodlights. Detectives were standing around in small groups, talking the case, and uniformed criminalists were still sweeping the scene. They were thorough, and they were very good. A couple of guys that I'd worked with before caught sight of me and smiled, and I nodded back without stopping. I knew what they were thinking. That was one reason I'd left L.A. to lick my wounds in the middle of the Ozark hinterland.

The set was a fake villa overlooking the sea. A la *Cleopatra.* Lots of white pillars and marble floors and billowing white linen panels draping a platform bed. A painted Aegean Sea backdrop offered a sunset on the horizon. The victim sat upright on the bed, completely nude, rail thin, legs crossed demurely, arms folded over her breasts in a show of modesty. Tate was right about the blood. The killer either got sloppy or was in too big a hurry and let her pump out all over the place. The air was heavy with the sick-sweet, coppery smell of congealing blood. Could be he'd done the same at the lake, but the water had washed it up all clean and neat for him.

There was no doubt the head was Sylvie Border's. Her face was unmistakable, beautiful even in death, eyes open and staring, but Tate was right. It looked like the perp had intentionally smeared blood all over her face, except for a patch on the forehead that looked as white and waxy as the magnolia blossoms perfuming the front veranda of her parents' New Orleans home. She had been posed to stare out the window at the fake ocean sunset. Cameras were in place around the set, with directors' chairs just behind, and stage lights focused on her as if ready for the shoot to begin.

It had taken me over six hours to get here, and they were still processing the scene. That meant lots of evidence to collect. I moved to the bed, where a young woman wearing black pants and a white polo shirt with LAPD on the breast pocket was clicking still photographs of the body. I didn't know the woman, but she glanced up from her work and gave me the professional nod reserved for law enforcement colleagues gathered at the scene.

Silver duct tape had been used again, all right, about three rolls of it. Definitely excessive. Wrapped round and round the throat. It was the same perp, all right, or somebody playing awfully good copycat. And very few people knew the details of the crime scene at the lake. Somehow he'd managed to transport Sylvie's head fifteen hundred miles across country to Tinseltown without being seen. God only knew what unfortunate soul the body belonged to, but it had been a young woman, anorexic probably and not much taller than five-foot, very slight and small, like Sylvie had been. Who was he trying to kill over and over again? Why was he switching heads? If I could figure out why, I could figure out who.

The criminalists had been filled in on my case and were making damn sure they handled everything precisely by the book. Thank you O.J. Simpson and his Dream Team. Everybody in the LAPD had become better and more careful at their jobs, and they were damn good before. Nobody was going to make any stupid mistakes that'd come back to haunt them. I examined the body more carefully, then leaned close to the head, with its dead eyes staring at the camera, glad Black wasn't here to see Sylvie's last and final humiliation. If I hadn't known better, I would have thought the body and head belonged to the same person. We definitely had a serial operating here, one with flair and flourish, and if my guess was correct, he'd done many, many other crimes before we ran headlong into him, so to speak.

Tate came over and bent down to examine the victim's neck. "You're telling me that when they remove this tape, they're going to find out that this body is not Sylvie Border's?" Tate stood up and looked down at the bed, with his fists on his hips. "Why the hell does he do that?"

"One reason is that he wants us to know these two murders are connected. Wants to show his handiwork to the world. I think he was disappointed when the media didn't get hold of the gory details at the lake, so he came out here, where everyone is media mad and likes to leak to the press. He wants the papers to run with this, and he knows they'll have no scruples out here. Good thing about it is it's riskier for him. He's getting reckless. This is a messy crime scene, lots of hair and tissue. Maybe he got careless and left a part of him behind this time, and that's all we'll need to nail him."

Tate said, "Nicholas Black is our primary at the moment. He was seen here and had the opportunity. Ditto on your victim."

"Black's not stupid enough to come out here and commit murder when the last one went down at his resort. Much less allow himself to be seen lurking around."

"Maybe that's what he wants you to think. I hear he's a publicity hound who likes the spotlight. That fits with the killer's profile, too."

I studied Tate's face a moment and realized he could very well be right. Every time I thought I could eliminate Black, he bounced back like some kind of frickin' fickle finger of fate. "Yeah, maybe. I've spent some time interviewing him, and my gut tells me he's not the killer."

"Your gut was right about 99 percent of the time, if I remember correctly," he said, grinning. "Trust your instincts; that's what Harve always told us, remember?" I nodded, and he asked, "What about Gil Serna? True about him sleeping with Sylvie Border?"

"I interviewed him at the funeral. He's pretty torn up."

"We'll get another shot at him as soon as he shows up."

We discussed the scene with the criminalists for a while, asked lots of technical questions, but they were already turning up more clues than we'd gotten at the lake. Several hairs in evidence, and a bloody footprint was being cast. At least we'd have something to work with this time.

Outside, the press was swarming the sidewalks like maggots in three-day-old garbage, but these were exceptionally good-looking, well-coifed, sunny California maggots. Unfortunately, we had to leave the perimeter tape guarded by LAPD officers to get to Tate's truck. Once we ducked under it, somebody must've yelled fair game. In seconds we were surrounded and hounded down the sidewalk. Twenty feet from Tate's truck, we were brought to a standstill by at least thirty camera crews. When I saw Peter Hastings barging his way to the front, screaming my name, I knew the battle was lost. I had to take a stand, give them something, or I'd never get out of the fray.

"Okay, take it easy. Get back, and I'll answer a couple of questions."

Oh, the delight they showed then, but they did back off. This was the part I hated, the part that sent me fleeing Los Angeles and everybody in it. But they didn't recognize me, and chances were they wouldn't.

"Can we have your name, please? And spell it, if you would."

"And take off the sunglasses, please." That from a photographer.

"Detective Claire Morgan. Canton County Sheriff's Department." I spelled my name. I ignored the bit about the sunglasses.

"A source tells us that the body found inside belongs to Sylvie Border. If that's the case, who was found at Nicholas Black's spa in Missouri?"

"I'm not at liberty to divulge that information," I said tersely, trying to keep my head down enough to shield my face. "I'm out here to view the crime scene. You'll have to present your questions to the LAPD officer in charge of the case."

"What about your case, Detective? Do you know who the murderer is?"

"We are making progress in our investigation. That's all I'm willing to say at this time."

"Is Nick Black still a suspect? We understand he's here in town. That places him at the scene of both murders, doesn't it? Is he the killer, Detective?"

"As I said, you'll have to direct your questions about this case to the LAPD. Now if you'll excuse me, I have a plane to catch."

For one magic moment, I thought I'd gotten through unscathed, that they'd back off and let me go home, but then Peter Hastings came forward, with a knowing smirk on his face. I braced myself for his insistent man-whine, but instead he hit me with a bombshell that nearly blew me off my feet.

"Isn't it true, Detective, that your real name is Annie Blue, and that three years ago, you were an officer with the LAPD?"

Everything around me stopped, all motion and sound fading into one shrill shock wave. *Oh, God,* I thought, *don't let this happen, not again.* Then a fiery crackle of energy swept through the throng, so palpable I could almost feel it coming at me, like heat off summer asphalt.

"No comment," I said. My voice sounded strange, and I looked around for Tate. He'd made it to the truck, but I was stuck tight in the jumble of rolling cameras and pressing people. "Please let me through."

The jackals pressed closer, pushing me around. Dozens of microphones were shoved in my face. *Get it together, get it together,* I kept thinking, but Peter Hastings was up front now, and the look on his face was *oh yes, oh yes, I am God.* A CBS reporter beat him to the punch.

"Is it true you're Annie Blue, the L.A. detective involved in the infamous love triangle with her husband and police partner? The incident crippled your partner and killed both your husband and son. Can you deny that, Detective?"

"I have nothing to say." I pushed my way through the reporters, knocking a couple of them out of the way, but others stepped in front of me. I wanted to draw my weapon and shoot my way through, and was considering it when Hastings stuck his mike in front of my face and struck the fatal blow.

"Is it true you're having an affair with Nicholas Black, Detective? Are you the woman in the photographs we're running on our show?"

Now I stopped because he shoved a sheaf of eight-by-ten glossies in my direction. I looked down at them and saw myself kissing Black that night on my dock, saw another of us having breakfast on the deck of his yacht. I ripped them up, sick to my stomach, and pushed my way through the crowd. When a long black limousine turned the corner, I knew it was Nicholas Black to the rescue even before he jumped out and started walking toward us.

"There's Nick Black," I heard a reporter yell, and the whole crowd gave a collective gasp of delight, then shifted in his direction like a tidal wave. They headed for him with a scramble of cords and excited cries, pleased as punch that they would get to destroy two people instead of just one. Shakily, I watched Black move up a flight of steps to where they all could see him, and then I headed toward Tate's truck. Halfway there, John Booker stepped out of nowhere and pulled me toward Black's limousine.

I jerked free from his grasp. "What the hell are you doing?"

"I'm getting you out of here before they tear you to shreds. Nick's taking the heat so you can get away. He's got his jet waiting on a private airstrip to take you home."

Tempted, I glanced back at Black, now speaking to the crowd of photographers. He wasn't looking at us, but some of the reporters were. Booker said, "They're gonna hound you all the way home. On the plane, in the airport, everywhere. This is the best way, trust me."

He was right, and the photos proved I knew Black better than I was supposed to know him. I waved Tate off and pointed to the limousine. He nodded okay, and I climbed in the back as Booker stiff-armed two photographers trying to scramble in after me. As we drove away, the photographers were snapping pictures through the black tinted windows.

"Nick must think a lot of you," Booker said as he settled into the opposite seat. "He'd rather take a beating than face the paparazzi. He's sued 'em three times and won."

"How'd he know I was here?"

"He called the sheriff about this new murder, and Charlie told him you were in L.A. Then on our way down here, we saw you on the tube." He pointed at three nineteen-inch color sets built into the console. All three sets were tuned to different stations. The one in the middle was Fox News and had a close-up of Nicholas Black's face. I didn't have to ask; Booker turned up the volume.

"My relationship with Detective Morgan is strictly professional," Black was saying, very calm, very used to media attention, "though I wouldn't mind if it were otherwise. She can arrest you guys if you get in my way."

The reporters laughed like they loved him, like they were having a real good time, like they didn't mind him suing them. He smiled easily, as relaxed as I'd been tense.

"Did you know about her other identity, Doctor Black?" Peter Hastings asked, sounding smug and thrilled to be the one who broke the dirt.

"No, but anyone who's really lived has a past. Maybe even you, Pete? Wonder what my private investigators could dig up on you."

More laughter, but it was a subtle threat, and Hastings looked like his closets were locked good and tight and for a reason. But he was nothing, if not persistent.

"I'm not calling you a liar, Doctor, but I do have a picture here of you and the detective getting pretty friendly. It's hard to deny the truth when it's right here in front of your face. It's going on the air in a matter of minutes, Black, so now's your chance to tell us the truth."

Black took the photographs handed to him but barely glanced at them. "You can't blame a man for trying, but she wasn't interested. If you're the jackal who took these, you'll be able to vouch for the fact that I left her place minutes after these were taken."

"Is it true she has a death wish?" a redheaded female reporter yelled from the back. "Is that why she left the LAPD, because the department psychs said she was too dangerous to remain on the force?"

"I think that sounds like you guys have been watching too many Mel Gibson and Danny Glover films. I'm planning a formal news conference tomorrow about my association with this case. I'll answer any questions you might have at that time. My office will give out the time and place within the hour."

The limousine hit the freeway, and the driver smoothly merged into six lanes of speeding traffic without even running a single person off the road. "Aren't we going back for him?" I asked Booker.

"He'll meet us there."

"Does he always travel with Cedar Bend security guards?"

"This time he did."

I tried to read Booker without any luck, sensing he was much more than one of Black's security details, then looked back at the television screen in time to see Black making his way toward the street. I dropped my head back on the cushioned seat and closed my eyes. The worst possible thing had happened. Now all I had to do was figure out how to deal with it.

23

It turned out that Black had a ranch of sorts north-west of L.A. in the Santa Monica Mountains, a ranch of King Saud sorts. The limo drove past a road that led up into the hills, where I glimpsed the windows of another Black mansion overlooking another Black spectacular view. I shut my eyes. How much money did Nicholas Black have? Maybe I should've been a psychiatrist and written a few books, too. Maybe then I could afford a hot tub. My life story would be a best-seller all by itself, considering the money it'd rake in for the tabloids.

I wondered again what I was doing here in Black's limousine with the mysterious Booker. How did this happen? I didn't want to analyze it right now. I just felt real bad, all wrung out and depressed. I didn't want to talk, explain, justify, remember. I didn't want to function. Luckily, John Booker wasn't much of a talker, either.

"Nick said to wait for him on the plane," he said at length when the car slowed to a stop on a tarmac.

I opened my eyes, picked up my leather handbag,

and trailed him across a paved runway to the sleek corporate jet. We were down in a small valley now with mountains around us. Inside the jet, it was as grand as everything else Black owned, all tan and black and plush and expensive. I felt like I had flown back in time, with all the old feelings crashing around inside my head, smashing up barriers I'd erected so I wouldn't have to face my past again. Too bad, so sad, as they say. My inner attempt at flippancy fell pretty flat, so I sat down in one of the black reclining seats and shut my eyes. It helped to shut my eyes. If I couldn't see my life falling apart, it wasn't happening. I heard Booker moving around as if he owned the place, quietly giving commands to a woman I assumed was a flight attendant and then later to a male voice I assumed was the pilot's. Again, I wondered who Booker was and exactly what he did for Black. Cell phones rang now and then, my own twice, but I hid behind my closed eyelids. Nobody home. Don't call back. Maybe I'd never have to open my eyes again; maybe I could just let John Booker silently watch over me forever.

In time I heard Black's voice somewhere nearby, speaking in low tones. I opened my eyes and saw him at the end of the cabin with Booker, both tall and dark and in control, and two gray-haired, distinguished-looking men in pilot uniforms. I shut my eyes again until Black spoke directly to me, now very close.

"Buckle your seat belt, Claire."

He was sitting across from me, and Booker was gone. I obeyed and buckled up, then looked up as a young woman with a gold nameplate that said Mindy handed me a goblet and a white pill in a tiny paper cup.

"It's a sedative," said Black. "Take it. It's mild and won't put you out."

"Then maybe you better give me two or three more,"

I said with my razor-sharp wit. Black stared at me. No smile.

"Well, I guess you've figured out where you've seen me before," I said, putting the tablet in my mouth and chasing it with the water. Mindy took the goblet and paper cup away.

"I figured out who you were long before today."

That surprised me. "When?"

"The first day you paid me a visit. I had Booker look you up."

"So Booker's your private investigator."

"That's right. We ran missions together in the army. He's a good friend and one of the best men Special Ops ever saw."

That explained a few things. "So I guess you keep dossiers on everybody you meet, just like the KGB?"

"You had it in for me; I could see that from the beginning. I make it a habit to know my enemies."

"So now we're enemies?"

"Not at all. What I learned about you helped me understand your . . . attitude. You were hiding a painful incident from your past, trying to make a new future. Nothing wrong with that. I would've prescribed the same course if I'd been treating you."

"So you tell your patients not to face up to facts, but to go out to the boondocks of Missouri and hide under a rock."

Black contemplated me as the plane began to move down the runway. "As you know, I've got a few secrets, too. I ended up in the boondocks of Missouri. Nothing wrong with that, either." He pressed a button, and a door opened beside him, revealing a recessed liquor cabinet. He poured himself a finger of whiskey, tossed it back, and didn't look happy. Not exactly his old debonair self. His face was serious; his voice was serious. We were suddenly a serious pair. "Annie Blue. I'm Black and you're Blue. Pretty ironic under the circumstances, wouldn't you say?"

I guess it was a joke, but he looked way too serious to be cracking gags. The sedative was relaxing me, all right; my arms were resting on my lap like slabs of bacon. My head was lolling on the headrest, then was pressed back against it when we lifted off the ground and up into the clouds at a sharp angle. We leveled off, and I stared out the porthole at heavy white clouds and blue sky, glad to be leaving the great state of California behind.

"Thanks for taking the spotlight off me," I said after a minute, looking across at him. "I guess you have a lot of questions. I owe you some answers, so go ahead, ask."

"You don't owe me anything. Especially answers. I know what happened to you, and it makes you even more interesting."

Well, that hit me wrong. Ms. Flippant reared her ugly head. "Oh, I get it. Now I'm your brand-new specimen. You can pin me to your couch and analyze me for your next book. Annie Blue, husband killer, and—" I started to add son killer, but I could not say it, not even under the effects of Prozac, or whatever the hell it was that I took. Our eyes met, and he knew what I was feeling. He always seemed to know everything.

"I hate psychiatrists," I said, squeezing my eyes shut.

"I'm not your psychiatrist," he said.

I said nothing for a moment; then I searched his face. "Why're you doing this? You just got yourself in a war with the media, and now they're going to start probing into your life, trying to dig up dirt. They'll find out about your brother, just like they found out about me."

"Guess I'm just one hell of a nice guy." He was angry

now. His face was tight; his tanned skin was flushed shades darker.

"Well, thanks for whisking me away, just like a Calgon commercial. I won't forget it."

Black definitely no longer found me amusing. He said, "You can trust me. I want you to trust me."

"Yeah, that'd be nice, wouldn't it?"

Black looked at me, and then he actually laughed. "Go to sleep. You'll feel better if you rest on the flight. Because, my dear detective, Charlie's the one who's going to hammer you with lots of questions when you get back home."

I shut my eyes, and then I shut my thoughts down, and then I slept.

Black woke me right before we landed. Another private airstrip. Another tan-and-black uniform. A helicopter to take us home. Boy, this was the life. But I felt better, more myself. The sleep was the first real rest I'd had since Dottie's potion. The helicopter was a Bell 430 six-seater, deluxe model, I guess, with some more hand-stitched, supple leather recliners and a wood bar and plush, deep-pile carpet in shades of gold and black. To my surprise, Black climbed into the pilot's seat. Amazing, the depths of this man's talents. I wondered if he could cook, too.

"Put this on so we can talk," he told me, handing me a headpiece with earphones and a little microphone. He slipped his over his head, poked on a pair of black aviator sunglasses, and focused on the elaborate instrument panel. I was a little nervous since I'd never ridden in a helicopter, but that was the least of my problems. Black handled it calmly and expertly, the way he did just about everything. In minutes we were skimming over tree-cloaked Ozark mountains on our way to Cedar Bend.

"I'm going to do a pass over your place and see if the media's staked out your house," he said in my ear. I nodded. I hadn't thought of that yet. Unfortunately, the media was way ahead of me. There were three satellite dishes set up on the entrance road, and I could see somebody doing a remote newscast on my dock, with binoculars and a tripod camera.

Black banked into a turn and took us down to the other end of the cove to Harve and Dottie's place. More satellite trucks, and a couple of people outside Harve's chain-link fence. I pulled out my cell phone and punched in Dottie's number. She answered on the first ring.

"Claire, where are you? Harve and I've been frantic."

"Look out the window. I'm in Black's helicopter, hovering over your house. Has the press been bothering you?"

"Yeah, I hear the rotors now. They're coming out of the woodwork, the jerks," Dottie said, and I saw her walk out on the rear sundeck and look up at us. Harve's wheelchair came into view at the door, and she said, "Here, Harve wants to talk to you."

"Claire, get the hell out of here. They'll eat you alive if you come back. Find some place to hide out until I can get a gate up that'll keep them off our road."

"Tell him you're staying with me. I have the security you need," Black ordered in my ear.

I didn't have a lot of choice, so I made the decision quickly. "I'm going out to Cedar Bend for a little while, but I'll be home as soon as I can. Have they put together who you are yet?"

"Not yet. Dottie's been running them off for me, bless her heart."

"Okay, I'll see you soon. Take care."

* * *

When we swept into Black's resort over the lake, we could see about half a dozen boats and pontoons full of press people floating around the point. But Black was right. His penthouse was secure. They couldn't get at either one of us there. Black put down on the round helipad as if he'd done it a million times, and he probably had. He took my arm and hurried me swiftly into his private quarters. Once inside the deserted lower level, he said, "Now you know why I have all this security set up for my patients. They can't get to you here, no matter how hard they try."

My welcoming committee from the sheriff's office, on the other hand, had no problem piercing Black's ultimate sanctuary. Bud showed up at Black's private living quarters within thirty minutes of our arrival. When he saw us sitting on one of the long black sofas watching the boats watch us, he said, "Well, ain't this sweet?"

Bud was as angry as I'd ever seen him. I didn't blame him. I would be, too, if I were him. Peter Hastings and the reporters made it look worse than it was. Anyone who saw those photographs would assume I was having a hot and heavy affair with Black, and Bud wasn't an exception. Truth was, I ought to have gotten as far away from Black as I could. But then I'd have had to face the reporters, and I couldn't bring myself to do it, not yet. Tomorrow, maybe, tomorrow I'd be able to do it. I'd be stronger then, the shock would fade.

"I'm sorry, Bud," I said, heartfelt, embarrassed. "It's not true. Nothing's going on between us."

Both men looked at me; then Bud glanced at Black. "Could've fooled me. Pictures looked goddamned real, but, hey, technology's a bitch now. You sayin' the pictures of you and him together are doctored?"

Black stood up. He didn't look particularly happy, ei-

ther. He looked like he was going to knock Bud's lights
out. "If you'll excuse me, I'll let you two talk about this
in private."

"Gee, thanks, Doc. You're a prince," said Bud. Sarcastic
as hell. Black left the room without replying; then Bud
looked at me in utter disgust.

It hurt, but he had a good reason to be angry. "I
made a big mistake, Bud. But it was just that one time,
out on my dock, just a kiss and then he left."

"That kiss is gonna cost you plenty, Claire, or should
I call you Annie?"

He obviously felt betrayed. "Bud, I didn't plan for
this to happen. I didn't tell you the truth about my past
because I didn't want it to come out. I wanted to forget
it and start over. I didn't tell anybody. Please, try to
understand."

Bud paced back and forth in front of the windows,
then sat down on a chair across from me. Frowning, agitated, he jerked loose his tie and said, "Getting involved
with this guy, Black, is a mistake. I know you think he's
innocent, but what if he isn't? Have you thought about
that? Let me get you out of here before it gets worse. I'll
take you home. Or you can stay with me."

"My house is under siege, so is Harve's. So is yours
the minute I show up there. Black can keep the press
away from me, at least until I get my head back on
straight and decide what to do. This is tough, Bud. It's
real hard to have to relive all this right now."

Bud shook his head and gazed out over the lake. He
didn't say anything for a minute or two. "Okay, God,
I'm sorry." He swiped his hand over his jaw, and I realized he was unshaven. I'd never seen Bud unshaven. I
didn't know it was possible. "I got all bent out of shape
when I saw him sittin' here like some kind of spider in
his web, gettin' you all tangled up in his shit. I thought
you hated his guts."

"He's not as bad as I thought." That sounded so damn feeble that even I was embarrassed.

"Yeah, right." Bud looked away from me, then stood up and paced, hands on his hips. I knew then something bad was coming. I just didn't know how bad.

"The LAPD got an ID on the body out there."

"Already?" I was surprised it had happened so soon, and I didn't like the look on Bud's face.

"The bad news is that you probably know her."

I felt my mind recoil. Not again. I waited, afraid to ask.

"Her name is Freida Brandenberg. They said the two of you joined the force at the same time. That right?"

I nodded, thinking of the tough blonde with a dead-eye's aim on the shooting range. My heart fell when I remembered the two towheaded little boys she was so proud of. "I didn't know her very well. We went through the academy together. I haven't seen her in a long time."

"She disappeared while out runnin', and they ID'd her fingerprints."

I didn't think I could feel worse than before, but I did. Bud's next words clinched it.

"Now for the really bad news. I hate to be the one to tell you this, but Charlie's takin' you off the case." He stopped in front of the sofa and looked down at me. "Not just because of the publicity with Black, but because you know this victim. He said it's just a formality. You'll go on paid leave until things calm down. You should've told him about what happened in Los Angeles. He's mad as hell and fendin' off calls from all over the place, includin' the governor's mansion. That's why he sent me out here instead of comin' himself."

"If he'll give me a chance, I can explain."

"I gotta get your gun and badge. I'm sorry, Claire."

For a single moment, I couldn't believe it was happening; then I thought, *Well, why not? Everything else is falling apart. It's a temporary thing,* I told myself then, *paid leave until he hears my side of the story. That's not too bad. He'll reinstate me.* Where was all that female bravado when I needed it? I stood up and walked to where I'd left my bag on the bar. I got out my badge and tossed it to him.

"Man, I feel two inches tall," he said as I reached under my tan linen blazer, pulled the Glock out of my shoulder holster, and handed it over. I felt completely naked. I hadn't gone anywhere unarmed since I'd left California the first time.

"This'll blow over," he said. "Charlie's furious with you, but you know him. He gets over things after he's had time to think. Once he gets you in to explain what went down, he'll change his mind about this."

"Yeah, let me know when he cools down, and I'll come in and talk to him."

Bud nodded and paused a minute, but there wasn't much else to say, so he left, but I'd be damned if I'd cry. I'd quit crying a long time ago, hadn't felt anything in a long time, but I was feeling something now.

"Bud told me, Claire. I'm sorry."

Black was back, standing in the doorway and watching me. He was always watching me, as if I were a ticking time bomb, for God's sake. I had a feeling he was on the right track this time. I found myself wanting to collapse in his arms and quickly nixed that idea. Yeah, right, that'd make me feel great. "I'm okay. I've gotten through a lot worse than this. This is nothing."

"I know you have. You've proven yourself to be a strong woman."

I waited for him to ask me if I wanted to talk about it. I knew it was just a matter of time before he played doctor with me. Maybe I wanted him to insist on it; maybe I wanted my head to be probed and examined and analyzed. Maybe I didn't know what to do, or say, or feel. Maybe I was crazy.

"Let me know if you need anything," he said after a few moments of uncomfortable silence. "I'll be down the hall, in my office."

LIFE AFTER FATHER

Once, just outside Gulfport, Mississippi, on the highway that ran along the Gulf of Mexico, Brat was almost pulled over by a highway patrolman. But the brown Crown Victoria with blue flashing lights went ahead of them, speeding off after a black Cadillac that had passed them going eighty miles an hour. Brat never exceeded the speed limit; the new woman and the mother didn't like to speed. So they drove slowly and carefully along, and once, Brat took a job in a funeral home to help with the embalming. The funeral director was amazed at the skill Brat showed at such a young age and paid well, although the three of them didn't really need any more money. It was fun being around dead people in cold rooms again, like a family reunion, and once, Brat stole a black lady out of her coffin right before it was locked up for burial. The mother and the blond-haired woman were pleased to have a new friend.

Finally, Brat found the next person he was looking for. It was on a big lake, and the young man was dressed in a white T-shirt and swimming trunks and was fishing on the bank. Brat had followed him from his house and lay belly-down in the bushes, watching and swatting at gnats. When the young man stripped off his shirt and jumped in the water, Brat made sure that he couldn't see how Brat eased into the water, too. The young man was a pretty good swimmer, but Brat was strong, too. The water felt cold against Brat's naked body, and the cleaver was heavy as Brat came up behind the young man chosen to die.

The young man never saw Brat because he swam with his head down in the water, and it was easy for Brat to come up behind him and bring the cleaver down hard enough against his bare back to sever his spinal cord. The body twitched and floundered and bled, but Brat dragged it back to shore, hacked it up, and put all the pieces in a blue rolling Samsonite suitcase he'd bought the day before at Kmart. That was the day Brat realized it wasn't as messy to kill in the water, because there was no need to clean up. The liquid heat dissipated, and Brat felt good about this latest accomplishment. Their little family was growing by leaps and bounds. Now there was a brother, too.

The next day Brat burned some parts of the young man's body and reported into work at the funeral home.

Six months later, Brat killed the young man's wife. She always drove her teenage girl to school every morning and then returned home and stayed in the little white house with the porch swing for the rest of the day by herself. Brat watched every day for a month from across a busy highway, in a parking lot of a McDonald's restaurant. Then one day when it was raining hard and everyone was running for cover with newspapers over their heads or umbrellas, Brat ran into the backyard of the wife's house. The back door was unlocked, and once he was inside, the sound of a radio playing was all he could hear. The hot river boiled up, higher and higher, and Brat could almost hear the mother and the sister and the brother saying, "She's the one, she's the one, kill her, kill her, we want her in our family."

The lady was in the bathtub, just sitting there soaking, and Brat tiptoed up behind her and held her head under the water until she quit thrashing and splashing water all over the place. There was a razor on the edge of the tub, and Brat placed her hands under the water so the blood wouldn't spurt up and took the sharp razor blade and made a cut so deep on her wrist that her hand flopped down. The water quickly turned red and looked like the river of fire inside Brat, and Brat watched it for a while, fascinated, weak with satiation from the heat burning inside. When someone came in the front door and called the lady's name, panic surged, and Brat jumped up and fled out the back door into the pouring rain. Terrified of being caught, Brat drove quickly to the silver travel trailer. The others were disappointed that Brat hadn't brought a new friend, but they understood and forgave Brat. There were lots of others out there just waiting for Brat to make friends with them.

Brat was eighteen.

24

After Bud left Cedar Bend with my badge and weapon, Nicholas Black saw fit to make himself scarce. Maybe that was because I immediately retreated to a big, quiet guest bedroom at the far end of the wing, as far away from him as I could possibly get, and shut the door. He could take hints with the best of them. In fact, I didn't trust myself to be around him in my present mood. I'd been devastated before, lots of times, and I knew what I needed to do. Bury myself in a deep, dark hole and lick my wounds.

The chemistry between Black and me was alive and well, but it wasn't going to jump into a higher gear just because I was down on my luck. Maybe some other time, some other place. But here, now, in the middle of a murder investigation with him, the suspect, and me, the detective, it had complicated everything and knocked me off the case.

So I lay on the bed and stared at the ceiling for a long time. I thought of my dead son, my dead husband, the dead woman who died while baby-sitting my son that awful night, my dead friend Freida Brandenberg, and lots of other dead people. I wished I was dead, too, for a while, until I got sick of my morbid thoughts and jumped out of the bed. I thought I'd learned to cope, but this time it was different. This time I couldn't shut it down. Worse, I couldn't let go of the anger forming into a hard, tight knot in my chest and eating away at my insides.

I stood inside a huge black marble-and-glass shower enclosure under almost scalding water for so long, my skin came out red and wrinkled. When I entered the bedroom again, a bunch of shiny black boxes were stacked on the bed, all with the raised gold Cedar Bend logo on the top. Inside the boxes, I found enough clothes to last me a month, all in my size, including a red silk gown and matching robe. Looked like Black was still playing caretaker. Somehow that made me angry and resentful, but hey, everything was making me angry and resentful.

I put on the silly red getup and burrowed into bed again. Where the hell were Black's little white tranquilizers when I needed them? I ignored the big silver tray of fresh fruit and cheese and crusty bread someone had left on the bedside table. The same silent phantom who'd left the clothes, I suppose.

Black was being thoughtful, I guess, providing for all my needs but leaving me strictly alone to work through my problems. Which was exactly what I wanted, but maybe it wasn't what I wanted. I didn't know what I wanted, except not to think anymore.

By the time midnight announced itself on the bedside ebony-and-crystal clock, I was pacing the floor, my emotions in a jumble, my numbness turning into rage at everybody and everything.

I decided maybe I didn't like being alone so much after all, so I opened the door and walked down the hall to Black's private office. The door was open, a dim light coming from the lamp on his desk, where he was sitting and sorting through newspaper clippings. Clippings about me. I guess he was starting his own personal scrapbook with separate pages for every awful thing that had ever happened to me. I saw red and decided not to keep my feelings to myself.

"Well, well, let me guess. I bet all those newspapers are about little old me and my so sad life. Tell you what, you can quit snooping into my past on the sly. I'm here now in the flesh, in this cute little nightie you picked out, your latest head case reporting for duty." Not very nice, but somehow it made me feel better.

Black looked surprised to see me. Then he looked wary and for good cause. Maybe it was the scowl all over my face, which said I might be going to kill him. No gracious mood anywhere in sight. I guess he decided to ignore my sarcasm, because he remained quite calm.

"I hope you're feeling better now."

"Oh yeah, I'm much better now. Now it just feels like somebody ran over me with a cement truck. How do you feel, Doctor? Is your blood pumping hard with professional glee now that you know what a basket case I am?"

He stood up. Frowned, concerned, but that didn't stop his eyes from dropping down to the plunging front of the sexy little number I had on. "Have you eaten anything today?" Maybe he was just looking at my empty stomach.

"For some reason, I lost my appetite. Wonder why? You're the shrink. Why don't you tell me?"

"You've been through a lot. You need to eat. Why don't we go down to the kitchen and see what we can find?"

"What, Doctor? You don't want to stick your pins in me?" I waited a beat to see what he'd say. He said nothing, and that made me even angrier, as did the cautious way he was looking at me, like I had a bomb strapped on under my slinky attire. Somehow I knew I was taking my frustration and pain and anger out on him, even that it wasn't fair, but I couldn't help it. I needed to jump on somebody, and he was the closest, I guess. Hell, he could take it; he was a psychiatrist. "Let's see, where should we begin? What should I do first? Lie down on the *dreaded* couch, maybe? Or should I go over these nice little inkblots you hang around your office to help you spot the crazies?"

I turned to the wall where the framed inkblots were displayed and contemplated them, tilting my head and placing a forefinger under my chin. Sometimes I could get obnoxious down to an art form. "Wow, these are just fascinatin', Doctor Black."

Black said nothing again, which annoyed me some more.

I said, "Maybe we should finish what we started on the dock. Everybody in the whole US of A thinks we're having an affair. Maybe we shouldn't disappoint them."

"Is that what you really want?" he asked quietly. Man, now he was tiptoeing around me like I was a split personality or something. Maybe that's what he thought, that this latest catastrophe in my life had sent me plunging headfirst over the edge, and I had turned into my uncivil, unpleasant alter ego. Maybe he had a straitjacket hidden under his desk, just in case I went nuts.

I didn't answer his question, because I wasn't sure that's what I really wanted, wasn't sure why I'd just asked him to make love to me except that I just wanted him to do something to make me quit hurting inside.

He crossed the room until he was a few feet away and stood staring at me. He stuffed his hands in his pockets and said, "I'm not sure this is the best time for that. But I'm here for you. I'll help you any way I can . . . we don't have to jump into bed to make you feel better."

I stared at him for an instant and felt pretty damn humiliated by his polite rejection. I hid all that with an uncaring, unaffected, huh-uh-I'm-perfectly-in-control little laugh. I clamped my teeth and shoved my fingers through my damp, uncombed hair. "Well, Doctor, I should've known you'd turn me down flat. It's just been that kinda day."

Again, he was silent. Again, I was pissed. I guess I needed somebody to hold on to, and he was balking, wanting to analyze me instead. Maybe I could go down on the dock and pick up Tyler.

"Why don't you tell me exactly what went down that night with you and your husband and Harve? The newspaper clippings aren't very detailed."

"They always seemed plenty detailed to me."

But the question brought awful pictures back into my mind of my little Zack lying lifelessly in my arms, of Harve on life support. I shut out those images and perched on the back of a white divan, where he could get a better glimpse of the lacy, low-cut gown underneath the red robe. He obliged me by glancing at my cleavage, then looked at me with a question in his eyes that asked why I was baiting him, and I wondered the same thing. It wasn't my style. Well, maybe it was sometimes. I felt out of control of myself, and I was so angry inside that I couldn't stop with the attitude.

He sat down in a big leather armchair and crossed his long legs, the picture of serene, controlled manhood.

"If you're so interested in my story, maybe I ought to just set up house here with you and let you play Freud games all day and all night. Is that what you had in mind? Maybe I could be the star in your next book, huh, Doctor Black? What do you say?"

His jaw got all tight and started flexing, and I thought I'd finally gotten to him, until he spoke, still calm, still pleasant. "I think you hide behind jokes and sarcasm like you're doing right now, so you can bottle up all the real emotions you're feeling. Then you feel nice and dead inside, just the way you like it. You've got defense mechanisms built on top of defense mechanisms until you can't function like a normal person. I think you've made your job your whole life, because you won't let anybody within two inches of your feelings. And now your job's been pulled out from under you, and you feel alone and lonely and miserable and angry, but that's the way you like it because you're so full of survivor guilt, you think you deserve the bad things that happen to you."

I didn't like hearing any of that. "Here we go at long last: Super Psychiatrist flexes his muscles and heaves a five-cent diagnosis over his head. Bravo, Doctor." I clapped my hands.

"That's right. I am a psychiatrist, and that's exactly what you need at the moment, whether you can admit it or not. You need to talk this out and let someone help you before it completely destroys you."

"I'm not going to weep and rend my clothes, if that's what you're thinking. Sorry, been there, done that."

He frowned. "Why don't you just explain why we're going through all this? You came down here to find me; you obviously want to talk about it."

The fury inside me was building and I hated the way it felt. I hated the way I was acting. Why didn't I just leave and go back to my room? Or just get dressed and go home? Maybe I should talk about it. Maybe it would put out the magma fire burning under my breastbone.

"Okay, what would you like to hear first about the worst night of my life? Would you like to hear how my ex-husband looked after my 9mm blew a hole through his chest? Or would you like to hear how the lady who was keeping my baby that night looked after my husband beat her to death with a baseball bat and kidnapped my baby?"

Black didn't move a muscle, and our eyes held as my voice involuntarily dropped to a whisper. "Or how Harve looked hooked up on all those tubes and monitors at Cedar Sinai, with a bullet lodged in his spine? Or, most terrible of all, how Zackie, my little baby boy—"

I couldn't go on, not about my son, and I felt my arms and legs begin to tremble. Sick inside, I clamped my eyes shut and wrapped my arms around my shoulders, my anger dying away. I tried to get hold of the pain that held me every day and every night when I thought of him lying limp and tiny in my arms, and of the way his blood soaked my uniform on the way to the hospital, his big blue eyes staring up at me, hurt and confused, until they closed forever.

I felt Black's hand on my back, and I stiffened under his touch.

"Please, Claire, let me help you get through this."

"You'll never see me cry." I don't know why I always said that, but somehow it helped keep me dry-eyed and in control. "Nothing will ever make me cry again." I shivered all over and felt cold, suddenly drained of anger and energy and even pain. "I'm just so tired, that's all, tired of thinking about everything. Can you help me not to think about it? That's what I need from you."

He pulled me into his arms, and he felt strong and solid and like a haven to sink into. I put my arms around his waist and rested my cheek on his chest, then held him tightly, needing someone to cling to just for a little while. He stroked my hair and turned my face up and put his lips on my mouth, soft, tentative. My arms came up around his neck, and we kissed until it deepened into a release of our mutual emotion. Then the bad things came spiraling back into my head, and I pushed away.

Instantly, he dropped his grip on me and stepped back, giving me space. I kept my palms braced against his chest, separated but still connected. "I can't do this," I said. "People who love me end up dead, or hurt, or missing. I'm dangerous . . . You need to know that."

"It's already too late," he said.

We stared at each other a long moment, and then I went back into his arms. After that, neither of us thought much about anything but the warm, naked skin under our mouths and hands, and I held on to him desperately throughout the heat and urgency of our lovemaking, as if he were my only lifeline to sanity.

Later in his bed, Black slept peacefully, his arms loosely around me. I lay awake, worried, but glad, too. Tonight we had made our relationship even more complicated than ever, but I'd opened up to him in a way I never had to anyone else, and it felt surprisingly good. The knot in my chest had loosened a little, and when Black turned in his sleep and pulled me closer, I closed my eyes and snuggled into his bare chest. Who knew, maybe he could help me come to terms with myself. Maybe tomorrow I might tell him about the horrible nightmare that was my life.

25

When I woke up the next morning, Black was sitting beside the bed, fully dressed, black pin-striped Italian silk suit, starched white shirt, solid gold cuff links, in full regalia, ready for important things. We shared coffee and croissants and great big strawberries and smiled at each other a lot, but we didn't say anything much that meant anything. Maybe he was as uncertain as I was. Then he left, and I went back to bed and slept for about five hours. And I felt a hell of a lot better.

He called a couple of times to check on me, which sort of pleased me, and said he'd be back in time for a late dinner with me. I said, "Make yourself at home, really, I mean it," and he laughed, and then I fell asleep on the chaise lounge in the shade for four or five more hours. Yes, I was sleep deprived, and I had grown accustomed to the pleasure of being unconscious.

I didn't wake up again until I heard Black enter his office. I was lying on a big, wide leather sofa, covered with a black velvet blanket. It was dark outside, and I hadn't turned on any lights, so he didn't see me at first. I watched him snap on his desk lamp, then shrug out of his dark suit jacket, loosen the top buttons of his still-crisp white shirt, then jerk off his gray tie and head for the wet bar. He got out a bottle of Scotch and set it on the counter. He poured a short glass and knocked it back as if he needed it.

I said, "Do you work this hard all the time?"

He turned quickly, and I sat up on the couch, still half hidden in shadows. He looked distinctly relieved. "I thought you'd gone home without telling me. Nobody's seen you for hours."

"I fell asleep on the balcony, then came in here at some point. I've been trying to think everything through, the way you suggested."

He poured himself another drink, walked over, slouched down in the wing chair beside the sofa, and propped his foot on his knee. He rested his glass on the arm of his chair, but he didn't offer me one. "And?"

I'd been thinking about him all day, about us, about what I really wanted. And what I wanted was to be honest with him, quit hiding inside myself as he accused me, and if he could help me feel better about myself like he said he could, I was all for it. "You changed something in me last night. I can't figure out how you did it, and I don't know if I like it or not. But I think I do like it."

Black grinned, and I could tell it was genuine. I felt the urge to pull him down beside me and forget about everything else. Maybe that was because he was one hell of a good lover and made me feel things I'd never even dreamed of, or maybe it was more than that.

"Well, I know a good thing when I see it," he said.

"Speaking of news, have you heard anything else about the case?" I had a feeling I'd changed the subject because of the growing intimacy. Black would probably call that a defense mechanism.

"The networks can't get enough of it. We can turn on the television and listen to the experts if you want."

"You've been one of those experts, haven't you?"

"Yes, I have. At times."

I watched him watch me, but the quiet was not too bad or too uncomfortable.

"I feel okay today," I offered after a while. "I slept all day, longer than I have in ages."

"I wish I could have stayed here with you."

I did, too. I thought of all the enjoyable things we did through the night, and I felt myself wanting to do them all again. I sat up and crossed my arms over my chest, somehow feeling vulnerable. "I realize I came on a bit strong last night. I apologize for that. I'm not very good at seduction. I guess I looked pretty silly, didn't I?"

Black gazed at me a second, then gave a wry-sounding laugh. "You're not too bad at it, considering what happened."

That both flattered me and embarrassed me, so I changed the subject again. "Did you see patients today?"

He nodded. "Yes, and any colleagues in Paris had some complications with a case we've got over there. We confer on patients a couple of times a week."

"Do you consider me your patient now?"

He hesitated, and that put me off a little. He sipped his drink and relaxed into the chair. "No, I'm too close to you now to be effective, but I have excellent therapists working for me that I can recommend whenever you decide you're ready."

"No way. I won't talk to anyone but you."

"Well, we can always talk." He grinned.

"That was pretty easy."

"I'm pretty easy in lots of ways." He picked up my hand and kissed the back of it, and I shut my eyes when he turned it over and kissed my palm. But I didn't pull away, and he threaded his fingers through mine.

I had to know, so I said, "You think I'm crazy, don't you?"

"No, I don't."

"Do you think it'd really help me to talk about everything, you know, what happened back then and other things that I went through earlier in my life?"

"Have you talked about these things to anyone before?"

"No."

"Then, yes. I think it'd be helpful."

"Do I have to lie down on the couch?"

"No. We can talk wherever you want."

"Will you lie down on the couch with me?"

I was teasing, but it felt good to have him back, to have hope that I could actually grind to a halt the awful tape that had run nonstop in head for years on end.

"So long as you understand you're not my patient."

"What am I?"

"My lover, at the moment."

"At the moment?"

"As long as you want to be. I know I felt like a million bucks after last night."

"You may not after you get to know me better."

"I know you pretty well by now. I just don't know about your past."

"Do I get to ask questions about you, too?"

"Sounds reasonable."

I sat up, made room for him on the sofa, and Black set his glass aside and stretched out his long frame beside me. When he put his arm around me, I snuggled in close the way I'd done last night.

"You smell good, like the soap in my bathroom," he said. "You know, I think we'll do all our sessions like this, or maybe even in bed. What do you say?"

"Sounds good. How do we get started?"

"I'm going to let you make up the rules. Who do you want to ask the first question? Me or you?"

Instead of answering, I plucked at the buttons on his shirt, and when it gaped completely open, I slid my hand over the warm, hard muscles of his chest. "Shouldn't we discuss your fee? Bud said you charge a thousand dollars an hour."

"Tell you what, I'll pay you a thousand dollars for every hour you lie here and touch me like that. Does that work for you?" He kissed the top of my head, and I felt something shoot through me that was closely akin to *whoopee*. There really was something about this guy. I used to think he rang my bell, but the truth was he melted my bell down to liquid metal.

I smiled and said, "Okay, go ahead. Do your magic, mighty voodoo doctor. Make everything right in my head."

"Where were you born?"

"Oh, God, you're not going to start with my childhood, are you? Like the shrinks do in every movie I've ever seen in my life."

"Everybody's a critic," he said.

I smiled again and threaded my fingers through the hair on his chest. There was no way he could have a body like he did without lifting weights. I wondered when he had the time. "In Dayton, Ohio. You?"

"Charity in New Orleans."

"Your bio says Kansas City."

"I put that out to distance myself from the Montenegro name." He pressed a kiss to my forehead and said, "You know, this is quickly going down as the most pleasant session I've ever had, bar none." Then he said, "I have one older brother, whom you met in the worst possible way imaginable, and who I promise will never order a hit on you, not under any circumstances. No sisters."

I smiled at that, but I knew he wanted to know more about my family. I felt myself going all tense and uncomfortable at the thought of getting into a subject I'd never discussed with anyone, not even Harve. It was hard, but I finally said, "One brother. No sisters."

"What's your brother's name?"

"Thomas."

"Where's he now?"

"I don't know. My mother took me and left home when I was little."

"How little?"

"Kindergarten age, I guess. Five or six, maybe. I can barely remember back that far. I vaguely remember him pushing me on a swing, I think, but it's all cloudy in my mind. That could've been someone else."

"Why'd you and your mother leave?"

I shifted in his arms, so uneasy now I thought about pulling away and standing up. I didn't like telling him these things. I guess I was afraid of what he'd think of me if he heard all the sordid details of my life. Just do it and get it over with. Scrape up enough courage and just tell him the truth, as ugly as it was. Instead, I mumbled a half-truth. "She didn't like to talk about it. She said we couldn't stay there any longer, so she took me away."

"She didn't take your brother?"

I shook my head. "She left him with my father. I don't know why. I never understood why he didn't come with us."

"Do you remember your father?"

"Hardly anything, really. I think he was a doctor, and I don't think we lived with him very long."

"What about when you were older? Did you ever see your father and brother again?"

I shook my head and heard my own breathing hard against his neck. Suddenly, I felt like I couldn't get enough air. Dammit, I needed to do this, I did, and I was going to get through it. Black was different than the other psychiatrists I'd been forced to deal with, especially the idiots in the LAPD. I trusted him now. He wasn't going to hurt me or throw me into an institution. "I heard once that both of them died in a fire, but I'm not sure. My momma died not long after we left them."

I wanted to stop almost as much as I didn't want to stop. I caressed Black's chest some more, then slid my palm down over his flat belly. Black sucked air when I hit pay dirt.

"You never saw either of them again?" He sounded breathless, and I knew why. He had certainly risen to the occasion, so I kept caressing him, ready to end the talking and do something much less painful.

"Huh-uh." I lifted myself on top of him and sighed when he slid his hands up under the green Cedar Bend T-shirt I wore and kneaded my naked back. My blood began to tingle.

"Where'd you go after that?" he said, pressing his hips up against me.

I smiled but answered his question against his mouth. I sounded all breathless and aroused, which was true, to say the least. "I lived in Florida for a while, with my aunt and uncle." I nibbled at his lower lip until he pulled my head down for a deeper kiss, and when it ended, I said, "Then I went to school in Louisiana, just like you."

"You went to college in New Orleans? Tulane, like I did?"

I kept up what I was doing, close to victory now. "No, LSU in Baton Rouge."

I heard his breath catch when I pulled back his head and began to kiss his throat. "I know what you're trying to do, lady, and it's working admirably."

"You must have a doctor's degree," I said, sitting up and settling myself atop him, then stripping my T-shirt off over my head. I tossed it behind me and knocked something off a table, but our eyes were locked when he put his hands around my waist.

"How about answering one more question before we move on to better things?" he asked.

"Okay. What?"

"How about frisking me one more time? You know, kick my feet out from under me and punch me in the stomach like you used to? That really turns me on."

"So you liked that better than you let on, huh? You seemed a little miffed about the handcuffs and holding cell."

"I didn't know you well enough then."

I said, "Get down on the floor, Black, and spread 'em."

"I will if you will."

I obliged him, with delightful results. Our first session together, all things considered, was a huge success.

26

Early the next morning Black took off again for a bunch of business and other shrink stuff, but around nine o'clock, when I was getting all depressed about the state of affairs and feeling all naked and vulnerable without my gun, I got a pleasant surprise. Dottie called me on my cell phone from downstairs and said she'd brought over the files on similar cases that Harve had promised to send Black.

I was sitting out on the breezy balcony alone, with a great big breakfast buffet warming under silver domes on the glass and wrought-iron sideboard, when Dottie appeared between sheer white draperies billowing around in the warm wind off the lake.

I jumped up as I was so glad to see her, and she ran over and gave me a tight, I-really-mean-it hug. I hugged her back, then held her at arm's length, where I could look at her. She seemed more darkly tanned than usual, with her blond hair woven into two long braids hanging over her breasts. The hairstyle gave her the look of a Nordic goddess. She wore the snug black T-shirt with the University of Missouri Tiger paw print across the front, which I'd gotten her for her birthday almost a year ago, orange fluorescent cutoff shorts, and black-and-white Adidas running shoes. The outfit looked good on her toned body.

Dottie gave me a brilliant smile that shone very white against her tan. Her gold hoop earrings shook when she looked around the balcony. "Where's the good-looking Doctor Black? Am I ever going to get to meet him again?"

"He's working, but he'll be back later." I blushed and felt like a jerk for some reason.

"Uh-oh, looks like the two of you are getting along pretty well."

When Dottie hugged me again, I laughed. "We're getting along a lot better than before. He's been great, putting me up here and keeping the media sharks at bay."

Dottie gave me a knowing look. "Is he good in bed?"

"Dottie, would you stop? Who said I'm sleeping with him?"

"You didn't have to say it. You're not calling him names, so that means you've done the dirty, right?"

"Stop," I said. "He's been very helpful, very attentive."

"Yeah, I'll bet."

We laughed together, but I really wanted to change the subject. "Are you hungry? Look at this setup we get every morning. You name it, it's under one of those silver domes over there."

"You know, don't mind if I do. I am hungry."

"Dig in." I really wasn't hungry at all, but I watched Dottie pick up a plate off the buffet table. She paused and gazed out over the lake.

"Wow, what a beautiful view."

"It's pretty nice out here. Black says you and Harve

are welcome to come out any time you want and use the Cedar Bend facilities. No charge."

"I guess that has something to do with you, right? Now that he's your lover man."

I didn't say anything. She wasn't going to worm any details out of me.

Dottie said, "Look at all those reporters out on the lake. What'd they do, sleep out in those boats? They can't see us up here, can they?"

"Not if we stay back here in the shade. Trust me, I know. Is the press still outside your house? I'm worried about Harve."

"Yeah, they're around. Today I snuck out in my kayak and paddled straight in to Black's private dock down there. Hope he doesn't mind. There was some hot young guy in a uniform out there who called up to you for me."

"That's Tyler. He's okay."

"Harve said to apologize for him for not coming, but he's not feeling so good since all this happened. He's pretty upset and didn't get much sleep last night, so I gave him a toddy. He's resting now, so I really can't stay too long. I'm going for a quick run with Suze, but I don't want to leave him alone more than a couple of hours." She grew serious. "What about you, Claire? Or, should I call you Annie now?"

"No, no. I'm Claire now. Making that change was important to me."

She nodded, and her pigtails shook. "You know, I never had a clue, not for the last two years. You and Harve are pretty good at keeping secrets."

I stood and watched her fill her plate with pancakes and bacon and fruit salad and just about everything else. Dottie had an amazing appetite, but she had just kayaked across the lake. I got us both cups of black coffee and icy glasses of orange juice and sat down beside her.

Dottie sipped her coffee and looked at me over the rim of her cup. Her gaze was very direct out from under long eyelashes she'd thickened with a lot more black mascara than she really needed. I hated make-up. It seemed silly to glob it all over a nice clean face.

I smiled. "I'm so glad you came by. I needed somebody to talk to."

"I know. I had to make sure you were all right. You know what a worrier I am. Harve wanted you and Doctor Black to have these files, anyway, so I brought them myself instead of messengering them over. Here they are, before I forget."

She unzipped the red backpack she'd carried in and took out a large brown mailing envelope and handed it to me. I placed it on the sideboard behind us and watched Dottie dig into her scrambled eggs.

After a while Dottie said, "Harve told me that you were decorated for bravery once out in L.A., when you saved another officer's life. He said you were one of the youngest officers ever to get that kind of distinction, and that's why they handled the deal with your family with kid gloves, out of respect for you, and all that."

Harve had been talking too much, but I shrugged. "Yeah, but the press ate me alive."

"I'm so sorry this had to come out again. But Harve said it was twice as bad the first time, when he was in the hospital all those months. Wish I'd known him then. I could've helped."

Yeah, those were dark, dark months, and I didn't want to talk about it and suddenly found myself wanting Dottie to leave.

Dottie touched her napkin to her mouth and frowned. "Now you're upset, aren't you? I shouldn't be talking so much about all this."

"No, it's okay."

"Here, have one of these yummy croissant rolls," Dottie said, selecting one and dropping it on my empty plate. "And this fruit salad is outta this world. You got to have some of this."

Dottie was feeling guilty about depressing me and was trying to make amends. To please her, I forked a chunk of watermelon out from among the cantaloupe and peaches and put it in my mouth. It tasted ice cold and sweet.

"Have you and Harve been watching the news channels?"

"Yes, but there's nothing much new this morning. They got a few shots of you and Black yesterday in the helicopter, but you couldn't tell who you were because of the tinted windows. I guess there'll be a few of me in my kayak tonight at six. That's how hard up they are. Next thing they'll get is Harve cussing out the windows at them." Dottie laughed.

"Tell him for me that we're going to get through this, just like we did last time." I sipped some cold orange juice and realized my lips were a little swollen from Black's mouth. I hoped Dottie didn't notice.

"Well, I guess I better shove off."

"If you want to, I bet Tyler would load up your kayak in one of the Cobalts and run you out to where you want to go."

"Thanks, but I need the exercise. Got to keep my muscles strong." She flexed biceps that were more than impressive, and then was gone.

I sat awhile in the shade, staring into space, then heard the helicopter approaching. I stood up and moved to where I could see the helipad and watched the chopper land. John Booker got off, and I saw Black walk out on the dock to meet him. They chatted as they disappeared from my sight.

Eager to see Black, I walked down the hall toward his office. I stopped short when I heard Black say, "Tell me what you found out about Claire."

At that point I decided blatant eavesdropping was not below me. I backed up a little to where they couldn't see me but I could see them.

"Maybe you oughta sit down first." That was Booker.

"Cut the suspense, Book. Just tell me."

"The lady has not enjoyed a carefree life. According to hospital records, Annie Rose Baker was born at Lucy Lee Hospital in Poplar Bluff, Missouri. Mother's maiden was Regina Ann Baker. Father's name was not listed."

I frowned because that wasn't true. I watched Black frown and put his hands on his hips. "That's not what she said. She said she was born in Dayton, Ohio." Which was the truth, I thought.

Booker said, "Okay, then she's lying to you. I've seen the hospital records."

I watched Black dig in a desk drawer and pull out a Missouri road map, but I did not feel guilty about not making myself known. Hell, they were talking about me, weren't they? Resentment was beginning to build inside me, as purple and black as the thunderclouds forming out across the lake. Black unfolded the map and spread it out.

"Poplar Bluff's down near the Arkansas border, almost in the boot heel." He looked at Booker. "What about her brother?"

"What brother?"

"The brother named Thomas."

"That's news to me. He doesn't turn up in any records."

Black stared at his investigator friend. "Are you telling me she fed me a pack of lies? Why would she do that?"

Booker frowned. "Why do you think, Nick? Maybe to get you off her back? Or mislead you? Listen, I got a lot of this from a lady who she and her mother lived with for a while. Her name's Fannie Barrow."

Black said, "What'd she say?"

Yeah, what did she say? Since I've never in my life heard of anybody named Fannie Barrow. John Booker was just full of bogus information about my life.

"She said she had an upstairs apartment she rented out back then. Nice old lady. Fed me homemade gingerbread and a glass of milk. She remembered the little girl's name was Annie, said she was a pretty little thing with long blond hair, but real shy. The father was a doctor named Herman Landers, and he was an embalmer or undertaker or something like that, but Regina, the mother, took Annie and left him and rented Fannie's place."

"Are you sure she never mentioned Regina's son?"

"No, just a little girl with blond hair. Okay, here's where it gets dicey. The father apparently died in a house fire, and then, not long after that, the mother, Regina, just up and disappeared. Nobody knew what happened to her."

I shut my eyes. Here it came in all the gory details. I hated the eager interest I heard in Black's voice.

"What happened to Claire then?"

"Mrs. Barrow said that Regina's younger sister, Annie's Aunt Kathy, came and got Annie and took her to Pensacola, where Kathy and her husband, Tim, were going to school at the University of West Florida."

"Did you check that out?"

"Oh yeah. Tim and Kathy Owens lived in a town called Ferry Pass, not far from the university. They took her in, all right. I saw it in the newspaper accounts about Regina's disappearance and how her poor little girl was left all alone in Fannie's upstairs apartment until her aunt and uncle took her home with them to Florida."

"How old was Annie when all this happened?"

"Around ten or eleven, I think. Listen to this: she lives with the aunt and uncle until Uncle Tim disappears when he's out fishing at some lake. Less than a year later, Aunt Kathy commits suicide, apparently overcome with grief for her husband."

"Good God."

"Cut her wrists in the bathtub. Annie came home from school and found her dead and soaking in blood."

I put my hand on the door frame to steady myself, remembering that terrible day like it was yesterday. Pain stabbed into me, but Black didn't stop with the questions.

"Claire told me some people around her had died. I thought she just meant her ex-husband and son."

Booker made a little whistle. "Yeah, and that's way too much as it is. Anyway, she got passed around in foster care awhile until she graduated from high school in Pensacola and got a full scholarship to Louisiana State University."

"She told me she went to LSU. She didn't lie about that."

"Really? Well, guess what? Annie's college roommate at Louisiana State died, too. Her name was Katie Olsen. She slipped one night and broke her neck on a flight of stairs. That was ruled an accident, too."

I shut my eyes and clamped my jaw. I'd suffered agony trying not to think about these things, and now John Booker was tossing the intimate details of my life around like handfuls of confetti. But I kept listening, hoping maybe he'd found out something I didn't know about myself, something I needed to hear.

"Go ahead, Nick, listen to the rest of this stuff, then tell me it's all coincidental. Annie quit college after the Olsen girl got killed and headed west and looked up her Uncle Tim's mother in Orange County. A lady named Margaret Owens. Margaret was recently widowed and mourning Tim's and Kathy's deaths and gladly took Annie in as part of her family. That's when Annie went through the police academy, graduated near the top of her class, joined the LAPD, got married to some guy named Todd Blue, and had a son she named Zachary. All in that order."

That was all true. But the worst was yet to come, and I wasn't sure I was up to hearing it told aloud in such a cold, unfeeling way. Or maybe that was the best way to hear it, without emotion and pain and guilt and remorse. I didn't move, couldn't.

"So there were no more accidents during this time?"

"You mean corpses? Not for almost ten years, then things blew up in L.A., and you already know about all that."

"I don't know how it went down, just that people died. Claire wasn't comfortable talking about it, and I didn't want to force her."

Booker said, "I talked to a friend of mine at the LAPD. He said that that guy you told me you met the other night, Harve? He was Annie's partner. Her husband was insanely jealous of Harve and accused the two of them of having an affair. Said somebody saw them together. Of course, they were always working together, but the sex part wasn't true, according to my source. Still, Annie'd had enough of Blue's possessiveness by that time, so she and Zachary moved back in with Tim's mother. Margaret watched the kid while Annie was on duty."

"So she went to live with her uncle's mother, who really wasn't blood kin?"

I took a deep breath and forced myself to stand still.

"That's right. I guess she didn't have any other family to turn to. One night the husband snapped. Nobody knows for sure exactly what set him off, but he bludgeoned Margaret Owens to death in her bed with a Louisville Slugger baseball bat then took off with Zachary. He found Annie and Harve on patrol, opened fire, and hit them both before they could take cover. When Harve got a slug in the spine, Annie shot Blue dead. She didn't know her kid was in the car. The slug went through her husband's body and hit her little boy in his car seat."

"Oh God."

Yeah, Black, oh God. That's exactly how it happened. And I've relived it so many thousands of times that it's a waking nightmare. I was in a nightmare now.

"I'm telling you, Nick, this girl's gotta be screwed up after all that went down. Then the media got into the act and hounded her until she finally packed it in and blew town. Nobody knew where she was for over a year, and I haven't been able to find out, either, then surprise, surprise, she turned up at the Canton County Sheriff's Department under an assumed name, just in time to investigate Sylvie's murder. You know the rest."

Black didn't say anything, so Booker went on. "Nobody has luck this hard. It doesn't take a Ph.D. in psychology to know when death follows somebody around like a shadow at night, there's usually a reason to suspect foul play. I'm no shrink, but I think she attracts a little too much death and destruction to people around her. Is she mentally disturbed in your opinion?"

When Black hesitated, I watched him closely, sick to my stomach and afraid to hear what he'd say.

"She's got some issues, but she's no serial killer."

"Well, if I were you, pal, I'd cut bait and watch that lady from afar."

"She could shoot somebody in the line of duty—she already has—but there's no way she's capable of cold-blooded murder."

Booker said nothing, which, of course, said a lot to me. Then, "Well, you're the shrink, Nick, not me."

"What about the mother's background? Regina Baker?"

"When she disappeared, the newspapers said she grew up in a little place called Hartville, Missouri. That's not far from here. Mrs. Barrow remembered a lady up there named Helen Wakefield. Helen came down to Poplar Bluff when Regina disappeared and stayed with Annie until Kathy and Tim picked her up."

Black was scanning the map again. "I can get to Hartville in under fifteen minutes in the chopper. What's that name again?"

"Helen Wakefield. Her phone number's unlisted, but she lives on a farm along a creek called Walls Ford near the Gasconade River. It's a small town. Probably anybody can give you directions to her house."

"I'm going down there. I want you to find out where Claire went that year she vanished. There's a state psychiatric hospital in Farmington, about an hour north of Poplar Bluff. See if she might've checked herself in there for treatment. She hates psychiatrists; maybe that's why."

At that point I'd had enough with the eavesdropping and decided that neither one of them was going to harass my Aunt Helen. I stepped into the room. "Yeah, I hate psychiatrists, all right, and now I have another really good reason to hate them."

Both men jerked around. I watched Black, and he had the decency to look as guilty as hell.

"Hello, Claire. I didn't see you come in. How long have you been standing there?"

"Long enough to know you had me investigated behind my back, and that your sneaky little friend, Booker, here, thinks I'm a homicidal maniac who killed everybody in my family. Who knows, maybe I am. Maybe I want to kill both of you at the moment. Maybe if I had my gun back, I would. And maybe you'd both deserve it."

"Let me explain."

"Oh, right, Black, an explanation is definitely in order. But hey, Booker has already pretty much summed up every hellish detail of my life. I guess I ought to thank you, Booker. Now it's out, and I don't have to lie on the couch and be analyzed anymore. You can attend the sessions with Black for me and let me know later if I'm sane or not."

"I think I'll take off now and give the two of you some privacy," said Booker to Black.

"Privacy, Booker? Coming from you? I wouldn't think you'd know the meaning of that word. Besides, why would you want to leave now? The fun's just getting started. Maybe you can watch the good doctor strap me into a straitjacket and give me a lobotomy."

"Claire, don't do this." Black kept his eyes on me as Booker left the room by a different door. Drop the bomb and then run like hell, the Booker family motto.

I was so angry I could barely breathe, but I had a handle on it. I wasn't throwing things. I hadn't slugged either of them. "I can't believe I actually trusted you. That I was trying to get the nerve to open up to you about all this, when all the while you had Booker out digging up dirt on me."

"I asked him to check into your past when we were in California. At that time I didn't expect you'd let me within ten miles of you, much less sleep with you."

"Yeah, after this, ten miles is way too close."

"You've got to be reasonable."

"Reasonable? Screw you."

I started to turn around and leave, but he was right there, grabbing my arm. "Don't do this. We've got a chance to find out why these things happened. Everything's out in the open, and some of this stuff just doesn't make sense."

"You're telling me that? I've lived with it, pal, ever

since I was little. You and Booker both think I've been killing people around me. You can't deny that, can you? Go ahead, ask me if I have blackouts where I don't know where I've been or what I've done, and terrible headaches that nearly break open my skull, and two or three other personalities that like to kill people."

"Do you have blackouts?"

"Oh, God, you *do* think I did these awful things, don't you? I bet you even think I murdered Sylvie."

"No, I think you lied to me last night about where you were born and about having a brother, when you don't, and I want to know why."

"I didn't lie about anything. That's what I was told. And I do have a brother. I don't know anymore what to think. I don't even know this Barrow woman that Booker found."

"There's a way we can find out. Maybe Helen Wakefield knows something."

"Aunt Helen doesn't know any more than I do. And you're not going to go down there and get her all upset."

"Watch me. My gut tells me she knows something that'll help you."

"If she knew something that would help me, she'd have told me about it a long time ago. No way. I mean it, Black; you leave her alone. I love her more than anybody in this world, and I'm not going to let you hurt her."

"I'm going down there to talk to her. You can either come with me or not, but I'm going to ask some questions that should've been asked a long time ago."

"You're a bastard."

"I can be."

I watched Black pick up the telephone and order the helicopter to be readied for flight. I felt helpless to stop him. I felt helpless, period.

But there was no way he was going to go see Aunt

Helen without me. And there was one question I wanted an answer to. "Do you think I'm capable of killing people and not remembering it?"

"No."

"What do you think?"

"I think that experiencing so much tragedy at such an impressionable age could lead to severe psychological problems. I've seen it before. Sometimes the child grows up to be a killer, or is tortured by multiple personalities or disassociative identity disorder. Sometimes they don't. Sometimes they just become hard-assed detectives with awful memories that give them headaches and keep them awake at night."

I said nothing, but what he said was what I wanted to hear.

"No, I've seen the anguish in your eyes, and the compassion and tenderness you're capable of. No, you're not a murderer. You might need some help dealing with the terrible things you've experienced, but you couldn't kill anybody in cold blood, and you couldn't abuse anybody the way Sylvie was tortured. No way."

To my utter shock, I wanted to weep with relief, but I fought down the emotion. "Give me the phone. It'll scare her if we set down a helicopter at the farm without her knowing what's going on."

Black handed me the phone. I punched in Helen's number and told her we were coming.

LIFE AFTER FATHER

Brat killed often after that, sometimes because a man he passed in a car resembled the embalmer or because they had long blond hair like the cook who'd left with the little girl, but most of the time, Brat killed because the mother got lonely and bored with the friends Brat brought home to her. They traveled everywhere in the silver travel trailer, all over the country, looking, looking, looking for the best ones to kill.

Once they found the perfect one in Louisiana, where long gray moss hung from live oak trees and everyone talked with a funny drawl. They found the girl living on the LSU campus, and the mother liked it there around so many young people, so Brat found a place in a KOA campground where lots of college students lived in trailers during the school year. For over a year they lived there and watched the college girl while Brat worked in a mortuary on Plank Road and often brought parts of special friends home to the mother. She always loved each and every one of them. At least for a while.

Sometimes Brat walked around on the campus with

other young people around the same age, and sometimes wanted to be in college like the rest of them. But that was okay. Dead people were the only ones you could trust; they were loyal and quiet and left you alone when you wanted to be alone. One day in April, Brat decided to kill the college girl and bring her home to the mother. For three weeks Brat followed her everywhere she went, and then one night, she came outside alone and walked across the campus to the bookstore. Brat trailed her back to the apartment building she lived in, and when she climbed the steps to the third floor, Brat grabbed her, with a hand over her mouth, lifted her up over the railing, and hurled her down the concrete stairs.

Someone sitting on a balcony on the first floor saw her fall and screamed, and Brat quickly walked away into the shadows. The fiery river began to cool then, and by the time the ambulance siren wailed, Brat felt hungry. Brat stopped the station wagon at Taco Bell on the way home and got two Chalupa Supremes, one for Brat and one for the mother.

Brat was twenty-three years old.

The next one was an old woman in her bed. They'd been in California for a year, and it had taken Brat a long time to find this one. She baby-sat a child when the mother was at work, and the mother was a police officer, so Brat had to be very careful. The neighborhood was nice and quiet, though, and everyone went to bed early so they could get up and go to work in the morning or take their children to school without being late. Thus Brat could walk the streets at will and peep in windows without anyone ever knowing it.

The old woman lived in a stucco house the color of peaches. There was a window open in the basement, and Brat used a small penlight to find the way upstairs to the kitchen. The house was silent. The first bedroom held a crib, and there was a light on the dresser that sent stars and moons reflecting on the ceiling. In the crib a pretty little blond-haired child of two lay sleeping. Brat thought it was a boy, but it might've been a girl. Brat watched it for a while and the way the light reflected off its tiny head. The fire started to burn, and Brat's hand tightened around the baseball bat.

A gasp sounded from the doorway, and Brat spun around as the old woman ran down the hall toward the back bedroom. Brat took off after her, swinging the bat as she grabbed at the telephone on the bedside table and continuing to hit her until she lay still. Brat got out the cleaver but stopped as an arc of car lights swung into the driveway and made a slanted pattern from the Venetian blinds across the wall behind the bed. The car lights went off, and a man got out. Brat heard the baby screaming then, and the man must have, too, because he ran up to the front door. Brat took off out the back door and across the neighbor's backyard, and the man came out with the crying baby and squealed off in the car. Brat took off in the station wagon in the opposite direction but could not stop shaking. Brat had barely gotten away this time.

"You're getting careless, and now I don't have a friend to talk to," said the mother later.

Brat was over thirty years old.

27

Cattle scattered beneath us as we skimmed the tree-
tops over my Aunt Helen's verdant pastures, looking for
the best place to set down. I felt a familiar sense of
peace roll over me. The farm below was the closest thing
I had to home and family, and I loved it. The property
was beautiful and rolling, with a high forested ridge rising over the far bank of a wide creek called Walls Ford.
A gravel road formed the other boundary, running in
front of Aunt Helen's farmhouse and barn. I could see
a white sheriff's car in the driveway. That would be the
Wright County sheriff, Daniel Harnett, who'd given us
permission to set a helicopter on the Wakefield property. Black finally selected a dirt clearing near the weathered gray barn and we settled to the ground gently and
he cut the rotors.

Removing his headset, Black fixed the controls and
turned to me. "You ready?"

We'd said next to nothing during the trip, maybe because I was mightily ticked off at him for being so cavalier about snooping around in my pain, not to mention
my life in general. He now seemed to think he owned

me and could do anything he wanted, whenever he wanted. Wrong. Time for a wake-up call, Black.

Truth be told, though, I actually felt better since some of this was coming out. And maybe because Black said he didn't think I was responsible for all the death I'd seen. Maybe I wanted somebody to tell me that I had nothing to do with the accidents so I could believe it myself. Maybe he was right that I shouldn't have kept it all buried inside me for so long.

But none of this was any of Black's business. I was still highly miffed with him for taking liberties with my life, so I said, "She's not going to know anything that I haven't already told you. You're wasting your time questioning her."

"It's worth a try. If nothing else, it'll give me a chance to meet somebody in your family."

"Well, I can promise you one thing, Black, she won't tie you to a chair and knock you in the lake, like your family did to me."

"I thought we'd worked through that."

"Nope." I opened the door and jumped out. I could see the sheriff in his dark brown uniform and my aunt standing next to him, wearing a pink dress, her white hair vivid against the blowing green trees. They waited at a metal cattle gate that divided the yard from the sprawling green pastures behind the house. Forty head of cattle bunched together a good distance away from us and looked collectively pissed off.

I ran ahead of Black and gave my Aunt Helen a tight hug, very glad to see her again. We talked on the phone sometimes, but it'd been months since I'd spent time on her farm.

"Well, aren't you something?" said Aunt Helen to Black when he walked up, still wearing his aviator shades. "Landing out here like a regular George W. Bush."

Black laughed and stretched out his hand. Aunt Helen

took it in her firm, no-nonsense grip, and they stared at each other, obviously measuring each other up. Then he shook hands with the sheriff. "I appreciate your letting me set down out here."

"Are you sure you're all right, Annie?" Helen held my hand and looked into my eyes. She was a pretty lady, well into her seventies, with the unlined skin of women from an era that didn't cherish suntans. Her blue eyes were fixed on me; then she looked at Black in a way that said: Don't you dare hurt Annie, or you're dead meat.

"It's started up all over again, Aunt Helen."

"I know. I've been watching it on the news. You'll get through this just fine. Last time made you strong enough for anything. You know that."

"That's right," Black said, putting his hand on my back.

Helen watched me move away from his touch, then cut her gaze to Black's face. "You haven't known Annie long enough, I reckon, to presume so much. Flashy types like you cause more trouble for a person than you're worth."

Black took that well, like a psychiatrist should. "Believe me, Mrs. Wakefield, hurting Claire's the last thing I'd ever want to do."

I took Aunt Helen's arm and walked toward the house with her before she and Black got into fisticuffs. "I'm so glad to see you again, Aunt Helen. Let's talk on the porch, where it's cool."

As we walked around to the open front porch, which ran the length of the old farmhouse, then wrapped around the far side, Sheriff Barnett bluntly asked Black what his business was in Hartville, listened politely—obviously scoping him out to make sure he could leave Black alone with his Wright County constituents—then said he'd be on his way. I thanked him and took a seat in my favorite place, a long white swing at the end of the porch. Black stood leaning up against a porch pillar.

"You have a beautiful farm here, Mrs. Wakefield." Doctor Nick Polite all of a sudden.

"Thank you." Aunt Helen was nobody's fool. She eyed him suspiciously, like he was going to steal her porch swing out from under me. But she was being polite, too. We were in the middle of a war of polite, but I was abstaining from civility until I heard what Black had in mind.

Aunt Helen said, "Would you like some lemonade? I've got fresh-squeezed this morning in the icebox."

"That sounds great," Black gushed.

Jeez. I looked out over the quiet, peaceful pastures.

After Aunt Helen disappeared into the house, Black said, "I don't think your aunt likes me."

"And that surprises you?"

Black was on his best behavior, so he ignored this. "It's really peaceful out here."

"That's why I come down here."

"Is this where you went the year you dropped out of sight?"

"Yes. I sat out here on this swing most of the time, just staring out over the fields. Everybody around here let me alone, and the media never found me. I love all this peace and quiet. I wish I could live here."

"I can see why."

Aunt Helen came back outside a few minutes later and set down frosty glasses of lemonade with lemon slices floating on top, a platter of her famous two-layer red velvet cake with cream cheese icing, white serving plates, forks, and white paper napkins with red hearts on them. While she cut the cake, she said to Black, "I believe I've seen you on my television set a time or two. You do that kind of work, do you?"

"Yes, ma'am. But most of the time, I'm just a doctor."

Boy, he *was* on his best behavior. *Ma'am*, and everything. I sure never heard him call anybody else ma'am.

Aunt Helen said, "What kind of doctor?"

"I practice psychiatry."

Helen questioned me silently with narrowed eyes that asked: *Quack?* Then she sat down on a metal rocking chair beside the swing. She folded her hands in her lap. "So what do you need to know from me?"

"I told him that you can't tell him anything more than I did, but he doesn't believe me," I said.

Black took a green metal chair across from us and leaned forward. "Mrs. Wakefield, I think you might be able to clear up some things about Claire's childhood that only you would know. She's been through more than any one woman should have to endure, and I want it to stop."

Helen looked troubled. "That's true, and her mother, too."

"Clarie doesn't remember much about her mother's disappearance."

I said, "I told you everything I can remember. If there's anything more, Aunt Helen would've told me a long time ago. Wouldn't you, Aunt Helen?"

When Aunt Helen leaned back in her rocking chair and clammed up, I dragged my foot and stopped the swing. Uh-oh.

"Aunt Helen? You have told me everything, haven't you?"

"I don't know. Maybe there are some things I haven't mentioned."

I knew at once she was hiding something. By the look on Black's face, so did he. He said, "Do you know what happened to her mother? Did she really just disappear?"

"Yes." Helen rocked gently. "Did Annie tell you we're not really blood kin, Dr. Black?"

"No, something else she just forgot to mention."

"I didn't see any need to mention it." But I felt edgy and nervous, afraid I was about to be buried under another avalanche of hurt.

Aunt Helen looked at Black. "Annie's mother, Regina, was best friend to my daughter, Linda, all through their high school years."

Black said, "Did Regina's family live around here, too?"

"Used to, but most of them are dead now. Father was a minister, a good man but strict as fire with those poor girls of his. Both of them got away from home as soon as they could."

I said, "Why didn't you tell me this, Aunt Helen?"

"I didn't see the need."

Black probed deeper. "Regina had a sister, right?"

"Yes. Kathy. She took her own life years ago. Annie, you found her."

"Yeah, I found her." I put my cake down on the table, suddenly not hungry anymore.

"I guess the time has come to tell you the truth, Annie. I guess I've been trying to protect you all these years, too."

"Tell me what?"

She sighed. "The truth is that long before you were born, your mother, Regina, ran off with a boyfriend home on leave from the Marine Corps. When the boy shipped out, she came back home, but her father, your Grandpa Baker, disowned her and threw her out of the house. That's when she came here and lived with Linda and me for a while." Aunt Helen took my hand. "And that's when she found out she was pregnant with you, Annie."

I couldn't move, couldn't believe she'd kept this from me all these years. Aunt Helen shook her head. "It was so different back then; you just wouldn't believe the way it was. Such a terrible stigma to be an unwed mother, especially when your father was a clergyman. So, before she got big enough to show, I got her a job cooking and cleaning for some friends of mine who ran a soup kitchen down in Poplar Bluff. They had a place where she could live safely while she worked there, and I knew the people were good-hearted and would do right by her. Regina wanted out of this town more than anything. She didn't want anyone here to know she was having a baby."

I blinked and stared at her, then blinked some more, having some trouble taking this all in.

Black said, "So that's where Claire was born? In Poplar Bluff?"

I said, "Why did everybody tell me I was born in Dayton, Ohio?"

"Your mother didn't want you to know the truth."

I just sat there. Black got up and sat down on the swing beside me.

"Linda and I kept in touch with your mother as much as we could, mainly by telephone. Her family never really accepted her back into the fold."

Black said, "And Annie's father? What happened to him?"

"He never made it back home, got killed in some godforsaken place."

"How could you not have told me all this? Why did you keep it a secret all these years? Who was my father? What was his name?"

"His name was Scott Parker. I didn't tell you, because I didn't see the need to go into all the sordid details of the past, especially when Regina went to so much trouble to conceal it. You'd suffered enough without hearing about the unpleasant circumstances of your birth."

Black said, "Booker found out that Regina eventually got married in Poplar Bluff to a man who was an undertaker. Is that true?"

Aunt Helen's blue eyes studied us both, and she seemed reluctant to reply. "Well, his name was Landers, and he was an embalmer. She worked for him a while, but I don't know for how long. He offered her a little house at the back of his property where she could live for free if she'd do some cooking and cleaning for him. She went to work there so you'd have a nice, safe place to play, Annie."

"I grew up with the Landers name. Does that mean he adopted me after he and Regina got married?"

Aunt Helen leaned back and studied a cow looking at us over the fence. She was hesitating again. Gee, this just got worse and worse. "Tell me the rest of it, Aunt Helen, please. Did he adopt me? Where is he now?"

"The fact is, dear, your mother never married him. She just worked for him."

"But I thought they were married. I had his name."

"Regina didn't marry him. She just told everybody up here she did, including her sister. She was ashamed and didn't want her family to know you were born illegitimately, so she took his name for the both of you. No one was ever the wiser after Landers died in a fire, and even before that, because apparently, the man was a recluse his entire life."

"Oh, my God, I can't believe this."

"Then your mother just up and disappeared one day. Regina went outside one night to smoke a cigarette after she put you to bed and just vanished into thin air. Thank God, her sister, Kathy, took you in."

Black said, "Do you think Regina deserted Claire?"

"No, never. She loved you more than life itself, Annie. She would never have left you alone like that. There was foul play involved, but the police never figured out what happened to her."

I said, "What about my brother?"

For the first time, Aunt Helen looked nonplused.

"Regina never had a son. Just you, Annie. You were her whole life."

"But I remember him; I know I do. And his name was Thomas."

Helen shook her head. "I don't know who you're thinking of. Regina never had another child."

Black said, "So this embalmer, Doctor Landers, died in a fire. Do you know what caused the fire?"

She shook her head. "Regina told me that he was very weird and strange acting. Lived in a spooky old house and did his embalming in the basement. Maybe the chemicals he used caught fire, or something like that. Regina said he drank too much whiskey."

I kept trying to remember any of the things she was telling us about, but I couldn't. It seemed impossible. "Are you sure there wasn't a little boy that lived with us or played with me? I remember him. I know I do."

"Well, you know, now that I think on it, Regina did tell me once that Doctor Landers had a son. That's right. She went on a bit about what a peculiar boy he was, always whispering and sneaking around. She said he gave her the creeps, but you might've played with him, Annie. I bet he's the child you remember."

"Did she call him Thomas?"

"I just don't remember."

I waited, growing anxious and resisting the urge to pace. "Please try to think."

Aunt Helen shut her eyes a moment; then she said, "I just don't know his name, but I seem to recall that he had a nickname, and it was something bad, like Snot or Jerk or something. No, I think it was Brat that they called him. Regina said Landers and the boy were both so strange that she finally quit working there and went back to cook at the soup kitchen."

Black said, "Claire, it's understandable that you thought Thomas was your brother, especially if your mother took the Landers name and told everybody she married the man."

"I guess so. I'm not sure about anything anymore."

"Is there anything else you can think of that might help us, Mrs. Wakefield?"

"I know she's not a jinx, like she thinks."

"A jinx?" Black said.

"Yes, that's why Annie wouldn't stay here for long, afraid something terrible would happen to me if she did. Of course, that's a bunch of hooey. So I suspect she'll try to push you away, too, especially since she obviously likes you. I hope you won't let that happen, Doctor, not if you truly want to help her."

"I'm not easily pushed around."

Still reeling from the revelations about my past, I listened to them talk around me, glad when my cell phone rang. I took it and walked a few feet out into the yard. Behind me, on the porch, Aunt Helen said, "She needs somebody with the training to really help her deal with all the losses in her life. She hates doctors, you know."

"Yeah, I noticed."

"That's probably because after Zachary died, her captain at the LAPD kept sending her to the police psychologists, and she hated them and said they were all quacks."

Nothing like having your soul stripped bare and flogged to death right in front of your face. I usually do pretty well until somebody mentions Zack, then I fall apart unless I push the memory down deep in the dark, where I don't have to deal with it. There are some things I have to keep buried if I want to survive, despite what Black thinks. It was going to take me a lot of time to sort through all this. I almost dreaded answering the phone for fear it was just the next piece of horrible news crouching in wait for me.

It was Bud. "Hey, Morgan. Where the hell are you?"

"Hartville, believe it or not."

"Thought you could use some good news for a change, so I gave you a buzz."

"You are so right on. Tell me quick."

"Charlie's thinking about reinstating you, so get your butt back home and wait for my call."

"What changed his mind?"

"I'll tell you when I give you back your badge and weapon. Just get back up here ASAP and stay close to your phone." Then he was gone.

I walked back to the porch, feeling like a brand-new person, with a spring in my step. Even the shock of Aunt Helen's revelations faded at the prospect of getting back to work. I couldn't quit smiling. "Gotta go, Black. Charlie's having a change of heart, and I just might be back on the job before the day's out."

"That's great," Black said with zero enthusiasm.

Aunt Helen, on the other hand, hugged me warmly and told me how happy she was that I was going back on duty. Then she said softly, so Black wouldn't hear, "I'm sorry I kept all this from you, Annie. I thought it was for the best; I really did."

"It doesn't make that much difference, but I'd like to know more about my real dad someday."

"I'll find out everything I can about him and call you," she said.

Black said, "Mrs. Wakefield, I don't know how to thank you. You've helped us a great deal. If you remember anything else, will you call me? I can give you a number where I can be reached at any time."

"Well, I guess you're going to gloat and be obnoxious," I said to Black after we'd left Aunt Helen and climbed back into the chopper.

He concentrated on adjusting his headset and strapping himself in. He handed me my seat belt. "I like your Aunt Helen. She's good people."

"Yeah, so what do you make of all this? It seems pretty strange to me, especially the fact that Helen kept it from me all these years. I don't understand that."

"She probably meant well. But something doesn't sit right about that guy Landers and his boy."

"What difference does it make? I'm just glad he's not my father if he was that weird. He's dead, anyway."

"I still want Booker to check it out, see if the boy's alive somewhere. This time I'm asking your permission first. What do you say?"

"Do whatever you want. All I care about is getting back to work. Let's go."

Black took the controls, and as we lifted off and scared the hell out of Aunt Helen's cows again, I lifted my hand in farewell. Aunt Helen stood waving good-bye beside the fence, her dress whipping around in the wash of the rotors, her other hand holding down her blowing hair.

28

We made it back to Cedar Bend ahead of a massive storm front that promised strong wind and rain from the thunderheads building in great blue-black mounds over the entire south end of the lake. The air was heavy with humidity and full of the smell of rain and heat and ozone. I sat outside on Black's balcony, with my cell phone on the table right in front of me, and tried to will it to ring. Black was inside his office, canceling some appointments so he could keep me company. I told him not to, that I wasn't going to be staying much longer, but he ignored me, as usual.

I had crime scene pictures spread out in front of me and was trying to read through the reports Dottie had brought over, but all I really wanted was to hear the "Mexican Hat Dance" song. When it finally started up, I grabbed for the phone so fast, I almost knocked it off the table.

"It's a go, Morgan. I'll pick you up at your house in thirty minutes, weapon and badge in hand. Got it?"

"Got it."

I smiled, absolutely ecstatic, until Black walked outside and I saw the expression on his face.

He said, "I take it that was Bud."

"Yes. I'm meeting him at my house in half an hour. I'm now officially reinstated."

"Congratulations." Again, he clearly wasn't thrilled out of his mind at my good fortune.

I changed the subject. "I've been going over the crime scene reports Dottie left, trying to find something that ties them all together."

Black changed it back. "I guess this means you're shoving off?"

Yeah, that pretty much was what it meant, so I began to gather up the papers strewn all over the table. I spent some time stacking them all nice and neat and orderly and not looking at Black.

I hesitated, feeling guilty somehow. Then I decided to just get it over with. "Look, I appreciate everything you've done for me, I really do. I was wrong about you from the beginning, but it might be better to cool it between us as long as I'm working on this case."

"So that's it? Tough luck, Black. Nice meeting you, but I don't need you anymore, so kiss off."

"Don't make this difficult. I'm going to concentrate on solving Sylvie's murder. That's the best thing I can do for us—find the killer and bring him in—and then we'll see where we stand. Next time they could pull my badge for real. Surely, you understand that?"

"And I'm supposed to sit here and do nothing until you decide if you want to come around again?"

"I guess that's about it. Let the police handle it. I'll keep you informed."

Black stared hard at me for a moment, then said, "Okay, Claire, if that's the way you want it. Let me know if you need my help on anything else. Take one of my

Cobalts home. It'll outrun any reporters following you."

First, I was surprised, then relieved that he didn't plan to cause some kind of ugly, recriminating scene.

"Okay, I'll leave these reports here for you if you want. Thanks for lending me the boat. Thanks for everything; I mean it."

"Yeah. I'll call down to Tyler."

I left in a big hurry, feeling like a heel because I was so unabashedly eager to get home and meet Bud. Tyler had the boat gassed and ready, and within minutes I was away from Cedar Bend and on my way. The lake was choppy, the sky almost black and low with storm clouds roiling over the hills around the lake. It felt good to be out on the water, and I bounced over the waves at full throttle.

The wind whipped through my hair, and I prayed that Harve had been able to shut the media out of our private road. Everybody thought I was with Nick Black now, and the paparazzi would stick to him like glue. Now it was easy for me to understand why he'd bought a resort down here, away from major news outlets. But Bud should be waiting for me at my house, and he'd clear out any pushy reporters hanging around long before I even got there.

As I rounded a jut of land and headed into my cove, I saw Bud's white Bronco parked at my dock. He was leaning against the front fender, totally immaculate as always, both hands stuffed in his pants pockets. No reporters in sight. I smiled, pleased to see him. Things could get back to normal now. Black's face filled my mind, and I recalled the way he touched me, the way my body responded to him, his determination to make me face my past. He'd helped me already, making me get it out and talk about it. *Stop it, Claire. Put him out of your thoughts and focus on the case.*

Bud strode down the planks to meet me with his usual loose-limbed saunter and easily caught the lines I tossed to him. He was wearing his sheriff's department rain slicker, and I wished I had mine. I hadn't been able to find it for at least a month. Guess I was going to get wet.

"Another of Black's baubles, I presume?" he said, looking the boat over. "Wow. Think he'll give me one, too, if I bat my long eyelashes and say 'pretty please'?"

He was grinning, so I let it pass. "It's borrowed. Got my stuff?"

Bud held up a blue plastic grocery bag as I stepped onto the dock. "You're back in business, Detective."

"Thanks." It felt good to pull out my badge and clip it to my belt. It felt even better to have the weight of the Glock under my palm. I shrugged into my leather shoulder holster and slid the gun into place and felt whole again. "Okay, what's this all about? Charlie wouldn't put me back on this soon if something hadn't gone down."

"They found another body in Ha Ha Tonka State Park. He wants us both at the scene, pronto."

"Same M.O.?"

"Yeah. Decapitation, silver duct tape, the little, half-round flesh cuts, the whole works. Charlie and the crime team are already there. The whole park's cordoned off."

"Let's take the boat. It's faster."

Ha Ha Tonka State Park was a big draw with the tourists, especially hikers and outdoor enthusiasts. It was heaven on earth for geologists who got off on sinkholes and craggy caves and walking across natural bridges and peering off soaring bluffs. It had miles of trails with spectacular scenery and the ruins of a turn-of-the-century stone castle hanging at the edge of a cliff overlooking both the Niangua River and Lake of the Ozarks. The castle drew lovers like a king-sized bed in Cancun.

Devastated by fire decades ago, the shell of the old castle became visible in the distance, and when Bud and I got closer, we could see the great granite bluffs rising out of the water and the castle's white stone water tower, which was still intact. I slowed the boat as we neared the lower parking lot at the entrance to the park. Ha Ha Tonka was Osage Indian for "Laughing Waters," but I had a feeling nobody was laughing at the moment.

I killed the motor and let the wash slide us up onto the sand. Connie O'Hara saw us and started walking down the rocky beach in our direction as we scrambled out of the boat. There were reporters gathering behind the yellow crime tape blocking off the entrance road, with three police officers keeping them at bay.

"How you been, O'Hara?" I said when she reached us. She didn't look so good, tired, as if she hadn't been sleeping.

"Don't much like what's goin' on around here." O'Hara glanced at the press. I could hear the distant drone of their voices. *Hey, everybody, another dead woman! Happy days are here again! Roll those cameras; dance those jigs!* O'Hara searched my face. "Thought that was a pretty bad scene that happened to you out in California."

"Yeah, thanks. I've got it together now. Where'd he leave the victim?"

"In the old water tower. They've been waiting for you before they bag her."

Bud had already started up the footpath that led to the castle. I caught up with him, and when we reached the upper parking lot, we took a right and the castle ruins loomed up in front of us. Looked like the last scenes of *Rebecca*, after Mrs. Danvers set fire to Manderley and burned herself up in it. A hulking shell of white granite and limestone, one wall still rose three floors, with the chimneys and window arches intact. I was surprised Black hadn't bought the place and restored it. *Stop it. Don't think about him.*

Officers lined the trail that led from the castle ruins to the crime scene. The water tower lay farther up the cliff, on a path that wound very close to a bluff that gave new meaning to straight down. We walked quickly along the weathered board walkways, which had been constructed with side railings for the safety of park visitors. I looked over the precipice and remembered that some guy had thrown his wife over the side into the deep blue-green spring bubbling below, but that was before my time. Unfortunately for the hubby, she got caught on scrub brush clinging to the side of the rocks instead of sinking forever into the water and out of his life. Foiled by nature. Wish this case was that easy.

Charlie Ramsay stood at the base of the fifty-foot water tower. An iron gate usually closed off the interior steps to discourage tourists and hikers from climbing to the top of the tower, but it was open today, the black metal chain and lock lying on the ground. It was a square stone structure, reminiscent of Tuscany bell towers or the English keeps of King Arthur's time. I half expected to see Merlin standing in one of the three windows high atop, a black robe with lots of crescent moons and stars swirling around him, his hands outstretched to work his wondrous magic. Or was that the guy in Harry Potter?

"Well. About time, Claire. Annie. Which is it gonna be?" People were definitely having problems knowing what to call me.

"Claire."

"You doin' okay?" Charlie added for my ears only. His way of apologizing for taking my badge. I nodded.

A couple of Missouri State Highway patrolmen were standing around inside. Dueling jurisdictions and clashing sabers. I recognized O'Hara's husband and gave him the obligatory solemn nod. He was a big, broad-shouldered man of German and Irish extraction, who looked like he should be on top of the Matterhorn wearing a black-and-red argyle sweater and blowing on a long pipe about cough drops.

I concentrated on Charlie. "Is it Brandenberg's head?"

He made a little shrug, took a nervous draw on the pipe he was holding. "Young woman. Blond. Sorry, you'll have to ID her."

I said, "Okay, but I haven't seen her in years." I saw Shag inside, edging around the body with his camera. He moved to his right, and I could see the body propped against the back wall, long blond hair flowing down over the face and nude torso. This time the duct tape was crusted black with blood. I could see some of the little half-moon wounds cut into her breasts and stomach. He'd struck again, all right, and right under our noses.

"Have they moved her?"

"Not yet."

Bud and I slipped on gloves and protective booties and watched where we stepped. There was a lot of blood pooled around inside. The enclosure was about twenty feet by twenty feet, and a flight of steps led up into the tower. Nothing was in the room except the victim. She sat on the dirt floor, looking straight at us. It looked like the perp had combed her hair down over her face. I recognized the duct tape and the tilted angle of the head.

"He must've taken a vacation in sunny Southern California, killed Brandenberg, then brought her head back here for this one." Bud scratched his chin. "He targeted an old friend of yours for a reason. Do you think he's after you because you're investigating?"

"I don't know." I looked at Charlie. "Has Gil Serna turned up?"

He nodded. "He finally showed up at a private rehab

clinic in Acapulco, Mexico. So he's pretty much off the hook. This victim's probably from around here, looks in her thirties, athletic. Should have been able to put up a fight."

I moved closer and squatted beside the body. Just like in the bayou, bluebottle flies had found the corpse and were everywhere, their buzz loud in the stone room. The heat was oppressive inside, and the smell of congealing blood was enough to rock me back on my heels. It was like being buried alive with the victim. "It's the same perpetrator, no doubt about it."

Shag nodded. "The tape's wrapped the same. I think it's the same roll. We finally got the L.A. evidence, and it matches up, too. This perp gets around. Likes blondes with long hair, like me." He grinned. Halfheartedly, though, no Ha-Ha in the Tonka today.

"Are you ready to pull back the hair?" Charlie said to Shag.

"Yeah."

Bud lifted it up and held it, and my breath left me. I looked away. The face was damaged some and smeared with blood, but I recognized her. "Yeah, it's Freida."

"Are you certain?"

"Yes, she had that scar on her chin. She gashed it when we ran the obstacle course."

I was glad when an excited shout came from somewhere up the trail. I stood up, and backed away from Freida's staring eyes, and went outside, eager to get out of there. I sucked in fresh air. The wind was brisk now with the impending storm and heavy with the smell of rain and the sound of fluttering leaves.

"We found the victim's clothes," said O'Hara's husband. I think his name was George.

"Maybe he finally slipped up," I said, as a young deputy headed toward us with a brown paper evidence bag. "An ID on the body might tie him to the victim."

Bud took the bag and pulled out a red backpack, then unzipped it and took out a black T-shirt. I looked down at the T-shirt, then grabbed it out of his hands. My mind reeled in horror. I staggered back, my eyes on the fluorescent orange cutoff shorts that Bud pulled out next. Bile rose and burned the back of my throat, hot and caustic.

"What?" Charlie asked me. All the men looked at me, and when Bud took a step in my direction, I turned away and leaned over, bracing my hands on my thighs. I felt like I was going to throw up. "These are Dottie's clothes. Oh, my God, this is what she had on the last time I saw her."

"No, it can't be," Bud said, frowning down at the shorts in his hands.

I looked at the University of Missouri Tiger paw print on the shirt, brought it to my nose, and smelled Clinique, Dottie's perfume. I looked toward the water tower, visualized again the woman left in the dirt, the lean athletic body, muscled hard from kayaking and running and lifting Harve. "Oh, my God, it *is* her." Then I thought of Harve, alone at home. This would kill him. It was killing me. I put my palms over my face and took deep breaths until Charlie came up close to me. His voice was gruff. "You're absolutely sure? There are lots of shirts like this around here."

A glimmer of hope. *Please God, don't let it be her.* Bud was examining the shorts. "No ID."

"He's definitely going after your friends," Bud said, his eyes holding mine. "That means it's probably someone you know."

"And Harve's home alone." I jerked my cell phone out and punched in the number with shaking fingers. Nobody answered. "I've got to see if he's all right. He could be in trouble."

Charlie said, "Go on; take off. We can handle things here till you get back."

I looked around at the others, fought the idea of leaving Dottie lying there in the dirt. I'd just seen her that very morning. I thought of the way we'd laughed together on the balcony, how she'd enjoyed having breakfast with me.

"You want me to go with you?" Bud said, walking beside me as I turned and headed back down to the boat at a fast clip.

"No. Give me your keys, and I'll drive your car back over here after I make sure Harve's okay. I want to break the news to him when we're alone."

"They're in the ignition."

"Okay." My voice clogged, and my sense of urgency was staggering. I started to run when I hit the lower parking lot. My phone rang about the time I reached the boat. I flipped it open as I climbed aboard and moved into the cockpit. It was Black.

"Listen, Claire, I just heard from Booker. He called that psychiatric hospital in Farmington and found out that embalmer guy your mother worked for named Herman Landers was committed for psychological evaluation years ago, when he was around twelve or thirteen. The neighbors found him wandering around naked and bloody and dragging a disemboweled dog by its tail. The records show he stayed a couple of months, then his parents came and took him home."

"Black, I don't have time for this, something terrible's—"

"Claire, listen to me; this is important. Herman Landers did have a son, and his name was Thomas, just like you thought. Nobody knows what happened to him, and there's no death certificate for anybody named Thomas Landers or any mention of him in news accounts of the fire that killed his father. Don't you see, Claire? He could still be alive somewhere. He's got the violent background and the connection to you . . . he could be the one!"

"I don't care about all that. Dottie's dead. We just found her at Ha Ha Tonka. Oh, God, she's dead, Black."

"What? When? Is it the same guy?"

"Yeah." My voice broke, and I swallowed hard as the storm began to break up the reception. "I gotta get to Harve and tell him. Oh, God, I can't believe she's dead; this can't be real."

The static got too bad to hear him, so I shut the phone and opened throttle on the Cobalt and was heading home within minutes. This just couldn't be happening. Not Dottie. I thought about her wide smile, the way she was always telling me to eat, worrying about my health, worrying about Harve. Now she was dead, like everyone else I'd ever let get close to me. Black was trying to blame it on some poor kid from my past who'd probably been dead for years, but I knew better. This was my fault somehow. I just didn't know how or why.

It took me about ten minutes to reach home, and I kept thinking it had to be a mistake, but then I'd see the dead body in the tower, the lean, long muscles, the small breasts, and I knew it was her, and I'd get sick all over again. Oh, God, what'd he do with her head? He'd have it somewhere. He'd keep it in the freezer to put on his next victim. Now I knew how Black felt when I'd sprung the photograph of Sylvie on him. I felt ashamed to have been so heartless, but I couldn't think about Black now. *Think about Harve, think of Harve.*

I roared past my dock and reached Harve's house a couple of minutes later. The Cobalt was gone and so was Dottie's kayak. The killer must've gotten her when she was out on the lake or alone at the park. She loved to run on the Ha Ha Tonka trails, did it all the time, usually by herself or with her friend Suze. I forced my-self to calm down as the Cobalt came into the berth too hard and hit the dock.

I tried to steady myself. I had to be in control when I told him. The old bass boat was bumping against the dock in the Cobalt's wake when I jumped out. Harve wasn't at his desk by the windows. I ran up the sidewalk and found the back door unlocked. There was a note taped to the glass. *Gone fishing with Dottie. Be back soon.*

I stared at the note. If he'd been fishing with Dottie, the killer might have accosted them together. Harve might be dead, too. Or lying somewhere wounded or dying. Fighting a terrible sense of foreboding, I ran back to the boat and switched on the tracking system. Harve's boat was on the screen, a green light blinking on and off in what looked like Possum Cove. Dottie's fa-vorite fishing hole. That's where the killer got them.

29

The pleasure boats and fishing craft had pretty well cleared off the lake, taking no chances with the weather. Far away in the distance, around Osage Beach, thunder rolled threateningly, and lightning spiked the thick gray cloud layer that blocked the sun and cooled the air. The storm was gaining momentum. All I could think about was Harve's safety, and I headed south, praying he'd not met up with the same fate that Dottie had.

I had his boat in a fixed position about two miles ahead in Possum Cove. That was Dottie's favorite fishing hole, and that's where her friend Suze Eggers lived. It stood to reason they'd fish there.

The sky had dropped so low, it seemed to hang in the forested hills and bluffs along the shoreline, and I breathed a sigh of relief when I glimpsed Harve's Cobalt tied at an old, half-submerged boat dock. Veering my craft to starboard, I headed there, growing more alarmed when I saw that the Cobalt and beach were deserted. I cut the motor, guided the bow in close beside Harve's boat, grabbed a line, and lashed the boats together.

"Harve! Where are you?" I yelled, climbing aboard

the other boat and looking up a narrow, rocky path that ascended the hill through thick vegetation. No answer, just the splashing of wind-driven waves against the shore. I went below but found nothing until I saw what looked like a spray of blood droplets on the floor. Chills played up my spine, and I pulled my weapon and held it up against my shoulder. I climbed on deck and outside found the wind growing wild and whitecaps racing across the cove perpendicular to the boats. The Cobalt's hull rocked hard enough to make me lose my footing.

I held on to the cockpit roof and scanned the tree line above the water. Through the tossing branches I saw a black-shingled roof. Suze's house, it had to be, with Harve's boat docked down here. The rain began to pelt me in earnest, and I ignored the stinging drops and pulled out my cell phone to request backup. I couldn't get a signal and remembered there were only a few communication towers in this undeveloped part of the lake, so I tried the Cobalt's equipment, but the electrical storm was playing havoc with all means of communication. I looked up the steep hill. The cellular might be able to pick up a signal at the top. More importantly, Harve might be up there.

I kept the Glock ready, finger near the trigger, as I climbed the steep incline. The path twisted around bushes and undergrowth, and I searched the sides of the trail as I went but didn't want to admit what I was looking for. If the killer had assaulted Dottie and Harve out here, he might've gotten Suze, too. Or maybe *Suze* might be the killer. I'd never trusted or liked her. She'd given me the creeps from the first day I met her. Dottie had been her best friend, and now Dottie was dead. Suze had been on duty the night Sylvie was murdered at her bungalow. She had been first at the murder scene, so she had opportunity. . . .

I came up behind an old barn at the top of the path.

It was weathered and dilapidated, and the roof had
seen better days, but it was the structure I'd seen from
the water. I edged along the side closest to me, glad the
wind obscured any sounds I was making in the dead
leaves and debris hugging the wall. I stopped when a
two-storied brick farmhouse appeared in my line of vision. It was in better shape and looked occupied. The
back of the house sat about thirty yards out in front of
the barn and had an open porch with a swing. A dirt
road curved around the house through the woods. This
looked like one of the old homesteads that had been
built generations ago and never sold to developers, like
Harve's land, which had been passed down in his family.

Keeping out of sight, I searched the windows of the
house. There were four upstairs and two on either side
of the back porch. The bottom floor had dark-colored
drapes, but the top story had white sheets blocking the
old-fashioned sash windows. No sign of life. I backed
out of sight, leaned against the barn, and tried to get
Bud on my cell again, but the phone showed no signal.
The rain was beginning to pour now, drenching my
white polo shirt and khaki slacks to the skin. My sense
of danger was up and running about a hundred miles
an hour.

When I heard a bang, I crouched and trained my
weapon on the corner of the barn. It sounded again,
and I took a quick peek in that direction. The front
door of the barn rattled in the wind gusts. I observed
the house for a few minutes, saw no movement inside,
then took the barn door fast and hard in police stance,
arms extended, ready to fire, my back to the wall as
soon as I gained the interior.

Inside, it was dark and dead quiet, except for moaning wind invading rotten plank walls and drumming
rain on the roof and splashing water where the roof had

lost shingles. Daylight was fading quickly, and the heavy storm clouds filled the barn with gloom. I took a step and almost tripped over Dottie's kayak. She would never put it in somebody's barn. She always kept it handy near the water. I knew then that I'd stumbled upon the killer's lair.

There was a vehicle covered by a dark green tarp. I looked around, then went down on one knee and pulled up the edge of the canvas. The Porsche Black had reported stolen. The killer must've stolen it when racing away from Sylvie's crime scene. I took a deep breath to steady my nerves. Okay. I had to go on. The killer liked to spend time with his victims, torture them, and arrange the bodies according to his fantasies. Harve might be inside the house, hurt or dying.

My heart hammered inside my chest when I stood up, adrenaline pumping through me. Still no sound, no movement, except for the sporadic thudding of the barn door. I inched around the back of the Porsche and found a beat-up green Ford station wagon. There was an old-fashioned, bullet-shaped silver travel trailer behind it, in the back of the barn.

Keeping low and alert, I checked out the interior of the station wagon. Lots of trash on the dashboard and in the backseat—McDonald's wrappers and sandwich boxes, donut sacks, soda cans—but no Harve, no Suze, no dead bodies, thank God. The travel trailer was ancient, about a thirty-footer, with plenty of dings and dents on the aluminum shell. One metal step led to the door. It was locked. I tried to see in the windows, but frilly blue gingham curtains covered them. I looked around for Suze's red Ford Taurus but didn't see it. Either she wasn't home or the car was parked out front.

The rain was coming down in sheets now, loud and hard and with the fresh, pleasant smell of summer electrical storms. I moved to the door and observed the back of the house for a minute. I tried to call for backup again but couldn't get through and knew I wouldn't be able to until the storm abated. I considered whether to go in alone and look for Harve or take the Cobalt back for help. But there was no real choice because I knew Harve might be inside. And he might not make it out alive if I took off and wasted time getting reinforcements.

As soon as I made the decision to act, I took a deep breath and ran across the backyard. The dirt was beginning to turn into mud, which sucked at my tennis shoes, but I hardly felt the cold rain. I bounded up the back steps, flattened my back against the wall, and listened for sounds from inside. The porch swing creaked back and forth on its rusted chains, and the wind had blown a dead philodendron plant off the banister and scattered dirt on the floor. I heaved in a breath and wiped the rain out of my eyes, then reached around with my left hand and tried the doorknob. It turned easily.

My nerves were dancing around like crazy, and I wet my lips and got my act together for a second or two. Chances were that Dottie's killer was inside this house waiting for me, and I could get him if I kept my cool and used my training. Chances were, too, that he had no idea that I was anywhere around. Unless he'd heard my boat, but I figured the wind and rain had probably drowned that out.

I pushed open the door a little, then entered the house quickly. I stopped just inside and let my eyes grow accustomed to the dusky light. Everything appeared neat and orderly. A living room on the left. A dining room on the right. Both were fully furnished with funky, modern stuff that didn't really go with the old house but looked like the kind of decor that Suze Eggers would choose.

No lights on. Silence. A steep wood staircase led upstairs right in front of me, and I could see the kitchen down the narrow hall behind it. I waited a few seconds, fully expecting somebody to jump out and charge me like in horror movies, but nothing happened. Maybe I was wrong. Maybe Suze Eggers didn't live here. Maybe it was just a harmless lake home owned by people from St. Louis or Kansas City or somewhere, and I'd scare the hell out of them when I jumped out and held a gun on them. But I knew better, and fear climbed up my spine and tapped me on the shoulder.

I moved cautiously down the hall, past an empty bathroom with an old-fashioned claw-footed tub, and stopped in front of a closed door beside the kitchen. I sucked air, then shoved it open. White sheets covered the windows, making it hard to see. When my eyes grew accustomed to the filtered light, I saw Suze Eggers's Cedar Bend uniform thrown across the end of the bed, along with lots of other clothes. The room was empty.

Relieved, I retraced my steps to the bottom of the staircase and listened. The storm was beating the hell out of the windowpanes. If somebody was upstairs, they'd never hear me coming. That was a good thing. I started up the steps, both hands gripping the gun out in front of me.

Upstairs, it was shadowy, but enough light came through the covered windows for me to see where I was going. A long upstairs hall ran toward the back of the house, with three closed doors. I hesitated again, listened for killers creeping up on me. Nothing but the weather. Thunder cracked not far away, and I jumped a foot, then moved quickly to the first door. I was wasting too much time; Harve could be in bad trouble somewhere.

I opened the door and peered around the door facing. It was even darker inside, but I could see a shape lying on the bed across from me. I held the Glock steady on it while I fumbled around on the wall inside for a light switch. I found it and flipped it on, and when the light flared, I saw Harve lying on his side on the bed. Relief hit me, but I didn't run to him. I kept my eye on the closet door and moved slowly across the floor, gun swiveling from closet door to bedroom door.

I turned him over and found him breathing. I couldn't see any injuries except for a shallow cut above his left eyebrow. I whispered his name, still watching the bedroom door, but I couldn't get him to wake up. He'd been drugged, but he was alive and unhurt, and I had to get him out of here. But first, I had to make sure the killer wasn't lying in wait for us somewhere in the house.

Fairly certain I was alone, I made my way quietly down the hallway to the second bedroom. It was empty. Two down, one to go. I opened the third door at the very rear of the house and found the window undraped, so I could see. Somebody moved on the bed, and I almost pulled the trigger. When they didn't move again, I crept to the bed with my gun trained on them.

"Don't move a muscle," I warned, but when I saw who was in the bed, I faltered and nearly dropped the gun. I couldn't believe my eyes at first, but it was Dottie, drugged, too, but still alive, still breathing. Joy filled me, and I grabbed her and shook her. She screamed and came awake fighting, so I clamped my hand over her mouth and said, "Shhh, Dottie, I'm here to get you out. Where's Suze?"

Her eyes were wide and terrified, but when I took my hand away, she murmured in a slurred, frightened voice, "She put something in our coffee, and I can't keep my eyes open. My muscles won't move right."

I looked at the door. "It's Suze, Dottie; she's the killer. We gotta get you and Harve outta here now before she comes back."

Dottie kept trying to focus her eyes on my face, and I said softly, "Oh, God, Dottie, I'm so glad you're all right. We thought you were dead. We found another body and then we found your clothes and we all thought it was you. I'm so glad you're all right."

"Harve . . . Harve . . ." Dottie said weakly, struggling to sit up.

I kept my voice low. "Harve's okay, Dottie. Try to listen to me. Do you know where Suze went? Is she coming back here tonight?"

Dottie didn't answer, and I gave her a hard shake to wake her. "Dottie, c'mon, I've gotta get you and Harve out of here before she gets back."

Her eyes popped open, and she blinked hard. "She sleeps in the cellar. Don't go down there alone, don't . . ."

Then she slipped out of consciousness again, and I couldn't wake her.

I hadn't seen a cellar door, but I had to check it out, so I left them sleeping, descended the stairs, and went looking for it. If she was in the cellar, she could probably hear my footsteps on the creaky old floor, so I tested each footfall before I put down weight. I left the lights off and kept against the wall. I found the cellar door under the staircase, hidden behind a drapery.

I opened it and looked down the narrow, enclosed steps. There was a light on, and I could see a naked lightbulb hanging from a chain near the bottom of the stairs. I started down the steps and immediately felt colder air, which made me shiver in my soaked clothes.

At the bottom of the steps, I looked around the unfinished concrete cellar. There was a picnic table and several lawn chairs in the middle of the room, and a small chest freezer against the far wall. My eyes became riveted on a narrow cot near a slanted concrete coal chute. Suze was asleep under a red-and-white quilt, lying on her side, facing the wall, but I'd know her spiked hair anywhere. I had the advantage of surprise, so I moved quickly across the room and stood over the bed.

"Suze! Don't try anything or I'll shoot you. I swear to God, I will."

Suze didn't move, and she didn't wake up. I frowned and held the gun on her as I jerked the covers off with my left hand. A scream tore out of me when Suze's decapitated head flew off the bed along with the quilt and bounced with a spray of blood onto my shoes. I jumped back in horror, knocking into the lightbulb and sending shadows careening crazily around the cellar walls in disorienting patterns of black and white. There was no body on the bed, just rolled-up blankets, and Suze Eggers's head came to a rest on her left cheekbone and stared at me out of wide, frightened eyes.

Oh, my God, my God, my God . . .

30

I stared down at Suze Eggers's head lying on the cellar floor and tried hard not to panic. My God, if Suze wasn't the killer, who was? Where was he? I had to get Harve and Dottie out of this house. I ran up the cellar steps and found the door at the top locked. I kicked it hard, twice, and when it gave, I came out into the hallway, with my gun leading, and heard someone running up the steps.

"Stop or I'll shoot!" I cried, then took the steps two at a time until I reached the second floor. Everything was silent again, so I moved to the bedroom where I'd left Harve. The light was off, and I reached around and flipped it on. Harve was still on the bed, but now Dottie was standing beside him.

I ran to the bed, relieved Dottie was awake and able to walk. She could help me carry Harve. "C'mon, Dottie, we've gotta get Harve out of here. The killer's somewhere in the house."

I shook Harve's shoulder, keeping my weapon trained on the doorway. My hands were shaking so badly I could barely hold the gun. "Dottie, help me pull him off the bed. Hurry!" When she didn't answer, I turned to look at her and glimpsed the eight-inch meat cleaver she held high in one hand. Before I could react, she knocked my gun arm aside and chopped the cleaver down hard against my left upper shoulder. I screamed as it cut deep, the top of the blade lodged into my collarbone.

Then she was all over me, cackling the most awful laugh I'd ever heard and grabbing for my gun. The weapon went off, slamming two slugs into the wall. The struggle made the embedded blade twist in the bone, and I went woozy with pain. I almost blacked out, and my knees buckled weakly to the floor. Dottie wrestled the gun away and threw it across the room, where it hit the wall and slid under a chair.

"Oh, Annie, Annie, you shouldn't've come out here. I didn't want to hurt you. Lie still, sweetie, and I'll fix you up."

I groaned in agony when she lifted me bodily and carried me to the bed. She laid me gently down beside Harve and ran out of the room. I fought to stay conscious and looked down and saw that the cleaver angled out of my upper chest just under my collarbone. It looked like it had pierced my muscle at least an inch deep. My shirt was cut open, and my bra strap was severed. The wound would've been worse if my leather shoulder holster hadn't taken some of the blade. My white shirt was already turning red with blood.

When I tried to move, the pain was so bad I almost fainted. I shut my eyes and clamped my bottom lip with my teeth, groaning and turning my head until I could see Harve. He hadn't moved, still deeply drugged.

Oh, God, I had to get my gun. I set my jaw and tried to sit up, but that drove the blade deeper into the wound. Then Dottie was back, and I tried to think how in God's name I'd ever get away, but she was standing over me and pushing me down into the pillow.

"Dottie, please . . . help me . . . I'm bleeding . . . The pain's awful. . . ."

"I know, I know, honey, but don't you worry that pretty little head of yours. I'm gonna take good care of the both of you. You're my best friends, and you'll be Momma's best friends, too, you'll see. Dottie's gonna make you feel better."

I shut my eyes and heaved in some deep breaths, but every time I moved, the pain overwhelmed me. When I looked at Dottie again, she was threading a big embroidery needle. Oh, God, I had to get away from her, but I couldn't move, and I watched her pick up a fat roll of silver duct tape. She pulled out a long length with a sharp shriek, tore it off, and quickly taped my wrists together.

"Dottie . . . why . . . why are you doing this . . . Please stop. . . ."

"Hush, hush, now, darlin'. You're gonna understand everything soon enough. I've got a big surprise for you. Now hold real still while I get you all stitched up."

When she suddenly reached down and jerked the cleaver out of my shoulder, I came off the bed in sheer agony, but that was nothing compared to the pain I felt when she suddenly dumped a bottle of iodine into the open wound. I screamed and writhed on the bed until she held me down.

"I know, I know, poor baby. It hurts so bad," Dottie said soothingly as she cut off my shoulder holster and shirt with the bloody cleaver and tossed them on the floor, "but it's gonna feel better once I get it all sewed up."

She picked up the needle and pinched the edges of the bleeding wound tightly together with her thumb

and forefinger. I groaned some more and clamped my
jaw when she pushed the needle through one lip of the
wound and out through the other. Oh, God, I couldn't
stand it, I couldn't, and everything went black for a moment, but not for long enough. I gasped for breath and
moaned as she slowly and methodically stitched up the
six-inch gash.

"There you go, all better." She gave me the big, familiar Dottie smile, and I could only lie there and stare
dully up at her. Nauseated, I wet dry lips and tried to
breathe.

"See, I'm taking good care of you, just like always.
Don't worry so much. I love you guys, ya know that. I
don't like having to hurt you, but you forced me to."

For a moment I could only stare at her in absolute
shock; then I shifted my eyes down and saw the neat
line of large black stitches she'd made across my bare
flesh. Blood was still seeping out between the sutures
and dripping on what was left of my bra. Dottie moved
away from the bed, then came back a few seconds later
with a hypodermic needle. "This'll help the pain, so
you'll feel all better for the party. We've been waiting
for you to get to come to our party for ever so long. Did
you know that, Annie? Everybody's so excited to have
you home again, just like old times."

"What? . . . I don't understand . . . what party? . . .
home? . . ." I kept trying to think straight, but the pain
was throbbing and hot, and I couldn't think about anything else. When she brought the hypodermic needle
down close to me, I shook my head. "No . . . don't give
me that . . . don't . . ." Then I cried out when she
jabbed it between the stitches and injected God knew
what into my wound.

"Now, now, be a big girl. It's just a little morphine to
help ease the pain. I'm so sorry I had to hurt you. I
never wanted to, but you were gonna shoot me, and I

had to. I'm pretty good with that cleaver, don't you think, Annie? I practice on bodies I don't need, sometimes with knives and hatchets, too. It's fun. I'll teach you if you want me to."

The drug was taking me quickly, but I struggled to get out something first. My plea was slurred and breathless. "Bud . . . Black . . . they'll come looking for me . . . Let us go, Dottie . . . please. . . . You can get away. . . . I won't tell them what you did . . ."

Dottie bent over and spoke very close to my face. "Oh, that's so sweet, darlin', and I know you wouldn't tell on me. You never did. God, I've missed having you at home with me like this. I promise you, Annie, I'm never going to leave you again, never, ever. We're gonna be together forever. Just like me and my mother."

Then I felt her lips press down on mine, and the smell of the Clinique she wore filled my senses as the morphine took hold of me and dragged me down into a dark and murky ocean of oblivion.

31

I awakened slowly, groggy and disoriented. My eyes were heavy, and my shoulder was burning up. I couldn't think straight, couldn't quite grasp what was the matter, though I knew something awful had happened. I could hear rain beating down somewhere and rumbling thunder. I lay still, but the pain was so terrible that I lifted my right hand to see what was causing it.

When my hand wouldn't move, I opened my eyes and tried to focus and saw the silver duct tape securing it to a bedpost. Then I remembered and groaned with the realization of where I was and what was happening. I examined the wound in my shoulder, not sure how long I'd been unconscious. The black stitches were swollen and red, the edges puffy and puckered and oozing blood. The morphine was wearing off.

Blinking away the confusing effects of the drug, I tried to figure out where I was. I was lying in the middle of a double bed, and my feet were taped to the spindles of the footboard. No lights were on, but I could see flickering lights at the foot of the bed and realized there were about a dozen red candles glowing in front of a long mirror. Above the candles and mirror, pinned to the wall, was a computer-generated sign with lots of big yellow smiley faces on it and big black block letters that said: WELCOME HOME ANNIE.

Oh God, oh God, Dottie, Dottie's the killer. I remembered Harve then and Dottie attacking me with the meat cleaver, everything. Frantic, I turned my head to the left and looked for a way out. I froze. Beside me on the bed was Suze Eggers's head, carefully balanced on a Blue Willow dinner plate. A green party hat shaped like a derby sat atop her blond, spiky hair. Congealed blood pooled around her neck like a maroon collar. A second Blue Willow plate sat in front of the head, with a knife and spoon to the right, a fork and salad fork to the left. In the middle of the plate was a precisely folded white linen napkin and one of those curled-up New Year's Eve party favors that blows out long and makes a whistling sound.

I heard an awful, low moaning and realized it came from deep inside me, and I began to struggle violently against the duct tape. I kept my eyes shut tight, not wanting to see any more, fighting my descent into absolute panic. *Don't, don't, don't scream, don't go to pieces,* I kept telling myself, but I was petrified with fear. Where was Dottie? What was she doing? Where was I? I had to get hold of myself. It took me a few minutes, but I finally willed myself to lie still. I opened my eyes and looked around for a means of escape.

At the foot of the bed were two more Blue Willow dinner plates, and each held horribly mummified human heads. Both heads had long blond hair that had been neatly braided, but there were patches where the hair had fallen out. Some of it had been glued back in place; some had been stapled with artful precision. A fourth head, one that looked like it might have belonged to a man, was sitting on the bed to my right. All the heads had a place setting, silverware, and a party favor directly in front of them. All of them had different colored plastic hats beside their plates. There was a chair drawn up to the bed beside me, and there was a plate there for me and one probably meant for Dottie.

Oh, Jesus, please, please help me, I thought for a couple of minutes in utter despair; then I clamped my jaw and forced myself to calm down. I had to get away. That's all I could think about, getting away. I couldn't think about the heads or what Dottie was going to do to me, or where she was or where Harve was. She was gone for the moment, and I had to escape before she got back.

I looked around again and realized it was a very small room. The bed took up nearly the whole area, leaving little room for a built-in dresser, where the candles were burning. I couldn't figure out for a moment where I was; then I remembered the old travel trailer in the barn. That's where Dottie had brought me. My left hand was untied because of the wound, and I reached across and tried to jerk off the tape holding my right hand. I was so weak I could barely pull on it, but I got it loosened a little, then stopped when I heard a door open in the next room. I held my breath.

Dottie breezed in, smiling and dripping rainwater off my black sheriff's rain slicker. So that's where it went. She must've stolen it out of my car. I wondered if she used it to trick her victims.

"Oh, man, it's become a flood out there, and there's a whole front of storms coming through. Oh, good, you're all awake. I guess you've been getting to know each other while I've been gone?"

I stared up at her and tried not to shudder. I watched her shrug out of the wet slicker and walk to the bed. "How's that shoulder, sweetie? Oooh, look at all that swelling; I'll have to give you another dose of iodine."

She put her face close to mine, kissed me on the mouth, and smiled. "Well, aren't you gonna say hi?"

"Hi, Dottie," I croaked out of cracked, dry lips.

"How do you like my little surprise party? Did everyone yell 'surprise!' like they were supposed to?"

"Yeah." *Play along, play along.* She's insane, but she's not threatening to kill me yet. Maybe I could buy time or talk her into cutting me loose. "You know how I love parties," I said and forced a caricature of a smile.

Dottie clapped her hands in delight. "Oh, Annie, I knew you would like it here with us. You can be the sister and my friend. I've always loved you so."

I tried to think who she was and if she'd really known me before, but I didn't know her, hadn't met her until Harve hired her. She had somehow woven me into her psychotic fantasies. I watched her move around the bed, kissing each head on the lips. I almost gagged but forced myself to lie quietly.

"My shoulder sure does hurt, Dottie. I think it's the way I'm lying. Could you let me sit up? Maybe it'd feel better."

"Okay, but not until after we eat. I've got everything about ready in the oven. I'm just starved, aren't you?" She suddenly turned to the man's head and said, "Just hold your horses; it's almost ready. I've got rice and meat loaf tonight, if you must know."

Then she was gone, and I heard her rattling pans and running water in the next room. Okay, she's not violent at the moment. Black knew where I was going, he'd be out looking for me soon, and Bud would go to my house to see why I hadn't shown up with his car. One of them would find Harve's note. They were probably out searching for me already. They knew I'd be looking for Harve, and they knew I was in a Cobalt. Black knew Dottie fished in Possum Cove, and that's where he'd look. It was just a matter of time before they showed up, and I had to survive until they did.

"Here we go. Time to eat."

I watched Dottie smile and smile and talk to each head as she forked up slices of meat loaf and put them on each plate. Rice came next in a matching Blue Willow bowl, then coleslaw and one half of a dill pickle for everybody. I felt like I was going to vomit. I couldn't move; the horror kept rising up and overwhelming me, and I kept forcing it back down.

I watched her move around the bed, tucking snowy napkins around the heads. When she had everything exactly the way she wanted it, she sat down beside me. She looked at me and said, "Let us pray."

Closing her eyes and folding her hands together, she began a long prayer about friends and family and staying together always, then looked at her watch and said, "Now we can begin. First, we'll all eat a bite of meat loaf. Everybody together now." She took a bite herself, then said, "Umm, yummy, if I say so myself."

Then she cut a piece of my meat loaf with my fork and held it poised in front of my face. "Open up, Annie. It's so good. You always did love my cooking."

"Dottie, I'm not hungry. My shoulder hurts."

Suddenly she got angry, and she slapped my face and said sharply, "Quit complaining, you brat. This party's for you. Now open your mouth and eat this, or I'll stuff it down your throat."

I opened my mouth and chewed the meat loaf. My stomach rolled, and I forced down the bile burning my throat. Dottie patted me on the head. "Very good, Annie."

She fed the other heads bites of food, which fell down onto the white napkins and bedspread, talking and smiling all the while. When she smiled at me, I smiled back. When she fed me, I ate. *Cooperate; do everything she says; don't make her angry.*

"Well, you're sure not very talkative tonight, Annie. I thought you'd be so happy to see us all again, but you act like you don't give a fig about any of us."

"That's not true," I said. "I love you all. I've missed you all."

She looked at one of the heads with blond braids. "Well, now are you satisfied? She loves us. See, I told you she still loves us."

I watched her have a long conversation with the heads; then suddenly, she jumped up and said, "Okay, everybody! Time to put on our party hats like Suze and bring in the cake! This is a big celebration! Annie's home at last!"

Dottie moved around the table, putting the hats on the heads, and she put mine on last. "I know it's not your birthday, Annie, but I put some candles on the cake, anyway. I love you so. I'm so glad you're home."

I looked around at the decapitated heads in their colorful hats and closed my eyes. Oh, God, I was never going to get out of here. Nobody was ever going to find me.

LIFE AFTER FATHER

This was the happiest day of Brat's life. The little girl was back, and they were special friends again. When she was asleep, Brat had taken the two big Cobalts docked at the bottom of the hill and set them adrift in the middle of the lake, so no one would know where Brat lived. Brat had kayaked back through the storm and had gotten drenched to the skin, but now no one would come looking for the little girl and take her away again. She would be Brat's forever.

Brat smiled just thinking about it. The little girl was in the mother's room now. She was having fun with Brat's mother and her friends, and she was smiling at Brat the way she used to do, before she left Brat all alone with the embalmer. Now they could be together forever and ever, and Brat was going to make sure that she was always happy and laughing.

Dinner had been a great success, and the little girl had told him that she liked the meat loaf very much. She was complaining about her shoulder, and Brat felt so badly about having to hurt her. But she'd be okay.

Brat would nurse her to health, and they'd go outside when the storm was over and swing and play and feed Mr. Twitchy Tail again. Happy, happy, so happy, Brat hummed and spread caramel icing on the special chocolate cake still warm from the oven. She was going to love this cake. Brat lit the candles and carried it back into the mother's room.

The little girl was still lying on the bed, and she smiled at Brat. Oh, good, she liked the cake. Brat knew she would! "Chocolate cake's your favorite, isn't it?" Brat asked her. She nodded. Her eyes looked scared, and Brat didn't like that but ignored it because it was wonderful to have her with them.

"I don't like her," said his mother all of a sudden. "You love her better than you do me."

"No, I don't," said Brat. "That's a terrible thing for you to say."

"You like her better than me, too!" said the brother. "You gave her the biggest piece of meat loaf, and you sat by her and fed her and ignored the rest of us."

Brat put his hands over his ears to block out their complaints. They were yelling now, all of them at once, all the voices loud and strident until he couldn't think straight.

"What's the matter, Dottie? Are you sick?"

That came from the little girl, and Brat looked down at her.

The mother yelled, "She doesn't even call you Brat anymore. She calls you by that made-up name that you've been going by. She doesn't love us. She hates us. And I hate her!"

"Don't say that about her!" Brat yelled and then did something he'd never in his life done before: he hit his mother and knocked her off her plate. Immediately contrite, he grabbed her up and held her cuddled close in the crook of his elbow while the little girl stared at them from the bed. She looked scared again, and that made Brat mad.

"You made me hit my mother," Brat cried. "I'm sorry, Momma, I'm sorry, but she made me do it."

"She's evil," said the mother's friend. "She must die; then she'll be nice to us. I had to die before I was nice to you. Don't you remember that, Brat? We all had to die before we were nice and could live here with you."

"I don't want to kill her yet. I love her," Brat cried, tears burning, then rolling down his face.

"Dottie, please, don't kill me. I love you, too. I like it here," the little girl said, her face white and strained. She was trying to pull loose. She was trying to get away.

"Yes, you must!" said Brat's mother.

"Kill her, kill her, before you serve the cake," said their new friend, Suze.

"Now, now, do it now, so she'll be nice to us," said the brother.

"Kill her now, kill her, kill her, kill her!" they all shrieked together.

The voices kept up no matter how hard Brat tried to stop them, to explain about the little girl and how much he loved her, but Brat finally couldn't stand their harping any longer and doubled his fist and punched the little girl in the face, so his mother and her friends would all shut up and leave him alone. Her head lolled back and blood ran from her nose, and she lay very still, but Brat hadn't hit the little girl hard enough to kill her. He loved her too much, and she hadn't even gotten to feed Mr. Twitchy Tail again or let Brat push her on the tire swing he'd bought at Wal-Mart to hang on the big oak tree in Suze's backyard.

32

Sscccccrapppe . . .

Somewhere far away a strange sound pierced my stupor. I was at the bottom of a very dark place, and I had
to stay there, where I was safe. I didn't want to swim to
the top, where the light was, where something horrible
was waiting to get me. I had to hide deep in the shadows
and sleep forever. But the light beckoned, pulling me
up and up out of the black sea, and when I was in the
wavery gray layers close to the top, I began to feel pain.
My head, my arm, and chest, and fear gripped me so
hard my muscles went rigid.

And the sound that frightened me went on, slow and
drawn out. . . . *sscccccrapppe* . . . Then it would stop for a
heartbeat . . . *sscccccrapppe* . . .

I gathered the courage to open my eyes and face my
terror. I saw blurry shadows moving around. My heartbeat charged into a staccato, and I knew I had to fight
this unknown danger. Where was my weapon? *Think,
think, focus.* Where was I? Why couldn't I move?

Sscccccrapppe . . .

Panic hit me with an empowering flood of adrenaline. I blinked hard, trying to see better, and realized one eye was swollen shut. Then I made out Dottie Harper sitting across from me, and images hit me in rapid succession—the macabre candlelit room and the severed heads and the party hats and that she was insane and that I was her prisoner. Her hair was wet, and she wore a short white terry cloth bathrobe, as if she just stepped out of the shower.

Something large and unmoving lay on the table between us. I squinted painfully out of my good eye and realized it was Harve. His eyes were closed, but his chest was rising and falling. He was still alive.

"Little, silly sleepyhead. It's about time you opened those eyes," Dottie said, not in her regular voice but in the spooky, singsong little girl's voice she'd started using right before she punched me in the face and I'd lost consciousness.

I tried to think. I realized that we were no longer in the travel trailer but down in the cellar, where I'd found Suze's head. We were sitting under the naked lightbulb hanging from a chain, and my arms were stretched up tight over my head, turning the stitched-up wound in my shoulder into unbearable pain. I tried to pull the injured arm loose, but Dottie had the ropes tied to a metal pipe in the ceiling. *Stay calm, stay calm, don't panic, play her game, talk her out of whatever she was planning to do.*

With a beatific smile on her face, Dottie watched me struggling to free myself. I stopped fighting the ropes when I saw Dottie draw the razor-sharp, eight-inch meat cleaver down the length of a long razor strop also attached to the ceiling. My blood was still on it, and there was a baseball bat crusted with blood on the table in front of me.

"That's right, Annie. Stop fidgeting and sit still like a good girl. Dottie's special matinee's about to get started." I licked dry lips. She had descended further into madness now; her eyes didn't look right, looked black and empty. She was ready to kill us. My mind raced out of control. My feet weren't tied. I could use them to disarm her. *Think, think, reason with her, make her stop, make her talk.* Oh, God, oh God, she was sharpening the cleaver because she was going to behead us.

"Dottie, please." I barely recognized the hoarse, raspy croak. I wet my lips again and forced down rising nausea. I could *not* panic. I could *not* give up. It was Dottie sitting there. Dottie, who'd been my good friend. There was a reason she was doing this; she thought we were someone else, someone from her past maybe. *Find out who, find out why, talk her out of it.* "Hey, Dot, why do you have me all tied up? I thought we were friends. Untie me; the ropes are hurting my shoulder."

"Annie, Annie, everybody thinks you're so bright, but you're not, are you? In fact, you're pretty stupid. For two years I've been right here under your nose, and you were still clueless about who I am and what I've been doing." Dottie's face changed, tightened until she looked like a completely different person. She was angry now, her face flushing dark red. I tensed all over. I didn't want her angry. Her voice went an octave higher, and the singsong intensified. "All Harve could talk about was Claire this and Claire that. Claire's the best cop in the state. Claire's been through some terrible things. Claire's the best friend I ever had. It made me sick to listen, because you both were lying to me. I knew you weren't Claire. You were Annie. You were my little girl, my friend, not his."

"Dottie, listen to me, please. You've got my arms strung up too tight. It's killing me, and the stitches are coming out. Please, loosen the rope a little so it won't hurt so much." Behind Dottie, I could see lightning flash in the small window in the door above the coal chute. It was dark outside, and I wondered how long I'd been unconscious, if it was the same night or the next night. Thunder rumbled, and the rain started in earnest again, sluicing down the glass. I could hear the wind banging something in the night.

Harve groaned, and both of us looked at him.

Dottie said, "Goody, goody. The star of the show's gonna wake up, and we can get started."

Suddenly, she leaned over and slapped Harve across the face. The sharp crack made me flinch. "C'mon, big guy. You're on. Curtain time."

Fury flooded me, and I struggled to keep it out of my voice. "Cut it out, Dottie. Harve's never done anything to you. He adores you. This is about me, not him, right? You and me. Leave him out of it." I kept my eyes locked on her face while I estimated how far I could kick out; maybe I could get her in the head and knock her out or disorient her. But that wouldn't do us any good if I was tied up.

The singsong disappeared. "Aha, now you're talking. You're finally getting it through that thick head of yours. It's about you, all right. It's about making you suffer. Tell me, Annie, what in the world would make you suffer more than me filleting your best friend alive right in front of you? We'll pretend he's a great big bass, and we'll clean him. What'd you say?" She picked up a large electric fillet knife and plugged it into a white extension cord. She flipped the switch, and I watched the sharp blades vibrate and heard the low buzzing sound it made.

I stared at her in abject horror. We were out in the middle of nowhere. A storm was buffeting the lake, making the search for us difficult, if there even was a search. Nobody knew where we were. Nobody was coming to rescue us. Nobody could hear Harve's screams, no one but me. "Dottie, listen, don't do this. I'm begging you. We're your friends. Harve and I both love you. You *know* that's true; you have to know it. Please, don't hurt him. Let him go."

Dottie's teeth flashed, and she looked almost normal for a second or two. Then the singsong was back. "Oh, okay, sure, you talked me into it. I know what. I'll untie you and Harve; then you can call Bud and tell him where I am, and he can put me in jail for killing Suze and Sylvie and all the others." Her forehead crumpled in a deep frown, as if she was suddenly annoyed. She turned off the electric knife and concentrated on sharpening the cleaver. I looked down at Harve. He was untied but still heavily sedated. I saw his eyelids flutter, and my heart stopped. Oh, God, he was coming around.

I had to get her attention off him. "Why are you doing these terrible things? Tell me, Dottie. Why'd you kill Suze? She was your best friend, for God's sake. The two of you were together all the time."

"Suze was a stupid bitch, but I needed someplace to keep my things where nobody would find them. Her house's out here in the woods, and she didn't have any family or friends. It was too perfect until she started snooping around in my trailer and found my mother and her friends. Then she had to go, but I didn't like her, anyway. After tonight's show is over, we'll have to move on, but that's okay. Momma and I like to travel." Dottie placed the strop on the table. There was dried blood on the buckle; there was dried blood all over it. Her face metamorphosed into the big Dottie smile, but the eyes remained dark and empty. "Ready for the show to begin? I'm good at this. Lots of practice through the years. I just love it every time. I wish you could've seen all the friends I brought home for my momma. There's been twenty-two in all. Counting your mother."

"My mother?" I didn't believe her. Nothing she said made sense, but I had to keep her talking. People would be looking for us; I had to believe that. Bud and Charlie would search for me, and Black, Black liked to keep tabs on me. He'd track me with the Cobalt's satellite system, or would the storm interfere? Unless he obeyed my wishes and stayed away from me. Oh, God, I'd told him to leave me alone and let me handle the case. *Stay calm, play the game, keep her talking. That's all you can do, bring her back to sanity somehow.* "Dottie, you need help, is all. You're sick, and Black can help you. . . ."

Dottie suddenly raised the cleaver and slammed it down toward Harve's head. I cried out, but she drove the blade hard into the wood picnic table inches from his ear. It quivered from the impact. I quivered from the relief.

"You little bitch," Dottie ground out through clenched teeth. "How dare you blame me for this? This is all your fault, yours, not mine. You're the sick one. You make me sick!"

Oh, God, she was completely crazy, living inside some kind of psychotic delusion where I was someone who'd hurt her. How could this be happening? How could we not have seen signs that she was so dangerous?

I made my voice soft and soothing. "I promise I won't tell anybody if you let us go. I won't tell Bud or Charlie. I'll help you get away."

"Oh, there you go again. But we both know that perfect little police officers like you don't do bad things. You're too perfect and pretty and wonderful. Annie doesn't have to whisper and tiptoe around. She doesn't have to be afraid."

"Who're you afraid of, Dottie? Your father? Did your father hurt you?" But it wasn't Dottie anymore who sat there staring at me. The eyes glittering in the dim light were mad. Dottie was gone. This was someone else. This was a monster.

Dottie leaned close to my face. Her eyes were so bleak and deadly that chills rippled up my back. "Yes, it was my father. Surely, you remember him from when you lived in the old coach house? I remember you. I've never forgotten you. We were best friends. You were like my little sister that I played with and ate cookies with. Then you went off with the cook and left me behind. I've been watching over you and your friends since I got away from him. I'm your own special avenging angel."

She grinned crazily; then she shook Harve's shoulder. "Harve's being a bad boy and won't wake up. I gave him too strong a dose. I could've killed you any time I wanted to, you know that? For years and years, I watched every move you made. I followed you everywhere you went and killed all your friends, one by one. Sometimes it took me a while to find out where you went, especially after I killed your Aunt Kathy and Uncle Tim in Pensacola. But I always found you. I lost you for five long years once, but I caught up to you in Los Angeles just in time to turn your husband against you. All I had to do was call him a time or two and whisper how you were screwing Harve behind his back."

Dottie threw back her head and laughed, then sobered instantly and said, "Then you got away from me that one year, and I couldn't find you. But you know what? I found Harve, and I knew you'd show up sooner or later to be with him."

She nodded, self-satisfied. "And you did, of course, and we became best friends again, just like when we were little. And I sorta liked that, being your best friend again and hanging around with you and having you trust me. Sometimes when I gave you toddies to make you sleep, I'd make them very strong. Then I'd walk down to your house and lie in bed with you while you slept, but you never knew that, did you? I made it really

strong the night you went out to Black's boat, but you
were already gone with him when I came back later to
sleep with you."

"Who are you?" I got out somehow, so full of dread
that I could barely speak. I tried to remember what
Black had been trying to tell me on the phone at Ha Ha
Tonka, who he thought had been killing people. I
couldn't think straight, and nothing made sense. Some
thing about the boy named Thomas, but this wasn't
him. This was Dottie. I fought down hysteria. "Why're
you doing this to me? What'd I do to you? I never laid
eyes on you until Harve hired you on."

"You'll see soon, little Annie. Everything will be all
cleared up. I've got so much to show you, Annie, so
much to share since we were little kids. I kept souvenirs
because I knew this day would come, and the truth
would come out and we'd share it together." She stood
up. "And I brought everyone down here to watch
Harve's show with us. Isn't that a super idea?"

33

When Dottie moved away into the shadowy part of the cellar, I struggled against the ropes and felt them give a little. Maybe I could break them or pull down the pipe. I jerked desperately until she opened a freezer chest against the wall. The light inside came on and illuminated her face where she stood almost invisible in the darkness. She said, "Family's important. I like to keep them close. I'm pretty disappointed that they didn't take to you right off, but they will. Once they get to know you, Annie, they're gonna love you as much as I do." She lifted the lid and reached inside and pulled out one of the decomposed heads with blond hair. It was still resting on a Blue Willow dinner plate and still wore a red party hat. *Oh, Lord, please, please help me.*

"I didn't really introduce everybody at the party. I was just so excited that I forgot. Maybe that's what got you off on a bad foot with everybody. But I'm gonna fix that right now. Momma, this is Annie. Annie, this is my dear momma. Father made me watch him embalm her down in the cellar. I held her hand, but I didn't cry. He got mad and threw her down the stairs, and he said it was my fault, so I had to help him make her smile again. Doesn't she have a lovely smile?"

Dottie set the plate on the table beside Harve's head. "All that happened before you and your mother came to cook for us. But Momma was always with us. Father made me kiss her good night before I went to sleep. Don't you remember me at all, Annie? The way I had to run home before dinner so he wouldn't know we were playing in the creek? Don't you remember the way I cried and beat on your front door the night you went away and left me?"

Realization finally dawned, and I cried, "Oh, my God, you're talking about Thomas. How'd you know Thomas?"

"And look, Annie, here's your momma. I got her, too. I punished her for taking you away and leaving me behind with Father."

I groaned and shut my eyes when she pulled out the other decapitated head with blond braids, frozen now and unrecognizable. *That is not my mother*, I thought frantically. *It isn't; Dottie's lying.* Dottie slapped me hard across the face and held my head so I had to look. "Oh, no, you're not going to pass out on me, sweetie. You're going to see everything I went through after you left me there with him, every little thing he did to me after you left."

Gripped with unspeakable revulsion, I began to shake, couldn't stop until Dottie grabbed my hair.

I twisted against the ropes, pulling desperately. "Let me go, let me go. You aren't Thomas; that's not my mother. You're sick. You're talking about your own family, not mine. . . ."

She slapped me again, so hard I tasted blood at the corner of my mouth. I stopped struggling and hung limply against the ropes. Everything was silent except for the sound of the pouring rain. "It wasn't so bad when you and your mother were there, but then you had to leave. I thought you were my friend. We used to feed Mr. Twitchy Tail together. Don't you remember that, Annie? Look, I've still got him for us to play with."

I watched her pull a dried-up animal carcass out of the freezer and hold it up by its tail. "Don't you remember how we played with him, and how we laughed and ran through the hose? How I pushed you on that old swing? You were the only friend I ever had, and you left me there with him so he could do awful things to me!"

Dottie was getting increasingly agitated. "You wanna see what he did to me after you went away? Do you? I want you to see what you did. Then you'll understand, then you'll know why I had to kill your friends and make you suffer, too." Dottie jumped to her feet and jerked open her robe. She was naked underneath, and I groaned and squeezed my eyes shut tight. "Look, Annie, see what he did to me so I could be a woman like he wanted. I was a boy, I was Thomas, and he made me a girl because you went away and left me there with him."

"Oh, God, Dottie, stop, stop. I can't stand to hear this. . . ."

"So *now* you remember me? I'm your friend Thomas. I loved you and your mother and her chocolate chip cookies and apple pies, but you left me, you left me alone with him!" Enraged, Dottie jerked the cleaver out of the table and hysterically hacked the squirrel carcass into bits of fur and dried hide. Then she fell to her knees, panting for breath and still clutching the cleaver. I held my breath and could not move.

When she was calm again, Dottie stood up and looked at me. Blood was running down her arm where she'd cut herself in her frenzy. "After your mother took you away, all I could think about was finding you. I got her first; she was the very first one I did after I killed my father. Did you know that? I hacked him up with a cleaver. Then I followed you and made sure you suffered like I did, and that everybody you ever loved suffered the way I did. And now it's Harve's turn, and I hate it, sort of, because he's a pretty good guy, really. But then again, this time is very special because this time you get to watch."

"Please, please, Thomas, I was so little then, I didn't know," I pleaded, my voice growing desperate and shrill as she leaned over Harve and raised the cleaver. "I'm begging you, Thomas, please don't hurt him! He didn't have anything to do with this, nothing. Do it to me, kill me! I'm the one you hate!"

At that, Dottie went completely still. She lowered the cleaver, a shocked expression on her face. "I don't hate you, Annie. I love you. I've always loved you. That's why I never killed you." She leaned down close and kissed me on the forehead.

"And I love you, Thomas," I muttered hoarsely. "I begged my mother not to leave you there. I said you were like my brother and we couldn't go away without you." I saw Harve move slightly, and I knew he was coming around. I went on quickly, "I said I wouldn't leave without you, but she made me. I was little like you were, don't you see? She made me do things I didn't want to do, just like your father made you do things you didn't want to do!"

Dottie stared at me, affected by my words, and then we both looked toward the window as the low buzz of a motorboat filtered into our hearing. It was close, in the cove below, and when the boat's air horn began to sound short emergency blasts, Dottie dropped the cleaver on the table and ran up the steps. It was Black or Bud, I knew it, but I didn't move until I heard Dottie's footsteps cross to the front door and go outside. Then I put my foot on the table and jabbed at Harve's shoulder.

"Harve, Harve, wake up, wake up; we've got to get outta here!"

Harve shook his head, trying to listen to me. It took a few seconds for him to awaken, and I kept yelling at him until he turned his head and looked blearily in my direction.

"The cleaver's on the table. Get it, quick, get it, and cut me loose."

I groaned when he laid his head back and closed his eyes, but then he tried to sit up. He knocked into the decapitated head, and it fell off the table and shattered the Blue Willow plate.

"There, Harve, there beside your head; grab it and cut me loose!"

Groggy from the drug, Harve moved so slowly that I twisted on the ropes, no longer thinking of the pain in my shoulder. When he got hold of the cleaver, I screamed, "Cut me loose, cut me loose!"

He pushed himself on his side, then raised up enough to slash at the ropes holding my arms. He missed them, chopped at them again, and missed again, and I looked at the door at the top of the steps and tried to lean toward him so he could reach me with the cleaver.

"Harve, hurry; she'll be back any minute!" He swung at the ropes again, and they finally gave way, but he lost his balance and fell headfirst off the table. I scrambled to the floor and held out my wrists to him. "Cut through the tape. Quick, quick, hurry!"

"What's Dottie doing? Why'd she tie you up?" he said in confusion.

"Just cut through the tape. Now!" I cried, and he cut through the tape, and I was free. I stuck the cleaver into my belt and grabbed the bat, then stood paralyzed when

I heard footsteps running across the floor upstairs. I backed into the darkness away from Harve, but Dottie ran past the cellar door and into the back of the house. A door slammed somewhere; then I heard her footsteps running to the front door again, and then she was gone. Somebody was coming to help us, but I couldn't count on them getting her before she got us.

My shoulder was killing me and bleeding profusely now, and I knew I couldn't best Dottie in a fight injured the way I was, even with the cleaver. She was too strong, and I also knew we couldn't escape through the house without running into her. I ran to the coal chute and climbed the concrete incline to the low door with a window. I looked outside, but it was too dark to see anything. It was still pouring, and I turned the latch and shoved the door open. I waited a second, rain stinging my face, cleaver gripped in my hand, waiting for Dottie to see me. But she didn't come, and I jumped back down and grabbed Harve's face with both hands.

"Harve, listen, listen to me. You've gotta help me get you up that ramp over there. Can you drag yourself?"

"What's going on? . . ."

"Just do it, Harve. Can you move?"

He began to pull himself with his arms, and I put the bat under my arm and got hold of the back of his shirt and dragged him along with all my strength. He was still under the effects of the drug, and every few minutes he'd stop and become deadweight, and I'd prod him and pull him again, until I got him up the ramp and to the edge of the door, and we both dropped out and hit the ground together. I felt the stitches tear loose, and the blood was hot where it ran down my arm, but the back porch light was on, and I could see Dottie down on the path that led to the lake.

"Shhh, Harve, don't say anything. Just try to stay awake."

I crawled along on the ground, dragging him along with me and heading for the thick undergrowth that surrounded the house. When Harve collapsed in exhaustion, I knelt and got my hands under his arms and pulled him toward the woods. It took several minutes to reach cover, and I considered the barn as a hiding place but knew she'd find us there. The woods would be safer, so I half-carried, half-dragged Harve through the mud and kept my eyes on the path as long as I could. Then I saw her, a flashlight beam leading her to the back porch. Oh, God, she was going to find us missing. We had to hide, had to find someplace to hide.

I kept going, praying she wouldn't go into the cellar yet, giving us time to get away, but it was dark and pouring rain, and Harve was groaning. Then I heard her yelling my name in the distance, saw the flashlight beams moving from side to side in wide, sweeping arcs. She was coming.

I saw a fallen log and dragged Harve to it, then frantically dug in the soft ground with the cleaver. When I made an indentation, I pushed Harve back under the log and raked sodden leaves up over him; then, as the light beams got closer, I slid in with my back against his chest and desperately pulled leaves and branches over both of us.

"Annie, what's—"

"Shhh, Harve," I said and clamped my hand over his mouth.

I could hear Dottie's voice now. "Annie, Annie, you're being a bad, bad little girl. You're gonna get in big trouble when you get home."

She was getting closer, moving back and forth in the rain. I gripped the cleaver tightly and peered through the branches. Lightning flashed, and I saw that she was only about twenty feet away.

I lay still and waited for her to find us.

34

"Yoo-hoo, Annie, where are you?"

I kept still. Harve was unconscious behind me. The first time Dottie had come looking for us, she had stepped around the log in the darkness and had not found us. This time we probably wouldn't be so lucky. She had run back to the house when the air horn had started up again down on the lake, but I had stayed put and tried to stanch the bleeding of my shoulder with a scrap of Harve's shirt. I was shivering uncontrollably in my torn bra and pants and was getting weaker by the minute. I knew I couldn't drag Harve any farther, so I prayed whoever was in the boat would come up the hill and look for us. Now Dottie was back and getting closer, and the darkness was giving way to a misty gray light.

"I've got a new surprise for you, Annie," Dottie singsonged happily, about thirty yards away from the log. "You're gonna *love* it."

I tried to see her but couldn't without moving, and I was afraid to move. Harve groaned, and I stifled the sound with my hand.

"I don't have time to keep looking for you, Annie.

But I tell you what: I'm not gonna kill Harve, if that's what made you run away. I like him too much, anyway. I just wanted to kill a friend of yours in front of you, and he was the only one I had. But now that's all changed: I've got somebody else to kill now, and I don't even like him, so it'll be easier. I'll trade you Harve if you'll come in and watch me kill Doctor Black."

I shut my eyes and didn't move. She was lying. Please let her be lying.

"It's really him, Annie, and he came all the way out here to find you. You didn't like him much at first, but you ended up sleeping with him, didn't you? You're not much of a friend, Annie. You just forgot all about me and Harve and spent all your time hanging around with him. Well, guess what? He's hanging around on my porch now, just waiting for us." She gave a cackling laugh; then there was silence under the dripping trees.

I debated whether she could get the jump on a man like Black, but he wouldn't be expecting Dottie to be here; he'd be expecting her to be dead. If he'd been the one blowing the horn, she could have knocked him out with something or led him into a trap when he walked up the hill.

"Listen, Annie, hear this?" There was a crackling buzz over the sound of the drizzling rain, and I knew that sound well. I bit my lip. Oh, God, she'd gotten him with a stun gun.

"It's my new toy, and it works really good, Annie. You should see him jerking around on the ground, just like Mr. Twitchy Tail. I bet you never thought you'd see him get his, did you? And you know what? I'm going back over there right now, and I'm going to zap him every minute or two until you come out. When I see you, I'll stop, but not before. So you hurry up now, you hear?"

I put my face down in the wet dirt, and I tried to think what to do now, but I was all out of options. I'd been trained with stun guns and police Tasers. I'd seen demonstrations of what they did to people. A couple of seconds completely immobilized a grown man. Three seconds or longer felt like the victim had been dropped out of a building onto concrete. It wasn't designed to be used more than once or twice; Black couldn't take it over and over. Dottie wouldn't stop until she killed him with it.

I took a deep breath, then crawled out from under the log. Dottie was gone, so I covered Harve up with leaves and dead limbs. I kept the cleaver in one hand and the baseball bat in the other and stayed low as I edged through the undergrowth toward the opposite side of the house. Maybe she'd go inside for a moment and leave him; maybe I could find a way to get him away from her. When I was almost to the far side of the house, I heard a static crackle and then Black's agonized cry, then Dottie's voice.

"That's number five, Annie, but who's counting? You're not being very nice to your new boyfriend, letting me have my way with him like this. C'mon now, he's not that bad. Even I'm beginning to feel guilty shocking him so many times."

I could see her now where she sat on the porch swing. She had her right foot on the railing, pushing the swing back and forth as if enjoying a quiet, rainy morning. Then she reached out and hit Black's chest with the stun gun, and his body went into horrible, kicking spasms. I couldn't stand it, couldn't stand to see her hurting him. I placed the cleaver and bat on the ground and stood up, and when Dottie saw me, she jumped up and clapped her hands.

"I knew you couldn't stand to see him suffer. You love him, don't you?"

Black was still convulsing a little, and his eyes were

shut, and he was groaning, and I wanted Dottie to get away from him.

"Dottie, come help me." I clutched my bleeding shoulder and dropped to my knees. "I'm too weak to make it any farther. I've lost so much blood; you've got to stitch me up again. I think I'm bleeding to death."

"No, you aren't. That's just a trick. You think you're smarter than I am, but you're not."

"Please help me, help me, and I'll go with you, Dottie. I'll be part of your family. That's where I belong, with you and your family. That's where I want to be forever."

Dottie hesitated, then moved to the top of the steps. Behind her, I saw Black coming out of the shock and trying to swing back and forth so he could kick her.

I said, "I love you so much, Dottie. I didn't realize it until you gave me that wonderful party, and I got to be with everyone again. It was great, and I wasn't sad and lonely anymore. I was happy, truly happy."

"Do you mean it, Annie? Really, truly, that you'll come live with us and meet the new friends I bring home?"

Black was ready to strike now, and I held my breath as he pulled his knee up and kicked her as hard as he could with the heel of his foot. He got her in the back of the head, and she went sprawling down the steps, and in my adrenaline rush, I grabbed up the cleaver and charged her. She rolled and came up on her hands and knees and lunged at me with the stun gun, but I dodged it and swiped a gaping wound across her back. She screamed in pain but got up and ran for the path. I took the cleaver and chopped through the rope holding Black suspended. He fell, and I knelt beside him and cut his wrists apart. He was still half-dazed, but when I saw him clawing at his ankle, I realized he had a gun strapped there. I grabbed it from the holster and took off after Dottie. All I could think about was stopping her, making her pay for what she'd done to me and everyone I'd ever loved.

By the time I reached the top of the path, she was halfway down the hill. I drew up, aimed, and fired but missed, then half-ran, half-slid down the hill after her. She was going to escape in Black's Cobalt, and I wasn't going to let her get away to kill again, not even if it killed *me*. I fired again but couldn't hit her through the trees. Then she was in the boat. Seconds later, I jumped into the bow after her, gun out in front, but when she rammed the motor in reverse, I fell forward and the gun spiraled out of my reach. The motor died, and I scrambled after the gun, and then Dottie jerked off a boat paddle clamped to the side and hit me in the leg with it so hard, I felt a shinbone crack.

Groaning, I lunged for the gun, but then Black was there, barreling out of nowhere, tackling Dottie and taking her with him over the side into the water. I got the gun and pulled myself up the side of the Cobalt to shoot her as sirens sounded above us at the house. But Black already had Dottie by the throat, choking her and holding her under the water, his face so dark and enraged that I knew he was going to drown her.

"Black, Black, let her go, let her go. It's over!"

Black didn't let up, didn't even hear me, so I fired a shot in the air and that brought him spinning around to me and back to his senses. He let her go and left her floating facedown in the water. About the time he heaved himself onto the stern platform, Bud showed up on the path, gun in hand. Black crawled up to me, still shaking with rage, and I collapsed on the floor, in relief and pain and exhaustion.

"Good God, we've got to stop the bleeding," Black muttered, stripping off his shirt and holding it against the gaping hole in my shoulder. He stretched out and yelled over his shoulder to Bud, who was dragging a limp and lifeless Dottie out of the water.

"Call an ambulance. Claire's hurt bad!"

I caught hold of Black's arm and whispered, "Harve's out in the woods beside the barn. Tell them he's hidden under a log. Tell them to get him out of there."

"Okay, we'll get him," Black said, examining my swelling leg.

I said, "Now, tell them now."

Black yelled and told them about Harve, and that's the very last thing I remembered before I got pulled down into that safe, dark hidey-hole of unconsciousness again, where I knew no pain and nobody chased me with a cleaver.

EPILOGUE

Nicholas Black insisted that I recuperate at his villa in Bermuda. I objected, of course, telling him that Harve was going to need me after what had happened with Dottie. He said Harve could go, too. Could have his own private guesthouse and his own private nurse who wasn't a goddamn eunuch in disguise.

So away we went on Black's Lear jet and found Bermuda was a beautiful, lush paradise with turquoise waters and balmy winds and pastel villas. Black's villa was pale pink stucco, with a pool overlooking the ocean and three guesthouses strung amid the verdant flowers and glades of trees above the beach.

Thomas Landers, aka Dottie Harper, didn't die and was locked up in a hospital for the criminally insane. Poor Thomas had killed his last victim, and I still remembered very little about him when we were childhood playmates. Black had a whole team of colleagues treating him, mainly because Black wanted to know why he'd chosen poor Sylvie Border as a victim, but also because Black would probably kill him with his bare hands if he ever laid eyes on him again.

So far Thomas had been quite forthcoming about his murderous past and said he had wanted the publicity Sylvie's death would bring down on me, wanted me to be exposed and to suffer through a public revival of my son's death. Sylvie had died as a means to an end. It was a tragedy, all of it, and I didn't like thinking about it, so I didn't, except when I awoke in the dead of night in a cold sweat and looked to see if decapitated heads on Blue Willow plates were in bed with me. But it was always Black in bed with me, and he came in very handy at nightmare time.

I was reclining in a chaise in the shade, feeling a bit like Madonna or Barbra Streisand, or any other rich, pampered woman. Except my lower leg was in a cast, and I had about fifty stitches in my upper chest and arm. We'd been in our little Garden of Eden for over a week now, and Black had canceled all his appointments and rarely left my side. He had gotten over his own encounter with the stun gun and was angry he'd let a she-male get the jump on him. I told him he should've used the old duck-and-weave boxing technique he liked to tell me about. He told me that we both needed practice in that regard, and that he was enjoying my company now that I couldn't kick his legs out and frisk him. I said I thought he liked that, but what I really thought was that he wanted me around to make sure I hadn't gone completely bonkers after spending the night with my old friend Thomas.

Truth was, I probably did need some intense psychological care, and one good thing about Black was, he didn't mind doing it in bed with lots of other pleasurable things going on at the same time, too. It didn't hurt, either, that he was a doctor and could prescribe all the painkillers I'd ever want or need. I think he probably thought it a good way to keep me quiet, too.

"Time for a painkiller."

Black sat down beside my legs. He was wearing black swim trunks and had his shirt off, and despite his dark tan, I could still see all the little snakebite bruises where the stun gun had gotten him. He handed me a pill and a glass of iced tea, then laid a cool hand on my naked thigh. The cast stretched from below my knee to my toes. I was wearing a yellow string bikini because Black thought it was easier for me to get it on and off around all my casts and bandages. Off, mainly. But I was okay with it. I was okay with everything now, especially with Black.

"I'm feeling pretty good."

"Maybe I should check your bandage."

"Maybe you should quit worrying so much and relax. I'm not used to being pampered and taken care of."

"Get used to it," he said, his mouth finding mine in a kiss as slow and thorough as the rest of his lovemaking. I put my good arm around his neck and drew him down beside me on the wide chaise.

Yeah, okay, so I had been wrong about him. He wasn't so bad after all. In fact, he was pretty damn good.

LIFE AFTER DOTTIE

Brat liked the big hospital pretty much but was angry that they took his mother and her friends away and buried them, just as if they owned them. The mother didn't like the dark, and she hated bugs. She must have been so angry. Sometimes the smell in the wide, shiny corridors reminded Brat of his father's embalming room down in the cellar. Brat spent his days talking to the doctors, who were nice and hung on his every word, even the big lies he told them. They said Brat would probably never get out and be free again, but Brat knew better. Brat went to the hospital library every day and read all about psychiatry and mental illness and disassociative disorders and psychopaths and personality disorders and listened to everything the doctors said about Brat's own case.

When the time came, Brat would know what to say to get out of this place, even if it was sort of pleasant here, and then Brat would go looking for Annie again. Brat loved her so, and right before the man named Black kicked Brat in the head and ruined everything, she'd said she'd come live with Brat and travel in the trailer with them and meet all the friends he brought home. Why, there was one special nurse that gave Brat medicine who had long blond hair twisted into a crown of braids. She would be a perfect friend. Brat had been watching her ever since they locked him up. And he could find more Blue Willow plates at any flea market around.

Oh yes, Brat couldn't wait for that day to come. It would be so perfect, just Brat and Annie in the trailer together, driving all around the country and finding friends for their mommas. Heaven couldn't be any better than that; he was sure of it. He got all excited just thinking about it! He hoped that his mother knew he was coming to rescue her . . . very, very soon.

More Nail-Biting Suspense From
Kevin O'Brien